MW01016891

Alter Egos

by

Lee F. Patrick

Javari Press
Calgary, Alberta
2017

Alter Egos

Javari Press,
Calgary, Alberta, Canada.
http://www.javaripress.ca/

ISBN: 978-1-895487-18-3

First Print edition, August 2017.

Set in Gentium Book Basic
Printed in the United States of America

Acknowledgements

Thank you for buying this book. Yes, you. I hope you enjoy reading this book as much as I enjoyed writing it. I had a lot of fun thinking up ways for Barrat to get into trouble.

Please consider letting others know what you think of it by leaving an online review, or raving to your friends how much you enjoyed it.

Thanks to Swati Chavda and Michael Thompson for reading earlier versions of the book and providing excellent commentary.

And a special thanks to my wonderful Gary, who is always here for me. Especially with technical bits with computers. Formatting for ebooks is a mystery requiring much effort to develop a template. The skill set for preparing ebooks and print books has been made easier with his wonderful aid and explanations. It should get easier. I hope.

Some readers wonder where ideas for a particular book come from. This story started in late October of 2014. It started as a tale of a rich father and the son who really didn't get along with him because they were too much alike. Barrat's family situation was similar to what you're about to read. In the earliest version he joins a mercenary group as a sniper once he's released from police custody. Numerous changes occurred and developed over the next few years and I kept coming back to the story to flesh out details and rework plot and add characters such as Kerit. I tend to start with plot and dialogue to learn more about the characters and their journey, then add settings, other characters and specific character descriptions.

Other parts of their adventures will appear as short stories, novellas and more novels as I figure out what other problems the team gets into.

Enjoy!!

Lee F. Patrick   Calgary Alberta, August, 2017

Works by Lee F. Patrick

Novels:
Alter Egos:
(Victim, Analyst, Predator)

Coming:
Mind Games: The Alanyo Heir

Short Fiction:
All at Sea
Spellbound Fall (Eggplant Production 2001)

Return
The Okal Rel Universe Anthology 2 (Fandom Press, 2007)

The Fire Mage
Enigma Front: Burnt (Analemma Press 2016)

Shadows in the Mist
Polar Borealis #4 2017

Chapter 1

The comm chimed and Barrat answered it absently. The battered, improvised desk in his tiny apartment was covered with papers and his portable computer's screen showed the home page of a major corporation.

"Hey, Barrat, do you some time to chat?" Kerit asked. "Just got back into town two days ago and thought it was time to check in."

"A few minutes for you, always. Anything of interest?" He leaned back carefully in the chair. It wasn't the sturdiest one he'd ever sat in. It was the best of the ones that he had available.

"Couple of jobs showing on the dark net. Thinking about contacting them, but wanted to chat with you about the targets first. What are you up to? Working yet?"

"No such luck, Kerit. But I do have an interview in two days. Just doing some research on the company at the moment."

"Any chance they'll hire you?"

"I don't know. But getting *any* interview is a good sign compared to being ignored. Or being told that I'm a stooge for my father to get access to their inside data. Just hope it isn't like the other three. Be a puppet, not an analyst. Stand around at corporate functions and spew the lies the top floor wants everyone to believe. Don't actually examine the data to find the truth, which might be inconvenient." He took a deep breath, trying for calm. It didn't work very well. It hadn't helped in months. Still didn't.

"You could go to work for your father. He's mentioned that a time or two, you said."

"I endured two summers there," he replied dryly. "Remember how I bitched about them every time we talked back then? The analysts I met either ignored me or sneered at me. Wait. The new hires wanted to be my best friend so I could help them with their assignments in between delivering the mail. Volunteering for several years of that attitude before the ones who matter realise I do know what I'm doing is not an attractive future." Another not quite calming breath. "So, what are the jobs you wanted to talk about?"

"None were sent to us specifically, but I thought maybe killing someone might help your mood. You've been grouchy lately and that's not good for the calm and detachment you need in a job like ours." A hint of a chuckle.

"That's a good guess. What's number one?" It would relieve so much stress in Barrat's life. Targets, even the picture cut-outs, didn't give him the same release. He'd tried to hide his misgivings and frustration from Kerit, but as usual, his mentor knew more about his inner turmoil than he wanted to admit. He wanted and needed a legal job, and soon.

"An angry client. He says the target wrecked his company with some bad reviews. Completely unfounded, he says. He's pissed and the existing customers are starting to listen to the target, not him. I looked at the reviews still on line. The target started out calm and their concerns were ignored. Then both parties started to escalate and now the public is choosing sides. Both were contemplating lawyers but backed off from that when they got quotes, it seems. The client's going with a more permanent option from the posting. Eight thousand for a covert hit. The target backed off but didn't take any of his reviews down. Just stopped responding to the client's diatribes."

"That sounds like revenge, Kerit. Any details on who the target is and why the client wants him dead instead of recanting the reviews? And the fee seems..." He tried to find a civil description for pitiful. "Low." *Inadequate might also be appropriate.*

A snort of laughter. "Good questions, lad. Same as I thought. I did a search in the news reports for some background. Seems the target found some odd things in the client's business practices. And I also think the client's trying to buy the death on the very cheap."

"So the client's more the type of target we'd take on. However, most of the others in our field would take the job in a heartbeat. "

"Truth. Any ideas how to circumvent the client?"

"Leak his request to the local police. Warn the target. Not much we can do. And we can't expose that we did anything or our competitors will not be happy with us. Bad for our reputation. Does the client know you looked at the posting?"

"No. He doesn't have a lot of experience in the dark net, I think. We could post a general link and provide the evidence that I found. A warning from us will deter our honourable associates. You're building a good reputation for Justice." Barrat heard the pun on his chosen pseudonym. He shrugged. It was appropriate, given who his preferred targets were.

"But not the rest, who also wouldn't balk at the small fee. And they'd probably botch the job so the client would still end up in jail for conspiracy and whatever else the police could toss at him."

"I can arrange a warning to the target to get his ass and his family into the local police station. I'll check our list and direct him to an honest cop who needs a high-profile case to help his career along."

"What's the other one?"

"More your style, actually. Wanted to see how you'd deal with the first one. I'm not going to be around forever. I might want to retire someday, after all."

"You keep saying that but you're still here." Barrat didn't bother repressing his smile. "How are the joints today?"

"Moderately creaky. Went for a steam yesterday when I got in and that helped." Twenty years in the army as a sniper had given his friend a legacy of health problems, but his mind was still at full strength.

"The job?"

"A piece of work in Snathard. A complete asshole who likes to target and abuse kids under the guise of helping poor kids see that there are greener pastures to come. He is also very rich. He's just bought out another jury and walked on the charges."

"That's more like it. How much are they offering?"

"Fourteen. A little low, but I think they scraped up all the cash they could get. I think a few other families in the same situation have chipped in to bring it up to a reasonable rate. It's still below normal but not many would risk getting this guy angry. We'd need to be very covert as well. The clients are going to be under scrutiny if anything odd results in this guy turning up dead. And any poison has to have a very fast breakdown rate with nothing left to raise suspicions."

"True. Same with a car accident. I'll have a look at his on-line activity and the society magazines to see if there's a way we can arrange something accidental, but I think we'll make some folks very happy. And poor kids won't have to worry about him ever again."

"Not as much fun as shooting someone, but you sound better already."

అకఅక

Barrat strode out of Vegathic's monolithic corporate headquarters in a mood that was beyond foul. He didn't pay attention to the people milling around on the broad plaza unless he was about to run into them. He dodged elderly men and all women. Men his age and slightly older were targets. Especially if they were wearing expensive suits. They were all shit-droppers.

"Hey, Barrat. Calm down." He managed to stop in front of one of his few real friends from university before hitting him. "What's the rush? A problem? Everything okay?"

He took a deep breath to steady his heart rate. "Told another crony of my father's that I don't want a do-nothing job looking pretty for their stockholders, Connil. I got Honours in Corporate Analysis, the same as you did. I can *work* but no one's willing to let me!"

Connil was employed as soon as the ink on his diploma started to dry. There were three serious offers in his hands just before senior finals and he picked the one that gave the best employee perks. Oddly, that was Vegathic Corp. One reason he'd thought there was a chance here for a real job.

"I'd love to come help drown your sorrows but my boss handed me a huge project with a deadline the moment I got in this morning. I came out for lunch to clear my head from sorting all the data. Why don't you go to the gym and pump it out? You've been spending way too much time in the bars lately. Not like we did in university. Serious drinking, I've heard. That's not like you."

"You're echoing my father, Connil. I got enough of that at home, which is why I moved out two months ago."

"Doing what to pay the rent? Is your allowance that good? I remember you complaining about how small it was last winter."

"No, it's now gone completely. I got cut off once when I graduated. To encourage me to take a scat job at Industries, I think. You remember that apartment building I inherited from my grandfather?" Connil nodded.

"There was a vacancy two months back. It's only a small place but big enough for me. I've got three rooms that were furnished in shabby chic when I moved in. All I have to do is pay the utilities and the building runs a decent profit. I'm even learning to cook, if you can believe it. Managed to find a cookbook called 'Beyond Boiling Water' in a used bookstore." He managed to grin.

"Real cooking?" Connil's blue eyes widened. "I just figured out how to make my blasted oven's delay start work." He glanced at his watch. "Damn. I'm going to be late. The boss is looking over my shoulder on this one. I think I'm up for a promotion or something, but the report seems to be fairly standard from what I've seen so far. Seriously, go lift something for a few hours. I'll message you if I can get away this evening or the next. You can cook me dinner. Or I'll buy to celebrate."

"Sounds good." Barrat paused, then headed for the nearest taxi stand at the edge of the plaza. He didn't have the patience to wait for a bus and didn't care how much it cost at this moment. Later, he'd count his change.

Grethel's Gym. If only he'd been the one to inherit it, Barrat mused as he paid off the cab and started to cross the street. He wouldn't be as worried about finding work. Not with the profits this place generated. He would still want a real job, but he'd be able to afford a nicer apartment and food that he didn't have to cook for every meal while he looked for one.

The gym wasn't an upscale place or retrofitted to include a juice bar. People came here to work out, not be seen and admired by beautiful people who were also there to be seen and admired but not sweat much. His next older sister Erithe had inherited it. She gave him a free lifetime membership when he graduated and moved home. She was just coming out of the women's change room so he stopped and tried for a smile.

"Hey, Barrat." She smiled at him. "How are things?"

"Hi, Erithe. Came by for a workout to relax. How's number five doing in there?" He pointed at her rounded stomach.

"Excellent. Dantil and the other kids are doing okay too." A gentle reminder. "Things still crazy?"

"Always in my life, it seems. I had another "we want a talking doll, not a real analyst" interview this morning."

"Thus the need to lift heavy weights?"

He nodded. "Father will be pissed. Again. Still."

"It's been five months since you graduated. Why hasn't someone snapped you up?" She seemed honestly confused by his unemployment. At least that attitude was better than Father's sneering and pointed comments about how lazy he was.

"It seems that no one who sees my last name dares hire me because they either think they can't afford me or that Father's getting ready to take them over and wants an internal assessment without showing his hand." She smiled at him and he tried to relax with a deep breath. None of his bad mood was her fault.

"I do know some folks who might want some work done. I met them in university and we keep in touch off and on. They need an outsider since too many internal egos are involved. A small company who doesn't have anyone who can do a real analysis to help them decide on how to expand. Much too small for Father to bother with. Can't guarantee any-thing, but I'll give them a call when I get home."

"I love a chance to do *something*. I've been playing with the public in-formation of a few companies that tickle my interest to keep my skills up. Seeing how much one can learn from their public filings and news re-leases helps keep me busy. I was thinking about investing in some of them to expand my portfolio from nothing but Trelner Industries. Mind you, Father's insisted on keeping it pretty diversified, but I want to add companies with potential that Father's been ignoring. Ones that aren't big enough for him to bother with."

She affected a shocked expression. "Not reinvesting in the family company? The horrors! The world will..." She started laughing and so did he. The tightness in his chest eased a little more.

"Better?" she asked.

"Some. I still need to sweat out my mood."

"Come over for dinner later this week. The little ones missed seeing you at the visit we made to the ancestral compound last week."

"I'll call soon and let you know if my calendar has any openings in the near future." She smiled at him and patted his cheek, then headed toward the business offices.

❧❧❧❧

The light-hearted exchange helped his mood but as he went into the men's change room, the idiocy of his situation returned. Why his parents thought another child would bring them closer together was beyond his comprehension. Maybe for the conception part, but by the time he was old enough to recognize his parents *as* parents, they'd drifted back apart even though they lived in the same house. They'd kept separate bed-rooms as far back as *he* could remember. The main house in the com-pound was huge so it wasn't rare to see anyone but the servants, making sure everything stayed immaculate. Most of them lived in one of the de-tached buildings hidden behind a row of trees. He wasn't sure how long the family had lived there. He hadn't cared. All he'd wanted to do lately was leave and never return to it.

He never saw either of his parents on a regular basis until he was ten and was allowed to join the family for dinner, except when there were important people visiting who wouldn't want to interact with a child when there were more *important things* to be discussed. That was about four nights out of eight, and never on the weekends. There were parties with the right people to be seen with. A few of his siblings still living nearby were out at those same parties, learning by doing and watching father as he made millions. The rest were at school or working at subsidiaries in other parts of Matheir and travelling to the bordering countries to look for opportunities for father to exploit.

He'd been sent to an exclusive boarding school at twelve, the same one his siblings and now all his older nieces and nephews went to. Then to university after graduation. To study business, of course. At least corporate analysis was fascinating, once he'd gotten beyond his father's "this is what you are going to study and excel at" lecture.

He slammed his locker shut and headed for the weight room. Maybe exercise would help burn off his anger.

He felt better after the steam bath. He'd overdone a couple, well, most of his usual routines. Wenthal, the weight room supervisor and coach, shook his head a few times but didn't try to talk him from changing up the weights. No one else wanted to talk to him and that was a good thing. He couldn't endure another sympathetic conversation right now.

Chapter 2

Nartig Haltarn watched his target speak to a man in his early twenties who'd just come out of the Vegathic headquarters. The two were about the same age. The analyst spoke to him, and it seemed they knew each other well. He got a decent shot of the man's face with his eyeglass camera and sent it to the office for facial recognition. The analyst headed into the building and back to work. Good. Someone else would keep an eye on him inside, via the internal camera network. And their employer would be alerted if it looked like he was leaving early or wasn't working on what he should be. The report was crucial and it had to be done on a specific day. No one had bothered to tell him why and it didn't really matter to his assignment.

Following someone to make sure they did their work was one of the odder things he'd done in his fifteen years with Branson Security. But any assignment helped paid the bills, so he'd followed the target once he left for lunch. The idiot knew absolutely *no* trade craft. He sighed, but that also meant he didn't have to really worry about being spotted unless he did something dumb like bumping into the target. Multiple times. From the front. He sighed again.

"Nartig, you'll never believe who that contact is," Jula said via his earpiece. "Barrat Trelner."

"Trelner? Of *The Trelners*? Any idea on how he and the target know each other?" Nartig asked.

"University, according to the info-pack on the target. They had adjoining rooms and were in the same program. Did you see the target pass anything to him?"

"Unsure. I could only see the target's back so I couldn't tell. Nothing big if he did. A memory chip if anything. Maybe. It looked like a random encounter to me. The target didn't call anyone from the restaurant. Hard to arrange that specific a timing without it. They were about halfway across the plaza, so he couldn't have been waiting just inside the doors. There's a lot of people heading back from lunch."

"Mr. Branson says to follow Trelner for now and he's going to call our employer. The inside man will have the target on screen by now. See if this one passes anything on."

"Got it." He turned to see young Trelner get into a taxi. "Need a destination on a taxi, Jula. Number 435809." The taxi pulled out into the dense traffic around the plaza and caught a go light on the first right. He lost sight of it among the stream of other almost identical vehicles.

"Wait one," she said. He went slowly to the taxi stand and waved. One pulled in quickly. Must have just dropped someone off. Dark hells. He should have...

"Grethel's Gym. 2357 Patters Ave." Jula said. Just in time. He let out a breath and smiled.

He relayed the address to the driver and they were out in traffic almost before he done up the safety belt. With any luck he'd be right behind Trelner when he went in so he could see who he talked to. Jula gave him a quick rundown on the gym as he travelled along the busy streets. It was *just* a gym, not a spa. He didn't smile openly. He hated spas and the idiots who went there to socialize, not sweat.

His driver stopped behind Trelner's, without prompting to make it obvious and memorable. He gave the man a good tip with a smile and started up the stairs just as Trelner entered the doors.

Trelner stopped to talk to a fashionably dressed woman in the spacious foyer. He sent a picture and Jula identified her as Barrat's next older sister before he passed them. Neither carried anything in their hands but he heard them plan a visit for later in the week before the clerk at the desk asked how he could be of help.

"It looks like I'm being transferred to Herithan and I thought I'd look for a new gym while I'm here," he said with a smile. "I don't want a lot of frills and fluffs or a coffee bar. Just a place to work out. The concierge at my hotel suggests I come here first."

"Then we may be the right fit for you, sir," the clerk said. He was short but looked like he spent a lot of off hours using the facilities. "We're old fashioned by design. We've got weight machines, stationary bikes, treadmills, small ball courts and a pool for laps. Steam and massage are included in the membership. The fee is two hundred a month, but the first two visits are free. To see if our gym is what you want and need."

"That sounds good. I dropped in just to see..."

"We have complimentary exercise gear for our members, sir. There's no way to test us out without testing our equipment."

Nartig smiled. "I do have some time free this afternoon," he said.

"Excellent. And your name, sir?"

"Jarth Kinnsol." That's what his current identification said, anyway. If he needed a membership to keep an eye on the kid, they could charge it to the client. A win-win for him. He signed the guest register with a scrawled signature.

A young man with a name tag came out of the men's change area. The clerk gestured and he came to the desk.

"Mr. Kinnsol is checking out our services today, Karth. He'll need a medium set of gear."

"Glad to help you out, sir." Karth smiled. "The men's change room is this way. What are you interested in doing today, sir?"

"Maybe a quick tour once I get changed. Then some weights. I haven't had a chance to do my usual routine in a couple of days with all the blasted meetings I've been scheduled to attend. I know that doing them when I'm half asleep is a recipe for disaster."

"Good choice, sir. We're open from five in the morning until nine in the evening. There's always at least one person on duty in the weight room to spot for you or to give some advice about routines." They entered the men's change area. He saw Trelner at a locker down the row.

"Looks like all the staff use the services here," Nartig said.

"That's right, sir. We're walking advertisements, plus we need to be able to spot our members and give them advice. Let me get you a set of gear. What size shoe do you wear?"

"Eleven wide." Karth headed into a room labelled Supplies and came out quickly with light green shorts, a matching shirt and a pair of shoes with white gym socks tucked in them.

"Most members leave their personal shoes in their lockers, sir. The shared ones are cleaned between uses and retired every two months." Gear in hand, Karth led him to a set of lockers near an exit. "The three on this end are for guests or visitors like yourself. I'll be back in a few minutes to give you the tour."

"Thank you." Nartig took the gear and saw that Trelner was just finishing dressing in the same type of green gear. He turned slightly so his face wouldn't be seen. Trelner didn't pay any attention to him. He did look pissed about something. The dratted analyst might have told him something. By the time he left maybe Jula would have some extra background on their relationship and why Trelner was in the plaza today.

Nartig glanced at the locks on the adjoining member lockers. Built-in electronic units. Expensive and hard to crack. Dark hells. He didn't have time to crack Trelner's combination to check for a memory chip. The escort would be back soon to keep an eye on him.

He'd barely finished tying the second shoe when Karth came back in. "All ready to go, sir?"

"Yes. Thank you. How do I lock this?"

Karth pulled out a personal lock out of his back pocket. This brand used a fingerprint to seal and open. No one else could get into his locker unless they destroyed the door or took off his finger. And kept it warm.

"Very fancy."

"It's easiest for our non-members and guests, sir. Once you join, one of the member lockers will be keyed to your personal code. None of the staff know them to ensure your personal effects are always safe."

"You don't have any frilly amenities, you implied. But these locks are top of the line. Seems a bit odd."

"True on both counts, sir. The previous owner passed away about five years back and he hated spas with frills so he vetoed any suggestions that might change our image. He was also very interested in personal security. That's one thing he was willing to invest in, other than keeping all the equipment in excellent condition. The current owner is keeping the tradition going. Our clients highly approve of our attitude so there are no plans to change what's working extremely well."

Nartig smiled. "Then let's start the tour!"

The place was wonderful. He didn't let his amazement show too much since they might be curious if he didn't come back. This was a place he'd *love* to have a membership at, no matter what the price was. He went to the weight room and saw Trelner doing an impressively heavy routine. An older man, still very fit, seemed to be unhappy about it for some reason, but wasn't stopping the kid.

Nartig dialled back his own routine to what a relatively fit corporate desk jockey might be capable of. He asked the older man to spot for him on the bench presses. When Trelner finished his routines and left, he glanced up at the clock and sighed.

"Need to head out soon, sir?" the man asked.

"Yes. I've got a meeting with my bosses this evening and the wretched report is only mostly done and isn't going to finish writing itself." The man, Wenthal, smiled. "I'd just stopped in to enquire on memberships. Didn't expect the opportunity to get a work out."

He quickly ducked through the shower and made it outside before Trelner did. No sign of him on the street. Maybe he'd gone to the steam room after his shower. Oh well, Nartig couldn't go back in now. There wasn't much traffic around here and thus no convenient place to stand and watch the doors for his exit. He pretended to be scanning for a taxi to stall for time in case someone was watching him. Not likely but he didn't take idiot risks while on any assignment, even one as banal as this one.

"So, Jula. What does the boss want me to do now?" Talking without moving his lips was second nature after fifteen years.

"Martan should be nearby. You're to follow Trelner and see where he goes next. Anything else to pass on?"

"That gym is great. Too bad I don't make enough to afford a membership. Two hundred a month is steep, but it's a great place. Think there's any chance of the boss coughing up for some employee benefits?"

"I doubt it," she said. "Not when we have very nice set up in the basement. Martan says he sees you. He's parked up the street a half block east and has the doors in sight."

He started walking and soon spotted Martan in one of the nondescript dark green family-style vehicles they generally used for surveillance. "Got him." Now they'd see where Trelner went next. Home or to visit someone else?

Chapter 3

Barrat felt better after the workout and a quick steam. He managed to find another taxi a half block down from the gym. As he rode toward his apartment, he sighed. His mind travelled old thoughts.

His family was never going to change. Maybe he should change his name. Or maybe the analysis Erithe mentioned could turn into a consulting business. That might be easier to build up into something that would provide a decent income and give him time and opportunity for his work with Kerit. Those owners still might think he'd pass along information to his father. It's what he would suggest, after all.

But Father seldom bothered with smaller companies who wouldn't already have an analyst or ten on staff. Too much effort to do a decent investigation for too little return. Tiny fish to be thrown back until they were big enough to eat. Smaller companies also tended to be private or family corporations, not public ones. Less attractive and harder to take over if their management was mostly competent. There were rumours that his grandfather Barrat had done some very shady things to acquire companies of all sizes that he wanted to buy up, including sabotage and paying off suppliers not to have what the target needed for a big order. He sighed again. He wished he hadn't been named after the old man. That might be another reason no one wanted to hire him. That kind of reputation tended to linger in people's minds.

He really needed to figure out how to transfer money from his other accounts so he'd have some visible income to keep anyone from guessing how he was really supporting himself. If he was doing consulting for small businesses, he could invent a company name, pretend to do some work for them and get paid in cash. He'd have to think about that. Decide if the paperwork was too much trouble and might reveal too much about what else he did. His mentor never mentioned how he managed. Maybe he needed to push on that front. Even a twenty year army pension wouldn't be much, he guessed.

Kerit would tell him more about their new job later tonight. In Snathard, just across the border. He'd need some of their currency for an emergency stash in case they were forced to go to ground, but Kerit would be able to manage it easier than he could. He spoke softly: translated his ruminations into Snatharin. Mainstream for now. Their slang varied depending on what part of the country you were from and how rich you were. The official classes he'd taken in university meant most business people would understand him. He did like their method of swearing. Calling someone a farmer in the wrong tone of voice was always sure to start a fight. A good way to break contact when someone was following you.

Duck into the right kind of bar and pick the two meanest guys there. He'd used it twice now. The first time, he'd gotten caught up in the ensuing fight until he dropped to the floor and got out by rolling to a wall, then crawling to an exit. The second time he'd left a lot quicker. Kerit had laughed and called the first incident a learning experience.

There wasn't enough money in his other accounts for true independence, but the demand for his services was going up now that his reputation was building. He just needed to get some of that money into his current pockets and maybe into his investment accounts. He also needed to do a grocery run soon. Very soon.

None of his family knew anything about his ability with a rifle. All they knew was that he'd been at a camp when he was fourteen that boasted a rare paintball program. If any of them remembered anything about where he'd been that summer, or any other, that is. The ex-military sniper tried to teach the boys and girls about being a predator with honour, not a mindless killer. When he started university, Kerit came to visit him with a proposal to train him and he'd jumped at it.

The taxi pulled up in front of his building. Time to try cooking pasta. The book *swore* it was easy.

At a few minutes after ten, he left the mess in the kitchen for tomorrow. The idiot book never mentioned that the sauce would bloop and splatter all over the stove if you put the temperature too high for too long. It would take at least an hour to get the dammed stove, counter *and* the floor cleaned up. That was first, and then he had the rest of the cleaning and tidying he'd put off for the past week. He'd spent the past two days on more important things: He finished reviewing what Vegathic's various divisions produced for the interview. That was the easy part and only took a half day.

He'd discovered by searching on various celebrity news sites that the target in Snathard liked a particular brand of liquor and he always drank a glass or two before and during his evening session in his hot pool. Alone. Always. There was a tasteless drug that would help him have a nap during that time. With multiple cameras on the area, Barrat couldn't go in and push the target's head under the water to be sure he drowned. No one seemed to come out and get him into bed, from their access to his home security system. Looping the feed was possible but getting onto the property would be difficult with multiple reports of fans being escorted off the property well before they reached the main house.

The drug alone was easier and sure. The target would be found in the morning and the reporters would pounce. As soon as the bottle was exposed to air the drug started to degrade. The small amount at the top would be an inert gas when they were done with the bottle. Nothing would be left to identify in the glass or bottle by the time the police arrived. The medical labs would take another few days to get to the analysis, even with a rush order, given the slime's celebrity status.

He glanced up at the clock and swore a little. Later than he planned. He needed to get to his meeting with Kerit and it would take time to ensure no one followed him. Not that he expected anyone to be interested in *him*. But Kerit insisted that in this business, the ones who survived and thrived took precautions all the time. So he would walk from here, and pay attention to his surroundings to ensure no one followed him from the building. He would head toward the club area first. Lots of people flocked there so that would help him lose a possible tail from the building. Moving through the drunken patrons without being noticed was also good practice for the times he might have to inject someone with a slow acting poison.

He didn't see anyone in the building's parking area and started to walk slowly at first, then sped up a little. It was a good way to stretch his leg muscles, still a little tired after his workout. There was a light breeze and he smiled in the dark.

The two blocks around the clubs would be packed with lots of people and an incredible decibel level to confuse anyone who tried to follow him. Anyone who did follow him into a club would have a horrible time figuring out which door he left by. That there was an entrance to the tunnel system in the alleyway behind of the middle club wasn't common knowledge. He needed to go further this time before going into the tunnels to get to the meeting place so he'd continue on and take a bus at the next major street. Down three stops and he'd be in the tunnels on his way to another bar that wasn't nearly as noisy.

Going to Snathard would be a nice holiday away from the family. He might invent an interview for somewhere near the border if anyone asked where he was going, or where he'd been. Not that he expected any of his family to really care, that is. He'd managed a lot of training trips and jobs over the past few years because no one really cared where he was unless Father wanted him. If he did start his own company, he wouldn't have anyone supervising his leisure time. A definite bonus to the idea. He'd just have to schedule any work around the annual summer holiday with the family and any other commitments, but he'd been doing that all through university so he was used to it.

His past summers were a mix of vacation places with the entire family and other courses or camps that would "enlarge his horizons." For his last two years at university he'd been Told he was interning at the main offices of the family business. Still, he'd been able to get away most weekends to train and eliminate some profitable targets.

His siblings were all twelve or more years older than him. People with their own careers and families who didn't have time to play with their little brother. When he was young and might have wanted to play with his nieces and nephews, they were either far younger than he was or they didn't want to associate with him so he didn't really know them either. Alone. As usual.

He walked on in the darkness. Maybe he'd move out of this city once he had enough money. Sell the apartment building and never see his family again. That had appeal on many levels.

❧❧❧❧❧

Nartig crouched behind a large shrub on the other side of the road from Trelner's apartment building. "He's leaving the building," Nartig reported. Martan left him the car once they followed Trelner to this location. It belonged to him, according to Jula's search. His suite was on the top floor on the west side. When the lights went out at ten, he assumed Trelner was going to bed early. He almost missed the figure coming out the side exit. Should he follow by car or on foot? The kid didn't have a car, but he might have called a taxi from the apartment. He slid into the front bench seat from the passenger side and pulled the door closed with only a tiny click. The interior light was already disabled so any sudden illumination wouldn't give him away.

"The boss says we're going to take him," Jula said. "The client is in a tizzy about possible collusion between the analyst and the Trelners. We've got to find out if it's true. The plan was to pop in and question him while he's sleeping but if he's heading for a meeting, he might have the information on him. You'll need to search him and then bring him in."

"The mugging scenario?" He asked quietly.

"Yes. Martan and a team are on their way: four minutes out, if not sooner. Do you have a dart gun?"

He risked speaking longer and louder since the kid wouldn't hear him from inside the car now. He was at the edge of the parking area, swapping to the sidewalk. "There should be one in here. Looks like he's walking wherever he's heading to rather than use a taxi. He just left the parking area. Do you want us to take him on the way back?"

"No. As soon as possible. The client wants everything he's carrying." Jula said after a moment. The boss must be in the control room and on the comm with the employer. Unusual, but plenty of things about this job were not according to their normal procedures.

"On my way." He pulled the small carry-sack from under his seat and unzipped it quickly. The dart gun was already loaded and he slipped it into his shoulder holster, leaving his regular pistol in the bag. He slipped out the passenger side and quietly shut the door, then stayed on the sidewalk on his side of the street to get closer before he made his move. The kid would never see him coming. His soft shoes made no sound as he ran, bent over slightly to keep his profile lower than the tops of the cars. Trelner wasn't dawdling on a walk before bed. He was going somewhere important by how fast he was walking. A meeting? Delivering the information from the analyst? His computer might yield something of interest. It didn't matter now. They'd soon know for sure if he carried anything related to the client. Another team could get into the apartment in an hour or so.

"Boss says if he's not carrying anything we may run a ransom scenario to explain his disappearance while we question him about what he knows about the report."

Nartig didn't reply since Trelner might hear him now. He was close enough to fire when the kid turned suddenly and saw him, halfway across the street. His dart gun was already out, so there was no chance to turn this into a friendly, late night walker encounter. Then he jerked and Nartig saw a dart in his shoulder as he spun toward the other threat. He fired another as the kid pulled the first one free. Then Martan was behind the kid and took him down the rest of the way in a choke hold.

"He didn't yell for help," Martan said when the kid lay unconscious on the sidewalk. "Why in the dark hells not?"

"We'll find out," Nartig replied. "There's more to this kid than meets the eye." He turned slow*ly, scanning for witnesses. No one. Good. Or else they'd have to bring* them in, long enough to block their memory and figure out if the kid knew them.

A dark van pulled up beside them and the side door opened. Nartig and Martan picked up the limp form and set him down on the van floor. He was pulled farther in and the door shut a moment later. Then the van eased into the street and headed off at a sedate pace with the headlights on. The driver even signalled his turn. They'd search the kid and find out if he did have anything on him. Otherwise, things became complex.

"I hate kidnappers personally," he said. "But officially, now I am one. Dark hells. Not how I expected today to end." Martan shrugged.

Martan picked up the fallen dart and tucked it into his jacket pocket, then slid his dart gun into a waist holster in the middle of his back. Nartig tucked his into his shoulder holster with a sigh. They turned back toward the green car. "Let's see what's further along this street," Martan said. "Maybe we can guess where he was heading to before he tells us. The boss said finding his contact's very important to the client."

There were three large bars in the next three blocks. All upscale and trendy in converted storefronts. No one *lived* in these blocks, he was very sure of that: not unless they were completely deaf. Loud music with louder, mostly drunk, patrons staggering across the streets. They parked in the middle of a block when someone left a parking spot. Hopefully the police would get the drunks before they'd driven far. Too much alcohol on board by the way the car weaved from side to side.

"Any ideas?" Nartig asked Jula as they surveyed the street. "We can each take one place. With the cameras we can record who's here. But there's enough people that we might miss someone in the third bar if they leave before we get there."

"Try them each anyway," Jula said. "Act like you're looking for someone. Quick in and out."

"All right," Martan said. They stowed their dart guns and holsters in the carry bag. Having someone bump into them and discover the weapons would be an annoyance and provide a place for the police or Trelner's family security to start checking once the family knew the kid was missing. "Check our cameras." They both put fashionable glasses on.

"Both cameras are streaming well," Jula said. "By the sound level in the car, you might want an earplug on your other ear. There should be some in the carry-sack."

The earplugs were in a side pocket of the carry bag and they both grimaced as they got out of the car, wincing at the assault on their eardrums. This would not be enjoyable. The doors to the bars were closed and the earplugs didn't give a lot of protection against the loud thumping and shrieking lyrics. Nartig couldn't tell if there were actual words involved or if the singers were being tortured.

A half hour later they were back at the car and shut the doors, muting the sound to something reasonable. "Anyone suspicious on your end?" Nartig asked.

"No one of interest," Martan replied as he pulled out the earplug and glared at it. "Just a lot of drunk people destroying their hearing. He must have been going to change direction at a cross street. Or he could go through any of them to lose a tail. But that's unlikely. I think. We'll have to ask him where he was going."

They pulled out around a gaggle of drunks holding each other up and stopped at a traffic light. A transit bus passed by and they looked at each other, considering the options.

"If he was going further and didn't want to use a taxi to be suspicious, a bus might make sense," Martan said. "Go through the club area to ditch any tail. Well, he'll talk to us later. Let's just head back to the office." The kid wouldn't have a chance to lie with the drugs they'd use. Just like the ones at the Interrogation Clinic.

Chapter 4

Barrat woke and tried to move. It didn't work. The room was dark, or... There was cloth on his face. He'd been blindfolded. Another of Kerit's training experiences? No. He didn't think so. Kerit could have easily guessed his route. There weren't many options from his apartment to the nearest tunnel access point or the bus he'd been heading for. His only glimpse of his attacker was the top of the man's head as he'd run across the street with the dart gun. They were pros. The big question was *why* had someone decided to kidnap him. Perhaps they thought Father would pay to get him back. That didn't seem reasonable to him but few people outside of the immediate family knew the true state of their relationship. So he might die in here when Father declined their demands. A shiver went down his spine.

"Good morning," came a somewhat distorted voice. He didn't reply. "I know that you're awake, Mr. Trelner. This can be quite civil or very nasty. It's your choice. I'll be satisfied with either."

"So I'm awake. Kidnapping for fun and profit?" Trying for bold. To get respect and humanizing himself to the kidnappers. Less likely for them to kill him if things didn't go as they planned. How he behaved could save his life. At least, according to all the training he'd gotten. Kerit might have other ideas, but that option was gone. He must have been missed at the rendezvous. What would Kerit do next? Backtrack him or go to ground, thinking that the police had found them?

"Very astute. Your father will be cross that you didn't have any security people with you tonight."

"No job, no responsibility in the company, no knowledge of their access codes or even a work account of my own there. I don't have a lot of cash but I'll give you the access codes to my accounts. Drain them all. No need to involve the family."

"Such a dutiful son. We do have a few questions for you."

"Such as?"

"Why didn't you take the job at Vegathic Corp earlier today?"

"Really? Your men kidnapped me and all you want to ask me about is a job offer I turned down?"

"Really. Maybe I'm bored. Just watching you sleep almost sent me into a nap. Need to do something to stay awake. So. Vegathic. Big company, lots of perks, good salary. Sounds like a dream job anyone would want. But not you, it seems. Why not?"

Barrat considered for a moment. That information wouldn't increase the advantages they already enjoyed. "They wanted a puppet with my last name to appease their shareholders if there's any bad news. I'm an analyst. That's the job I want and am trained to do. I don't want to stand around at parties or be trotted out a shareholder meetings being a good little drone chanting the company position, even if it a pack of lies."

"And the person you chatted with outside the building?"

"A friend from university. He works there. We sort of planned to get together last night but he was up to his ears in a report."

"Did you ask about it?"

"I learned nothing beyond that he was very busy and might not get any sleep last night or for the next week or so. I *do* understand about confidential material despite what some people think. Your men were following me all day?"

"We've been tracking your movements, kid. How about your late night ramble? Where *were* you going if not to one of those noisy bars down the street from your apartment?"

"That's where I was actually heading. The middle bar of the noisy block. The staff will sell full bottles out the back door for cash. I wanted a drink and I'd nearly run out at home. Didn't feel like being with people or dealing with the noise levels to drink in those bars. They should require hearing protection be worn. Workers Safety and Health should shut them down. They would in a heartbeat if they were factories. Maybe the staff should unionize."

"Interesting. We'll chat again later."

There was a clicking sound. They were running distortion software. The man wasn't in the room, he was sure. Another way to keep the kidnapee from identifying the kidnappers through a mistake. He refused to think of himself as a victim. Kerit taught him that one. He only thought of himself as the victim of his family. Nothing else. He tried to move but the restraints on his wrists and ankles were tight enough to prevent escape and the straps didn't have any play in them. Webbing, he thought. Impervious to moisture and friction. One needed a knife or a very sharp piece of stone and be able to use it. Dark hells. He let out a deep breath, to show the kidnappers that he knew they possessed the power in this situation. So they might make a mistake. Eventually.

There was something else he needed to do before anything else happened. He couldn't risk them or *anyone else* finding out about Kerit and his other trade. He just hoped the commands the elderly hypnotist inserted into his mind two years ago worked. They should. She'd been employed by the army's covert teams before a forced retirement. Carefully he whispered the nonsense phrase that would erase all memories of his other life. He had to hear the phrase for it to take effect, she'd said. That way reading it or repeating it in his head wouldn't activate it.

'Apricots nestle within the fealty of geology.'

⚜⚜⚜⚜

Nartig stretched before he got up from the microphone. He'd gotten a decent nap in the break room but wanted to see how the kid behaved on their first real encounter. A little bravado but he wasn't stupid. However, he'd muttered something the microphones weren't able to parse once their conversation was over. The cameras showed him just sitting there. Not struggling against the restraints. Occasionally his head moved. Listening for any hints on where he was or where a door might be. Possibly. They'd have to be careful when untying him. Maybe a dart to knock him out again. Just in case. The weight routine he'd seen at the gym meant the kid was strong. But was he trained to fight? Hard to tell.

"He's gotten some training on how to behave," Martan said from the doorway. "Pretty standard for families like his. I don't believe the answer on the lack of security. Do we send a message to the family now?"

"Not directly," the boss said from behind them. "Let's arrange something for when they figure out he's missing. Gives us more time to question him." He turned to Jula. "Did someone access his computer?"

"Yes, sir. A team went in through the balcony. Fairly easy and there was no real lock on the sliding door. They couldn't break the password up there so they brought the computer back with them. The techs were forced to strip out the drive's contents directly and even those files were encrypted. There's limited data in the machine's storage. There aren't any appointments listed in the computer's open calendar for the next week. His main files must be somewhere else and there's no sign of their location in the transfer history. It gets wiped fairly often, by what they can determine." Branson shrugged.

"If he is hiding documents off site we'll need the locations and codes from him. There were no storage devices on him. A wallet, keys, some change and a screamer for a security pickup from Daddy." The boss nodded. "Wherever he was going tonight, it wasn't to pass anything on unless it was completely verbal."

"I overheard him say that his sister wanted him to come to dinner later in the week so she may be the one to discover his absence. Do you want the team to leave a message in his apartment?" Nartig asked.

"Good idea. Better now than later. Take what he was wearing tonight and bring a good suit back with you. The one he wore today will do. Finish searching the place in case he stashed anything there. Tonight or early tomorrow the neighbours will expect to hear some noise. The ransom letter should be on his computer screen. Bugger it up proper. It shows we took him from a safe place. It should say we'll send a message where to drop the ransom once they put an ad in one of the papers. Think up something odd, will you, Jula?"

"And the amount of the ransom, sir?"

"Two million. Enough that they'll take us seriously and low enough that they won't involve anyone outside their own security. We don't want the police or anyone official involved. Our client wouldn't be happy with us. The whole point to this operation is to remain covert."

"I'll compose a message for you to approve at once." She left the room and closed the door.

"We've strayed over the lines before, sir," Martan said. "This is further over than we've ever been. How far are we going?"

"We won't take the money," the boss said. "Once we're sure he has nothing to do with our assignment and the client agrees, we'll pump him full of Zeltin to mess with any memories of his time here and let him go. No one uses him as a punching bag unless he tries something and he'll be fed and left to himself as much as possible. Minimal trauma so he'll recover quickly. A tame adventure that won't have any lasting effects. He'll be more careful in future about going out alone late at night. "

"When do you want us to untie him?"

"Give him another two hours alone in the dark, then ask about something else. Where he learned about kidnapping protocols, maybe. Or family dynamics. That's always good for background information we can use later. Then undo the cuffs. Give him an exercise shirt and shorts to wear. He can take the blindfold off once you leave the room. Martan, take a shock stick in case he tries anything brave and idiotic."

"Very good, sir. Any word on the analyst? Is he behaving?"

"Nothing of interest, which is a good thing, considering. He spent the evening at the office and kept hard at work on his report. Headed home in a taxi and is in bed at the moment. Alarm is set so he'll be back at work in good time tomorrow. No sign that he's compromised. The client is feeling less stressed since the kid didn't have anything on him."

"But he wants to be sure," Nartig said. "So we keep the kid until we're sure there's nothing going on."

"True. Shouldn't take long to find out what we need to know. Then he'll be back safe with his family. No lingering side effects. We don't want Vanthin Trelner to come after us."

❧❧❧❧

Erithe frowned as she sat at her desk after breakfast, toying with a report in their home office as they organised their day before heading out to their real offices. Her husband Dantil looked up at the tapping of her pen on the marble top. Their desks at home were now at right angles from each other so they could work and not get distracted by each other. That's how her latest pregnancy began. Not that she was sorry about it, but she'd wanted to wait another year or so.

"Problems, dearest?" Dantil asked. She looked over at him.

"Barrat hasn't called about coming to dinner yet. It's been three days now. He's not usually this slow in arranging anything."

"And he has friends his own age and is single. Spend significant time with his older sister, husband and two grubby urchins? We're far down the must call list on his social calendar, love."

"He does like the kids, Dantil. We all ignored him when he was little. Nothing in common to talk about and then we were all so busy with university and work. I feel bad for him now that we've got kids and see how much they enjoy playing with each other. Barrat never had that. At least, I don't think he did."

"Is that why you gave him the gym membership?"

"Sort of. Gods know it doesn't make much difference to the profit margin. I think we could double the fees and we'd still have all the clients they can handle. If more people keep showing up, we're going to have to expand or buy up another gym. Then tear out all the frills. It might be easier to start with an empty lot." She wrote a reminder in her planner.

"Your father would double the fees, I think. Back to Barrat. Give him a call if you're worried. I've got a meeting near his place this afternoon so I can drop by there on my way home if you don't hear back from him by then. I'll thump him for making you worry."

"All right. I'll make sure your driver has the address and entry codes."

⊸⟨⟩⟨⟩⊷

Barrat could barely sit up with the drugs in his system. The men kept asking about Vegathic and his interview. Why were they bothering? He kept giving them the same answers. He'd tried not answering and that meant no food or water. He wasn't sure how long he'd been here. The drugs to make him sleep or talk must be airborne since he didn't feel any effects immediately after eating or drinking. How many days was it now? No way to tell here in the dark room. Only a tiny light ever stayed lit. He still hadn't spotted the cameras he was sure were there.

He slipped to one side and let gravity help him to the floor. Would they send someone in to help him get back up? He passed out instead.

When the drugs wore off enough that he could move and think coherently, he climbed slowly back onto the cot.

"Now that you're more awake, we have some other questions," the voice asked. It was a different one than the first. Three of them so far, all male, he guessed. The speech patterns were slightly different but all were using the same distortion system.

"Tell me about your sister."

"I've got three," he said carefully. His jaw ached. "Which one?"

"Start with the youngest. We've got time."

They did. He didn't have much of a choice. "Erithe. Married to Dantil Hathner. Four kids so far. Number five is on the way."

"We know that. How do you get along with her?"

He sighed. How much longer would this go on? Would Father pay any ransom to get him back? Maybe. It wouldn't look good in the news if word got out that he'd abandoned a son. No one knew that was old news.

⊸⟨⟩⟨⟩⊷

Dantil's guard and driver escorted him into the building from a visitor space in the parking area. The driver used the code to enter the building but the same code on the apartment door didn't work. He thumped on the door. Several times. No response. The door at the other end of the hall opened and a female head emerged. The other two doors on either side of the hallway remained closed. Either not home or didn't care about their neighbours.

"Good afternoon," Dantil said with a smile. "I'm Barrat's brother-in-law. Have you seen him lately? He was supposed to come over to dinner this week and hasn't returned any of his sister's calls. Your name?"

"Narylla. Last time I heard him was three... I think it was four nights ago now. There was a burnt smell too. He can't cook but keeps trying. He should take an actual class or two. I offered to help but he said he wanted to experiment by himself."

'*Cooking?*' Dantil wondered. In Gods' name why was Barrat cooking on his own? What state *were* his finances in? Maybe that was why he always agreed to come over for dinner.

"Do you know the code for his door? It's been changed from what our security were given when he moved in."

"No idea. The management company must. They have all the door codes in case of emergencies." She darted inside her apartment and came back with a card. "This is the person we deal with for repairs and so on. He'll know how to get the code for you. That one's an extra so you can keep it."

"Thank you," Dantil said. She vanished back into her apartment. His guard pulled out a comm and took the card.

Ten minutes later they were told the new code. It took that long for Barrat's company rep to contact his and Erithe's rep and verify who he was. The driver punched the number in and the door opened. Dantil was relieved until they got inside.

The tiny apartment was a mess. The dark, dried stains of the food experiment were all over the stove and kitchen floor. A dirty plate, cutlery and a wine glass were by the sink, almost overflowing with other dirty dishes.

"Not a good housekeeper, it seems, sir," the driver said with a neutral tone. The guard came back into the living room.

"Nothing obvious in the bedroom or bath, sir. The bed isn't made but I wouldn't bet it ever is made by the state of this place. He might have left here any time of day. Impossible to tell."

"At worst the morning after he made the mess in here," the driver said. He rubbed a reddish spot on the stove and it was dry and hard.

"We need to check for his luggage, sir. I didn't see any in the closets, so unless there's a storage unit in the basement, he could have gone on a trip and planned to clean up once he got home," the guard said and turned to the driver. "I'll stay here. You check the basement. The code should be one of the ones we have. I'll check his desk for his passport and the computer for any travel purchases on line. Maybe he went out of town for an interview and forgot to mention it to you, sir."

Dantil held out a hand for the comm unit. "I'll call Erithe and let her know what we've found so far."

He'd just finished reassuring her when the guard swore. He rushed over to the desk and saw the message on the screen.

"Get word to your father, dear. Barrat's been kidnapped." The driver came back in just in time to hear him.

"Two large and one small suitcases in the storage unit, sir. Not much else beyond a few empty boxes down in there. They must be the ones he used for moving in here."

"I'll call security first. They may want to come over there to look for more clues," Erithe said. "Then I'll call Father."

❧ ❧ ❧ ❧

More questions, more drugs. Barrat couldn't keep his eyes open. Didn't really try any more. Just answered whatever they asked him.

Then it got quiet. He tried to lift his head from where he lay. Someone stood next to him. Dressed in dark clothes with a doctor's mask covering his lower face and head. Only the eyes showed. Brown. Darker eyebrows

"Time to go to sleep and forget all this happened, kid," the voice said. The figure held a syringe.

When Barrat could see anything in focus, it was the brick walls of an alleyway in a business district. He sat in something damp. The smells were noisome and barely registered above his own stench. He swapped to breathing though his mouth, not his nose. It didn't help much. He looked up past the tops of the buildings. Night. A few lights shone at the businesses' back doors and he seemed to be wearing his good suit, same as the day of Tarla and Kennet's wedding...

What *had* happened to him? A mugging while he on his way home? He reached for his wallet and it was there in his front left pants pocket as usual. There were two twenties and all his ident and cash cards were in place. So was the screamer. Push the button and twist and a signal went to the compound's security office. They'd send a car to take him home. Eventually. He stared at it.

Father would be pissed if he called in for a free ride home after a night of drinking. He didn't usually drink much but sometimes he couldn't say no to a round. Or buy one for his friends as they celebrated their new jobs or other successes. He couldn't afford many trips to any bar with his friends since their graduations and the surprising loss of his allowance.

The aroma of cheap whiskey made it through the other smells as he raised his arm. He managed to stagger to his feet, leaning against an industrial waste container that smelled possibly worse than he did. His stomach roiled but thankfully he didn't spew. Likely nothing was left in there. After a few minutes his guts settled and he looked either way down and up the alley to decide which direction to go.

The road to his left seemed a more major one by the light level and semi-constant sounds of cars. It was more likely he'd find a taxi to take him home there. He managed a few steps by leaning on the wall and glanced into a window set in a service entrance. The sight shocked him. Dark hells, he'd *never* get a taxi looking the way he did. The beard was barely acceptable, but his clothes were a mess. Plus the stench of the alley would deter any cabbie unless they kept a sheet of plastic for drunks like him to sit on. He'd have to walk. Or use the screamer. Dark hells. Two equally bad choices. No good ones. As usual in his life.

He reached the end of the alley and headed left again. There were traffic signals visible in the distance, so hopefully it was a major intersection that he could recognise. There should be street signs at the very least. Maybe a map and a bus stop. If he was lucky. Of course Father always said *no one* was ever truly lucky. Their extensive plans took into account all the relevant variables so that to the uninitiated, their success seemed to appear with no background or relationship to their current situation. Well, he needed to hope for some real luck, given his life so far.

"Great," he muttered as he spotted a bus stop at the intersection. Squinting was the only way he could make out the route numbers. "Wait. That one goes near home." About three blocks. He tried to muster any enthusiasm but failed. A headache of epic thunder hit him. "Dark hells." The streetlights hurt his eyes and if it felt like someone was using a sledgehammer on his cranium. He reached the shelter and leaned against it.

"Which way is home? And are the buses even running?" More squinting to read his watch. Two minutes after one. "Yes. Lucky to be me tonight." He staggered toward the street and looked either direction. A few cars sped past but he didn't see any buses.

Barrat went down the street slightly, then recognized the next intersection because of a coffee shop he'd stopped at occasionally on his other trips on the bus. He was only maybe eight blocks from his apartment. He could get home on his own and not have to chance even a bus driver turning him away or getting mugged for real while he waited. That was a relief. He looked, and felt, like a victim.

His legs were aching when he finally reached the building. Keeping a hand on whatever parked vehicles or walls he passed was the only way he managed to stay upright after the halfway point. What *had* he been doing for the past few days? He'd never gone on a bender like this before. He punched his code in and the door clicked so he could open it. The sole elevator never looked so inviting. Usually he ran up the four flights of stairs but that was *so* not happening tonight. The slow ride up only gave him time to get sleepy again.

He kept one hand on the corridor wall so he wouldn't make too much noise bumping against the walls when his feet wouldn't move properly. The tenants had to get to their jobs later this morning and wouldn't appreciate an early wake up with him crashing into their walls. At least with carpeting on the floor, it muffled his steps.

His fingers punched the code to his door and he stumbled inside and it swung closed. There was a little light from the half open drapes on the balcony door so he didn't bother with the overhead one. Dropping his suit coat on the back of the couch, he headed for the bathroom. A quick shower, painkillers, and as much water as he could hold. Maybe the painkillers and water first.

"Clean everything else up later. If I have a later." He put the hall light on rather than the bathroom one to keep his head from exploding. Looked at himself in the mirror. Dark hells. Maybe it was a good think he had nothing important to do this week. Just like every other week.

༺❀༻❀༺

The boss waved the three men into the conference room and they all took seats. Nartig stifled a yawn behind his hand. It had been a long day. And night. He might grab a quick nap in the break room before heading home. Falling asleep at the wheel was not on his 'to-do' list.

"The kid made it home on his own, boss," Martan said. "I thought it was possible he'd use the screamer but once he got out of the alley, he must have recognised the street. I guess he didn't want daddy dearest to know he'd been that drunk."

"And his computer? Was there anything we can use?"

The tech seated to his right shrugged. "The off-site servers held nothing of real interest, boss. Analysis of various small companies who weren't associated with the client and some resume letters. I'm not sure why he bothered with the added security."

"Maybe to keep daddy dearest from spying on him?" Nartig opined. "When I was talking to him, it showed that he really doesn't like his father. More neutral for his mother. The siblings are all older and distant. None seemed to spend much time with him outside of the family vacations each summer. The sister who owned the gym seems to be the only one he visits routinely, and even that is only in the months since he graduated. Poor little rich kid." Everyone shrugged. He wasn't their problem any more.

"And the Zeltin?"

Martan sipped his coffee before answering. "We gave him enough over the last two days so the kid won't remember anything about his visit here or our interest in what he was doing that day. He'll attribute his condition to an epic bender. At least until the family catches up with him. Not that it will matter then either. Screwed up memories never come back to cause trouble down the road."

"Too bad Zeltin is illegal," the tech said. "The inventor would be swimming in royalties from the sales. Then again, maybe he, or she, is the sole manufacturer and makes their money that way."

"Is there anything else relevant to this case?" Branson asked. No one spoke. "Then I'll relay all this to our client, who will also be happy. Head on home. Not a bad week's work. We started billing bonus money to the client once we took young Trelner into our custody. Everyone involved will share in that. Dismissed."

As they left the room, Martan looked over at him. "Any downsides to this cluster you can think of?"

"The only one I can think of was that I won't get a membership to that gym unless I pay for it myself."

"Two hundred a month is pricey, even with our salary and bonuses. Plus if their security looks at where he was during that day, they might wonder who you are. That identity wasn't properly backstopped. Just the wallet and ident documents, really."

"I know. Oh well, it was just a thought." His assignments involved a lot of travel, so maybe it was better to just use the totally adequate equipment in the office's basement. But working a kidnapping was never high on his list of job assignments. At least the kid wasn't harmed like others in that situation, he told himself. Mostly they'd helped get the victims back to their families, not been those who took someone away. He straightened. A week or so to get his muscles back into shape and the kid would be fine. He'd be more careful walking alone at night in the future.

"All's done here," he told Jula when they reached the op room. The boss never referred to new assignments. "What next? A week's holiday?"

"Home to bed yourself," Jula replied. "Come to the office in two days around noon for a new job. We've got a quirky client who needs his hand held on a trip. Bring your passport and clothes for two weeks. You'll be going directly from here to pick up the client and then to the airport. It might qualify as a holiday as there are no real indicators of trouble, just nerves."

"Okay. Where am I going?"

"Warm and sunny, I heard. I'll call you with details tomorrow night so you can pack your favourite bathing suit."

"My lucky day." Jula smiled at him.

Chapter 5

Barrat's eyes opened slowly. His head still ached, but it wasn't as bad as the drum corps from last night. Maybe. He rolled onto his back and his bladder vied for attention. That must be why he'd woken. The water he'd forced down earlier obviously hadn't been sufficient to clear all the alcohol byproducts out of his system. And he needed to clean the apartment and arrange to get his suit cleaned. He sat up on the bed and stared at the clock until he could focus on the numbers. Near noon. Damn. It smelled funky in here. Maybe he still smelled the alley's detritus from himself or the suit. He'd have to wash the sheets too, in case he hadn't gotten everything out of his hair. There was a very bright light on the other side of the curtains. He went over to the window and shut his eyes against the glare to open the window to let some fresh air circulate.

A pair of mostly clean exercise shorts on the dresser would be enough clothing for now, then he staggered to the bathroom with one hand on the wall. Sitting on the toilet relieved his bladder and he didn't have to try to balance to pull the shorts on. "Glad I got some water in me last night. Not enough to clear everything, but..." He managed to focus on the vanity after he stood up. The bottle of painkillers was still out. He chased a pair down with a large glass of water before leaving the bathroom.

"Need to open the balcony doors for a good breeze to clear the air." As he crossed the living room, squinting a little in the brightness, he noticed his computer was gone from the improvised desk in the corner. "Dark hells. Did I take it with me? And why would I take it to a bar?" At least if someone had stolen it, the password wouldn't be easily guessable and would completely lock up on the third wrong attempt. The breeze once he opened the doors was cool against his bare legs. He didn't care.

He sat down on the couch, waiting for the drums in his head to go away. Or for the volume to ease.

Slipping to one side woke him up. His stomach rumbled and the drums were muted. Food was his next priority. He'd have to go buy a new computer tomorrow. He could afford it. Barely. At least he stored everything on a remote server farm. Not under his own name or easily guessable aliases. One site held all his research on the various companies he'd applied for jobs with. Sometimes he never bothered sending a resume once he finished that cursory look. Other small companies intrigued him. Those he might invest in once he got enough of a cash flow to be *able* to invest, that is. That meant finding a job. Any job at this point would do a lot for his budget. He'd actually be able to stop worrying about every coin he spent. He managed to stand up and walk almost normally. "Yippee."

He stared into the lower kitchen cupboards after opening the small kitchen window. The smell of the air coming in was much better but the contents of his food cupboards weren't cheerful. Cereal. Dry. Some cans of various soups and vegetables. "Cereal should be easiest to eat." He pulled the box out and went over to the fridge. There was a small jug of milk, some cheese in the upper drawer and three bottles of wine bought after a special dividend paid out. He opened the milk and gagged. Closed it and put it in the mostly empty freezer. He'd toss it later, when he got around to taking the garbage out.

"Soup for breakfast?" he muttered. "Or should I just call this brunch since it's past noon?" He went back to the storage cupboard and knelt so he could see everything. He spotted a half package of crackers in the back corner. "Excellent!" He had one clean bowl remaining in the upper cupboard. He'd have to wash a soup spoon. That wouldn't be hard.

"Okay. First, start heating the soup. Where's the dratted can opener?" The obvious drawer was where other kitchen tools lived, but it wasn't there. He quickly checked the other drawers. Nothing. He sighed. "So I'll start by loading the dishwasher instead. Might just have crackers for breakfast. Easier on my stomach. Maybe." A gurgle from down there. Hungry. Better than throwing up for the next ten or more hours.

The box of cleaning packets lived under the sink. Opening the box, he stared at the can opener. Sighed again and put one of the packets on the counter above the dishwasher and opened the soup can after reading the directions. It was a beef vegetable soup, so it only needed a can of water added, not a cream based one that would need milk. Maybe he should get some dried milk on his next shopping trip. If he could afford the extra expense. Without his computer, he had no way to check his account unless he called directly.

While the soup heated, he started loading the dishwasher. Multi-tasking. He managed not to burn the soup. Lower heat settings were best, the dratted book said. By the look of the stove and floor, he'd been too eager for something to heat. Pasta sauce by the small bottle in the trash bin. More mess to clean up. There was a mop in the bathroom closet. Later. Maybe tomorrow. Not a lot of rush. No one ever came over. Especially not his relatives.

When the soup was hot, he took the bowl into the living room, put it on an old news sheet to protect the already distressed table and turned the viewer on. Time to check in on what he'd missed while he was drunk. Then he'd call Erithe and apologize for not calling the day after the wedding as she'd asked. Maybe he'd feel more like socializing tomorrow night. Today was about surviving the hangover and having enough clean clothes and dishes to survive the next few days.

He stared at the screen in shock. His hangover was forgotten in an instant. The markets were in an uproar.

"Vegathic's common and preferred stocks are both plummeting as a result of a report leaked late yesterday evening by a junior analyst," said the stocky, mostly bald pundit standing next to a monitor showing Connil's graduation picture.

What was Connil up to? He loves his job at Vegathic. How or why had he gotten involved with something like this?

"The analyst is currently in a safe location pending an investigation by the Securities Services," the report continued. Barrat hoped so. Connil was one of the few people he considered a real friend. Not someone only interested in him as a way into his father's notice and a cushy job offer.

The rest of the segment was full of histrionic pundits, male and female, arguing it was a great time to buy Vegathic stock, for everyone to hold onto their stock as it was obviously a hostile takeover attempt, and the most shrill: the entire market would tumble to new lows. Everyone should sell everything right now or preferably yesterday morning and put their money in their mattresses or sock drawers. Or buy gold and silver, which were going up in price as small investors panicked.

The market in general was starting to dive and it seemed to be getting worse with each passing minute. He stared at the sidebar that showed the composite index, fascinated at how fast the drop was. His classes had covered the recent ups and downs of the markets, of course, but this was far beyond anything he'd heard of in the past from any country. The professors needed to completely revise this part of their lectures before the next term started.

One pundit mentioned that Vanthin Trelner of Trelner Industries was busy buying up companies on the cheap and the hysteria reached new highs and the market was aimed at new lows. On the plus side, their company's stock price was starting to soar as people jumped onto his father's bandwagon. Father must be releasing more shares from the reserves, to ensure a steady supply for the new and nervous investors. It would also give him enough money in the accounts to buy more bargains without needing to dip into the cash reserves, or worse, borrowing. Father hated to owe anyone money, especially a banker.

His stock, also inherited from grandfather Barrat, could be worth at least double yesterday's value once the fuss died down if the trend continued. Or there might be some special dividends once the market rebounded and Father sold off some of these stocks. He wondered if Father had some buy orders on file in case there was a "correction" that caught everyone else by surprise. Barrat wouldn't be surprised if that wasn't the case. Father always took a long view. Buy Low and Buy Smart were his two basic rules of investing. Buying Low was certainly possible today, at least until the Securities Services closed the market. He wondered why it was still open. They should have shut it down hours ago. Even he could see that and he was badly hung over.

He shut the viewer down and looked at the messy living room. There was nothing he could do about the market. If his computer was here he'd have to consider how much he could syphon from his living funds to buy some of those interesting stocks he'd found before the market shut down. Right now, he didn't have that option. He could and should finish cleaning up and not tease himself with doing the impossible. He should be used to constant failure by now.

The dishwasher rumbled on through the rinse cycle. The Plan: Finish off the pots and pans in the sink, the mess on the floor and stove, then get started on his clothes. At least the breeze through the balcony window had taken the musty smell away. Or most of it, anyway. He took his dirty dishes into the kitchen and refilled the glass with water to keep sipping. He hadn't realized how much work just *living* was when he'd moved in here. Servants to cook and clean for him were now a fond memory unless he wanted to subject himself to Father's dominance again. That was not in any of his plans. Ever.

There was a message on his comm unit according to the blinking light. He hadn't looked at it before. Few people ever called him. He pushed play before starting to stack the pans on the counter so he could fill the sink.

"Mr. Trelner, we've found a way for you to increase your income from the building." The bright and cheery voice of his usual representative, Fargril. *What flight of fancy had he come up with this time?* "We've sourced general quotes on converting your basement storage area into another apartment. There's considerable demand for housing in your neighbourhood. Please call us as soon as possible so we can start the construction. Have a great day!" He deleted the message.

He'd call and tell them *No*, once he finished cleaning up, he decided. Hearing washers and dryers going all the time in the evening meant a tenant in that space wouldn't stay long. The windows were small and high up on the wall as well. Messing with the walls that held up the entire building seemed an expensive set of renovations, even with his minimal construction knowledge. Dim and dingy also meant hard to rent. Advertising cost money and so would the construction costs. There was no way he could afford it out of his personal accounts and he doubted any bank would lend him the money when he had no job to pay even the interest.

He had to put more than half the revenue into the contingency repair fund when he first took control of his inheritance. In case the elevator, heating plant, or other big ticket items failed. Grandfather never bothered keeping up that funding and his father hadn't changed the paltry amounts going in there while he'd controlled Barrat's inheritance. The rest of the income he needed to survive away from his father's influence, not waste on idiotic renovations.

He filled the large hamper with clothes that were washable and found the detergent and the small jar of coins he kept for the washers and dryers in the bathroom cupboard.

Narylla was just coming out of her apartment when he got back upstairs after starting two washers. One light colours, the other dark. He'd learned not to mix them up after the first time. The elevator ride down and up was a great thing since his legs were still wobbly.

Her eyes went wide in shock. Confused, he looked behind himself. No one there. "Barrat! You're okay! Thank goodness! We've been really worried about you!"

"Of course I'm fine," he said. Well, relatively so. "Went on a bender for a couple of days. Not sure why or who I was with."

"No, you didn't," she said. "You were kidnapped! Last week!"

"What?" He stared at her. She wasn't making any sense. Was he still that badly hung over?

"Call your family right now! Your brother-in-law came and found the note on your computer."

"But..." She pushed him toward his door.

"Call them. Now. When did you get back here?"

"Really late last night. Past one. I was very drunk, Narylla. I know drunk." She pushed at him again and glared.

To humour her, he called Erithe once he shut the door. And he'd been going to call her anyway. "No way I'm going to bother Father, not with the decisions he was making today. I'd be lucky to get fobbed off on the sub-minion to the minion's second assistant." Instead, he got Phonbul, Erithe's butler. At least he transferred the call quickly. Maybe a little too...

"Barrat?" Erithe's voice broke. "Where are you? We've been so worried about you. Are you all right? They didn't hurt you?"

"I'm fine. At home since last night, or early this morning," he said. "Sorry, but I've been..."

"Dantil, get a car over to Barrat's! They let him go!" He heard someone running over her quick breathing.

"What? Erithe, what *are* you talking about?" His head ached in the confusion of her statements. It must be time for more water and pain pills. Maybe a double dose.

"Don't go anywhere, Barrat. Lock your door. How did you get away?"

"I woke up in an alley near my place after a bender, Erithe. No kidnapping, no men in dark suits." Barrat paused. "So... how long have I been gone? What day is it today?" The news on the viewer hadn't mentioned a day, not even the day of the week. There was too much hysteria about the market's fall.

"We met at the gym on the eighth. It's the seventeenth. You were at a job interview that day. At Vegathic. You told me they wanted a puppet, not an analyst and turned them down." Her voice got calmer as she spoke. Barrat turned the lock on the door. Just in case.

"The last thing I remember is the wedding I went to for some friends from university. Got a ride home with one of the other guests. Then I woke up in an alley last night. That was over *two* weeks ago?"

"We'll get a doctor here as soon as possible. I'll call Father on the other line. Don't hang up on me."

"With the market meltdown he's busy with? Don't bother," Barrat said. "He won't have the time to waste turning the market's disaster into his new triumph. Not for me."

There was a soft knock at the door. "Hold on," he said. "Someone's at the door."

"Don't open it," Erithe said. "It might be them!" He moved the handset so she could hear what happened. *Though why would kidnappers come back for him today if they'd released him last night?*

"Who is it?"

"Narylla. Are you going to see your family?" Her voice was a little muffled but recognisable.

"Looks like. There's a car on the way to pick me up."

"Do you want me to get your laundry when it's done?"

"Sure," Barrat said. "That would be great. I used four and five. I'll come by or send someone by later today or tomorrow morning to pick up everything." He wasn't standing in line with the door. The guards hadn't trained a total fool. He needed to think, and quickly. It was normally about twenty minutes from Erithe's office to here. The guards would break or at least severely bend all traffic regulations necessary to get here in the shortest possible time. Then he'd be in the middle of a herd of people with long lists of questions. He needed to have *some* sort of answers to give them instead of just more questions.

"All right. I'm just glad you're safe." Her door closed a few moments later. He checked the spyhole and no one was visible in the hallway.

"Who was that?" Erithe asked. "It sounded like a woman. Do you know her? They might have used..."

"Calm down. She's my neighbour from down the hall. She talked to Dantil last week. I'd just put my laundry in the washers after doing the dishes. She saw me in the hall and said to call the family and let you know I was okay. She just said she'd take care of the clean clothes for me. I was trying to tidy up my place. Did someone take my computer? I saw it was missing earlier." He hoped they'd taken it, not the kidnappers.

"Yes. I think it's at the main security office at the compound. The ransom note was up on the screen. Dantil found it when he went to see you on a couple of days after we met at the gym. You were supposed to call and arrange a day to come over for dinner. You didn't and didn't answer your comm. I was worried."

Dark hells. How could someone have circumvented his protections?

"Erithe. I'm going to get dressed in something other than exercise shorts, so I'm hanging up. Don't call Father, okay? I need some time to figure things out and he'll be very busy today."

"All right." He hung up and went into the bedroom. *Did* he have anything clean and decent left to wear?

Barrat managed to find a cleanish shirt and underthings and an informal suit that he didn't usually wear in the back of the closet. Everything else needed the cleaners. Multiple items got a discount so he'd thought to wait and take all of them in at once. He glanced at the clock. No time for another shower. Or shaving. He turned to the mirror.

Erithe said he'd been missing over a week. But the stubble on his face was maybe three days long, not over a week. He turned to the clothes. One thing at a time.

He didn't get much chance to think after he got dressed. There was a quick knock at the door and he heard Dantil's voice. He unlocked the security bolt and opened the door. Dantil's arms wrapped around him in a surprise bear hug. He'd never thought this brother-in-law was that fond of him. Or was it the mess that would result from his demise or the hysteria of the tabloids that he was happy to be dodging?

"I'm fine," he wheezed, not entirely for effect. Damn, Dantil was strong. Or his muscle tone was non-existent. Maybe both.

"Let's get you back to our house. Do you need anything from here?"

"Erithe said my computer is at the compound. My clothes are mostly in the laundry or need cleaning. My neighbour will take care of the laundry if someone can come back in a couple of hours. And give her enough to cover the dryers."

"We'll send someone back to get anything you need later, sir," Svent, Dantil and Erithe's lead guard, said. "Right now you're the priority, sir." Another guard was facing toward Narylla's door. He hoped she didn't come out suddenly and startle the guard. His hand was on his pistol.

"Okay. Let's go."

The four of them fit with room to spare in the elevator but both he and Dantil were at the back corners while the guards stood in front of the door.

Dantil didn't say anything as they were driving, still fairly aggressively, toward their house. The driver took a sudden turn.

"New orders, sirs," he said. "We're to go to the compound instead. Just got word from main security."

Damn, thought Barrat. He'd have to face his father still suffering the effects of the hangover. And scruffy. That would be worse. Far worse.

Chapter 6

Vanthin Trelner was a fighter, as he always liked to say. Stocky when he was younger and now stout with age, he still liked to put on the fighting gloves. At this point, he did battle with other corporations rather than a single opponent in a square, but he still liked to stand over the inert body of an opponent. Enemies were his preferred target but family was acceptable if they didn't do as they were told.

"Mr. Barrat and Mr. Dantil are in route, sir," his aide said, standing just inside the door. "Mrs. Erithe, Mr. Carthan, Mrs. Hethane and all their young children are also inbound. All other family members are in safe zones and accounted for by their security. The older children are also under guard at their schools and at the university. Do you have any other orders, sir?"

"Let me know when Barrat arrives here. I'm swapping all my feeds to the market. My idiot competitors are going to try something else and I'll need to counter it quickly. I've locked everyone else out of the purchase system. Call the office so no one starts to pout. If they have any good recommendations for buys, have them sent to you. I'll consider them if I have time."

Three large screens on his desk filled with numbers. He sat at the keyboard and swapped indexes and groups for several minutes.

"Got the bastards." He typed quickly and put in buy orders for five different major companies at prices considerably below what the screens showed as the price they were now selling at. The market dropped another hundred points as his orders hit the markets' computers. Soon all the orders were listed as filled. He smiled. It was so easy to make money with this level of confusion and panic. One needed to keep their heads and remember their priorities in the face of others screaming and panicking. Buy Low and Buy Smart were the two he had today. And just about every day, come to think of it. He checked another pair of listings on his mental buy list. Excellent. They'd be down to his price level in a few minutes if the drop remained steady.

The Securities Service finally shut down trading ten minutes after he added those last stocks to his purchases. Idiots. They should have shut the markets down three hours ago. Or when the first rumours and confusion about the earnings report hit the public's awareness. He stood up, stretched and smiled. It was a great day. Possibly the best trading day in the history of the market. His smile faded suddenly.

What in the dark hells was Barrat involved with? Had it been a real kidnapping or did his son think to extort money out of him to keep up his alcohol-fuelled lifestyle? And *had* his erstwhile friends panicked and done something to mess with his memory or was that a lie as well? Two million would have given him a lot more play time before he was forced to join the real world. They'd negotiated down to a single million. That was still too much money to let Barrat access without supervision in his opinion. Too long until he would be forced to deal with the real world.

The baby of the family always grew up spoiled, his father told him multiple times: when he'd told the old man about the pregnancies of the last three of his children. And after, there were reminders every time Barrat cried because of some idiotic reason. It was his job to make sure his youngest was tough enough to survive the cutthroat world of big business. That's what he'd done.

Now that his university training was over, the boy was being obstinate, refusing to come to work for him, as all of his other children did without protest. The plan had been for Barrat to spend maybe a year or so in basic analysis at the main offices, then be sent out to one of the subsidiaries to finish filing off the idiot ideas he'd learned from people who didn't have the guts to succeed outside their classroom cocoons.

He glanced at the clock. All the local family would be here soon. He needed to decide how to handle the boy. He was still unemployed nearly five months after graduating. He'd done nothing in the meantime but work out at Erithe's gym and drink. Live in that tiny, squalid apartment building he'd inherited. That was going to stop. Now. He would be useful in sorting out the aftermath of today's trading. The boy's analysis of several of the smaller companies he'd bought over the course of the day gave his analysts a good overview for further investigation. Their agreement with those analyses proved the boy had a good head for finding investments. Now he just had to be motivated into using it for the company's good. Vanthin wasn't going to live forever and his legacy had to be protected.

A soft knock on his door and his aide came in. "The cars are pulling into the garage, sir. Mr. Barrat and Mr. Dantil are in the second one."

"Bring everyone to the large parlour."

"Mastren has already arranged for refreshments there, sir. Your doctor is also on route to give Mr. Barrat an examination to determine the extent of any injuries. The chef is prepared for everyone to join you for dinner and housekeeping is also preparing for the family to stay for an indefinite time."

"Good. I'll head down there in a minute. Since the markets are closed now, we don't have to worry about any further trading until the idiots in Securities change their underwear. Mid week at the earliest. There will be people calling me to arrange off-the-books trades. Get their names, what they're offering and how much or what they want in trade. I'll decide later which ones are worth calling back. Anything important from the main office?"

"There were a few suggestions, but they were also ones already on your buy list, so I did not wish to disturb your concentration. I'll continue to monitor the news programs for the rest of the day. There might be a hint of what that inflammatory report actually said rather than the vague hysteria we've seen so far."

Vanthin headed past the aide. "Do so." The outer office was tidy, just as he preferred. The corridor to the family section of the main floor was empty. He heard happy child voices up ahead. The children, excited to see him as usual. Their nannies could take them up to the nursery suite after they had a hug and a snack.

He passed two guards outside the parlour doors and stopped just inside. All five children were hugging Barrat's legs. Ignoring him.

"So you escaped," he said. All conversation ceased. The children came over to him and hugged him but their eyes kept going back to Barrat.

"I don't remember what happened, Father," Barrat said. He stood tall, at least: not cowering or making excuses. He'd beaten that into the boy whenever he had a chance. For a few years, those chances were frequent, almost weekly. Not very many lately. Mostly because he'd snuck out. He should have warned the guards not to let him do anything that stupid, but once it was done, he'd ignored the slight. "I woke up in an alley about one last night and walked home. Didn't know what happened until I met a neighbour who said I should call in. I saw part of the market coverage when I woke up and knew you'd be busy. Have they shut down trading yet? I was surprised Securities let it stay open so long."

"They finally did that a few minutes ago." He turned back to the children. "Have you had your snacks yet?" They got smiles and he got more hugs.

Vanthin didn't ask the harder questions yet. Not with the children here. They didn't need to hear his displeasure with his youngest son.

෫෨෫෨

Under the excuse of the medical exam, Father got him out of the parlour in record time. Barrat had barely finished a pastry and his coffee cup was still half full. He hadn't been able to figure out how to use the coffee maker he'd bought. Maybe he could get Mastren or one of the cooks to show him how one worked before he moved back home: if he was allowed to, that is. He might have to sneak out. But this time the guards might be more vigilant about his movements.

"Come with me," Father said. As soon as his back was turned, Erithe frowned at him. Barrat shrugged. He knew the interrogation would be coming. He just wished he had answers to the questions instead of more questions. Father would be pissed no matter what Barrat said, as usual.

They walked in silence to Father's office suite in the public section of the house. The head minion sat at the outside office desk. He started to stand but Father waved him back to his seat. Very important things were happening in the market. Barrat was an unfortunate side-note. Father never delayed or shirked an unpleasant task. Or allowed anyone else to do so.

Father waved him into the chair in front of the desk and closed the doors behind them. "You remember nothing of the last two weeks? That's what Erithe said when she called."

"The last thing I *do* remember clearly was attending a wedding of some friends from university apparently two weeks ago. Nothing of more recent events. She said the ransom note was on my computer?"

"Yes. You turned down a position at Vegathic earlier that day. A good choice, in retrospect. You on staff would have allayed some fears that I might bail them out. The market wouldn't have fallen as far."

"Less chance of profit for you."

"I did fairly well." The smirk Barrat hated was in full force.

"Did you pay the ransom? Erithe and Dantil didn't say anything about it. How much do I owe you?"

"There were some negotiations but those broke off two days ago. They started with two million. We were down to one. They must have let you go, unusual as that seems. Any thoughts on why they would do that?"

"Not at the moment. I was going to stay with Erithe and Dantil until their driver got the message you wanted them here. I need some time to think about what happened and what I don't remember." And for the residue of the hangover to go away so he could think clearly.

"You will stay here from now on. You obviously need security and that won't happen in your hovel. You're moving back into your old room. I'll send someone for your things later today. You'll rent out that apartment and increase your revenue. The whole place needs refurbishing or you'll drag the value of the other properties in that area down. You don't want that to happen."

"I like living there." A faint hope. And he'd already decided to start a refurbishing plan for next spring. The contingency fund would finally be at a reasonable level so he'd have the cash available to do so.

"I won't have this happening again." Hope crushed, again. "You'll start working for the analysis department at headquarters. We need to sort out how long some stocks that I bought today will be held. It's about time you took on some real responsibilities." And so his future was decided. No choices left for him. Father knew best. Of course.

"You'll also tell security where you woke up. Maybe they can access some camera feeds through our police contacts to see how you got there. Doctor Rethennel should be in the med suite by now. Go see him." His father turned on his screens and stopped looking at him. Dismissal.

Barrat got up and left the room. Outside the closed door he halted for a moment to think. He could put on an insignificant show of spite and go back to the parlour or to his old room, or be a good boy and go see the doctor. He glanced over at the minion's screens.

The minion looked over at him, then back at the news feeds. There was still a lot of hysteria and pundits shouting at each other, it seemed. He headed for the med suite. He wanted to know what drugs might still be in his system. *Anything* to understand what happened to him since he went to a simple wedding.

The doctor was already in the med suite, which he expected. Dr. Rethennel: Father's personal doctor who'd also taken care of him when he was younger. Still gave him an annual physical. That he also reported everything Barrat said and the results of all his tests to Father didn't bother him any more.

"I'm glad you managed to get away from the kidnappers, Barrat," Rethennel said as he gestured Barrat to sit on the exam table.

"I don't remember anything from the past two weeks, Doctor. There might still be some remnants of any drugs in my system." He shucked his jacket and rolled up his left sleeve. "I need to you see if there is. And if there are any puncture marks from injections. I didn't really get a chance to check and wasn't thinking of it as a possibility when I showered last night. My legs were really wobbly after I walked home and I could have run that distance without breathing hard two weeks ago."

"And the clothing you wore should be examined for any evidence of where else you might have been. Are they still at your apartment?"

"Yes. The suit needs to be cleaned but I put everything else into a washer this morning. Thought I'd been on a bender. If I was taken a week ago, they cut my beard or shaved me at least once about three days ago."

"You seem to be thinking clearly now. When you woke in the alley, how did you feel?" Rethennel went to a cupboard and pulled out a needle set and a handful of blood collection tubes. He wrapped an elastic tie around Barrat's upper left arm and Barrat squeezed his fist to enlarge the vein in his elbow.

"I felt like I drank way too much," Barrat admitted. "It has happened before so I recognised the symptoms. I could smell the whiskey on my clothes. Considering I was in an alley that possessed its own abundant aromas, I'd spilled a lot of it on myself. But," he paused. "I didn't see a bottle anywhere near me. There should have been. Didn't think of that until now."

The second tube was filling now. "Or the kidnappers splashed it on your clothing and face just after leaving you there. There are drugs that interfere with the transfer of immediate memory to more permanent storage," he said. "Illegal, so they are not readily available, except to the criminal element, of course. The most common one is called Zeltin."

"I've heard of it in the news sheets off and on. Like backing up your computer. Send the memories off and if something stops them from uploading to the new site, you don't have any of the data anymore."

The doctor nodded. "A good analogy. Those drugs do tend to break down quickly, so we may not be able to find them at this point. There are some breakdown products that do linger so that will also be definitive as to what happened and give us an idea of the dosage they gave you. Two weeks of memory loss would indicate they gave you a fairly high dose or lesser ones over several days." A third tube and Rethennel removed the needle and put a wad of cotton against the puncture site.

"Just hold that a moment or two while I write up some instructions to the lab. One of the guards will take these over to a testing clinic with a rush order. And we'll keep one tube here for reference later." He turned to the small desk and pulled a blood tests sheet from a pad. He looked over. "I'll also want a urine sample. Some drugs and their byproducts are processed via the kidneys. It will give us a more complete list of what drugs the kidnappers used to keep you quiet."

"I could do that now," Barrat said. He lowered his arm and removed the cotton. No new blood welled up. "Are there some cups in the wash-room?"

"There should be supplies in there." Barrat hopped off the table and went further back into the med suite.

He came back to the exam room a few minutes later. Doctor Rethen-nel smiled. "Now for the rest of the physical exam. I should have sugges-ted that you take a gown to the washroom." He extended one.

Barrat sighed and took it. Left the half-full cup of piss on the desk and went back to the washroom.

An hour later he went back to the parlour in search of food. The soup and the small stack of crackers at noon hadn't really filled his stom-ach and one small pastry hadn't been enough to fill the void. All the food was gone. So was the coffee service. Dark hells. Everyone else must be in their rooms. He sighed and checked his watch. Near four. Dinner would be served at seven, as always. Maybe he could mooch a snack from the kitchen to tide him over. Maybe he could ask one of the footmen to bring him something if he spotted any of them.

No luck there either. He didn't recognize any of the busy current staff in the vast kitchen. Mastren looked very disapproving at his suit, so he went up to his old room and shut the door. He didn't see anyone on his way there to ask for food and coffee. His stomach grumbled.

The same furnishings were here as when he'd moved. He hadn't lived here much outside of summer breaks from school. Not that he had any input in decorating the room at any point in his tenure here. The last time was when he'd gone off to university. Someone was hired to make this a more mature room now that he wasn't a child. He hadn't bothered to comment on anything that changed. It was easier not to fight for *everything*, just the things that were most important to him.

Like moving out.

Father was away the week he'd escaped, touring some subsidiaries and terrorizing the siblings who managed them, so it was fairly easy to take his things, one or two suitcases at a time, over to the apartment on the bus, it being cheaper than taxis.

His computer and power cord sat on the desk. He went over, plugged it in and started it. The ransom note was still visible on the screen. The people who had grabbed him had completely trashed the start up protocols. He turned it over. Tool marks on the screws suggested the drive was removed recently so they could strip out the contents.

That wouldn't have done much good since everything was encrypted. Depending on what drugs they gave him, he might have told them everything about his codes and storage locations. Not that there was much on his secure servers. But that was in the past.

The combination of talents meant money and expertise. But why kidnap *him*? Then let him go with no ransom paid? He honestly didn't think his father would have paid even a million to get him back, unless he could repay it from his inheritance from Grandfather by selling the apartment building. Or it would be deducted from what he'd inherit? If he did inherit anything, that is. Given Father's ongoing attitude toward him, he seriously doubted it.

The timing was bizarre, though. If he'd vanished the same day he'd been at Vegathic, did they think he was responsible for glitching their computers or what? He stared at the note on the computer screen. Pretty simple. How much they wanted and a way to open communications. He tried rebooting the system and the note still came up. He couldn't trust this computer any more. Not unless someone did a hard wipe and reinstalled the operating system. The recovery disk was in his desk back at the apartment. He shut the computer down and closed the lid. If he'd been at Erithe's he would have asked to borrow one of hers to log in and check his bank accounts. Maybe father's minion might arrange for the wipe and installation. It would cost less than a new computer. He took out his bank card. There was a comm code for enquiries. Good.

A knock at the door and he started. "Yes?"

"The tailor is here for you, sir." Mastren's voice. Somewhat deferential, always a surprise when he was alone.

He went over and opened the door. "I didn't request anyone," he said. Barrat looked at the well-dressed tailor. An older man likely from father's usual store. *Not* the styles he preferred. And his presence explained why Mastren was so polite. "I'm very sorry you were called by accident, sir. I have no need of your services today."

"There is no mistake," Mastren said. "Your father sent for him. Your current wardrobe was acceptable for your university needs but it is not adequate for your new responsibilities."

"I have other suits at my apartment. Sorry for your trouble." He closed the door. He tried to listen if there were any comments but neither spoke and the carpeting outside muffled their footsteps.

Ten minutes later the door flew open. Father stood there, jaw set.

"What do you think you're doing?"

"Waiting for my things to be brought from my home, Father," Barrat said. He debated a moment and stood up. He was slightly taller than his father and needed all the advantages he could get at this moment. "Why did your minion send for the tailor?"

"You need clothes for the office."

"No, I don't. I never agreed to your proposal. I am *not* working for you or for Industries in general, Father. So I don't need to waste hundreds or thousands that I don't have on suits I don't need and don't want."

"You are going to work in two days," father snarled and sneered at his suit. "That thing isn't worth ten."

"And it was the only thing readily available in my closet this afternoon that didn't need cleaning." Barrat forced himself to walk over to his father. "I'd worn my best suit to the interview, it seems. Got kidnapped in it and after the whiskey and detritus from the alleyway were absorbed by it, it needs cleaning before I wear it again. Should I just return to my apartment and stay there? I'll keep the door locked. I'm sure my not being here will do wonders for your blood pressure."

"You aren't going anywhere," Father growled.

"So I'm a prisoner here?"

"If you want to think of it that way, go ahead. You're staying *put*. Where I can keep an eye on you for now."

"And if I managed to call the police, there would be no response?"

"Dammed straight. I don't want to see you in that *thing* at dinner." A sneer as Father looked up and down at him. Somewhat expected.

"Then I hope someone returns shortly with some of my other clothes," Barrat said. "Or I'll be in my underwear and a shirt."

His father stormed out, both hands clenched into fists. Barrat almost wished Father had thrown the punch he'd threatened. Maybe he'd get some respect from the old man if he'd taken the blow. Or not. The door remained open and his next older brother poked his head in.

Carthan was the youngest until Barrat had been born. Twelve when that title passed and he'd ignored the infant and little boy who wanted to play. He was married and had three kids now. His children seemed to be enjoying a happy childhood. At least they had each other to play with.

"Dad's beyond pissed, it seems." Carthan leaned against the door jamb.

"How is that news?" Barrat replied. "He has to deal with me. He's dragged *everyone* back home over this?"

"Just Erithe and me. We live too close to justify staying away. Everyone else is safely hiding out in their homes, or at least that's what their security is reporting for them. You look like shit, by the way."

"Feel that way too. I'm going to shower and get rid of the fur. That's about all I'm going to do to placate him."

"We're about the same size now, I think. If you don't have anything here or that's wearable at your apartment, I've got a suit in my old rooms that should fit you. Left it behind the last time we got dragged back here for the weekend. Hethane suggested I loan it to you so we don't take it home. It's okay, but I seldom wore it."

"Thanks. Has Father been like this since I vanished?"

"Not that I heard. Cold as usual. Don't know why just seeing you pushes him into that frothing anger all the time. More than during the university breaks, I think."

"I think I preferred it when he ignored me."

"Maybe seeing you reminds him of Mom. You favour her more than the rest of us. She's back from the latest trip for her foundation. Raised a pile of money for some important cause in Hallaway. I'm not sure which one offhand. She didn't know you were missing until Erithe realized she wasn't here a few days after we discovered you went missing. Dad neglected to call her."

"That should make dinner interesting."

Carthan grinned. "Just love family dinners. Actually, we've been alternating with Erithe and Dantil for monthly get-togethers. Just us, and our kids. Sometimes Mom comes if she's in town. You should start coming as well, now that you're done with university."

"I promise I won't cook if you all come to my place. If I still have one after Father gets done yelling at me, that is."

Chapter 7

Captain Lagrath of Corporate Oversight was near to tearing what little hair was left out of his head. There was *no reason* the markets should have cratered the way they'd done two days ago.

The "damming" report everyone was talking about as the actual cause mentioned a one percent drop in revenue for one of Vegathic's major subsidiaries. It was a significant amount if you talked about the height of a stack of hundreds, but as a percentage of total company cash flow it hardly raised a blip. So why had everyone panicked? Was there something else going on? The radio in the outer office was on, so he listened for a while.

Everyone was telling everyone else their theory in loud voices and not listening when someone tried to bring rationality into the conversation. There simply weren't any solid facts to back up *any* of the theories. That's why half the people in the building were now sifting through reams of data getting eyestrain and headaches. Buys, sells and who had ended up owning what.

He looked at the accumulated trades listing his sergeant just put on his desk. Trelner Industries scooped up a lot of bargains as other investors panicked. Some on margin, others bought from their "rainy day" cash pool. The markets were scheduled to re-open in two days and it would be interesting to see how much profit Trelner made on the crash.

There were others who'd taken advantage of the hysteria, some with pockets as deep as Trelner's. Five of them, to be precise. But none of their children were interviewed for an analysis position at Vegathic a week *before* the crash.

And, according to what information was available, the boy was left alone in an office long enough to access their computer network and give the log-in information to someone outside the company. However, there was no direct evidence that he'd done anything of the kind. But many idiots were adding him into their wild theories. Added to that was that no one had seen him in the past week. Why anyone *should* have seen him was not being discussed by any pundit or reporter.

The analyst who'd written the report that started it all, who was also totally confused about the fallout, spoke briefly to the son as he left the building. They were friends from university and planned to get together that night. The analyst called to cancel due to the pressure on him to get started on the report but everyone was looking at that seemingly innocent interaction with big, distorted, paranoid magnifying glasses. The analyst was somewhere under guard. Hopefully still alive so he could answer questions. If he vanished completely or turned up dead, different questions would be raised.

Lagrath's boss, Major Peterren, came into his office. "Anything new come to light? We've got all the upper levels hovering around with not a lot of patience on any delays in figuring who's responsible."

"Not really, sir. The only really new information is that Barrat Trelner reappeared today. Or last night, depending on whose version you trust. Says he doesn't recall the past two weeks. There's blood and urine samples in at one of the testing labs. We'll get copies of the results."

"I saw the earlier report you sent up. I don't know if the kidnapping story is true." Peterren took his visitor chair. "It was, however, a very convenient way to get him out of the public eye if he did do something while he as in Vegathic's headquarters. I'm glad you managed to turn one of Trelner's people in the police force."

"I am too. He's nervous but the pundits are already on the kid's disappearance as a major lead. Someone *else* leaked the kidnapping story. I don't know if young Trelner is involved or was really kidnapped. Nor does his father, by what I was told. There are *no* records of a kidnapper just letting someone with his value go with no payment. They were dickering and were down to a million for the ransom. Might have gone down further. Hard to tell. Kidnapping victims escaping, maybe three of them in the ten years I checked. One of my officers went to the alley the kid says he woke up in. No physical evidence was obviously from him. No cameras caught anything but coverage is spotty around there. A good choice of a place to dump him. It's eight blocks or so to his apartment. I have people checking for any sight of him on the possible routes. That late at night, not many crowds so we should spot him on at least one camera to give some credibility to his side of the rumours."

"Vanthin Trelner might have paid the ransom in other ways. A big favour, information, loaning his security people for something off the

books. Buying someone some stocks during the free fall. Hard to tell
what it could be. He always plays side games with his investments and
this could be just another one of them."

"None of what he does is technically illegal. And we have no way to
tell from the outside," Lagrath said. He shook his head in frustration.
"And none of the Trelners, especially the father, will talk to us voluntarily."

"Everything we have boils down to there being no proof for any of
the current theories on the kidnapping. Do you think it was him and
some friends looking for money?"

"I don't think so, sir. I have someone examining his financials but so
far he's clear. Spends a fair bit in bars, but that's common with his
crowd. He moved out of the family mansion during the summer. Guess
dad didn't like his lifestyle. He doesn't have a job, by the way. Hence the
interview at Vegathic, according to the report analyst."

"Do we have legitimate cause to question young Trelner about the
crash?" Peterren asked. "Or the kidnapping?"

"If he doesn't remember anything about the missing weeks, even
the Interrogation Clinic's drugs won't help, sir. Zeltin's very common
these days to hide all sorts of inconvenient facts from us and the police.
The lab results might show proof if he'd been dosed in the past few days.
Depends on how much they used and when they injected him."

"But if he's faking the memory loss, the interrogators would find
out quickly. And we'd know exactly what he did at Vegathic."

"I'd like to see a little more evidence, sir. Getting Trelner Industries
cranky with us isn't a good career move for either of us."

"True. Or maybe his dad wouldn't mind handing him over so *he'd*
get the truth." Peterren smiled.

"Interesting angle, sir. I should know more in two or three days."

"Let me know. I know someone I think we can use to approach his
dad. We'd be able to question him about anything else he might have
done and say we're helping Dad to find out if the kid and some of his pals
arranged his own kidnapping."

They smiled. Once someone was in the Interrogation Clinic, there
was no scrap of information that could be hidden from them.

❦❧❦❧

Barrat appeared for dinner in Carthan's suit. All of his needed cleaning, and his shirts needed ironing, according to Mastren. Another task
he'd never learned how to do and didn't want to keep paying the clean-

ers to do for him. His clothing would be dealt with and his second-best suit would be ready for his first day at work. He wondered if two or three guards would just pick him up and carry him into an office if he kept thinking he possessed any power whatsoever. He *could* just sit there all day drinking coffee and playing card games on the computer if it came to that. Surely Father would get tired of pushing if he didn't react. Or maybe he'd have a heart attack when his blood pressure went too high in the rage that Barrat was sure to be blamed for.

His mother stood at her end of the table. Her dark brown hair, a match in colour for his own, was in a new up-swept style. Carefully applied makeup gave the impression that they weren't that far apart in age. She actually looked younger than Erithe usually did.

The footmen must have put an extra leaf in the table to seat all the adults. The children were left up in the nursery as usual. They would be distracting. That's what he'd been told when he was their ages, anyway. He'd rather be up with them than down here, but he didn't have any options that simple. There were even cards to indicate who sat where. Dantil sat opposite him. Carthan's wife Hethane was to his left.

"Hello, Mother," Barrat said, giving her the required kiss on the cheek. "You're looking well tonight. Carthan said you had a good trip for the foundation."

She held his arm so he couldn't move away. "Are you all right, Barrat? Tell me the truth."

"I'm fine," he said. "The headache's gone, finally. Dr. Rethennel said he couldn't find anything really wrong with me. He thinks they kept me well supplied with sleepy drugs the whole time and that's why I've lost some muscle tone and weight. I'll be back in shape in another week or so. I won't overdo any routines but I need to start working out tomorrow. The gym here will do since Father doesn't want me out in the world with all the fuss going on."

Father bustled in from the other entrance and everyone started to sit. Once Father's butt hit his seat, Mastren would start serving. Barrat reversed his wine glass after he sat down. Mother looked at him with a raised eyebrow. So did Erithe.

"Dr. Rethennel suggested I drink nothing with alcohol for the next few days. He wants another blood sample late tomorrow to double check on compounds I can't pronounce and don't want to try to spell. Any extra alcohol could skew those results, he said."

Father glared at him but didn't say anything about the borrowed suit. The temperature was on the low side for this room. If he *had* shown up in his underwear? Likely.

Some of his clean clothes showed up the next morning. Enough so he could give Carthan's suit back. His mother didn't appear but that wasn't unusual. She usually breakfasted in her suite.

"You should just keep the suit," Hethane said. "The colour never really flattered Carthan. It looks far better on you. And it will keep Father's shouting to a minimum. I hate it when the kids have to hear him yelling at some idiotic thing."

Barrat nodded after a few minutes. Everyone was on each others' nerves here. Maybe that's why his other siblings lived far away, managing their sections of the family holdings. He'd thought he'd been the only one who felt the tension in this house. He hadn't realised everyone felt the same way and they'd run away long ago. Successfully.

Unlike him.

"I will. Any notion how long he's going to keep everyone here?" He hoped they could escape. Maybe Father would let him stay with Erithe if he couldn't go back to the apartment. He wouldn't bet much on that possibility, but it would be better than living here.

"Another few days, I fear. The younger kids generally like visiting here, so they aren't as upset as we adults are. We do need to know if you were really kidnapped, Barrat."

"I know. You don't want any of the kids at risk. I haven't remembered anything. Might not ever remember, the doctor said. The drug they probably used is common for making people forget what others don't want revealed."

Father passed by him and gave a snort of semi-approval at his second-best suit. The best was still at the cleaners. The alley's residues were proving challenging, Mastren reported to him on his way down to the dining room.

"How's your apartment building doing?" Hethane asked. "I was surprised it went to you. Grandfather owned most of that block, you know. Each building went to a different grandchild. Carthan and I have the one across the alley from yours."

His building was the smallest on the block. Not entirely a surprise. He knew most of the other buildings all had the same management company from the signs outside but hadn't realised what that meant. He was fifteen when his grandfather died. It was mostly expected and he hadn't liked the old, cranky bastard. It seemed to be mutual, but he didn't understand why. Maybe because he'd been named after the old man? His siblings and their children all seemed to get along well with the obnoxious curmudgeon. Maybe that's why they'd all more or less ignored him

up until then. They didn't want to risk losing out on their portions of the
estate if the will was changed. Most of them still ignored him.

Father, of course, managed his inheritance until he reached twenty
and was finally forced to transfer the ownership documents and control
back to him. A minor minion from the company's legal department
showed up, pounding on his dorm room door just as he woke up on his
birthday, held out a sheaf of paperwork, then vanished after getting a
scrawled signature on a delivery form. It took him most of the weekend
to truly understand what he owned and to arrange the profits from the
building to go into a new bank account and transfer the joint one's balance. That was also when his allowance was cut in half. He should have
expected it. The average monthly income was close to the previous
amount of his allowance. Then he realised how small the contingency
fund was and that swallowed up more than half the available cash. That's
when he'd started being very careful how much he'd spent so he could
start to save for independence. He was still saving.

"I didn't realize that," he said out loud. "Well, the building's in decent shape and most of the tenants have been there over five years. Next
spring or summer I was thinking to start some refurbishing. New paint,
carpets, maybe appliances, that sort of thing. Do one unit at a time with
hopefully a spare available so people can move into it while theirs is being worked on. Minimal fuss and then I can really justify a rent increase.
That area is getting more expensive and I don't want anyone to think
that I'm hauling their investment value down. Especially if they're
mostly family."

"Is that what you want to do? Just be a landlord?"

"No. I want a job in analysis. Father informed me I'm starting to
work at the Industries main office next week to help sort out all his purchases yesterday. He's tired of my lifestyle, it seems."

"Nose to the books."

"That's true. I did some basic work on my own, just to keep my hand
in, as it were, once I graduated. I need to get a new computer or have the
company techs scrub my old one. I can't get that dammed ransom note
off the screen."

"I'd get a new one instead," Hethane suggested. "The prices came
down again and the new models are all better and faster. If the kidnappers messed with your old one, you can't ever trust it. Unless there's data
on there you need?"

"I use off-site server storage," Barrat said. "Manual update and
memory wipe so there's no trace left on the computer where the stored
documents are. I can get everything back. Just need a new machine to ac-

cess it from."

"Father's aide should be able to source you a new computer. Same day, most likely."

"And what will Father have installed for my own good?" He shrugged. "It doesn't matter. I shouldn't care if he's looking over my shoulder all the time. It'll happen no matter what I manage to do."

"You're far too cynical for your age, Barrat."

"Long practice." Erithe and Dantil came in with their kids. Carthan chivvied their three in the door after them.

"Grand-papa!" and other variations as the children ran to the other door as his father entered. The source of treats and ultimate power over their parents. Barrat went over to the laden side table and got a cup of coffee. He wasn't sure what activities his father planned for the rest of the weekend. He probably wouldn't enjoy them. Maybe he could hide out in the nursery for a few hours and play with the kids.

⊱⊰⊱⊰

Captain Lagrath stared at the illegally obtained document. Their computer techs were among the best in the country. Most decided to work for Corporate Oversight instead of going to prison with a side trip to the Interrogation Clinic to find out what other laws they might have bent or broken.

He picked up his comm to call Major Peterren. "Sir. Just got those drug test results. Barrat Trelner was dosed with a *lot* of Zeltin. Enough to account for the two weeks of memory loss we've heard he has. Our doctors figure they wanted some information from him and got it. Eventually. The decay curves match him first getting it two days before he reappeared. Nothing was left of any interrogation drugs, but that's to be expected given the time frame."

"The big question is what were they looking for?"

"If it happened within the past two weeks no one is ever going to know unless there's another source of that information. Any ideas?"

"Can we get his movements during that time frame? Without letting the family know what we're doing?"

"Possibly, with traffic cameras and our access to his financials. He tends to use taxis if he's going somewhere fancy and the bus or walking if he's out on his own. We did manage to track him from the alley to his building after his release. A dark van with no plates went near the alley about three hours before he shows up on a camera down the street. Then it vanished. He must have been unconscious, since it was a couple of hours before we have him on camera. Drugged for the drop off, I'd guess."

"Professionals, not buddies," Peterren said. "Dark hells. It was likely a real kidnapping, not a set up to get fun money from his father."

"True. I'll get some men on the extended parameters. The day of the pickup might have nothing to do with Vegathic or the crash."

"Or he was the root cause of the crash. That's the most popular rumour out in the forums at the moment."

⋰⋱⋰⋱

So he'd been pumped for information. On something. Maybe. Father cancelled his new job. One minor win for him. He wandered around the mostly deserted mansion while everyone else headed to their offices. He ended up in the guards' basement workout room. He dialled back his usual routines and still ended up sweaty and exhausted. Went back upstairs to change. At least he could rebuild his muscles. He obviously wasn't going to be allowed to do anything else while he was here.

He'd just finished a shower and was mostly dressed when there was a knock at his door. Mastren came in, looking somewhat agitated. Not a common occurrence.

"The police are here to speak with you," he said.

"And my father allowed them in?" He knew the police wouldn't be allowed in the house otherwise but figured asking would give him a few moments to think.

"He said they could speak to you."

"And is a lawyer is on the way to supervise the interview?" He finished buttoning his shirt cuffs.

"Your father suggested that would send the wrong message."

That his family actually cared for him?

"Well, I don't want to disappoint him further. Where are they?"

"The small guest parlour, sir." Wow. He'd gotten a sir out of the old fart when no one else was around. A sure sign the end of the world was coming fast and hard. And he was in the way.

Barrat slipped his jacket on and waved in dismissal. "I can find them and I'm sure you have many more important things to do." He headed for the more public area of the house.

The two men wore decent off-the-rack suits. Neither was sitting nor had poured a coffee from the tray a footman provided. He went over and poured for himself before sitting down. Letting the coffee get cold was the only crime he could think of right now.

"I'm Barrat Trelner. What can I do for you, officers?"

The older one spoke and the slightly younger took out a notepad and pen. "I'm Captain Lagrath and this is Sergeant Cranter. We're from Corporate Oversight. We have a few questions on your recent adventure." The tone put quotes around *adventure*. "Your father apprised our commander of the details and suggest that we speak with you."

"So I'm sure you've been told I have no memory of the two weeks leading up to my re-appearance. I'm not sure how I can help with any enquiries of that time." He sat back in the comfortable chair. If he was going to spend the next few hours saying variations on *'I don't remember anything'*, he wanted to be vaguely at ease while he did it. The captain took the seat opposite him and the sergeant moved one so it almost blocked his route to the door.

"When you woke in the alley, you thought you'd been drinking?"

"Yes. I smelled the whiskey on my clothes and an epic hangover was starting to impinge itself on my skull."

"Your wallet was still in your possession?"

"Yes. I was a little surprised, given where I woke up. All my cards were in place, two twenties in cash, a little change. Not what I recall having in there but with the length of the memory loss I'm fairly sure the amount was reasonable if I'd been out drinking."

"And your security screamer was still in your pocket. Why didn't you call for them to pick you up rather than walking home?"

"My father disapproves of excessive drinking, Captain. If I called security to take me home, they would, of course, inform my father immediately. I didn't want him to know that I'd lost at least a full day to alcohol poisoning. In retrospect, I could have saved myself the walk. I'm very out of shape and it was worse that night."

"Did you check your purchases on your cards?"

"When I got here the day after I woke up. The bank said I'd last used my card for a taxi ride from Grethel's gym, where I usually work out, to my apartment. The day I vanished, it seems. If the kidnappers asked for my account information, they did nothing with it. None of my accounts were accessed or drained. That seemed odd to me."

"And earlier that day you were interviewed at Vegathic. Why?"

"Why did I take a taxi from there or why the interview?"

"The interview." A small frown. The captain didn't like him. Would probably describe him as a smart ass. It wouldn't make much difference. Father working with the police meant he was in trouble.

"I don't want to work for any of my family's companies, Captain. Too many would see any praise, or any positive notice of me as caused by being my father's son, not because of the quality of work I was doing. My siblings and their spouses endured much the same reaction when they first went to work for my father. I heard stories when I was younger and experienced it first hand when I was an intern there in the main office mail room during university. Volunteering for several years of that particular dark hell didn't really appeal to me. I would guess I turned down the offer Vegathic made because they wanted a puppet, not an analyst. At least that's what happened at the few other interviews I've been to since graduation. I don't recall anything about being offered the interview. That would have been several days, at most a week before the event. You'd have to check with Vegathic's personnel department in regard to that timing."

"You've had only a few interviews? Even though you graduated with Honours? That seems unlikely, given the respect that degree is given."

"Only four of them so far. From cronies or those who want to suck up to my father. Many other companies don't want to hire me because they think I'll help Father take them over once I get access to their internal documents."

"One of them said that to you directly?" A frown.

"Yes. The head of an analysis division of a major corporation, in private, at a business function we were both at. I'd wondered why there was no response to my resume and asked him directly. When he told me why few if any companies like his might want to hire me, I apologized for wasting his time and left. That's the day I decided to move out of this house. To try to build a life of my own."

"And to leave your security behind." The sergeant. Barrat stared at him for a moment, then nodded.

"That too. I enjoyed living at my apartment, even though cooking was a mystery I was learning. Slowly." He got up and went back to the side table. "Coffee? I never got the hang of the coffee maker I bought. It has way too many knobs and adjustments." He refilled for himself. Neither of the others moved. Their loss. It was very good coffee. Father wouldn't permit anything else in the house, at least for the family. He'd never considered what swill the staff might be forced to drink. *Maybe that's why no coffee service sat out for long. The footmen wanted the good stuff before it got cold. Or they managed to reheat it.* He set down the spoon. *Whatever happened to the leftover coffee was irrelevant at this point.*

"You moved out to dissociate yourself from your father," Lagrath said.

"Yes. Isn't a young man, or woman, supposed to move out when they finish university and find a job? I thought it was past my time to go." He seldom saw either parent when he did live there and was tired of the servants watching his every move. He sat back down and sipped his coffee. He needed to get *someone* to teach him how to make it before he moved out again. Buying it all the time from shops was an added cost he could trim. Maybe. Perhaps Erithe's staff would teach him if those here wouldn't. He had no idea why making coffee wasn't covered in his basic cookbook. It was a critical skill for living. Maybe he'd write to the author and suggest they include it in a future edition.

"That is true. Generally they have a job when that happens."

"I own the building I live in, Captain. I'm sure your people know what the cash flow there is by now. I might be able to move back in a few weeks, once everyone here, especially my father, calms down. There was a vacant, furnished apartment that needed a tenant when I wanted to leave here. My living there didn't affect the profit margin too much. Sounded like a reasonable plan to me. A sign from above, even."

"What condition was your apartment in when you returned to it late that night?" Lagrath asked. At a tiny jerk of his head, the sergeant poured two coffees and brought one to his captain.

"It was a mess but that's not unusual. I tend to clean up when I can't find anything clean to eat from or wear. I was so hung over and fuzzy when I first got there all I wanted was a shower, a lot of water in my system to blunt the hangover and sleep. The next morning I was a little confused. The mess was messier and quite different from I remembered. And there was red stuff dried all over the stove and kitchen floor. I saw a pasta sauce bottle in the trash but I didn't remember heating it or cooking the pasta. I found a few strands in the sink."

"So you started to tidy up and didn't realise how long it had been since you were last in your apartment."

"True. After I ate some soup and crackers. Which I did not burn or make into another mess. I was quite proud of myself, despite the headache. It was near noon when I woke and the milk was off. So cereal, my usual breakfast, wasn't happening. I put the milk in the freezer so I couldn't smell it. It's still there. Oh, well. As long as the freezer stays on it shouldn't get much worse. I hadn't gotten around to taking the garbage out when I met up with one of my neighbours. She told me to call my family immediately as I'd been kidnapped. I didn't believe her until I talked to my sister Erithe. She sent her husband Dantil over to help pick me up and I was brought here when my father found out I'd been released. End of the story of my kidnapping."

The sergeant glared at him.

"The one thing I did notice missing at the time was my computer. I didn't know why I would have taken it with me on a pub stroll and figured that I would have to buy a new one. That made me cranky."

"It was brought here for the note on the screen, we've heard."

"Yes. I know that *now*. It's in my room, frozen up. All it shows is the note even after I tried to reboot it. I'm probably going to get a new one. Sometime soon, I hope. I have to ask Father's minion to arrange it. I don't think the guards want to let me out of the house at the moment, with or without their escort."

"Could you leave on your own?" An eyebrow raised.

"I could try, but Father would be unhappy. More unhappy than he's been, that is. So I will task one of his minions to procure a new computer. With the market still closed I'm sure one has a few minutes to spare. Or that one can send a sub-minion. There are plenty of them lurking around the main office. No idea what they actually do other than jump when my father says to do something."

"What are your other plans?"

"My father said I'd be working at Industries' main office, but that's been put on hold once my drug test results came back. The same day you and the sergeant arrived. Isn't that a coincidence? Or not?"

"Not chance but with a request. Your father contacted my superior to suggest that you come with us. Our Clinic doctors have ways of discovering hidden memories."

"You think they can beat the Zeltin? I was told those memories are gone for good. There is *no* way to recover them."

"It's an outside chance. Mr. Trelner is concerned some instructions have been added to your brain by those kidnappers. And you might do some things that are not in any of your family member's best interests."

"And you can find them? It doesn't make sense. The Zeltin would erase those memories as well, wouldn't it?"

"It is a grey area," Lagrath said. "It is possible according to the experts I consulted. My office, as well as the Securities Services, has an overwhelming interest in determining what happened to cause Vegathic to fail on such a minor report. Then the cascade of many other stocks started. Obviously, some fell just on the panic of that day but other companies might have also been targeted. You might have been, I don't like to use the term programmed, but it fits, or set up to do something to Vegathic's computer network to compromise their response to the reports. That might have happened outside the two week window that the Zeltin erased. That's more what we want to look for."

"So you think all of my interviews over the past five months were chosen by a nefarious conspiracy to allow them to access the computer nets of four large companies? So someone could crash the market and make a series of quiet purchases at bargain prices? You should take my computer. It might have something your people can find. Our experts gave up."

"We wish you to come with us. The computer might be useful. You are much more likely to have the information we're looking for."

"Am I under arrest?"

"Of course not. Our doctors, and your father, want you to check into our secure facility so they can determine if you have been compromised in any way."

He knew that was a Very Bad Idea. The secure facility, shared with the regular police divisions, had a reputation. A very bad one. The Interrogation Clinic. The public and popular news media usually called it Insanity Central for a very good reason. Those doctors could find out all the things he didn't want Father to know. With their truth drugs in his system there was no way he could keep *anything* secret. Whatever they asked about, he'd tell them. The police loved it since it gave them a very high rate of clearing cases. Sometimes they guessed wrong about who was guilty but those stories never lasted long in the news sheets.

"I decline, Captain Lagrath. I am quite content to manage my apartment building and my few personal investments. I will not seek to gain access to any major corporate computers in the future. Goodbye."

He got up and headed for the door. The sergeant stood and moved in front of him.

"Do I have the right to leave or are you going to arrest me since I won't surrender my brain to your interest?"

"We have no grounds to arrest you at this time, sir. We are asking for your cooperation in our investigation into the crash." The sergeant moved to one side at a signal from the captain.

"I will not allow anyone to rummage around in my head for fun. I will have someone show you out." He opened the door and spotted one of the footmen headed down with corridor away from the room.

"Welker?" The man turned and waited. "Could you show the police out? They have no further reason to remain." The footman nodded and Barrat hurried back to his room. He got there, shut and locked the door. Leaned against it. *Dark hells.* If he tried to leave the house and vanish now, they'd all assume he knew about a conspiracy and would hunt him forever. Arranging an "accident" to get free meant having help from outside, which he didn't have available. All of Father's guards here would refuse to aid him, then sit on him, and tell his father immediately if he asked for help in leaving. Then the guards would bundle him up hand him over to the interrogators. They might even deliver him personally.

Even if he did manage to get out of the house, police resources were too great for him to escape notice with the surveillance he was sure was now on the compound from inside and out. And his personal accounts had a pittance in them, according to the total he was given when he'd called to check on his more recent purchases. The end of the month would see a deposit from the rental revenue, but that was over a week away. He was trapped here.

He couldn't access his external storage here because all these computers would have a direct feed to his father's desk and he'd have to reset all his passwords and log-ins. The guards wouldn't let him out of the compound into any bar where he could hope to get some cash by his usual method of asking a waiter to ring in a higher amount than he'd spent on his card and give him the difference in cash. He could do nothing to protect or free himself. As usual. He stared at the window, not looking at the garden beyond.

❧❦❧❦

Welker indicated the way to the front door and the two men started to follow him. He hadn't been able to hear much of what the police asked Mr. Barrat. Just something about the market crash and his loss of memory. Things he'd already heard from the rest of the staff. No new tidbits to pass along.

"Do you know anything of what happened during the kidnapping or that related to the crash?" the captain asked him. "There could be an ongoing payment, if you chose to do the right thing. We need help to identify who was responsible for so much turmoil. It might be young Mr. Trelner. We aren't sure his memory loss is real."

"I have no knowledge of that, sir," he said, since another footman was within hearing distance. They stopped near the front door and he looked around quickly. No one was nearby. "But I have heard a few things, and might hear more with all the family staying here now."

The sergeant handed him a card. "Contact me if you want to set up a contact method. We'll take very good care of you." They left and he closed the door. A quick glance around. No one was in sight, or within hearing range. Welker stared at the card. He heard footsteps from the service corridor and tucked the card into his vest pocket for now. Mastren came into view and he started walking toward his boss on the way back to the small parlour.

"I'll tidy up the small parlour, sir," Welker said. "Mr. Barrat asked me to show the officers out after their interview."

Mastren nodded. "Very good. I'll inform Mr. Vanthin when he returns that they were here."

⤙⤙⤙⤙⤙

The rest of the day was quiet. He'd managed another session in the gym but his muscles were still weak. Another reason he wouldn't be able to escape on his own. The storm began when Father arrived home for dinner and someone, probably Mastren, told him the result of the interview. Or maybe the captain had commed him right after they left and the storm was just another excuse to shout at him.

"You should *want* to know if you're being used!" Father stormed into his room without knocking. Barrat was reading one of the novels he'd left here when he moved out and sipping on a mug of excellent coffee he'd asked Welker to bring. This tale of adventure was one of his favourites. When, or if, he managed to move out again he'd take at least some of his books with him. Harder to move without notice but he could relax and enjoy himself when there was a chance.

"I don't want my brain scrambled any more than it has been," he replied. He stood and faced his father. Another stupid dominance battle. One he couldn't win but had to try to.

"It would be perfectly safe for you, they said." Barrat heard some noises out in the corridor. His mother came in a moment later.

"Any time someone says that, they're lying, Vanthin," Mother said.

"That's not true, Carithe. Their commander assured me personally that there would be no physical or psychological damage. They have the experience to ensure his safety and find out if he was used."

'*Oh good, I get to be in between another epic fight between my parents. Can I sneak out of the room?*'

"Is that why several thugs are in the corridor by the main stairs? To take Barrat away against his will?" The chill in her voice was evident.

"I am over twenty, Father. Or did I miscount the years? You don't have the right to speak for me or to arrange anything for me." There was no secret passage in this room. *Dark hells. He was trapped.* His stomach, slightly relaxed by reading, seized up. Again.

"You're not thinking rationally, boy. You need to get this done." Both turned to face him then Mother came to his side.

"I told the police I'd give them my old computer so they could dissect its storage. I don't want anyone messing around with my brain. I have no idea what the kidnappers did to me. No one, except them, can tell anyone what they did to me during that week."

"You don't get the choice to refuse. Not now. There's too much riding on your cooperation."

"Riding on *what*, Vanthin?" Mother asked. Barrat nodded, letting her take the lead for now. He didn't know how to change Father's mind. he'd never managed to before, so how could he think to triumph this time?

"All the other companies he interviewed at are saying they'll launch civil suits if Barrat can't prove he didn't do anything to their computer networks while he was in their buildings."

"How can anyone prove that?" Barrat asked. "It's impossible to prove a negative. You know that, Father. Haven't they checked their recordings of the time I was in their building and seen that I hadn't even tried to gain access to their network?"

"Vegathic did that already. Nothing showed. No one else still has that footage. So they aren't convinced. They want proof. And that means getting into your memories. They're asking fifty million in damages if we don't comply. Each."

"So I'm the sacrifice to save your company. Giving in is a sign of weakness, Father. You taught me that very clearly. If you let the police take me, then you're admitting they have power: it's their game." He paused. "Or are you playing your own? I'm still the sacrifice, though. The captain said *you* called them to offer my brain for their amusement. Is that what you've been saving me for? A pawn to bring you even more wealth?" His father glared at him. Mother glared at Father but didn't say anything for several seconds.

Barrat turned to his desk. He got out a sheet of paper, ignoring his parents' renewed argument. He wrote quickly. A slim chance to keep Father from controlling his meagre assets and implementing changes he didn't want to make. Like the basement apartment renovation. He'd be in favour of the increased income and ignore the eventual problems. It wasn't *his* building, after all. If it fell down it wouldn't be his fault.

He waved the paper to distract them. "This power of attorney assigns control of all my assets to Erithe. Not you, Father. I don't want you stomping all over my tenants or investments. Agree and I go willingly. Else the police will have a fight as long as they keep me. I might make a mess in this lovely house or they may cause permanent damage to my brain that *you'll* have to explain to the world. What's your answer?"

"Fine. Do as you like. Just go with them and let Erithe do some work for a change." Vanthin stormed out.

"Would you give this to Erithe, Mother?" She nodded and he gave her the document. He hoped it contained all the required information but she'd know a judge who would grant it with no questions.

"A good plan, Barrat. He'd object more if it was me. Erithe and Dantil will look after your things." She took the paper and tucked it into her skirt pocket. "I still think this is a terrible idea, Barrat. I've heard things about the people they've questioned and released as innocent."

"So have I, Mother. But I can't see any way out of this. Not with Father on their side." He looked at his suit. "I'm going to change. I don't want the police to ruin my good clothes. I can't afford to replace them." She smiled with a tear running down her cheek. *As if she really cared now that he was an adult. She'd mostly ignored him for years. Her foundation was the most important thing in her life, not her children.* "Go now and call Erithe. The sooner she files the paperwork the less time Father has to mess things up. Could you have someone tell the police I'll be out in a minute or two?"

She kissed his cheek and hugged him. "Come home safe and soon," she whispered in his ear.

"I'll try, Mama." The word he'd used as a child slipped out. She left and he headed for the closet to strip off his shirt and pants and replace them with exercise gear. Comfortable and practical.

Three low level police goons, the sergeant and Captain Lagrath waited outside his room when he opened the door. He handed the captain his computer, then extended his arms toward the sergeant. "Do you want to use handcuffs, Captain? I did promise my father that I'd behave. You don't have to believe that promise if you don't trust me."

"We wish to be discreet, Mr. Trelner. There some reporters and protestors outside the compound walls. I don't know who tipped them off that we were coming to visit but taking you out of here in handcuffs sends the wrong message at this time. The public is looking for a reason behind the crash and isn't interested in verifiable facts, but we prefer them to wild speculations."

"Well then. Let's get this over with." The three goons were behind and on either side of him. The sergeant was just in front and the captain was in the lead. Welker opened the door, looking shocked at the extent of his escort. He must not have been nearby to let them in.

The waiting limousine had dark tinted windows and two outrider cars, one in front and the other behind. "Very fancy," Barrat said. "All this for me? Am I such a danger to the markets and society in general?"

"They're for dealing with the press if we need them," the sergeant growled. "To show escort, not arrest."

He was sure it sent the opposite message. Just the captain, the sergeant as escort and maybe a driver in a sedan would be a friendly chat. All these goons meant nobody could get to him and he couldn't get away. Maybe not arrest, but serious interest and distrust in anything he said.

He was directed to the back seat, with the captain and sergeant on either side of him. Two goons faced them. The other goon was up with the driver. As they left the compound, he caught sight of the growing crowd. Some waved signs denouncing the police, others suggested he or the family pay them for their losses and for starting Vegathic's collapse. The rest were reporters with cameras and microphones who shouted questions no one in the car could hear. Only a few people seemed neutral. One looked almost familiar but the car sped past the crowd too quickly to get a good look at the older man. Barrat hoped his mind was still intact when this ordeal was over with. If it ever ended, that is.

⋘⋙⋘⋙

Erithe stared at the document for several moments. "He gave you this? What does he expect is going to happen to him?" she asked her mother. Mother was in the parlour, perched on the edge of a chair when she and Dantil arrived from their offices in response to her call.

"He gave it to me just before the police took him away. They're going to rip his mind apart looking for someone else's plans, Erithe. And your father is allowing it. He might have instigated it to find out if Barrat was behind his kidnapping. There's no proposed lawsuits by the other companies Barrat interviewed at. Vanthin made it up to convince him there was a real threat to the family. I have my own contacts in those companies and *none* are planning any legal action against us. They also realized considerable profit in the collapse. The same way your father did."

"I'll call my lawyer to have this filed as soon as possible. Who has Barrat used in the past? Do you know?"

"One of ours, I believe. He wanted to set up another, I think, but may not have been able to do so. I would have offered to help if I'd known he was so low on funds. His allowance dropped on his twentieth birthday and ceased when he graduated, I found out yesterday. Unlike the rest of you. Your father said it was to toughen him up from being the baby of the family. And once he came into his inheritance, he possessed another source of income so didn't "need" much of an allowance. I would have replaced those funds from my own holdings if I'd known what was going on. He never said anything about his finances when he moved back here after he graduated. Did he ever mention any of this to you or Dantil?"

"I don't think he wanted any of us to know, Mother. He's been aloof since he went to boarding school. Maybe even before. I think I've spent more time with him since his graduation than in the entire rest of his life." She took a deep breath. "Mom, do you think he helped to engineer Vegathic's collapse? Either knowing what he did or as a dupe for someone else?"

"Neither, dear. I think he wanted to get away from us, certainly from his father. Have some independence. Have his own friends without any family looking over his shoulder. Did he tell you he was learning how to cook?"

"I did hear he wanted lessons in how to make coffee," Erithe said with a smile that faded as she looked at the document in her hand, then at Dantil. "We need to talk to Carthan. And everyone else in the family. Father's gone too far this time. We can't let him get away with what he's doing to Barrat."

Carithe nodded. "As soon as we can set up a conference call, dear."

⚜⚜⚜

The two outrider cars left them on the speedway. Barrat raised an eyebrow and looked toward Captain Lagrath. "Are we safe from the evil machinations of the reporters now?"

"In a manner of speaking." He nodded and Barrat felt a sharp pain in his upper arm on the other side. The sergeant put away an injector unit. One of the goons knelt in front of him and grabbed his arms so he couldn't move. He was almost flattered they thought him such a danger to society. It got dark quickly.

His eyes opened slowly. The light was dim enough that he didn't mind the level. He sat up slowly in case his balance was still affected by whatever drugs they'd given him. The injection in the car was the first, not the most recent, he knew from the stories in the news sheets. He looked around. He sat on a hard, solid metal bench about knee high. It was cold except where he'd been lying. The walls and floor were covered in large beige tiles. A small floor drain sat in one corner. A solid ceiling with a single light in a cage above a beige metal door with no knob or hinges on this side. A tank-less toilet in the opposite corner and there was no sink. Easy to clean, cold to be kept in.

No clothing. A tight, wide silvery band on his right wrist and a bulky mitten on his left hand and partway up his wrist. He looked closer. A port with four tubing connectors was on the back side of the mitten. He turned to check the rest of the cell. There was something in the wall behind him. The other half of the port? He pulled it and a thick cable came out of the wall. He let it go and it retracted. *Great.*

He used the toilet and realised it was like one on an airplane. No water in it, but a little clear liquid flowed in when it flushed and the trap at the bottom opened. There was no source of liquids but what they allowed him to have through the port. He looked at the other walls. A strange set of fixtures were set into the wall near the door. About person sized for all of them. There was another of those port things. He went over and pulled on the chest-high tongue of metal and a wide piece of webbing came out of the wall. A restraint system? Why did they have someone tied to the wall when they were questioned? Did it matter, or did they just use it to intimidate their prisoners? Or did they like to make their prisoners suffer, just because they could and no one on the outside cared enough to protest?

"Good evening, Mr. Trelner," came a male voice from the ceiling. He started a little.

"When does the brain sucking start?" he asked. "The sooner you all realize I don't know anything about the market crash or have someone's evil plan in my brain, the sooner I can leave your delightful rest spa."

"We will start soon. We're going to go over some rules first. If you do things we don't like or refuse to do as you're told, you will be punished."

"How?" His right wrist spasmed from the pain. He grabbed the silver cuff with his mittened hand. Collapsed forward in agony. Then the pain vanished. He was on his knees when he could finally see. His breathing took longer to return to normal. He blinked rapidly, trying to clear his eyes. Eventually the room came into focus.

"That's how. What you just experienced was level five for five seconds. There are eleven levels in total and the timer can reach five minutes. Do you understand me?"

"Yes." He managed to say that one word and to get up to sit on the hard bench. More time passed and his brain started to work better. "And the mitten?" He waved it. There must be at least one or more cameras to observe his every move, he just hadn't spotted them yet.

"An access port for nutrients and for the drugs we'll use to question you. You will tell us everything we want to know."

"Tied to the wall? Very medieval."

"Very perceptive. We'll start the questioning in a few hours. Lie down and hook the port to your hand."

"First," came another voice. Deeper. Barrat stopped reaching for the port. "We don't like to clean up the mess when our clients piss on the floor. It stinks and it's very unsanitary. There's an item on the right side of the bench. Pull it up."

Barrat looked down and saw a limp plastic bag with a large bore, clear, flexible tubing coming from it. Some kind of sticky tape around the top of the bag and extra for wrapping it around his penis.

"Put it on. As tightly as you can on the top or it could leak and make a mess. You'll clean it up, not our staff." It was difficult with only one functional hand but he managed. "Now the port. It will click into place if you have the correct orientation."

One end of the port was square and the other rounded, like many computer cables. It did click. "How do I get it out later? Or do I?"

"There are two prongs. When they are pushed together the connector releases," the first voice said. He saw them but didn't touch it, not wanting to risk another shock. "Lie down now."

He did so quickly, in case they shocked him for not obeying. Felt something cool running into his hand. Drugs, nutrients or plain water, he was soon asleep and didn't care what was pumped into him.

⸙⸙⸙⸙

"All good so far, sir," the tech reported to his supervisor. Each monitoring station watched over four cells. It was a slow week so far. Only two of the ones under his control were currently inhabited. The police, Corporate Oversight and the Securities Services were running around trying to figure out why the market crashed and hadn't arrested anyone yet. Trelner was involved, the lunch room gossip said. "He didn't give us any trouble so far. I gave him the eight shock and told him it was five. I don't think we'll have cause to use it seriously. Just for some quick reminders. He might be smart enough to behave, unlike most of our clients."

"Good. The interrogation team is still reviewing the case notes. Give him three hours of sleep, then shut down the sedative. We need to calibrate his reaction to the drug mix. I was told we can't take the chance of damaging this one permanently. The rest of his family would never let it go. And the press could start looking at others the interrogators decided were actually innocent. Keeping that from happening is a priority, the director told me. Several times, in fact."

"Right, sir. Someone will be monitoring him at all times, of course."

The supervisor left. The tech turned back to the monitors. There were other things that would help break the rich asshole that weren't obvious. A few high level shocks while he was drugged wouldn't show on the monitors and no one ever looked at the raw data from his or any console in this building. The asshole would tell the interrogators everything they wanted to know and would suffer for his arrogance. And he'd never be able to stomp on any ordinary people ever again.

Chapter 8

Erithe entered her father's study after an uncomfortable dinner during which no one spoke much except to acknowledge the footmen. He did look up when she came in, which surprised her.

"I now have control of Barrat's assets by the power of attorney he signed before the police took him away. My lawyer just finished the paperwork and it's been approved. You should be getting the notification by tomorrow morning. I just wanted to let you know: As a courtesy."

"And?" He looked down at a document. Ignoring her. Not for long.

"And I also know there are no lawsuits threatened against us. Mother told me what you'd said. I've checked with my sources and we've let everyone in the family know what you've done. I hope Barrat survives whatever you've arranged for him, Father. We're moving back home tomorrow morning after breakfast. So are Carthan and Hethane. All the kids, of course. We won't be stopping in next weekend. You're too busy sorting out the stocks you bought to spend any time with them. The children will understand that. They've heard it often enough."

Vanthin stared at her for a long moment, then turned back to his screens. She left, leaving the door open. Dantil met her outside the main office door.

"How did it go, love?" he asked.

"He didn't really say anything. Maybe we just sent the wrong message, Dantil, but Father crossed a line I hadn't realised was there when he gave Barrat over to the police. I just hope my little brother will be someone I recognise when Insanity Central finally releases him."

"I hope so too. I wish he'd refused, no matter what your father said."

ᡣᡒᡣᡒ

Welker sat at his usual coffee shop three days after Mr. Barrat was taken away. It was near enough to the compound that he didn't have to waste a lot of time in travel. He didn't have much free time during the day. Mastren made sure of that. He tried not to look around for his contact. The sergeant from the other day, he'd been told.

He blinked. The sergeant, Cranter, was fixing his coffee near the checkout. Wearing casual clothes, not a suit or his uniform. Covert work. Like he'd read about in most of the novels he enjoyed. He relaxed a little.

"Share the table?" Cranter asked.

"Sure," Welker said and moved the rest of his news sheet to clear more space. An envelope came out from Cranter's news sheets and slid under his. Cranter turned slightly to watch the traffic and sipped his coffee.

"This has your first fee and instructions on how to send us word that you've got a report to deliver. We're thinking every two weeks as a regular schedule, unless you find something urgent. Then you'd send word to us and come here. We'll send a car here to pick you up if we need to get you out of the house."

"The Trelners hate informants. You won't ever tell them what I did? Even after the trials?"

"No. And we'll relocate you with a new name and excellent references when this is over. We mostly want to know what the family thinks and does in relation to the crash and young Mr. Trelner's possible complicity in those events. Any other information you can find out on the time he was missing is also very important. We need cross checks on some events." He folded the news sheets and picked up his coffee. "Thanks." He walked away into the crowd.

Welker shifted his own news sheet to pick up the envelope, then glanced at his watch. Dark hells. He had to get back to the compound soon. Mastren was such a martinet to work for. He gathered up his news sheets, tucking the envelope into his pants pocket, and headed out. He smiled once he was well away from the coffee shop.

ᡣᡒᡣᡒ

Kerit shook his head as the police cars took Barrat away from his family's compound. There were too many rumours about the market collapse and his possible involvement for the boy to stay safe, especially if he vanished. He worked his way to the edge of the crowd and headed down an alleyway with no surveillance coverage. There was still work to do. He hadn't realized that Barrat had been kidnapped when he'd missed their rendezvous, just that he hadn't arrived nor answered any messages in the days following their planned meeting. The police might have picked him up then but he'd heard nothing on the dark net about either of their identities being compromised or later, any chatter that wasn't about the market collapse.

Two days after the aborted meeting he'd moved all of Barrat's other identity assets and gear into new locations. And now he'd shift to a residence that Barrat didn't know about. Had he tried the memory repression technique when he'd been kidnapped? And did it work? He grimaced. There were stories of the technique working, but he couldn't count on it being true. But on his end, he'd be safe. Dark hells.

Until Barrat resurfaced and could send him a message, he'd have to treat the boy as a possible enemy. He would finish that contract in Snathard they'd agreed to, but pretend to be Barrat in any communications with the clients. Easier when it was a simple poisoning that he could arrange without abusing his creaky joints. Some people made it easy to be eliminated through the illegal drugs they used. Death by drowning while mentally incapacitated wouldn't raise many concerns. There were stories like that in the news often enough for those who were more famous than this denizen of the dark hells. He didn't like men who picked on kids either.

Soon he was on a bus headed the wrong way to anywhere he actually wanted to be. A brief jaunt on the subway and then into one of the most crowded malls in the city. Few of the citizens who thronged those stores knew that the basement provided an access point to the underground levels he'd taught Barrat how to find. There were enough tunnels that he'd be safe even if the boy told the police all about it. He'd encountered enough other people down here to know the knowledge of them was very widespread in some circles. The unwritten rule was that you didn't make eye contact with anyone or speak to them. They had their reasons for being here and you had yours. And no one ever mentioned anything to the police.

✥❧✥❧

Barrat wasn't sure how long he'd been in this tiny cell. He didn't know what questions he'd answered already and which were new. They seemed to repeat a lot or the drugs were doing very weird things with his brain. His stomach growled with almost constant hunger. Why were they starving him as well? Nothing about these interrogators made sense. His stomach roiled again. He thought it might be happening more often but with the myriad drugs in his system he couldn't be sure. Sometimes the room's light was very bright and other times he could barely see anything. Yet size of the light by the door didn't seem any different.

A click from the speaker heralded an order. He tried to open his eyes. It was completely dark. A nice change from constant light. Maybe.

"The blindfold is necessary. Don't try to remove it."

"'Kay," he mumbled. Nothing else happened. They must have come in while he slept to put it on. Sometimes when he woke his beard or hair were shorter. And damp. How did they get him cleaned up? And how often? Did it matter? At least he hadn't been shocked lately. Maybe.

They'd shocked him several times during the questioning, he thought. Just because they could, not because he'd done something they didn't like or refused to get into the restraints on the wall. What did the shock do to his mind? Things were always fuzzy for some time afterwards. Enough shocks or a high enough one and he'd be a vegetable. Maybe that's what Father wanted them to do to him. A good obedient son who didn't do anything to make him mad.

His tears were absorbed by the cloth across his eyes. At least he was lying down at the moment. The chest webbing cut into his armpits when they sent him to sleep standing up.

He managed to doze off when a gust of colder air meant the door opened. He didn't move. That would get him another shock. Hands grabbed his arms and hauled him upright. The port and the little piss bag were removed and he was shoved into a wheelchair and a strap went around his lower chest and upper arms. His feet were put on supports.

"That cuff works anywhere in this facility and I've got an activation unit," came a voice beside him. Not one he recognized. "You gonna cause us any trouble, rich kid?"

"No." No power, no control. An inconvenient extra son. He left his hands in his lap to provide a little modesty. They went down a long corridor, then turned left. There were three men with him by the sounds of the footsteps. One on either side and one pushing him. Another turn, this one to the right. Echoes said this was a small room.

"I'll call when to come take him back," a voice said. Captain Lagrath? The blindfold vanished and he was right in the identification. A beige room, painted, not tiled. A grey metal desk in front of him, one chair on the other side and one against the far wall. The captain stood beside the desk and put a file folder down on it.

Barrat didn't say anything. The voices on the speaker trained him not to ask anything. He was there to provide information, not request it.

"We need some answers from you, Trelner."

"You haven't gotten them?" It felt strange to use a full sentence without the drugs in his system. Of course, they could have given him a small dose just before they'd come for him, just to get him talking but not enough to shut down his ability to think the way it usually did.

"No. You've been saying things that don't add up. So you get a choice. Tell me now or they'll use the cuff until you do. There's a set, you know. All four limbs. They're being nice at the moment."

"What's the question?" No way to escape, no way to stop this. All he could do was submit and hope they didn't destroy his mind anyway.

"Your financial records say you spent considerable sums in bars during university and after. Yet when my men have asked about your consumption, some of your friends seem to think you actually don't drink much. An occasional whiskey or glass of wine, but most of the time you had a soft drink or juice with them at the bar than get falling down drunk. Same once you graduated, they've said. Where did that money actually go? You haven't provided adequate answers with the drugs. The interrogators haven't been able to ask the right question to unlock the answers they were looking for. So you get a chance to bypass some very unpleasant procedures. This is a very limited time offer, so I suggest you tell me the truth now."

He let himself blush. "Girls. Professionals. I... ask the bar staff to put through a higher amount on my card when they bring the tab and give me the cash difference. They got ten percent as a tip and I got money I don't have to account for."

"Girls? *You* couldn't get a date? On campus with your name and family well known? Try again." A snort of derision.

"You're right. I could have dated a different girl every night. But I didn't. Getting married right out of university wasn't how I wanted to start my adult life."

"Keep explaining." The captain sat on the corner of the desk and swung a foot. At least he was still listening.

"Most of the girls in my classes and dorm building were looking for a husband who could keep them in the style they wanted to live. They saw my last name and assumed *I* was rich. I'm not. Very much the opposite if you consider just my cash flow, not my asset list. Love wasn't necessary to the future they were planning. If I asked any of *them* out on a date, it would encourage that one and all the others to keep up the pursuit. So if I wanted some," blushing again, "female companionship, I went off campus and took cash. That's the truth." He didn't bother to look up to see if the captain believed him. It wouldn't matter. They'd drug him and ask all these questions again, he was sure. Make sure he wasn't lying.

Captain Lagrath snorted in amusement. "Now it makes sense. I take it you continued this practice through your university career?"

"I did. And when I was home during the summers. And then at the apartment. I don't trust my bank not to report everything I spend to my father. He's very controlling, as you might have guessed." He dared a question. "Do you think I was taken from inside my apartment?"

"It isn't clear. They did gain access but that might have been via the balcony. Or they grabbed you on the street and got the door codes from your mind. And they buggered up your computer. We haven't gotten anything useful from it, by the way."

"Maybe I was on my way to one of the nearby bars to suck some more money out of my account. There's several within easy walking dis-tance of my apartment. The kidnappers must have been watching me and made their move while I was either there or on my way."

"How much were you paying for your female company?"

"Forty for the evening, sometimes I left more for a tip. Didn't use the same girl more than once or twice so *they* didn't get ideas. The ones here in the city want more cash for less time, so I didn't get out as much. Last time was about three weeks before I was kidnapped."

"We'll make enquiries here and near the university." The captain stared at him. "Any other secrets you'd like to share now?"

"That I hate my father? I'm sure the interrogators have figured that out. I don't know why my mother stays in that house with him, unless it's to prevent the old bastard from doing something to her matrimonial agreement. You'd have to ask her on that."

"Did you ever think about running away from your family?"

"For a while, all the time. I was sent to boarding school when I was twelve and all the kids knew each other. They'd been together for three years. I was the odd one and they started picking on me the first day I was there. My father said it would toughen me up for life in the corpor-ate world and to suck it up. He refused to let me leave that school. And he instructed the staff put a tracking device on me for the rest of that year. So yes, I thought a lot about running away. Then I got smart and played his games back at him and started planning. I moved out this summer in a vain attempt to build a life away from his influence. That didn't work. I should have moved further away but didn't have the cash. The apartment in my building was the only place I could afford given my pitiful income level. That's why I wanted to get a job. But no one wants to hire me for my expertise, just as a puppet." The headache was coming back. Again. The light level dimmed slightly, which helped him cope with the pain.

"You've dropped out of sight a number of times over the past few years," the captain said. "Where did you go?"

"Motels with no cameras and no contact with family. Rented car. A girl hired for an extended romp. Never a repeat there."

"You're cooperating. I'm a little surprised, given your comments at the compound when we first spoke."

He lifted his right hand. "This is a powerful inducement to behave." He let it drop back into his lap. He was tired. And hungry. The headache ramped up and he partly closed his eyes.

"It seems to be. You're not looking well."

"Feel like last week's garbage," he admitted. He leaned slightly forward and rested his hands on his knees. Some nausea returned but it wasn't bad enough to make him spew. Increasing pressure throbbed in his temples and he shut his eyes against the suddenly bright light of the tiny room. "Are we done?"

"For now." The captain passed him and the door opened. The guards put the blindfold back on and took him back to the tiny cell. The headache worsened. He flopped onto the bench as soon as they got him sitting. Didn't care about the piss bag or the port. The guards or the techs could come back in to hook them up if they wanted. He didn't care about what they did to him now. If they let him die, at least the pain in his head would go away.

⊱⊰⊱⊰

Captain Lagrath stared at the monitor for Trelner's cell in the observation room down the hall from the cells.

"What's wrong with him, doctor? He's not behaving the same as others I've seen in here."

"He seems to be having a long term reaction to the drugs," The doctor on duty said. "An allergy, for lack of a better term. It could be idiosyncratic or he's been prepared for this kind of interrogation. Hard to tell which at this point." A figure in white entered the cell to attach the port and put a small bag on Trelner's penis. Lagrath frowned.

"To keep the mess, down, Captain. When he urinates while unconscious or during questioning, it is sent down the tubing instead of splashing on the floor. He's able to use the toilet when he's conscious. We can analyze either source to check the progress of drug breakdown. That's usually once a day. I'll have the techs take a sample the next time he pisses so we can compare it to the last one as well as a blood sample." The white figure left but Trelner didn't move.

"We'll see if something odd is happening. Some people don't react in the usual ways to our drugs. We've moved slower with him and that might be why it's causing problems. Any sensitivity is mostly hereditary but sometimes it just shows up after a week or so. I'll have someone double check all of his medical records to see if he's exhibited other sensitivity issues. Right now, he's just getting nutrients. He seems to be losing weight and that isn't usual either."

"When will you be convinced he's harmless?"

"Another day or so to be sure, the interrogators said when I checked earlier today. They'll bring up the questions and answers he gave you to see if they get the same story when he can't lie to us about it. I'll let you know when he can be returned to his family. If he is having a drug reaction we may need to keep him a few days longer to let him finish stabilizing once the questioning is over."

Lagrath shrugged and turned to leave.

"Is there any progress on your other investigations? He can't be your *only* lead for the market collapse," asked the doctor.

"We're getting nowhere fast," he said. "Everyone now agrees that they don't understand what happened either. The drop should *not* have started. The Securities Services is more confused than I am, and that means they have no ideas at all." He left the building. Sergeant Cranter waited for him by the car in the underground parking area.

"Looks like the kid is completely innocent," he said. "Dark hells. Proving he was responsible would have meant promotions all round."

"Now we have to backpedal and do it fast," Cranter said as they got in. "Back to the office, sir?"

"Yes. Call ahead to have the squad meet while I report on this cluster. Maybe they can brainstorm a scenario that fits, even if we don't have any real evidence and can't get a confession."

❧❧❧❧

Kerit sighed. His back hurt. Moving all of Barrat's and his gear from the storage unit the boy knew about to another one had stressed his body. Unfortunately, there was no one he could truly trust to help him now. But it had to be done in case Barrat told the police about their association and locations of their very expensive and necessary equipment. And now it was finished. He looked at the second key and tucked it into a pocket. With any luck, he'd give it to Barrat sometime soon.

The first unit's rent would run out at the end of the month. Good enough. His apartment rent would run an extra month but he could hire movers there. Strong young backs. Bah. Youth was wasted on them.

The electronic work was much easier. He leaned against a heating pad and sipped some coffee. New passwords for all of their accounts. He went down his checklist of things to do. House hunting was next. He decided to stay in Herithan for now but swap to the other side of the city. The capitol was one of the largest cities in the country and that meant it was easier to stay invisible.

⛤⛤⛤⛤

Welker sighed as he looked at the scant half page of information he'd been able to glean over the past two weeks. One of the guards had finally talked about what he'd overheard when Mr. Vanthin talked to Mr. Barrat and Mrs. Carithe before the officers took him away. That other companies would sue if Mr. Barrat couldn't prove he didn't mess with their computers. It was false, he found out later that day, but maybe Corporate Oversight could find out if there was some other collusion going on. Mr. Vanthin might have done something illegal during the crash. Welker was sure that was likely. Had Mr. Vanthin set Mr. Barrat up to provide a cover for his illegal activities? His anger at the kidnapping might be a ruse to confuse everyone else, especially the Securities Services.

This pitiful amount of information wouldn't get him any bonuses. The real problem was that none of the family really talked to each other here. If he was able to listen in on their comm calls or intercept their messages, he might have a better idea of what they were discussing. Now that the local family members were back at their homes the dining table conversations were nonexistent.

Half the time Mrs. Carithe ate in her suite or went out to an event. And she always had breakfast in her suite. Any time they were both in the dining room there wasn't any conversation. He made a note on his report about his idea. If they could teach him how to set up a repeater box like he'd read about in the spy novels he enjoyed, he'd get copies of all messages sent and received from the compound. That should provide some real information that would get him some large bonuses and out of this rat hole to a better job. He smiled. In the meantime, some tidbits he knew about the family would keep them happy. Things that they wouldn't want anyone to know about.

❧❧❧❧

Erithe stared at the boxy, stainless steel thing on their kitchen table. "What is it?" she asked, moving to see it from another angle. "I've never seen anything like this."

"It's Barrat's coffee maker," Dantil said. "I heard that all his things had been brought over to the main house and asked Svent to fetch it after he and the boys dropped me off at the office."

"It is for espresso," Carlon, their chef, said with a wide grin. "Very small cups with much flavor: very thick and strong. Is this what Mr. Barrat enjoys drinking? I don't think he's ever asked for any special coffees when he's visited here."

They looked at each other. "I don't think he drinks anything special," Dantil said. "I've heard of it but never tried it. Why don't you make us each a cup and we'll watch."

"I need a special grind of coffee first," Carlon said. "And there are special cups needed. A cup of espresso is much stronger than the coffee I usually prepare for you and your visitors. I will make us each a cup, once I have what I need."

An hour later they returned to the kitchen to watch the process. It did seem overly complicated. The cups were tiny and the coffee was thick.

"Bitter," she managed to say after the first sip. Dantil, the wretch, just smiled at her. She managed maybe half the cup full only after adding more sugar and replacing each sip with more cream.

"Not for me," she said, pushing the cup and saucer away with a shudder. Dantil was grinning now.

"I like it. Maybe it's conflicting with the baby," Dantil said.

"Possibly." She shook her head and shuddered again. "Dark hells. I think waiting until after the baby's weaned to try another cup would be a very good idea."

"Keep the machine in the kitchen for now, Carlon," Dantil said when he finished his cup with evident enjoyment. "When Barrat gets back we'll see if he really does like this kind of coffee. If he does, you can teach him how to make it. If not, I'll buy the machine off him and you can teach me. And teach him how to make a regular cup with one of the smaller units." Carlon nodded and sipped from his own cup with a smile.

When they returned to the study, an envelope lay on her desk. She slit it open and sat down. From the management company by the letterhead.

"These idiots again," she muttered as she skimmed the wordy prose.

"What?" Dantil was examining a file but looked over with interest.

"The management company for our apartment buildings," she said. "His representative wants to convert the storage space in Barrat's building into another apartment. He's being really pushy about it. Barrat didn't mention hearing from them, but it sounds like he already told them to forget about the idea and now they think I'll just approve it. This is the second letter I've gotten on the proposal in the past week. I ignored the first one. I don't like the idea."

"What do you want to do about it?"

"Tell them no. Very firmly. I want to talk to Barrat first. Anything done to that building is going to be his decision, not mine."

"They're being a pain about our building as well, remember? Want us to up the rent and there's no real reason. A generic 'rents are going up in that neighbourhood' speech but no details, unless they told you." She shook her head.

"Their revenue *is* a percentage of the rents," Erithe pointed out. "And the company is probably getting a kickback from the construction company they want to do the renovations on Barrat's place. I think it's time to shake things up a bit. I'll contact Legal and find out if there are any contractual issues in finding a new manager."

"Always possible. Everyone else might want to swap as well, if they're getting the same kind of harassment. Six buildings full of people could get us a discount on the fees."

She picked up the comm and smiled at him.

෧෨෧෨

Barrat woke at the flash of pain in his wrist. He started to sit up but realized he was still hanging from the wall. The headache pounded and his eyes ached. He mostly shut them. There wasn't anything here he wanted to see anyway.

"Disconnecting now." He didn't reply. There was a click near his right wrist. That catch released. He moved his hand out from the wall and tongue of the lock came out of the holder and the webbing retracted automatically. Next he removed the port and freed his left wrist. Then the waist and chest straps. The little bag stayed in place but the tubing retracted as he neared the bench. He sat down, his head dizzy and throbbing. The light seemed so bright and that made his head ache more. Completely closing his eyes was the only way it was bearable.

"Reconnect the port." Reaching around to pull it from the wall made his head worse. He managed to get it in place before he passed out again.

He was on his side when he woke, on something soft instead of the hard bench. He tried to see any details but his eyes didn't work right. Some moments he could see just fine, then the things near him went out of focus. Or away from him. Each eye was on a different schedule so he just kept both shut. It was easier. The mitten was still on his left hand, the tubing leading to it. He slept again. The dreams weren't as bad as his current reality. He dreamed of a lake. Splashing in the water. This nanny, not his usual one, made sure he was happy and enjoyed himself.

Someone was standing over him again. He kept his eyes shut. Didn't want to see them. Didn't want to see anyone, or talk to them. He heard voices yelling at him again. Father was mad. He'd must have made a mess. It was all his fault. He was always a bad boy and had to be punished for making messes.

⋘⋙⋘⋙

"What the hells is wrong with him!" Vanthin yelled. The four doctors pulled back slightly. "Your idiot commander told me he'd be fine! *No damage.* That doesn't look like my definition of fine!" He stared at the lump in the bed that was his youngest son. Cowering in fear. A coward now. The doctors said the boy was awake moments before he'd come into the room. His hiding was deliberate. Ignoring his own father. That wouldn't be allowed once he got the boy back home.

"He *will* be fine," one of the doctors, an older man, said. He took a half step forward, asserting his own dominance. His facility. His fault. "Your son's reactions to our drug regimen aren't normal. We didn't realize it how badly he was affected by the testing regime until these symptoms began. The onset of his reactions was quite sudden."

Vanthin doubted that. They just hadn't expected him to show up in person after the official call that their questioning was complete. *Did they hope to keep Barrat here until he recovered so no one would know how badly he was damaged?* "Someone got to him in here to shut him up?"

"Not at all. The interrogators have all the answers that you, the Securities Services and Corporate Oversight needs. He was not involved in anything to do with the market collapse or his own kidnapping. His reaction to the drugs is most likely genetic. Without testing all of your family, it's impossible to tell. A day or three of rest should get the rest of the breakdown chemicals out of his system. We've increased the fluid flow rate to speed that up. There are no other drugs being administered. Just fluids and nutrients."

The other doctors scattered at a signal from their leader. Barrat hadn't moved, even with the shouting. Not a good sign, to his way of thinking. Had they burned out his brain? Turned him into a useless liability? He'd sue them if that was the truth and the boy didn't recover. Get enough money to keep him in an institution for the mentally weak until he died. *Dark hells. What a waste of time this had been.*

"What about the interrogation on the computer scare? *Did* someone implant any instructions in him to disable Vegathic's system?"

"As far as our people can tell, no. Nor did he conspire in anything to do with any computer system. The memories of those two weeks are completely gone. No one can access them. The other company interviews were just that. He put nothing into any of their computers. He is a solitary person, sir. That's one reason he moved out after he graduated, it seems. He was trying to build his own life, on his own terms. Doing what he wanted for his life, not what you thought best for him." The doctor looked at the lump in the bed.

"He was experimenting with women. Paid ones, so there would be no surprise weddings to annoy you or the family. That's where his extra money went and why he seemed to drink a lot but, in fact, did not. The police found several very attractive professional ladies who recognised his picture in this city and in the area adjoining his university. He used false names to them to ensure they didn't come looking for a wedding."

"You swear he will recover?"

"He will, sir. It may take a few weeks or so before he's completely well. Do not push him to do anything or yell at him. Low stress and therapy are the keys to his recovery."

"So, not in the compound, then. There's a retreat we've used for holidays in the past few years. You can send him there once he wakes up. Ship in a therapist to sort him out from this." If they could.

"Give him the choice of where to go," the doctor cautioned. "The inmates here have no control over anything in their lives. He needs to redevelop his sense of self and take back control of his actions. The drugs we use here are extremely powerful weapons in searching for the truth, Mr. Trelner. Most times we don't really care how functional the individual is at the end of our questioning once we know they are guilty. That's why we were working slowly and stopped when your son started to show the symptoms you've seen. So he *would* recover from this. He is completely innocent of any wrongdoing."

"Call me when he can be moved." He took a last look at the wreck remaining of his son and left. The family would be more pissed about this development. But at least he knew the boy hadn't betrayed him.

❧❧❧❧

Barrat didn't move once he recognised his father's voice. Father was very angry at him. He was here because everyone thought he'd been bad but he didn't remember doing anything Father might not like. The tears came again and he thought the doctor bent over him but the man didn't say anything. A chill liquid entered his hand and he started to relax without meaning to. Maybe he would have a good dream.

When he awoke again, he guessed it was the next day. Brighter lights. More noise outside the room. He stayed curled up with his eyes closed.

Someone touched him on the shoulder and he screamed in fright. He stared at a face he didn't know, then burrowed back under the covers. Held them tightly in case the person tried to pull the covers away. He shivered, thinking of that bare bench they'd left him on before. Was someone from the family going to come and not yell at him? Would Mama come and rescue him? No, she wouldn't. She didn't like to make Father angry.

❧❧❧❧

Erithe glared at her father. They were in the family parlour. Mother came in with her. She wanted a witness.

"The police have decided Barrat's innocent of any wrongdoing in regard to the collapse or the kidnapping," Father said. "But he showed some odd reactions to the drugs used to ensure the subject tells the truth. They said it might be genetic. He'll be ready to leave there in a day or so, I was told by their director."

"And go *where*?" Mother asked.

"Here, until we're sure he's all right," Vanthin said, not looking at anyone. He was hiding something else, she knew. Was he now ashamed that he'd subjected Barrat to police interrogation and now had nothing to show for it but a damaged son?

"Did they find out *anything* about the two week gap in his memory?" she asked. Father turned to her.

"No. Whatever happened during that time is lost forever. He might have been going out that night to visit a sex worker when he was taken by the kidnappers, whoever they were. Apparently he's been wasting his money on them for years."

That surprised her at first. But she hadn't seen much of Barrat outside of family events until he'd started using the gym. Even then, they
never spent *any* time talking about his sex life. Their age gap and different gender was too great for that kind of intimacy.

"He can come to my house," she said. "It will be much less stressful
than staying here and he'll still be with family."

"Your security isn't as good. No outer wall like we have here. Some
idiots still think he's responsible for the Vegathic collapse."

"So you insist that the police to make a public announcement that
he's totally innocent and they'll provide outer security until that knowledge sinks in." She stared at father. He nodded.

"Once he's ready to leave their care."

❧❧❧❧

Barrat didn't want to be touched by the nurses or the doctors but
they kept coming in and doing things to him. Trying to talk to him. He
didn't *want* to talk to them. Didn't have to, maybe. He pulled the covers
up over his head and tried to hide again. The silver band on his wrist
meant they could still hurt him, so he couldn't try to get out of this room
by himself. He cried with the pain in his head and the worry about the
shocker. Why didn't they send him to sleep again so he could dream of
the lake? No one hurt him there and he could be happy and forget the
pain.

❧❧❧❧

"He's finally clear of the drugs," the doctor said. "But he's not coming back mentally as quickly as we anticipated. We're not sure what is
going on as he won't speak to us. He's been questioned by both female
and male nurses but he just cowers under the blankets when anyone else
is in the room. He will lower the covers and use the toilet if the lights are
dimmed and he's alone. The room microphones are at max to catch anything he says. We don't think he is speaking at all but he seems to cry a
lot. There are some nightmares but other dreams are neutral to good."

"Did you get him back onto solid food yet?" Captain Lagrath asked.

"Mostly. Breakfast shakes with added nutrients and new gut bac-
teria. His bowels started working yesterday. Physically, he could leave
but his father's going to be very upset at his continued withdrawal."

"We should let him go," another doctor said. "He'll recover better in a place that he knows. Here, there are only reminders of what we did to him. Having family around will give him reassurance instead of having him constantly wondering what we're going to do to him next."

"He could be just not talking to *our people*," another said. "Without using other drugs or pain as stimuli I doubt he's going to help us understand what his mental status is. Sending him home is the best course, I believe. He'll talk to his family. If he can."

"Another shock could do more damage and set back his recovery. I've scheduled a brain scan before we let him out," the older doctor said. "He sometimes holds his head as if it hurts so there might be some internal swelling. We've seen that a few times in those who were here for an extended period. Once that's done, you can contact his family."

Chapter 9

Three big male orderlies took him, strapped into a wheelchair, to a strange, tube-like machine. One of them held up a controller unit and tapped the silvery band on his wrist before they left the room. Behave or get shocked. Again. Tears ran down his face but didn't try to get away. When would Mama come? Would she? Father was angry and Mama didn't like to make Father more angry. He shut his eyes tight against the bright lights in the ceiling. They used webbing to hold him down on a hard bench and put things on either side of his head to keep it still. There was a humming sound and his head hurt more.

At least they took him back to the soft bed after. He'd behaved well enough not to get shocked. A female nurse brought a large cup of the tasty drink sometime later. Once she left the room and the door was safely closed, he drank it and pissed in the little toilet. Then he crawled back into the bed and cried some more until he slept.

❧❧❧❧

"There is swelling in his brain, sir," the doctor told Vanthin on the comm. "That's why his personality is affected. We think it's also affecting his vision, but we can't be sure because he still won't talk to our people. I'm uncertain that releasing him will change his recovery time. Another scan should be done in three or four days, to see if the swelling *is* going down. We could remove some fluid manually but I don't want to do anything that could panic him further. We can't do any cognitive testing without him answering our questions. One of the therapists on the list we'll give you will have to start that testing as soon as possible to track his recovery."

"Drug whatever you're feeding him and he'll be asleep when you op-
erated. Wouldn't be aware anything happened." The screen nearest him
showed another decent uptick in the markets. It might be time to take
more profits from the stocks he didn't want to keep for the long term in
the company's portfolio. He tapped a few keys to check on two particular
stocks and their price history for the past month appeared on the screen.
Coming up nicely. One hundred percent profit at the moment. They
would go higher, he was sure. Back to near the level they'd been before
the crash. Two hundred percent profit. A decent return.

"Lower fluid levels in his brain might help deal with the headaches
but not the actual tissue swelling. That's the real problem," the doctor
said, dragging his attention back to the comm. "We can do medically necessary procedures since he's in our care, but it could be argued that
he'll recover naturally without surgery or other interventions. There are
significant risks any time the brain is involved. We know his sister holds
his powers of attorney, not you, Mr. Trelner. Our legal people think the
chance of a lawsuit is too great if we do anything else. Captain Lagrath
wants him out of here as well. Send a car for him tomorrow. We'll have
him ready to go at ten."

"Fine. Tell the captain to make his announcement to all the news
services that the boy is totally innocent before he leaves there and to put
the security cordon around my daughter Erithe's house. Any attacks on
him will result in a lawsuit against them and you." He hung up the handset and checked on some other stocks, also rising in price as the ones
who'd sold in a panic tried to capture some gain from their losses.

At lunchtime, he sent word to Erithe. Let her deal with the boy. Take
him to her house. Gods knew his son wouldn't be any use to him the way
he was now. And maybe he'd never recover. Dark hells. What a waste.

≪ଈ∕ଈ≪ଈ∕ଈ

Welker snarled silently. Frustration filled him. He'd missed another
important conversation by the silence in the dining room after that
simple announcement. But since CO would get a report on Mr. Barrat's
condition anytime they wanted, his report was redundant. But Mr.
Vanthin seemed crankier than usual when Welker brought the coffee
service into his office after dinner. He thought about making a comment
but decided getting fired wasn't worth it. The sergeant told him at their
last meeting they weren't going to give him any electronic help. Maybe
he should try to find something on his own. There had to be shops that
sold such things. He'd show them how resourceful he could be. His next

half day off was in two days. He'd locate a store and find out what they had available to the public. Those wouldn't be as good as what the police used, but he needed another way to hear what went on when he couldn't just listen in.

Maybe he'd reread his earlier reports and add more details of the family's inner workings. Anything to make his reports better.

⊲⊱⊲⊱

Erithe stared at the office comm, then slammed the handset down. Dantil looked over at her. "That was Father's aide. Couldn't be bothered to tell me himself." She stared at the desk for a moment. "He's agreed that Barrat can come to our house. But he's still not well according to the doctors at That Place. I can pick him up tomorrow at ten. They don't think he's getting any better while he stays there. Apparently he's not talking to them and is having headaches. I don't blame him, but I wonder how much damage they've done to him. Maybe he can't speak at all." Tears filled her eyes.

Dantil stood up and came over to her. "Call your mother. And I'll call Phonbul and have him get a room ready. Mastren can have his things packed and over to the house before dinner."

"You're right." He kissed her tears away, then returned to his own desk. "We'll know more when we see him."

She was shocked to see Barrat. His head was down and he'd lost a lot of weight in the nearly four weeks he'd been here. Her mother gasped and hurried forward. For some reason he wore a set of exercise gear. Had he known what might happen and worn that here? She'd have to talk to Mastren to find out what he'd been wearing when the police took him.

"Barri?" Mom said when she crouched next to him. "Please look at me, Barri." Her hand stroked his hair. "Can you talk to me?"

"Mama?" His head came up a little and she saw tears running down his cheeks. "Please, Mama. Can I come home now? Will be good." His right hand came up and she held it tightly.

Erithe stared at his left hand. There was a wide bandage around his wrist and the back of his hand looked bruised. He didn't seem to want to move or use that hand. Why?

"We're going to Erithe's, Barri. So you don't have to worry about anything. You'll be safe there. No one will hurt you."

"Father was mad." His head came up a little more. "He yelled at me. Hid until he went away. Didn't want to rescue me from them. Be worse."

"I know. Did you look at him or talk to him when he came here?" A quick shake of his head and it dropped back down.

A doctor appeared beside her with a thick folder. "These are copies of his medical records from his time here. The recommendations for further treatment are very important. You'll need to have a therapist see him soon to do the cognitive testing since he wouldn't talk to our people. There's a list of those we've used in the folder as well."

"Our suit for unlawful detention is on hold pending his full recovery," she said. She smiled at his alarm and went over to Barrat and their mother. "Come on, Barri. It's time to leave here."

The driver pushed the wheelchair over to the car. Barrat was able to get inside by himself but he moved slowly and carefully. How much pain was he in? Mom got in after him and she went around to the other side. Handed the guard the medical folder and he opened the door for her.

She got in but Barrat was staring at the lap belt mom held up. His face said he didn't want that around him.

"It's for safety," Mom said. She put her own on and Erithe copied her. "There won't be any pain this time. No one's going to hurt you any more, dear." Barrat finally nodded and she clicked it shut, since he wouldn't touch the thing. How *did* they question the poor souls sent here? She wasn't sure she wanted to know, but they needed the information in order to help Barrat recover.

Barrat calmed down as they drove away from the boxy structure. His head came up a little and his grip on Mom's hand seemed to relax.

"We're going to my house, Barri. You know my kids. You'll be safe with us." A quick glance at her, then at the driver and guard in the front.

"Mama?"

"I'll stay for a little while, dear," she said. Barrat relaxed more. "And come over every day. No one will hurt you any more, Barri. Not like at *That Place*. You're safe now."

"Are you hungry?" Erithe asked. He'd been starved, she was sure. Why was another question she wanted an answer to. "We can have some milk and cookies with the kids when we get home. Then it'll be lunch time."

"Hungry lots," Barrat said. "Can have two cookies?" He glanced toward her, unwilling to make solid eye contact.

"Yes, dear," his mother said. Their gazes met over his lowered head. Two very pissed off women. Vanthin was not going to have a good year *or* decade if they had any say in the way the future would unfold.

❧❧❧❧

Barrat tried to act more grown up in the car but it was so hard. All he wanted was for the pain in his head to go away. The silver band was removed just before Mama and Erithe had come, just after they'd tossed some clothes at him and told him to strip off the gown and get dressed. The mitten on his left hand was on for so long that those fingers didn't work right and it was hard to pull things on with one hand. The shoes had been the worst so he just pushed the laces inside and forced his toes in while the guards all stared at him.

They stopped at the back door of Erithe's house so none of the people who loitered out across the street could see them. Dantil was by the door but Barrat only gave him a quick look. Being outside made him nervous so he kept hold of Mama's hand until they got inside.

"We've set up a room for you on the second floor," Erithe said gently. He nodded. "We brought all your clothes over from the compound. You can wear whatever you want, Barri. Do you want to see the room first, then have a snack?" Another nod. He'd agree to do anything they wanted so they didn't send him back *there*. He wouldn't make any messes or make them mad at him. He'd be a good boy this time.

They led him upstairs and into a bright room. Real sunlight, not the pale light of the little cell. He tried not to cry again but couldn't stop the tears. Mama helped him sit on the bed and sat next to him so she could hug him. The others went away.

"It will be better soon, Barri. Those people won't hurt you any more. You're safe here."

"Head hurts, Mama." She kissed the side of his head. Mama didn't ever yell at him. Father did. All the time.

"What they did to you made your brain swell. Remember when you sprained your ankle and it was so swollen that you couldn't walk very well?" He nodded. He'd been six and tripped in an animal burrow on their summer holiday. The older kids had laughed at him for being so clumsy. "It took over a week before your ankle was better. As your brain gets better, your head will hurt less." Her hand rubbed his shoulders, then his neck.

"The muscles in your neck and shoulders are very tight, Barri," she said. "That might be making your head hurt too. Do you remember Erithe's gym?" A tiny nod. "We'll get someone from there to come give you a massage after we have lunch. All right?"

"Yes, Mama. Warm helps tight muscles, Karth said. Steam is good."

"Good. Do you want to change clothes?"

"No. Not wear any there. Feels good to wear them."

"Then let's go have our snack and Erithe will send for a masseuse."

He followed her back down to the main floor. The nursery was on the same level as his room but he didn't hear any noise from there.

Two small children were in the family parlour with their parents. Barrat stopped as they ran over to him.

"Unka Barri, Mommy said you was hurted," the younger child said, taking his left hand from Mama. The older one held his right one.

"Hurt lots," he managed to say. "Hungry. Cookies." They smiled and towed him to the table.

"Mommy said we could have cookies too," the older child said. He couldn't remember their names or faces but they knew him.

He sat down and tried not to cry. Erithe put two chocolate chunk cookies on his plate and poured him a glass of milk. The kids got the same. When he'd finished those, forcing himself not to cram both into his mouth so no one could take them away before he could eat them, Mama let him have some more. He blinked quickly to hide the tears.

Barrat recognized the massage person who came after lunch, but couldn't recall her name. She knew him and that made his head hurt more. She set up the special table in his room and one of the staff heated a pad that she lay on his upper back. He'd taken off the pullover shirt with Mama's help but he kept the pants on.

"The warmth will help your muscles relax better," the woman said. He nodded. "I brought a relaxation disc. It's a beach one, with the waves and seabirds with an instrumental track. It helps people's minds relax so their muscles start to relax. Do you want to try listening to it?"

"Yes. Never any noise in the cell. Didn't like me to talk. Or make noise. Only allowed speaking to answer questions."

"Then this will help you feel better, Barri," his mother said. "I have to do some reading, dear. I'll be right here at the desk. All right?"

The warm pad settled on his upper back and neck. He could keep watching Mama to make sure she was still there. Then the disc started. Waves. They'd gone to the seaside on several holidays. Those were his favourites. The waves were so much fun to play in. Mama looked over and smiled at him over her papers.

He wasn't sure how long the massage was. He couldn't get up when the woman shut down the relaxation disk. A big man in a uniform came in with Erithe and helped him into the bed, which was also warm and soft. Mama covered him up and moved the hair from his eyes so he could see.

"Just sleep now, Barri. I'll be downstairs and will check on you in a little while. Sleeping will help you feel better." She kissed his cheek.

"When you wake up there will be some supper."

"Okie, Mama," he said. Then he slept, dreaming of playing in the waves when he was happy.

⊰⊱⊰⊱

Erithe saw her mom come down the stairs, tears streaming from her eyes. "Is Barrat okay?"

"He's sleeping now. His neck and back muscles were so tight it's no wonder he has terrible headaches." She took a deep breath. "I'm... so furious at Vanthin right now. What Barrat went through... And for *nothing*. We need to get Dr. Rethennel here to do a full physical tomorrow. I want to know how much weight he lost, for one thing. And we'll need a therapist. Not one from their list. I don't trust them."

"I'm feeling guilty," Erithe said, walking with her mom into the parlour. "We all ignored him when he was little. But I was eighteen and in university when he was born. I'd just met Dantil. I couldn't take even a few minutes to play with my little brother once he was older, even when we had the family gatherings and holidays. I don't think the older kids ever played much with him either. Several of them are near his age. I don't know why they didn't."

"And I ignored him too, dear." Carithe sat on the longer couch. "He was supposed to bring your father and me closer together. Once I was pregnant, your father became more involved in the company due to *his* father's illness. I cheered when that horrible old man finally died. It would have been better if it had happened far sooner. He ruined our marriage, you know."

"I didn't," Erithe said. "How?" None of the siblings knew much about their parents' marriage. Including why their mother had married him in the first place. There had to be a reason and maybe they'd been in love at one point, but none of them had any idea what the reality was. Fraklin was the eldest but he hadn't realised what was going on either.

"Your grandfather wanted lots of grandchildren. He'd only had two children and your aunt decided she wasn't going to play his games. She took her inheritance from your grandmother and married a man who couldn't have children. She was mostly disinherited and he never allowed her name to be mentioned. But that left Vanthin and me to take up the slack. He wrote the apartment building assignments into his will. Each child of ours would have one. Any left over when he died would go to house the homeless. That was the unspoken and real reason Barrat was conceived. I didn't know anything about it at the time, by the way.

His apartment building was the last property your grandfather owned in that block."

"That's not what Father said when the will was probated. At least not that any of us heard."

"Of course not. He didn't want any of you, especially Barrat, to know anything about that codicil. It also means all of you will have to agree to do anything that involves the eventual urban renewal project. Although you now hold two votes, yours and Barrat's."

"I hope I don't have to worry about his property for long, Mom. But I'll try to do what's best for him, not me."

"I know you will, dear. I'm sure Vanthin is going to try playing his own games with his will. That's one reason I've stayed in that house with him. If I move out or formally separate from him, certain legal doors close for me. I didn't like the idea of a matrimonial contract when it was first mentioned, but it's proven very useful over the years."

"That's very strange, Mom. What are the conditions?"

"I cannot take more than two suitcases when I go on a trip without him and the bulk of my jewelry has to remain in the house safe. Or I forfeit a considerable sum when he dies, no matter what his will says." Carithe sighed. "I have my own investments, of course, but I get some pleasure from smiling at him when we both know he wants me gone. And the sizes of suitcases has gotten larger in past years so it really hasn't really inconvenienced my travels."

Chapter 10

Kerit saw the news announcement about Barrat's release. No picture of him. No idea where he was. It would be simple to find out, though. Check the close family first. But... Should he?

He finished cleaning the sniper rifle after his practice in the hill country and put it back in the case as he thought. No. Not now. He'd seen the result of what the interrogators did to the criminals they took into that facility. Most came out unable to tie their shoes. It cut down on re-offenders, some pundits pointed out with a grin. The innocents suffered the same problems, the same damage, he heard. Or worse, because the interrogators kept trying to find evidence that their victims were guilty. Longer interrogations meant more exposure to the interrogation drugs and whatever else they used to force answers from the wretches in their custody. There were rumours, but no facts. Those who had been in there were very careful never to do anything that would send them back.

They would have taken care with Barrat's interrogation. Having his father as an enemy was a powerful inducement for them to be cautious. But it could be some time before the boy was able to think or act coherently. And be able to get away from the family without sending the wrong message to the world. Since he'd heard of nothing happening to Barrat's alternate accounts or alias, it seemed that the fail-safe worked. He'd have to arrange a "chance" meeting to release Barrat's other memories. In a month or two, so that other crises and rumours could blunt any interest in what the boy did and where he went.

The boy's investment portfolio, with the automatic buy and sell orders, had done well. He wasn't sure how Barrat chose those companies, but Kerit arranged to purchase the same stocks for his own portfolio with all his spare cash when the crash hit. Barrat never steered him wrong before. They were rebounding nicely. His hidden portfolio had never been so high.

Kerit looked out at the quiet suburban street from the bungalow he currently called home. Went over to his computer, swapped to different cable, hidden behind an electrical outlet, that connected him to a different server, then logged into the very dark account where people sought him and Barrat out to arrange a death. No new specific requests. That was fine. The job in Snathard had paid well enough. It had been fairly simple to swap a doctored bottle at the liquor store when the target's order came through. It had taken five days for him to get to the treated bottle, but the drug was quite stable in alcohol. Air made it start to break down. He smiled. A good method to keep any of their clients from becoming suspects. The funeral was lavish but rumours were starting to find listeners. In another year, the dead man's reputation would be in the sewers where it belonged. Another smile.

He had enough money to live on for a long time. Being an assassin was more a hobby now that age was catching up with his long abused joints. And a way of training Barrat.

He knew that Barrat could do the job from the first lesson in handling a paintball gun at that long ago summer camp. The determination to win, to be able to aim at a human being and never any hesitation in pulling the trigger. At fourteen, Barrat was good. At twenty-two, possibly better than he'd been at his peak. A worthy successor. His own code name was Silence. It had sounded good when he'd been young and in the army sniper school. It was also true.

Barrat chose a different kind of name: Justice. It fit with the types of jobs he was willing to take. Kerit agreed with him. No more deaths at the whim of his superiors. Just those who were truly evil. The monsters with enough money to buy protection from the legal system.

⸙⸎⸙⸎

Barrat sat in the sunlight that came into his room. He wasn't sure how many days he'd been here. Four, five? Mama said they were going to a special clinic today to see if his brain sprain was getting better. His neck and shoulder muscles were still a little sore from the latest massage. Lots of residual tension from being questioned, Mama said. The warm pad at night felt good and helped him sleep.

Erithe came up to the room to get him. "It's time to go, Barrat. We're leaving a little early, just so we don't have to rush if you need a minute or two to relax when we go."

"Ready now." He wore some older clothes. Just in case the police took him back to That Place. He stood up and Erithe held out her hand. "Brave."

"You are *very* brave, Barri," Erithe said. Soon they were at the back door. He paused a little at the outer door and Erithe didn't say anything. Mama was standing outside the car and she smiled at him. He got in and did up his lap belt without crying. Mama smiled again and so did Erithe.

Driving though the streets teased at memories. "Did I ever go along here before?" he asked. It was almost familiar but he wasn't sure.

"Not that I know of, dear," Mama said. "But you might have taken a taxi or bus along this road at some point in the past few months. Does it seem familiar to you?"

"Some. Mall there. Was in it. I think." To meet with someone or just shop? He wasn't sure.

"There are a lot of shops in there," Erithe said. "Maybe you bought things like clothes there to save money."

"Think so."

The clinic building was three stories and the walls were all glass. He liked the idea of always being able to see the outside. The guards got out and nodded, so they got out too. Mama wore large dark glasses and Erithe settled a floppy hat so her face was mostly hidden.

"Disguises?" he asked as they headed for the doors. Someone was waiting just inside and he took Mamma's hand so they wouldn't be separated.

"Your face hasn't been on the news but ours have been," Erithe said. The door opened and a young man smiled. "We don't want anyone, especially any reporters, to bother us today."

"We're almost ready for you," he said. "Please. Come this way." They went down a side corridor and up a freight elevator. The office they were ushered into was bright and welcoming.

"You made good time getting here," Doctor Laken sat behind the desk and rose as they entered. "We need to talk a little, then the scanner will be free. The results of these tests will be listed under Jakon Harther, to slow down any police involvement. The scan will be logged as occurring this evening, not now. That's the best we can do."

"But they'll figure it out," Barrat said. "What happens if they find out I'm better?" He tried not to shiver in fear.

"They will find out eventually, but they'll have to work to get the information. I think the IC doctors and the investigators are actually worried that you *aren't* getting better so they won't do anything to make you feel worse. Please, sit down." He gestured to an informal seating area. Mama stayed next to him on a small couch.

"How have the headaches been in the past few days, Barrat? Getting better or worse?"

"Better," he said, glancing at Mama. "Muscles in my back and neck were really tight. Still are some. Massage helps. Hot pad before sleeping and pills to make swellings go away."

"That's a good sign. How is your memory?"

"See things sometimes I should know, but don't. Couldn't remember Erithe's children at first. Things like that."

"Do you remember the children now?"

"Mostly. On the way here, a mall looked familiar but not sure why. Might have shopped there or met friends."

"Your records show that you were crying a lot just before the IC let you go. Do you remember why?"

Barrat paused. He really didn't want to remember That Place. "Was sad. Everything hurt. Wanted to sleep all the time but they kept waking me up. Wanted me to talk but I didn't want to. Lights very bright sometimes, then got dim."

"Barrat's been sleeping over twelve hours a day between naps and when he goes to bed at night," Erithe said.

"Another normal response to your ordeals. The amount of sleep should start to decrease as you get stronger. What about your weight loss? Any idea why it happened?"

"Hungry a lot there. Just fed through tubes. They'd hurt me if I didn't behave. Now can have a snack whenever I want. Doing some exercises to make muscles get stronger."

"A good thing." A knock on the door and their escort came in.

"The scanner's free now, Dr. Laken."

"Good. Let's see how your brain is doing."

The tiny room was like the other one. He changed into a gown and that was hard. Mama held his hand as the assistants put the blocks by his head in place.

"We need to hold your head still so the pictures will be clear," the doctor said gently. "Any movement could make them worthless to compare to the earlier set. It will only take a few minutes for the scan, then we'll get you out. All right?"

"Yes." He bit his lip and hoped they hurried so Mama wouldn't see him cry again. It made her sad when he cried so he tried not to, at least when she could see him.

The scanner made two passes over his head and then they took him out of it and let him sit up.

"Scary, Mama," he managed to say.

"I know, dear. It's over now. But we might have to come in to do another picture in a few days. To make sure that you're getting better." He nodded slowly.

"We'll see how this one looks first," Dr. Laken said. "You can put your clothing back on, Barrat. I'll contact your mother and sister tomorrow with the results. Then we'll decide if another scan is necessary in a short time frame. If this scan shows the swelling is going down, we'll wait to do another in a week or a little longer to ensure everything's back to normal. I think it will be better but I want to be sure."

Soon they were back at Erithe's house. He was so tired now. Mama let him go up to his room for a nap. He hoped the doctor would say he didn't need another scan very soon.

⊰❧⊱❧⊱

"He *is* getting better, Mom," Erithe told her mother when they settled into the parlour and the footman served coffee. "I can see the improvement. A few times now, I think I've seen the Barrat I've talked with at the gym. He's only present for a short time, but those times are getting longer. I think he'll be nearly 'normal' in another week or two. I'd like to get him a new computer so he can have something to do other than look at the walls. I don't trust one that father's aide would provide. He's been reading and playing with the kids but that can't be very exciting for him. He hasn't complained but I don't think he would right now. Going back to That Place is something he really wants to avoid. I'm not sure he understands at the moment why he went there in the first place."

"A good idea on the computer," Mom said. "We can't order anything for delivery. That would give the old fart a chance to load some spying software into it and I want to make him work at invading Barrat's privacy. Let's go shopping in a day or two. I haven't been anywhere since Barrat went into That Place. It will do us good. And we'll stop in a computer shop just before we come home and take a nice one off the shelf for him. He has some off-site storage system, didn't he?"

"He did. Does. That sounds like a good plan. I've got to call our apartment management company again tomorrow morning. The person in charge of his building want to do some changes to it and he seems to think nagging me is the way to get me to agree. I think he's working with a contractor and will get a generous kickback for the referral. I have another company lined up for my building and Barrat's and I've suggested that the rest of the family swap to these folks as well. They charge a lower fee and have properties all over the city, in most large cities and a lot of the smaller ones. We'd only kept the other company because Grandfather used it. There are no binding contracts to worry about. I checked with Legal before going looking for another one."

"Sounds wonderful." Mom looked at her watch. "I have a fundraiser to attend this evening. I'll call you tomorrow and stop by in the afternoon to discuss the doctor's report."

"And annoy Father some more?"

"Of course. Seeing his face turn purple truly gives my life meaning."

✥✥✥✥

Barrat woke. It was dark out and a small light on a desk let him see real bedroom furnishings, not the cold and sterile cell. Where was he? His last real memory was pain. The interrogators didn't like his answers to their questions of why he wanted money. They said he'd lied to Captain Lagrath about the girls he paid to be with him. He sat up slowly. A comfortable bed. Pyjamas. He didn't usually wear them. Shorts were what he'd bought for himself for sleeping in. He got out of bed slowly since he was stiff and his back and neck muscles were sore. He went to the window and drew the curtain open a little. The few lights he saw were urban. He was in a city. Which one? Could he still be in Herithan? He couldn't tell from what was visible.

He went to the bathroom and sat down carefully, blinking in the bright light. His balance was off and so was his strength. It made sense. Kind of. No exercise while he was in the interrogators not very tender clutches. He flexed his left hand. Much weaker than his right. The mitten for the port was to blame. He flushed, leaned on the sink to stand then looked at himself in the mirror. He'd lost weight. And his beard was fully grown in. He never went more than two or maybe three days between shaves. It was trimmed and tidy, but why did he have one? When had he come to this place, wherever it was? Too many questions. What was here to give him some answers?

He went to the next door and found a walk-in closet. Clothing he remembered wearing was revealed when he put that light on. Plus an extra suit. He thought he'd seen Carthan wearing it at a family dinner last winter or maybe the one before that. Was he at the compound? This wasn't his old room there. At least, it didn't seem familiar.

The next door led to a dimly lit corridor. He shut the door, breathing heavily now. Panic. Going outside was dangerous. They'd punish him for trying to escape.

He was glad that at least there hadn't been someone outside the door to see his panic. They'd tell Father he was just a whinger. Afraid of everything now.

Barrat leaned against the door until his breathing was back to normal. He looked but there wasn't a lock on the door. He told himself that he didn't need one. This wasn't a bad place. He was safe now. At someone's home, but *not* at the compound where Father would yell at him whenever he wanted to. He went back to the bed and climbed in. Stared at the outer door in case someone came for him, annoyed that he'd tried to leave. Eventually, he slept.

❧❧❧❧

Erithe finished dressing and went downstairs to the dining room while Dantil shaved. Svent, their lead guard, stood outside it.

"Something odd happened last night to Mr. Barrat. He seemed different when he woke. Would you like to see the recording?"

"Yes. Did he say anything?" He fell in beside her. Phonbul saw them go, so he would advise Dantil and the kitchen staff.

"No, but he looked around the room. Acted as if he hadn't seen it before. Checked all the doors. He panicked when he opened the one to the corridor. Took him several minutes to relax."

The segment was ready and the guard seated at the control station started it at her nod. When it ended, she brushed the tears away. "I think he truly regained himself," she said. "At least for a little while. There's a therapist coming in later today. She may want to see our records, Svent. She's to have full access to anything we have here or from the main house related to Barrat."

"Of course, ma'am. We'll help all we can."

"Has he woken yet?"

The seated guard switched the feed and she saw Barrat's room. He was burrowed under the covers again. Still. The guard shook his head. "I don't think so, ma'am, but sometimes when he wakes up he stays under the covers until he needs to use the bathroom. I think he feels safe under there. Like a small child. If no one 'sees' him, they can't hurt him."

Erithe nodded. "Let me know when he's awake. I'll be working at home today and Dantil will head in at the usual time."

"We'll be ready."

The therapist, *not* one from the list the police provided, was a spare, older woman with a sweet smile. Erithe handed her a copy of all Barrat's medical records after she'd been ushered into the office.

"We think Barrat's normal personality is slowly coming back," Erithe said. "The room he's in has an active camera system installed. I'll introduce you to my head guard, Svent, before you leave and he'll arrange for you to see or get copies of anything you ask for."

"I work mostly with adult abuse patients," Dr Halli Gretne said. "I'm not sure why you chose me to help your brother, Mrs. Hathner. The therapists on the police list have considerable experience with reconstructing those unfortunates the police decided were actually innocent."

"My father would have insisted that they not cause permanent harm to Barrat as part of the deal to get him to the IC voluntarily. So that should be a minor issue as he regains himself. No, the abuse is and was real. Covert rather than overt."

"Mental, not physical?" An eyebrow rose.

"Some physical to 'toughen him up' when he was younger. Barrat does weight training and was in very good physical condition when his journey into the dark hells started. He's lost over ten kilos during the past month. His muscle tone is shot. But that's something our guards are helping him with. He needs help to deal with his childhood. I've included a brief family history in the folder. Our mother will also be available to help you understand what this family did to him. Mostly benign neglect from our parents but..."

"For now, I'll just help him understand the damage that was done to him recently. Do you have a sitting room or conservatory here? Somewhere bright and cheerful. Sunlight and colours. I don't want to use his bedroom unless it's necessary. We will be discussing some very painful subjects and he needs at least one room, preferably his bedroom, as a retreat where nothing hurts him and he feels safe."

"There's a small parlour on the second floor that overlooks the gardens in the back. There isn't much to see just now. It's on the other end of the house from his bedroom. Will that do?"

"It should. I'd like to meet Barrat now. We'll start some real work in two days." She put the medical file into her briefcase. "Once I look over all this information. Any other things I should know immediately?"

"The drugs from the questioning caused some brain swelling that gave him headaches and affected his eyes. A drug sensitivity, we were told but I'm not entire sure they've told us the truth on the cause. It is going down, according to the scan we that was done a few days ago. That doctor wants to do another in a week to make sure. His back and neck muscles were very tight, probably from tension and fear, but are mostly better now with massage. The brain swelling and muscle atrophy seem to be his main physical problems at the moment. He's not quite the same mentally, but he had a short time last night when I believe he was the old Barrat. But he was frightened at the thought of leaving the bedroom, even though he didn't seem to recognise where he was."

"Well then, we'll get started."

⋙ ⋙ ⋘ ⋘

Barrat held Erithe's hand as she took him to meet the therapist. She was a nice woman, Erithe said. He wasn't sure he wanted to tell anyone what was going on in his head. They'd send him away again.

"Hello, Barrat. My name is Doctor Halli. I'm here to help you."

He glanced at her. She didn't look mean like the women at That Place. He nodded. Didn't let go of Erithe's hand.

"Please sit down, Barrat. Or do you prefer Barri?"

Looked at Erithe. He didn't want this woman to use Mama's name for him. That one was only for family. "Barrat."

"Can we talk by ourselves or do you want your sister to stay with you? That's all right if it helps you to relax."

Doctor Halli's voice was nice: caring and patient. But maybe that was just to make him trust her. Then she'd hurt him when he wasn't expecting it. But Mama would want him to talk to her alone. To show Father that he was better and then Father wouldn't yell at him for being clingy and a whinger. He let go of Erithe's hand. "Just me."

"All right, Barri," Erithe said. "I'll be in my office and there will be someone down the hall if you need any help."

"Okie," He moved away from her. She went to the door and left. Doctor Halli didn't do anything but sit there. He took the chair opposite her. Sat forward on the seat. "You're supposed to fix me, Erithe said." He didn't look at her. Couldn't.

"I'm going to help you get better, Barrat. Eventually, I hope, back to where you were before you were kidnapped."

"Don't remember that part. Never will, they say."

"Just because your brain doesn't remember what happened doesn't mean that your body has forgotten what you endured during that time, Barrat. You know about muscle memory, don't you?"

"Get better at things when you've done them before." A quick glance at her. "More practice helps reactions get faster and better."

"Between the kidnappers and the interrogators, they've set up a lot of bad muscle memories that won't go away without help. Like not looking directly at someone. Or not going places by yourself. Letting someone else dictate when and what you ate. Are these some problems you've been having?"

"Yes." He paused.

"Anything else?"

"Big men scare me. If they're too close. Think they're going to hurt me. Like at the bad place. Yelling at me and hurting with the cuff if I made them mad."

"Have the guards here been too close to you?"

He nodded. "Sometimes. Not bad after kidnappers, but now it's worse. Need their help to get stronger but it's so hard to trust them. Keep waiting for them to get angry at me. To hit me."

"They have a small gym here in the house?" He nodded. "Can you use it when most of the guards are on duty or sleeping? Just so that you're there with only one or at most two others. Would that help?"

"Should." He relaxed a little and moved back in the chair. Maybe Doctor Halli *could* help him.

"Let's see what other things you can do to get over the other bad habits they made you start."

He relaxed a little more.

After Doctor Halli left, he wanted to write down the things she said so he wouldn't forget them. There was a small desk in the room and he found a pad and pencil in the top drawer. He went back to the seat near the window and started to make some notes. His left hand was still very weak so he didn't try to hold the pad properly. The pencil was also hard to hold but he had to try.

There was a knock at the door and he startled.

"Can I come in, Barri?" Erithe asked.

"Yes." The door opened and she entered, not shutting it completely.

"I was worried when you stayed in here, Barri. Mom will be here soon for dinner. What are you doing?"

"Needed to think about some things Doctor Halli said. What to do to change to get better. Hard."

"I know. Is there anything we can help you with?"

He nodded and forced himself to look directly at her. "Gym. Only me and a spotter. Please?"

"That sounds easy to arrange. Have the guards here done anything to frightened or hurt you?"

"Not scared on purpose. But like the police. Big. Know how to hurt someone. Me." Sudden panic made him look down.

"All right. I'll let Svent know about the gym. He'll tell the others." There were sounds from down the stairs. "Sounds like Mom's here. Why don't you go say hello? Dantil will be home soon and then we'll eat."

Chapter 11

Two months had passed since the first time his brain worked normally after his release from Interrogation Central. Barrat still hadn't moved out of Erithe's house. Renting his former apartment allowed him to build up his available funds for a bigger move. As a bonus, his rep at the new management company didn't keep suggesting that he should replace the basement storage area with another apartment.

Their engineer had flinched when he'd mentioned the proposed plan at their first meeting. Barrat hadn't really understood the jargon the woman used, but he did get the distinct impression that cutting the bigger holes for the windows in the basement of a four story structure was not a trivial or prudent plan, especially with all the apartments fully furnished and occupied. The engineer ended her rant by congratulating him on his grasp of construction limitations. He'd just smiled and thanked her.

He finished the invoice he was working on and printed it, then bundled the whole report together and put it on top. The meeting with the clients would be tomorrow afternoon at their lawyer's office. One of Erithe and Dantil's guards would drive him. Some people still thought he was responsible for the market disaster and the buses took forever. Taxis were expensive and too many expenses would delay his move.

"This is your third analysis," Dantil said at dinner two hours later. "Are you still planning to set up your own office?"

"I think so," Barrat said. "But not here. Too many important people still remember the crash and think I was responsible. And a lot of others still think I'm targeting take-over potentials for Industries. I want to deal with companies so small they'll be safe for years if Father does get into my computer or records."

"True," Erithe said. "Have you decided where you want to move to?"

"Beranga is still my first choice. It's a good sized city with lots of smaller businesses and not a lot of analysts in the immediate area. There are three firms with about fifteen people total on staff. The city's been growing steadily in the past ten years and there's no sign it's going to stop any time soon."

"And no family live there."

"That's a big attraction. I like living here, but I need to be on my own to keep getting better. Doctor Halli thinks moving is a good idea. She knows a therapist there if I still need help occasionally."

"What about your building?"

"I've told the managers that I'll be moving and to contact you if they can't reach me. They have a branch in Beranga that I'll be contacting to rent somewhere to work and live so communication shouldn't be a problem. But it's a plan B. If that's okay with you, that is."

"It's fine. I'm so glad you're feeling better."

"I'm just glad your friends decided to wait until my brain was working well enough to hire me."

⋘⋙⋘⋙

Kerit checked in with one of his contacts in Herithan after a small but complex and lengthy job outside the capitol. News was always welcome. Sometimes a tidbit led to a decent contract. He met the man in a bar that wasn't renovated into a society party spot. Yet. It was also the one that he'd planned to meet Barrat in, the night of his kidnapping.

Merlg looked terrible. Saggy jowls and hair that couldn't decide if it was changing to white or just vanishing. He looked far older than his actual age. He was actually three years younger than Kerit. But Kerit looked at least five years younger than *his* real age without any effort. His clean living and exercise, no doubt. With a decent dye job, people would swear he was in his mid-forties. He hid a smile as he sipped his beer. That ability for disguise had come in useful over the years.

"The Securities and Corporate idiots still haven't figured out why the market crashed. Word is, they would love to pin it on some kid, but they wrung his brain out at IC once and found nothing. So the judge came down on them hard when they asked for a warrant to get the kid back into Insanity Central for another try. Heard there was a complete block so they couldn't go to another judge who's deeper in their pocket and get one that way."

"Hmm. Why did they fixate on him? Is he some kind of criminal mastermind?" They both smiled. Kerit sipped at his beer again, just tasting the excellent brew. Getting drunk in public was not on his list of things to do today. Or any day.

"Wrong place, wrong time, but he was missing for a week just before the crash. No one has any idea where he was except for maybe kidnapped, from what I heard. They let him go without an obvious payment, which is weird. Lots of speculation and some insane theories, but nothing solid. Somebody must know the truth but they're not talking."

"Any leads for a contract in relation to that incident or the crash?" He raised an eyebrow. "You know we pay well for referrals."

"That's come in handy a time or two, but there's no one I know of who is mad enough to hire someone. Not that would pay your rates, Silence. Plenty of people are pissed, mostly because they panicked and sold their stocks but no one knows *who* should become suddenly dead with no questions from the police. What's been going on with your protege? Haven't heard anything about him in a while. Is he still looking for your kind of work?"

"He's in the north at the moment. Minor job but a real piece of work. Unions. They used to be a good idea but it's getting more like they are old style crime bosses with the factories as their war zone."

"What did they do this time?"

"It's not in the news at the moment. Might be once he gets that bastard in his sights. Depends on how the union reacts to that death. I wouldn't buy any Flatrock stock in the next little while. The union wants all their workers to get voting stock as part of the settlement package. At a ridiculously low buy price. They'd end up owning the company in a couple of years if it went through. And the union would hold all their proxies. You can imagine what other companies with that union think of that contract going through would do all of them in a few years. Their president said he'd shut the place down if the union didn't behave. And he's got lawyers reading every sentence in the contract." On his suggestion. Those contracts were full of verbiage that made no sense to anyone. The document had gone from over two hundred pages to fifty with the dreck gone. Double spaced. Another small smile.

"Messy. Is he going to be free soon? I've got a rumour I'm checking out. Might be nothing, might not. You know how it is."

Kerit nodded. "My boy's always up to take the little jobs. He might be better than I was with the rifle."

"Or the rifles have gotten better over the years."

"True. He can outrun me at the moment but I can out think him. At least for now. I'm trying to fill out his education before I finally retire for good, so I look at all kinds of jobs for him."

"And these jobs build his rep." Kerit smiled.

They spoke of other topics for the next hour. When Kerit left he ducked into the back alley by habit and was down in the underground tunnels a few minutes later. He heard a multitude of sirens and came up a few blocks away in case these officers knew how to access the tunnels.

Who had called them? His erstwhile contact? Or was this circus about someone or something else entirely? There were a number of marked and unmarked cars and men running back and forth but no real sign of what or who they were looking for. Someone official must know about the tunnels but he'd never seen any trace of uniforms down there. He had taken the precaution of reversing his jacket so it was a different colour before coming up, and now pulled on a cap that hid his mostly sil-ver hair. A reasonable thing to wear given the cold wind. He hated the cold. But damp cold, like today, was worse on his cranky joints.

"One more little job," he mused. Merlg would be very cautious and vigilant for the next month if he'd been the one to call the police. He'd come back and settle this score. Eventually. The police would warn the union target if Merlg betrayed him but Kerit knew the type. He'd never think of how far the accurate shooting distance of a modern sniper rifle was. Or the chance encounter close up with a poison dart. A tottering old man stumbling into someone wouldn't be remembered five minutes later. The other two targets associated with the death would be found alive. At some point. He hated traitors. The new security detail were brainstorming some interesting ideas on their punishment. He smiled. That would be fun. A bonus for the employer.

A day later he noted that Barrat's apartment building was full as he walked along that street with a box stuffed with packing chips, pretend-ing to be a lost delivery man. None of the names on the call plate by the main door were his or any of his aliases. He must still be with his sister. He'd wander over that way tomorrow. See if there was a way to contact him. Though, if Merlg was right and the police were still trying to pin the market crash on him, giving it another month or so wouldn't hurt.

⋐⋑⋐⋑

The soon to be partners were thrilled with his analysis. Their plan to merge their two small advertising companies could go forward. They were both doing well, but were too small to bid on the level of contracts they all wanted and were capable of doing.

They also handed him cheques already drawn up. Half the amount of his fee from each. They'd done a coin toss to determine the new Chief Ex-

ecutive Officer. The other would be the Chief Financial Officer. Both possessed the training and had the mindset to do either job. Thankfully.

"We weren't sure it would work," said one president (and founder).

"You both have similar needs and expertise," Barrat said. "Merging
helps lower your admin costs and provides synergy." He turned to the
other president (and founder). "Your personnel head is much better
suited to running the art department, you know." Her counterpart was
good at his job and didn't have skills desperately needed elsewhere.

"I do. But we kept dumping the personnel stuff on her in the early
days and then we hired that wacko straight out of art school for the top
design position to give her a break. That was a serious mistake. But she
was able to juggle both departments once we finally got rid of him. We
were looking for an admin person when the idea of merging came up, so
that was put on hold. Now, of course, we won't have to."

"The idiot art director was a good friend of someone you knew,
wasn't he?" Both men nodded. "Pals are great to hang out with. Might
not be good to work with." They both nodded. They'd now seen the issue
first hand and would not repeat that mistake.

"I'm going to be moving around the end of the month but I'll still be
available for consults any time you need an outside voice. Now, go talk to
your lawyers about all the pesky details that are left." The lawyers
smiled. They'd already told him that he was on their list for referrals for
their other clients. One happy client often led to other happy clients and
that led to very happy bank accounts. His, by preference.

He put the cheques into his coat's inner pocket and picked up his
case. Now to stop by the bank and deposit them. He needed another job
like this to have the minimum he'd need to set up a small office and a
smaller apartment. At least he now knew how to make a decent cup of
coffee. Not that nasty espresso stuff. Although it would wake anyone up
or keep them awake all night. That might come in handy some days.
Dantil had liked his espresso machine and reimbursed him on the cost.
The sales person must have been laughing for days after selling him *that*
machine rather than the very simple one that just made regular coffee
and kept it warm. What he'd wanted in the first place.

✥✥✥✥

Captain Lagrath stared at the stacked files on his desk. His people
were no further along in determining why the market crashed that horrible day. The officers he'd consulted from the Securities Services didn't
seem to have any real ideas either. A few pundits still insisted it was an

act of the gods when they managed to corner a newsie with a camera. There was no way to predict when another catastrophic drop would start and no way to stop it without shutting down trading on a moment's notice. According to the office rumour mill, at least one person over in Securities was testing a panic switch in case whatever or whoever did it tried again. He hoped that would eliminate anyone from trying to profit from a deliberately crashed market again.

Sergeant Cranter entered the office after a brief knock. "We just received a report from our source in the Trelner compound, sir. Barrat Trelner is planning to move to Beranga within a month or two. He'll be setting up an office there to do business analysis for small companies. Guess he finally got tired of big companies not wanting to expose their secrets to his father."

"We can't touch him here and higher will not be happy if we grab him there. That dammed judge put paid to that. Without real evidence, we can't do anything else. He might be convicted if we found something the idiots at IC missed the first time, but otherwise our careers would be over and we'd be at IC to determine what else we'd done off the books."

"Should we keep the snitch on payroll, sir? It's not likely he'll have much to report if the kid's in another city. And he hasn't been able to get much in the way of real information. His reports are padded with trivia about the family. Mostly useless for this problem, but I haven't called him on it. He might still give us something useful. Maybe we should have gotten him access to the messaging system and comps access when he asked the first time. He's not really good at this job without more equipment or better training. And he doesn't have much time off."

"Keep him on for now, but reduce the payment rate. Maybe he can get a nugget or two from other members of the family. Vanthin Trelner made a lot of money for Industries from the crash. Maybe he knew something ahead of time and the snitch might get lucky and find some proof. If we just dumped the snitch cold, he might go to his boss and confess. That wouldn't be good. I don't think he's smart enough to hide any toys we could give him. We don't want to make an enemy of that family."

"Too true. Trelner has a bad rep for the continued health of employees exceeding his limits. I'll send the mole word on the extended parameters and the pay cut. That should motivate him to be more active in finding new information, not old gossip. We could link him into the messaging system fairly easily. Just flip a few switches on the lines going into the compound."

"We'd have to give ensure it doesn't get traced back here. I'll think about it. I'll also check the roster for Beranga's police department."

Chapter 12

Beranga. A nice city. Big enough to give Barrat a decent living and small enough to have a "homey" feel. Kerit smiled into the mirror as he finished shaving. He looked old enough to pass as an early retiree. With his cranky joints and going grey young, it made the facade believable. Might be a good place to relocate to, despite what the damp cold would do to his joints. He and Barrat could meet once he found out where the boy set up shop. He just hoped the memory block *was* reversible. The therapist responsible said it was, but he'd never known anyone who used it before. Maybe they should have tested it at least once.

Then he frowned. He'd have to pack up all the toys himself. *Again. Dark hells.* Maybe he'd just box or crate up everything in the storage unit and hire some strong young backs to get it on and then off the truck into a new unit. Then he could break down the boxes at his leisure, or if he needed a specific item. Or he might wait to unpack until Barrat could help him. Much better than doing it all by himself, he decided.

He went over to his computer and started searching for smallish houses with basements and underground utilities in Beranga. Easier to hook into the dark net if he could access the system directly with a discreet tap. Once he and Barrat were back in operation, they could set up something similar wherever he was living.

࿋ ࿋ ࿋ ࿋

Barrat looked at the small shopfront, then back at Maryl, one of the local reps from his management company. Another reason to move here. They owned or represented a number of properties in the city. He looked back at the door. It was wood, not glass, but there was a large window to the left of it for some natural light. Solid brick construction otherwise. The tan drapes were drawn, possibly to keep it warmer inside. Reasonable, given the current temperature. He looked up and down the street.

In fact, most of the stores on this street were made of brick. That also spoke to the age of the area. Forty to sixty years ago, he guessed. That was the pre-boom days of Beranga and the recent re-development had passed the area by for some reason. Was it a good reason or was there something wrong with this part of the city?

This was their fourth stop today. The winters this far north were colder than he was used to and he made a mental note to get a new jacket and boots, even though it would be spring soon. Technically, at least. Given the time of year, perhaps the department stores were focusing on spring fashions and the winter gear would be on sale. If not here, back in Herithan, where spring had mostly removed the snow and slush. People were not thinking of buying winter gear. Swim suits and shorts were more likely.

The streets here were well cleared and it looked like they removed the mounds of snow from the snowplows and dumped it somewhere else. There was a river and some wetlands not far away, he remembered from the city maps he'd looked at. Given the narrow streets he'd seen in this area, that made a lot of sense.

"This building has been vacant for just over three months now, Mr. Trelner," Maryl said. "The owner is motivated to find someone before much longer and authorized a small rent reduction for the first year. We might be able to go somewhat lower, since there isn't a mortgage or any other liens on the property."

"And the neighbourhood? It seems a few steps down economically from what I was hoping for." The businesses along here might not have any need for his services. But... they might know those who did. Or needed some help in order to compete with the large malls on the outskirts. That would be tough and he couldn't guarantee success with just one store promoting in a vacuum. The whole area might have to become involved. More risk of failure and that wasn't an option at this point.

He needed happy clients in the near future or he'd be beyond broke. He could make a mistake in a year or three and not have an early failure impact his future business. *Do I have enough in my reserves to last out a year?* If it took that long for him to start making money here he was in the wrong business. Would these business owners think he was targeting them for his father? That would kill any hope he had of success.

"Most of this area has small business with owner/operators, not a lot of chain stores. Some buildings have renters above them who don't want the hassle of travel. The biggest mall in the area is out to the east with all the major department outlets and the big supermarkets. Other malls are smaller and tend to be linked to the main supermarket chains and small local businesses. They're scattered around the city for ease of shopping. This area is central but not in the Core, so it has reasonable rents and available on-street parking that's still free. There's two spots behind the building for your car and a receptionist's or a second analyst. An office inside the Core will double or possibly triple your basic monthly costs and you said that was a concern at the moment."

At least for now, her look said.

"Then let's have a look inside." He glanced up and down the street. The stores looked to be in decent repair, no real sense that this area was going downhill. Or uphill. There was some pedestrian traffic but it was cold, mid-afternoon and a work filled weekday. People were at their jobs, not gadding about. He looked at either side of the empty storefront. A small art gallery on one side, and a florist on the other. A law firm down the street. If *they* could survive here, he might be in luck. Shops like that were places that attracted the moderately wealthy. Maybe they'd seen those shops as they headed into work or back home. And perhaps they'd see his sign beside theirs in the near future.

Maryl unlocked the front door. "A bonus to this location is that there is a small apartment on the second floor, like many of these build- ings. Originally, the people who owned the shop lived there. Now, it's ex- tra storage space or they're rented out separately. There are minimal amenities, but it does have a full kitchen and bathroom. If you take it, you won't have to commute or rent two places. Do you have a car at the moment?" She'd picked him up at the modest hotel he was staying at.

"Not at present. Haven't really needed one back home, but I do have my license. What's the bus and taxi situation around here?"

"A bus line runs down this street with stops every three blocks. The closest set is across from The Cozy Kitchen diner. They run very fifteen minutes during the Core's rush hours, thirty the rest of the time, includ- ing the weekends. Starts at five am and ends at one. Taxis don't tend to cruise this street but there's a central dispatch number that gets the nearest free one to your location pretty quickly."

He looked down the street and spotted the diner's sign.

"I might wait a bit to get a car, then. See how things pan out. I can rent if I need to for bulk shopping trips." More expenses. Well, he did have some extra in his budget. Not much, but if he didn't need a separate apartment and the furnishings to make it liveable, that would definitely save on his ongoing costs.

Maryl went inside and he followed along. Dusty, yes, but not in bad condition. He'd followed several of Erithe's maids around for a couple of days and learned the basics of how to clean when he decided he was moving out. There had been too many things he hadn't known how to do the last time. Erithe had laughed herself into hiccoughs at the sight of him with a toilet brush. At least the apron they'd given him didn't have frills, just several large pockets.

Since it was partly furnished down here that might also save him some cash for the other expenses he was sure would appear out of nowhere. A secretary's desk and small reception area with light wood panelling to help it seem larger than it was, a small kitchen with a basic washroom next to it, one smaller and one large office. A corridor led into darkness. He hoped there was a light back there. He raised an eyebrow.

"Along there is the back entrance to your parking area and the stairs up to the apartment and down to the basement. The furnaces, water heater and so on are down below. It could be used for some extra storage but there can be some dampness in the spring, so keeping paper files down there would not be a good idea. Wine, on the other hand, would probably love it."

"Does all the furniture comes with?" He mentally crossed his fingers.

"It does. The previous tenant was an insurance person who moved to the Core and bought all new for that office. Still doing quite well. He's in another of our properties. The owner here is an older lady who depends on the rents for her income. She has another four properties, including two medium sized apartment buildings, so she's doing fairly well." And so he wouldn't feel guilty about turning it down or trying to get a larger reduction in the rent.

"Let's see the rest of it."

A switch at their end of the corridor provided light to see where they were going. Another switch at the other end could shut it down when he went up to bed. The apartment's two medium sized bedrooms filled about half the upstairs space. There was a minimal but okay kitchen given his limited skills and a full bath with an older, larger tub than in his former apartment. There was another room currently set up as an office that overlooked the street. He could use this room for a small set of weights if he couldn't find a gym nearby or as a living room. Or both.

The last room was a smallish file/storage room that needed a real lock on the door for proper security. There was also minimal furniture up here, bland paint on the walls and carpeting that wasn't too threadbare. Some sort of tile in the kitchen and bathroom. Not as nice as downstairs, but clients wouldn't be coming up here. In fact, it was better than the apartment he'd had before. He could make do for a year or two.

"Plenty of room for company growth," Maryl said. "Three or four offices could fit in here if you live elsewhere."

"You know it's just going to be me for the foreseeable future," Barrat said. "This is a start-up, not an established business. I can't even afford a receptionist at the moment."

"For now. Being a newcomer will actually work in your favour here, Mr. Trelner. The existing independent firms, and there are three of them, as I'm sure you know, institutionally hate one another. For various reasons, some of which go back a generation or more, but it means they don't really work with or trust each other. Many smaller business people don't want to alienate any of them, so some owners have gone to other cities to find an analyst to help them out. Having you, someone who isn't associated with any of them, in the city means they'll tend to come to you to have someone local and easier to access. Once they know that you're here, that is. The Commerce Association meetings are very well attended. You should join as soon as you move in. The meeting schedule is monthly, with some events scattered through the month. All meetings are free to attend with your membership."

"Will the three firms all hate *me?*" Barrat asked. This information hadn't been readily available in his searches. Dark hells. Should he abort this move and find somewhere else? Beranga had been the most promising city he'd found, but there were others on his list that were almost as good. And further south with much less snow to endure every winter. Or he could tough it out for a few more months with all the smaller analysis companies in Herithan. Save up more for his reserves to have a better chance of success.

"They shouldn't. They don't have the smaller companies' business and don't really expect to get it. They each have major, mostly local clients who take up most of their time. They may start to use you as an intermediary once they get to know you. Stay neutral in their power struggles and you'll do well."

The last stop was the basement. He shivered at the sight of it. Dark, slightly musty and cool. He couldn't hear any noise from the street. Like the cell at Insanity Central in some ways. The wrong ones.

"Problem, sir?"

"Enclosed spaces still make me twitch, Maryl. Courtesy of the police." He'd come down here alone and explore so no one could see him shake while he found the water shut-off valve and the electrical box.

Phonbul had quietly shown him those critical systems three days ago and described how they could go wrong and damage the entire basement. Or burn down the building. Maybe the entire block. His breathing evened out as they went into the alley to see the parking.

Another advantage to this place was the back alley for parking and for clients needing discretion. There were no cameras that he could see on the neighbouring buildings at a quick glance. He might put in his own just to protect himself if the police came sniffing around here. Or if whoever kidnapped him came back for round two. He'd also talked to several guards, especially Svent, Erithe's lead guard, on what he might need to protect himself without tripping over and needing funds to pay someone to follow him around. That was far beyond his current budget.

He had enough in the bank to pay his own expenses for five months and that was about it. He had to get some well paying clients fairly quickly to last more than a year here. He didn't want to dip into the special dividend that would soon come into his pockets. Father was holding a lot of cash at the moment. His board was, no doubt, eager to see that cash in the pockets of the bigger shareholders like themselves to keep them happy. So they'd be nagging Father. He'd buy some other stocks for his own portfolio. Trelner Industries' share price was too high at the moment for him to think of reinvesting.

"It looks good." They came out the front. It looked like traffic was starting to pick up as people left work. She locked the door and dangled the keys in front of him with a smile. "I'll walk around here a bit, then head back to my hotel. I'll call you tomorrow with my decision." He already knew he'd take this place. Meeting some locals before he moved in would be a good idea. He'd start with the stores on either side of his and introduce himself. Get an idea of how prosperous they were. Then the diner for a decent, fairly cheap, he hoped, meal and then a taxi back to his hotel.

The next day he signed the lease. One year to prove he could succeed without his father looking over his shoulder.

Chapter 13

Kerit smiled as he walked by the now refurbished storefront. Trelner Consulting said the newly installed sign. The boy had done it. Left home and now had a great way to cover any further missions. No one watching to see if he punched the clock on time, or wasn't in his room at lights out. And the place he'd rented was possibly on one of the old tunnels he knew were under every city in this and every other country. There might not be an access hatch at the moment, but that could be dealt with quietly once they could triangulate the system. The location couldn't be more perfect if Barrat had planned it. He paused to look at the bright flowers in the shop next door. *Had* he known why this was the perfect place? Another few weeks and he'd make the approach. Bring back Barrat's memories if he could, now that no one was hovering over him. He'd missed the boy. And he did *not* want to unpack the toys alone this time.

⋖ঞ⋗ঞ⋖ঞ⋗

The meeting of the Commerce Association was held in a historic sandstone building on the outer edge of the Core, but still inside the limit. Another thing to get used to. A carefully delineated area of the city was The Core. Not downtown, or any other appellation for the business centre of a city. Berangans were determined to correct anyone who used a different term or were confused. There was status associated with having an address in the Core. Maybe someday he would move inside the limit. But he didn't want to run a giant company. Maybe one or two other analysts, all of them working together on major projects and individually on smaller ones. If he was that successful, he'd rent an apartment and could turn the upper bedrooms into extra offices, to go along with the two downstairs. Or he'd find another small office building to rent or eventually purchase. Living where he worked might, or might not, be a good idea in the long run.

Maybe Connil would like to join him when that happened. Right now he couldn't compete with Vegathic's pay or perks. Keep an eye on today and tomorrow would be closer to your ideal. A trite saying he'd heard over the years. He shrugged and went into the presentation room.

A few people came over to greet him after the talk on the proposed housing development to go with the industrial park being built on the south side of the city. The CA treasurer, eager to take his membership cheque, and the president, wondering if his presence meant Trelner Industries was taking an interest in their city and the aforementioned industrial area. Barrat declined to comment on his father's plans. He was very sure they didn't believe him. No one ever did.

The three analysis firms were represented and came over, glasses of whiskey in hand once they finished discussing something, or him, among themselves.

"We've heard some rumours about you, Mr. Trelner," said Mr. Daltons, the oldest of the three and head of the largest company. Silver hair and only a few age lines showing. A very nice suit.

"And you gentlemen *agreed* on something?" He'd learned a lot more about their rivalry at the diner down the street from his office.

"We do co-operate on occasion," Mr. Gandeth said testily. The second largest company and about the same age as Daltons, but he went to a slightly inferior tailor. Maybe because he wouldn't go to the same one as Daltons did. Or that his tailor was one of his firm's clients.

The third nodded. Mr. Martins, a younger man about ten years older than Barrat. His elder statesman didn't get out much, the diner rumours said. Age and illness were forcing him into a retirement he didn't want and the junior members of that firm might not be up to taking up the slack to keep the other two from snapping up their clients.

"And is the plan to starve me out?" Attack when they don't expect it was one business tactic he'd learned from his father.

"There's more than enough work in Beranga for all of us," Martins said. "The city's growing as you've seen by the talk today and we're all busy with our current clients. So there's room for another firm. Or two. Are you planning on hiring some staff soon?"

"Not until I have sufficient cash flow or a rush of clients," Barrat said. "And I'd probably hire from out of town. Just to keep clear of any rivalries or misunderstandings, you understand."

A snort from Daltons. "We'll spread the word that you're outside our differences. If there is someone local looking for work, we'll let you know if any of us have a problem with you hiring them. I did look up your university records when I heard you'd moved here. Honours is hard to obtain from that school." A slightly approving nod.

"It's what my father expected. He also wanted me to join the family firm and I declined. Several times, in fact. I do what's best for my clients, not what's best for me."

"And you don't tell your daddy," Gandeth said.

"I have the best security I can manage," Barrat said. "And that's *very* good. I also took a minor in computer security to help that become a reality. Daddy has to work very hard to crack my data."

As he headed home on the bus with a pocket full of business cards from other members of the Commerce Association, he wondered if Father *had* been able to access his computer for information on possible takeover opportunities or the simpler notion of future share purchases.

The fact that the kidnappers buggered up his computer meant it hadn't been as secure as he'd thought. As always, having physical access bypassed most of the protections that were in place to prevent remote access. And he'd lived at the compound for several months before moving out. Not to mention past summers and holidays. Dark hells. He'd changed his passwords on an irregular basis, but not that often.

Father's security people could have broken into the computer or traced his downloads through the house connections. Or put a concealed camera in his room to watch him type passwords and make note of the various sites he visited. That would be enough to spoof his security when he was out of the house at work or with his friends. *Dark hells.* He'd have to change all his passwords on the new machine, although he'd sensibly picked new ones when he set it up after Erithe and Mama bought it for him. Just in case. Maybe he should get a second one to handle the day to day communications that was always hooked up to the net?

That led to another thought.

What stocks *had* Father bought during the crash? The total list was part of the public record, though much harder to find than the top ten holdings, so he might do some investigating on that while he waited for a paying client to walk through his door.

Two days later he was positive that Father's people *had* hacked his computer and the access to his off-site storage. Father bought all four of the companies he'd listed as possibles for his own investments during the crash. They were too small to have been on Father's acquisition list otherwise. He'd made good to excellent profits when he sold some of their shares once the market bounced back up. At least Barrat would receive some of that profit when the special dividends were issued, but that wasn't really the point. What he'd ordered was very illegal.

After learning the method as part of a computer security class, Barrat set up a backdoor into Trelner Industries' computers when he'd been an intern after his second year at university. Delivering mail for the analysis department, mostly, for no pay, but for the "experience" and to let the people get to know him. Bah. Sneering at him was the most common reaction. Proving that he wasn't at the top by handing him all the worst jobs. How did they think they'd fare once he was *their* boss? Or did they assume that he'd never be promoted up that high? Did they realise what world of hurt might be in their future? The boy they'd sneered at being the one who decided their promotions and eventual fate?

That was the point when he decided he was not going to work for his father. He'd overheard stories from his siblings who didn't know he was listening during the family vacations. Their immediate supervisors either fawned over them or hated them, giving them all the worst and most menial tasks. Enduring years of this before they decided he *was* competent and promoted didn't fill him with any company spirit.

He'd only used the access code twice. Just to make sure it was there and that he could access everything in the corporate database. Was it *still* there? And should he use it? Did two illegal acts, his and Father's, make it all right? Yes, he finally decided late at night. He'd decide what to do with the information once he knew what was there. Some other analyst on staff might have suggested the companies, after all.

The backdoor was still in place. He finished the file transfer to his off-site storage and re-encrypted the files. Father *had* ordered the access, then given his preliminary data to his analysts for further investigation. Now Barrat had everything he needed to go to the police and charge his father with information theft and breach of trust. Maybe the police would take *him* to the IC to determine just what *he'd* known about the market crash. He smiled. A credible threat. That should get Father's attention. Show that Barrat wasn't a pushover.

He turned to his invoicing template two days later. Five thousand for each company's analysis would be a nice start to his success here. And give him a great cushion to find some real clients.

ঌঌঌঌ

Vanthin stared at the invoice. Twenty thousand? He looked up at the company name at the top of the sheet. Trelner Consulting. *What?* He glared at his aide, who wilted slightly.

"What drivel is this?"

"The material was sent to my attention from Finance, sir. They didn't have a purchase order to go with the invoice. They investigated the rest of the material in the envelope and they found a letter addressed to you. From Mr. Barrat. He's set up his own firm in Beranga, it seems."

"Go back to your desk. I'll look at the rest of this." The aide left quickly and he turned to the envelope.

He went through the other material swiftly at first. The companies the boy thought might be worthy of personal investment. The boy's analysis had given his own people a very good starting point. The smaller envelope taunted him. *How had Barrat learned that his computer wasn't as secure as he thought? A lucky guess or he'd checked the complete stock asset list and guessed. That information was hard to find for a good reason.* He ripped open the envelope and pulled out a single sheet of paper.

Greetings, Father.

This is to let you know that I have all the internal memorandums and documents that show your people stole data from my personal computer on your orders and used it for gain. Those stocks did quite well for the company portfolio, didn't they? Over a hundred thousand in profit so far, just from those four small companies. And surely more to come, since you still own a number of shares.

Congratulations.

The Securities Services will be sent the entire package if my invoice is not paid within a week of receipt. I wonder if they will invite you to visit the Interrogation Clinic, just to be sure that you were not involved in instigating that pesky market crash which brought you such a fantastic opportunity to Buy Low.

I'm sure that you're happy to learn that I did pay attention to all of your lessons on business ethics.

You need not respond to this letter personally. The cheque will suffice.

Barrat

He started to rip it up, then reread the line about paying attention to his lessons. Good enough. He'd pay. And keep this as evidence of blackmail. Two could play at this game. Of course, he couldn't take this to the police or Securities himself. Too much risk of them deciding to start questioning some of his other activities. He would not go into the IC voluntarily, especially now since he'd seen the effects of their questioning first hand. At least Barrat had recovered, unlike others he'd heard of. That possibility had bothered him while he thought about the offer from Corporate Oversight. But they'd promised him that the boy wouldn't be harmed. He snorted in derision.

Then again, this showed the boy had the drive to win to go along with a good head for investments. A potent combination for the future. The boy needed to mature a little more. To run Industries and make it prosper, he'd need to give over his hot temper, at least in regard to business. Vanthin smiled. He'd spent years under his own father's tutelage. Learned to channel his anger into something productive, like learning his enemies' secrets so he could bring leverage to force them into supporting his plans, or to learn how they thought and reacted to demands or internal crises. That's why the company had prospered. And would continue to do so. At least until he retired. Or died.

Barrat had likely changed all his passwords and log-in data by now. The tech department hadn't been able to physically access the boy's new computer or his passwords before he moved. The security on his new machine was much better than the original and since he'd been at Erithe's house when he started using it, it was much harder for his people to get a camera in place to observe his log in and site information. No matter. If he really wanted any information on Barrat's life or his new investments, he'd get it, one way or another. For now, he'd authorize the payment. A flutter of pride in the boy. He'd fully recovered and would thrive. Twenty thousand was pocket change in the corporate world.

❧❧❧❧

Barrat looked at the two young men seated opposite him in the diner. He'd finished a hearty lunch and they'd almost slunk in and ordered coffee at the counter. Sat where they could stare at him. He poured the rest of the coffee in his carafe into his cup. Stared back at them. They looked at each other. He leaned forward and tapped the other side of the table. They swallowed hard and came over. Another glance at each other when they sat down. He wondered who lost the coin flip to speak first.

"We heard you help businesses figure stuff out," the darker haired one blurted out. Both seemed to be in their mid twenties. Maybe two or three years older than he was.

"I do. What sort of business do you two have?"

"We're running a paintball range on the west side of town," the other said. Curly, lighter brown hair. A few freckles.

"And?"

"We need help to figure out what we need to do," Dark hair said. He wasn't happy about being here. "Our dads own the land and they've been charging us rent all winter and there's been no way to make any money now. We're just about broke."

"And the taxes are due soon," Curly said morosely. "We can't afford to pay them. Then we'll end up in jail, I heard."

"Do your parents want you to fail?" Astonished looks. Good. They didn't believe their fathers would cackle with glee if this business venture failed. Their aim wasn't to humiliate their sons to teach them a lesson in why any business was a cut-throat battle for supremacy in the market. Barrat envied them for that.

"No. They said they needed to keep away from the range's operation. Something about arms?" Both shrugged. Barrat tried not to sigh. Naive. No real research or training on running a business before starting operations: just like jumping out of an airplane without a parachute.

"Arms' length is the term I think you mean. It means you are responsible for everything that happens, not them." They now looked like the hopeful puppies he'd seen in the window of a pet store when he was seven. His nanny refused to let him even touch the glass. She said that all dogs were dirty and smelly and Father would never approve if he sought to bring one home. He'd cried back in the safety of his bedroom. Neither of his parents came to see what was the matter with him. Never interested in him, as usual. Unless he made a mess where outsiders could see and comment to their friends.

"Come on over to my office. We'll talk about some possibilities. The first hour's free." He paid his bill with his usual generous tip and covered their coffees. Bethie, the waitress, smiled at him. He'd ask her about the boys and their fathers later. He had a good idea who told them about his area of expertise.

Once the boys were sitting down in the reception area with more coffee, he retrieved a pad and a used copy of a book from his office. He'd spent a busy afternoon at all the used book stores back home searching for multiple copies of this and a few other titles on running businesses. His budget hadn't run to new. The ones he'd found were generally in pristine condition. Never opened or read, he thought. He'd sighed and bought them. He might be able to sell them for the cover price and earn a little income. Or give them to bigger clients and write off the cost. Either way he'd recoup the money he'd spent.

"What's your names?" Curly was Jessen, Dark was Hadren.

"Whose idea was the paintball range?" They looked at each other.

He hoped they would start using their brains soon.

"We've always liked paintball," Jessen said. "And we played in our woods by ourselves or with a couple of friends because we couldn't afford to go out to Krathell, which was the closest place we knew of. It's about an hour further west from here," he added at a kick to his foot from Hadren. "And we didn't have much spare money for gas before we graduated school and started working full time."

"We've been doing construction since we finished school five years back," Hadren said. "We were getting tired of being the low guys in the crew. No one ever listens to us, even when we knew what needed to be done or was going wrong. So last year around this time, which is the slowest time for building things around here 'cause of the cold and snow melting all over everything, we tried to think of something *we* really wanted to do. We were offered jobs in our dads' company when we graduated but neither of us want to work there full time, but we do some work for them when they need construction or painting help." Both had "oh yuck" faces.

What did that company do? Seasonal construction had been the better alternative? Well, it might be for these two. Whatever their fathers did.

"And your parents came on board for your venture. Did you have a good summer? Lots of patrons?"

"Really good, since we're so close to town," Hadren said eagerly, then the frown came back. "But we opened later than we wanted to because we needed to do some work on the trails and such so people could get around easier. A late cold front came through and snow stayed around so we couldn't do any digging til the ground thawed. We put money in the bank all summer, but we had to buy a load of guns and protective gear for the rentals out of our savings. Some people have their own gear, of course. Most folk who want to try it or come in a group don't. But winter's dead time out there. We both went back to construction once the schools started back up, but those companies slow down in winter and keep their full time people working over part timers like us. I'm working maybe two or three half days a week if I'm lucky. Usually if there's a few days of nice weather, there's a quick push to get the main structures further along: walls closed up, roofs on and stuff like that. So they hire anybody competent. And all the builders know we know what end of the hammer to hold." Jessen nodded. "But there aren't many of those stretches and lots of other guys who are as qualified as we are."

"I'm doing the same. Our dads are paying us to do some maintenance and such for them these past weeks, but it's not enough to cover the rent. And we've still got to eat. We've shared an old trailer with a leech field on my dad's land since we graduated. We've got a wood stove and lots of brush that he wanted to be cleared out anyway so we're staying warm. Filling the water tanks is nasty in the winter, and we don't want to stay there much longer. But we need money to build a real house and dig a well. We figured to put it near the paintball parking area, so we wouldn't have to commute."

"And you kept paying the rent for the range. When can you open it up for the spring paintball season this year?"

They stared at him. "Spring season?" Hadren asked. *What spring season is he talking about?* Said his expression.

"Of course." They were still not seeing it. "You need to develop paying activities on that land for each season of the year, not just summer. Especially this far north with shorter non-snow time. When's the earliest you can let people out to play? And when do you have to shut down?"

"Next month, depending on the conditions, for opening. It'll be a lot quicker, now that we've got the main trail work done," Jessen said. "Snow can linger under the trees. And it can get too cold to play all day. In the fall, well, it can snow just about any time, then come down hard a week or five later. No one will come out for just an hour or two after work when the sun sets so early. Weekends are about it to get folks out. Only if it isn't snowing or too damn cold to be outside. And once the kids are in school all week, they can't nag their parents to bring them out except if the schools have a teachers' day. Those helped in the fall, but no one will come out to shoot now. It's way too cold and you can see people's tracks in the snow. Or it's knee deep and you can't move fast. Harder to hide that way." He frowned.

"Do you have any type of shelter you can make available for people to take a break in if they come out on the weekend during the late fall or later in the spring? It doesn't have to be pretty at this stage, just somewhere people can warm up before they go back out and play."

More stares. They looked at each other, then back at Barrat. Total confusion. *Oh well. Drop another hint. Or get a club. Maybe two.*

"What about winter sports like flat skiing to get some revenue coming in for the next two months? Assuming paintball starts late next month. If there's still snow, that will keep the skiers happy. Or they can play paintball on skis or... maybe snowshoes might be better. You need to provide whatever gets people out to your facility and keeps money coming into your pockets. Check on what your competitors do during the winter if you can. They've been dealing with the same situation that you are and they're still in business, so it must be working."

They stared at him. "Our families have been skiing around in there

since we were kids and couldn't get out to one of the other parks," Hadren said after a few moments. "It's not bad. Like I said, we improved the
trails last summer to make it easier for people to sneak around. We'd
have to put location signs up and make a map, I think. Showing where
they are. Or new folks might get confused. Lost isn't good. There's a bog
on one side of the treed area. We couldn't afford to put up a real fence.
Just have some ropes with a "Don't go here" sign. We can take the location signs down once the paintball starts. Or leave them up for groups
who don't know the area."

"We have a disclaimer people sign about staying in bounds or it
wasn't our fault what happens. We still had people going into the bog
during the summer," Jessen said, rolling his eyes. "Had to pull three idiots out of the muck with one of the trucks when their friends couldn't
get them out. They were okay, just muddy."

"One of them lost a boot," Hadren pointed out. Jessen shrugged.

"And are there people from Beranga who might pay to go out to
your facility to ski? You could emphasize the shorter driving time in
your advertising. Put notices up in the local ski shops if you can. Have
some colour on the page so it stands out. Tell all the skiers in town that
it's easier to get out to your site for a quick loop or two and still get all
their weekend chores done than go out to the next nearest location.
Work in construction or whatever you can find during the week to make
some money to cover your own expenses, but getting paying customers
out to the land on the weekends and school breaks has to be your priority."

"Yes." More staring, but Barrat sensed that wheels were starting to
turn behind their eyes. *Excellent.*

"My dad's got that old cargo pod, Hadren. Remember? Behind the
wood shed. He said last summer he wants to get rid of it. It's ugly as hell
but we could put the older wood stove at one end and get a door in the
other. Plenty of scrap wood around the construction sites they'll let us
take to get rid of it so they don't have to pay dump fees. There's still lots
of brush to clear for fuel and we know how to build walls. I think there's
room to put the pod next to the shack where we store the rental equipment. We could move the rental stuff in the pod for the summer and we
could paint it up once the weather breaks so it looks nicer. It's more secure, I think." Jessen bit his lip. "Maybe charge five a person, ten for a
family? For now?"

"That's a good idea. See what price works and adjust. Check to see
what other places charge for a similar venue. Maybe a frequent skier
card. Come ten times and get the next visit free. And you should sell

snacks from the pod," Barrat said. "Hot drinks and pastries or energy bars you buy from a bulk store, mostly. No alcohol. That's a big step up in regulations and permits. You're already selling the paintball ammo and have rental guns and other equipment?" Hadren nodded. "And you should also keep selling soft drinks, energy bars and so on during the summer. The sort of thing that won't go bad so you won't have to worry about waste. Double the price you're buying them for and recycle the drink containers."

Jessen looked confused. "Buy everything when it's on sale, never at full price," Barrat went on. "Be sure you keep separate receipts for range expenses and your own groceries. I'm sure people get hungry and thirsty running around all day. They might forget to bring their own food or didn't bring enough. Provide free water for their canteens if you can."

"Would we need a some kind of license to sell the drinks and stuff?" Jessen asked. "We've got one for the paintball equipment, but I don't re-member seeing anything about food on it."

"That depends on local regulations. You might need one specifically for the food. The cost and bother should be minimal since everything will be in store packaging, not made on site outside of the coffee and hot chocolate. Call or drop by city hall when you have a chance and ask about the permits. If you're outside city limits the county's in charge and their rules might be different. They might have to come out to see how you store the food and so on. Make sure wherever you store those sup-plies is metal and completely mouse-proof."

Twenty minutes later his watch chimed. "It's been an hour," Barrat said. He flipped the book over and pushed it across the table. "Take that home and read it." Their eyes went round at the title. *Business Planning and Implementation.* It was an inch thick and on thin paper. "If you want to keep it, you can buy it from me later."

"Umm." They stared at it, then him and back to the book.

"Also, talk to your dads. Soon. See if they'll wait on the rent from the next few months so you can pay last year's taxes. You may need help with the business return from an accountant to maximize your expenses and minimize your taxable income. If your dads use professionals for their returns, check with them for a recommendation. I don't know any-one here yet." He looked them both directly and waited until they looked back at him. Their eyes were still glazed slightly. Information overload.

"I hope you kept *all* of your receipts. If you have increased revenue and from all four seasons of the year, you shouldn't have the same prob-lem next year. Sit down with your families in the next few days and brainstorm. Think way outside the box for more ways you can use that

land. Group camping for special events, birdwatchers, school trips during spring and fall to see the natural wetland..."

"What? The bog? People would pay us to see a *bog*?" Jessen seemed
to have a hard time seeing a bog as an asset, not a hazard they needed to
fence off to prevent the clients from falling in.

"School groups. Scouting badges. People who like to watch and
identify wetland birds. Look at magazines describing holiday destina-
tions. Why do people bother to leave the hotel pool? You won't be able to
do everything on your lists, but thinking of five or six and then how to
implement them should give you enough ideas for something to fill your
empty hours."

Jessen picked up the book. Slowly. "We've got a lot to think about
now, Mr. Trelner."

He didn't say it was past the time for business planning. That was
last year when they'd first had the idea. A very common mistake.

"Read the book and make the list of anything you can do on that
land to generate income. Talk to your dads and families to get their
ideas. You know where to find me if you want more help."

They put their snow boots on at the door and were soon heading for
a very beat up looking, dark, rust pocked car parked on the other side of
the street. He hoped its heater was in better shape than the body was as
the overnight temperature still dipped to well below freezing these days.

He had inserted a sheet showing his rates for various services in the
back of the book. They might not be able to afford his help. Maybe their
fathers would see the benefit and front them some money. And what did
their dads do for a living if they weren't using that land for income? Why
didn't the boys want to work for the family business? He knew why he'd
run from that future. What was their reasoning? Bethie or one of the
diner's other patrons would know the boys and their families.

He smiled as he went back to his desk. Real clients. Sort of, anyway.
A first step on the way to success.

Chapter 14

Kerit took advantage of the warm day to go to the diner near Barrat's office. He *could* legitimately meet with the boy. They'd met while he'd used this persona. His real name, oddly enough. Not that he'd used it for some years now. Kerit Kellman. He'd been out of the army for a few years at that time. Bored with sitting around all day, living off his pension. Not much of a family, few friends he cared to spend time with.

He'd done a few jobs and hadn't yet decided to make it into second career so he needed the income from the summer camps to avoid dipping into his reserves. It had been mostly fun. Some of those little brats were horribly spoiled and he couldn't jolt them out that mindset in the short time they were under his supervision. Barrat had made up for a lot of the grief the others brought in their wake.

Now, being in the boy's timeline meant they wouldn't have to hide their meetings. A minor chance that the wrong folk might associate with them with Silence and Justice by a guess at their ages. However, no one knew the boy had developed his skill with a real rifle, so that would deflect any interest. He'd have some coffee and a hot piece of apple pie at the diner, then wander by the office and see if Barrat was busy.

The pie was very good and he left a nice tip for the waitress. Then crossed the street and stopped in front of the office. Like a man who wasn't sure he should intrude in case someone was watching. He doubted there was anyone around, but he always took precautions.

The door to the back office was open and he couldn't see anyone else in the room or in the client chair through the partly opened drapes on the main window. He opened the door and went in. A gentle chime announced him.

Barrat came out and shut the office door closed behind him. "Can I help you, sir?" he asked.

"Might be. Are you Barrat Trelner?"

"I am." A pause. "Do we know each other?"

"From when you were fourteen," Kerit said. "Summer camp near Hallaway. I was one of the ..."

"Sports instructors. Paintball. Mr... Kellman, isn't it?"

"Kerit Kellman. You've a good memory for faces. You just moved out here?"

"Voices are easier after a few years. I arrived about a month back. Want some coffee?"

"Don't want to intrude. I'm retired now. Just wondered if you were the boy I'd known. Not many folk with that last name." The memory block had worked, he thought. Barrat brought out a coffee pot and a pair of cups from behind a door and set them onto the low table in the reception area next to a fresh flower arrangement. From next door, Kerit guessed.

"Things are still slow," Barrat said. "Oddly enough, I'm doing some preliminary work for a pair of youngsters trying to run a paintball range at the moment."

Kerit snorted. "That's a hard business."

"They found that out last year. But they're starting to think outside the box now that I've kicked it open. I'm hopeful they'll make it work for the long term."

"You still shoot?"

"Not for a long time. Convincing my parents to let me near a range proved harder than going to a gym was. It wasn't an option at the boarding school I went to." Barrat took his seat.

"*Filibusters die a lonely death in the sunlit country.*" Kerit said slowly and carefully. Before Barrat could pick up the coffee cup and spill the hot liquid on himself.

Barrat blinked rapidly, then turned pale. Kerit spotted a wastebasket near the reception desk and brought it over. The boy leaned forward, elbows on his knees and his head dropped. Several minutes passed while Kerit fixed his coffee, sipped occasionally and waited.

"Kerit? Dark hells. It worked."

He sighed in relief. "Yes. It's me, lad. How are you feeling?"

"Like shit. Memory cascade. It'll take a while to sort through them, I think she said."

"The army never warned me about any side effects. Neither did Lenia, for that matter. Sounds like she should have."

"She also didn't recommend keeping the split for very long. Any idea when I did it?" Barrat's head came up enough to look at him. He was still pale and a sheen of sweat glistened on his forehead.

"Early fall. Been five months, more or less. You were kidnapped and likely that's when you hit the panic button. Took a while for the police and public interest in you to ease off so I could come visit and not trigger any bad reactions from them."

"True." Barrat sat up a little more. The pallor was almost gone. "Wait. The kidnappers erased my memory. They used a lot of Zeltin, the doctors guessed. Why do I still remember getting grabbed?"

"That's a puzzle for later. Ready for some coffee?" Barrat nodded. "It may take a little while to get your brain settled down. I moved to Beranga about two months ago, once I knew you were heading here. We can be acquaintances, since I'm in your timeline under this name."

"Good. Not having to sneak around will make both our lives easier. But a smaller city like this means more attention from the neighbours. About the only downside I can think of."

"And that interest will make going to the jobs easier. Tell the neighbours you have an appointment out of town and rent a car or buy one if you haven't already. We can try to time those trips with real jobs you have outside the city. You picked a place that likely has access to the local tunnel system. Any sign of an access port in the basement? Wasn't able to nail the tunnel path down well enough from the outside. There's not as many access points around here, I think. Might need to do some digging and build a little tunnel of our own."

"Um. I'm not sure. I only went downstairs once, just after I moved in here, so maybe. There's not a lot down there except for the furnace and such. I found the water shut off valve and the electrical panel. In case. The agent said it sometime gets damp in the spring down there, so I didn't really care about using it to store anything. There's lots of room upstairs for my few odds and ends. I don't actually have much furniture of my own. Most of the things here came with the place. The previous tenant didn't want to move them and I can't afford to replace them yet."

"Well, it takes time to come back from the Insanity Central's rummaging, I've heard. Rumour was your father gave you up to them."

Barrat sipped at the coffee. "I think so. My memory's stuck near the kidnapping at the moment." He looked around. "So I did get away from him. Finally. Why did I pick here?"

"No idea. There isn't any member of your family within two hours on a plane. Maybe that was why. You've been here three weeks, maybe four. Second time I've been past here." Barrat sipped his coffee, then added another sugar cube.

"Maybe by tomorrow your head will be in synch," Kerit said. "For now, let me tell you about some new contracts that have popped up. One's near here. Seems to be a revenge thing. I plan to stay away from it until I get some more information. I have someone checking into the stories I've heard from the prospective client."

"Those are usually messy," Barrat agreed. "What about the others?"

"One back in Herithan, actually. Politician named Lothal Pregnor won't stay bought and is trying to shaft some good programs unless their backers come up with more money to keep buying his vote. Lots of good reasons to take that one. Thought about using a delayed poison on him. Matrinal. Don't know if you remember it. Causes clots that aren't stuck in the blood vessels for long. Usually gets treated like a heart attack or stroke and he looks like he's a prime candidate for it. Overweight, drinks a lot and has high blood pressure. Won't take medication or do anything about it by changing his diet or activities. Hasn't had a recent physical or a long time doctor to complicate the autopsy."

"A good choice for covert work. His morning coffee?"

"Toothpaste is a better option." Barrat snorted. "He's not married or with a live in at the moment. Or it can be layered onto a pill. A little more uncertain on the timing, but it means no one will connect anyone to the event itself. Some critical votes are coming up in less than a month, so we'll need to move fairly quickly on it."

"That rules out the pill unless there's just a few left in the bottle. You're thinking of a late night visit?"

"Ensures we know he's alone if we go with the toothpaste. You'd have to do the high angle work to get over the wall and inside the house. My joints are more getting cranky lately. One reason I was thinking to pass that one up. But it fits with your profile. I did some jobs *as* you so no one will get suspicious at you not being around, then reappearing. Tell you about them later."

"Thanks. The politician. My mother's birthday is coming up soon."

"A week from yesterday. Doable. You in?"

"Oh yes." Barrat smiled. "I'll let the family know I'm coming for a visit and book a flight first thing tomorrow morning."

"Third one is in Snathard. A crime boss who irritated off the wrong set of businessmen by trying to shake them down for protection at an exorbitant rate. There's a bonus payment if a majority of his people die at the same time. Decent money, even split between us."

"That could work. What sort of place does the boss have?"

"An older building. Used to be a factory: light industry, I think. It was condemned about ten years back but no one wants to deal with the demolition yet. There's some nasty chemicals leaked into the ground, from what I found out. The clean up cost is steep. More than anyone wants to pay. It's on the edge of the district he's annoying the most. We might be able to access the tunnels or use the sewer or underground transit to access the underpinnings. I hadn't looked at that aspect yet." Their extensive map collection was stored on a very secure server, hidden among a thousand others.

"A gas explosion might be the best way to arrange to eliminate everyone at the same time," Barrat said. "How many men does he have?"

"About twenty all told, from what the message said. I was thinking to pass on it since trying to manage everything for an explosion alone would be a bit more difficult."

"And now, that isn't a problem. I can use the cash. I can also launder it as an analysis. Do you have my Snatharin tapes?" Their slang was strange and each subgroup seemed to use the same words for different things. Anytime they went away from the bright lights, how they spoke became crucial. To blend in and not be identified as outsiders that were either robbed or killed.

"They're in the storage locker, along with all the other toys. We should go over there in a day or so, just to pick up what we'll need for the politician. And you should drop into a casino when you're home. Buy chips from various tables with money from our other activities but don't play for real or for long. Then you cash out at the wicket and take all your winnings home. Usually what I do. Declare it on your taxes."

"You could have told me that method years ago, you know. I was very short of cash last summer. That's why I went for the Vegathic interview. Really wish I hadn't met up with Connil on the way out."

Kerit smiled. "And now you have a fine backstop. Didn't waste any of your cash on silly things. Now that we've settled those points, go climb into bed and I'll see you in a day or so."

Barrat nodded. The conversation had helped beat back the memories, but he knew they'd all want to push forward again.

⊷❧⊷❧⊷

Barrat didn't recognize the older man at first. It was his voice that tugged at memory. Mr. Kellman, from one of the summer camps he'd been sent to over the years. He was surprised but since he was just playing around with a few "out of the box" ideas for the paintball range, he figured spending a little while with him wouldn't hurt. And he might have some insight into running a range or ideas on other activities. He could afford some money for consulting fees. And maybe the boys would hire him on as a part-time instructor and mentor once they got their cash flow under control.

The nonsense phrase unlocked everything. His head pounded. Nausea roiled in his stomach. Centuries later, he was able to speak.

"Kerit? Dark hells. It worked."

"Yes. It's me. How are you feeling?"

"Like shit. Memory cascade. It'll take a while to sort them, they said." He lifted his head slightly. The nausea receded, but his memories all wanted to be acknowledged *now*. He pushed them back for the moment. He needed an update on what was happening *now*.

Kerit described two good jobs but didn't stay much longer and suggested he lock the door and go lie down to let the memories sort themselves out. He'd be back in a couple of days so they could plan their strategy. Doing a job while visiting for mother's birthday would also help *his* cash flow. He'd get the new codes for his other accounts when they next met. It would be interesting to see if his trading orders had clicked in without any supervision.

He used both arms to keep himself in the middle of the stairway and the corridor to his bedroom. Proud of that accomplishment, he took his suit off and managed to hang everything up before falling onto the bed.

He dreamt the past. A recap of his training with Kerit, all the operations. All the deaths. The slightly sick feeling on the first one, seeing the blood spray from the target's body. Then joy in the hunt. Avenging those with no recourse through the so-called justice system. The poor always suffered at the hands of the rich.

Kerit taught him how to find the truth of some of those requests. Some were real and others spurred by malice toward an innocent. And he learned all sorts of methods, like poison in common household items like toothpaste, to hide a death, keeping those who sought them out safe from reprisals or the interrogators at Insanity Central. All the other skills and training he'd needed. And the equipment. Kerit's trunks contained most of what was necessary and other tools that were just fun to use. Other items were custom made by others and some Kerit helped him make.

He woke late at night and made it to the bathroom. His stomach growled so he found some cereal in the kitchen and ate enough to quiet the ache there. He looked at the coffee maker, then turned away. Not now. He needed more sleep.

When he padded downstairs the next morning he found a note with Kerit's comm number and address on the table in the reception area. He tucked it into his shirt pocket. While he tidied the tiny kitchen and started a new pot of coffee, he wondered if he'd subconsciously chosen this storefront with help from his hidden memories.

Really, the office on the second floor of the little mall on the west side was closer to the Core, but he would have needed to rent a separate apartment and get a car first thing. More expensive and more people to watch his comings and goings. Here, all he'd have to do was say he was heading to a nearby town for a consultation and his neighbours on either side would keep an eye on the office and pick up his mail. Once the cleaning was done and he was ready to open for business, he started a standing order for a small flower arrangement each week and was paying for a very nice landscape for the outer office on a monthly plan. The ladies, both married, thought he was a nice, polite boy. So did just about everyone else who knew him. It was a great cover.

Either way, this place *was* better. There was a tapping at the front door. He went into the reception area and saw a police vehicle parked outside. Great. The day *after* his memories unlocked. Start thinking everything was going well and the universe showed him it didn't care and wanted to let him know it. He looked out the window to see who was outside the door. Two detectives, both of them burly and cranky. One held his ident folder open.

He unlocked the door and held it open enough to speak. He left the security chain in place. "Yes, officers? I'm not open for business at the moment." All of his weight was on the foot preventing the door from opening further. It might stop one of them but if both hit the door at the same time, they'd be in.

"We'd like to speak with you, Mr. Trelner. May we come in?"

"Concerning?"

"The market crash."

"Do you have an arrest or search warrant in regard to that incident?" His stomach cramped up.

"Not at this time. Just some routine questions." The one on the right seemed grumpier than his companion.

"It was determined by IC and Corporate Oversight that I was innocent of any involvement in the crash, officers. Has any new information come to light that hasn't been released to the newsies?"

"Not that we know. We just have a few questions for you. Won't take long." The other one said. He was really not happy to be here.

"This sounds more like harassment, not investigation, officers. I am unable to assist in your enquiries without a warrant or the presence of my lawyer. When you produce the first, I'll bring the second with me to your station. Good day."

He shut the door and locked it, then slid the deadbolt closed. Went back to the window. They stood on the sidewalk for a minute, staring at the door, then climbed back into their car and sat there, now arguing. One spoke on a comm for a few minutes. Eventually they left.

Barrat went to his office to call Erithe and warn her. At least if they took him again, he knew the trigger phrase would protect Kerit and their secrets. He didn't want to use it again so soon, but he would if they tried to take him into custody.

Erithe fumed once he explained what happened.

"I have the whole thing recorded," Barrat said. He'd checked the camera feeds and the one aimed at the front door had recorded the whole episode. The continuous feed worked well and he didn't have to think about turning anything on or off. It wiped every week and there was an off-site backup of two weeks. "Shall I send a copy to you?"

"Yes. I'll have our lawyers prepare a harassment suit if they come back and find a local lawyer if you need one quickly. Do you think that idiot captain's responsible? Lagrath, I think his name was."

"Yes, it's likely his work to keep an eye on me. I wish I knew what happened in that week." But he did remember some now. Up until the moment one man came at him with a dart gun and another shot him from behind. "I was at the gym the day I was kidnapped, you said before. Did anyone new come in, like maybe they were following me?"

"I don't know. I don't think we have the outer door tapes anymore. Those only get kept a week, if that."

"If it was someone new, wouldn't there be a sign in record?"

"There should be. I'll have someone check the register later today to look for anyone new on that day. I don't think we bothered to check before. I didn't hear if the police ever went there to question the staff. We all assumed the kidnappers had taken you from your apartment or in the immediate neighbourhood. I didn't see you leave but once we knew you were missing, I was told that you left by yourself. The next person left about ten minutes or so later."

"Just thought of the possibility myself a day or so back," Barrat said. "I was going to ask you what the register showed when I came back for mom's party. If they were already following me that day, it makes sense that one of them might have come in to see what I was doing in there other than sweating."

"You are coming to visit for mom's birthday? You weren't sure last time we talked."

"I have some free time. And enough for the plane fare. Can I crash at your place while I'm there?"

"Always." He heard the smile in her voice. "I think everyone's going to be coming this year. Mom has scheduled a fund-raising dinner she wants all of us to attend. Father's annoyed but wants to use it as a "we're all happy" photo op, even though none of us are talking to him unless it's at a board meeting or about a specific problem. You should bring a stack of business cards. Never know who might need some help from an impartial source."

"Too true. And that lets me write off the trip as a business expense." He grinned. *If she only knew what business he was really in.* "I'll send a copy of the feed right now and let you know once I have my flight booked. Should be later today."

"Good. Stay warm up there, little brother."

"Sure thing, big sis. Tell Mom I'm doing fine."

Once he shut down the comm, he plugged the net feed cable into his computer and sent off the file. He never left this computer plugged into the outside world unless he was downloading information to his outside servers or messages like this one. His other computer was the one he used for the automatic updates and other day to day communications that he needed for the business. It had no other information on it and there were very sneaky firewalls in place. He looked at the net feed cable and unplugged it. He'd have to set up a sensor set and alternate feed line up through the basement. Just in case. Kerit would have the equipment he needed so no one would suspect his links to the dark net. And they might have to do some tunnel work to access the system.

Wonderful. Tiny, dark, noisome tunnels. But very useful. He did have some anxiety medication but didn't take it routinely. He'd try going down there without it first. And the job in Snathard might also require trips down dark tunnels. Finding out if the pills worked before going into one for an extended trip was a very good idea.

He started to turn back to the topographic map he'd downloaded on his other computer. A soft ping meant a message coming in. He opened it. Excellent. The boys and their fathers could be here later next week to discuss the extended possibilities for that business. And he might find out what other enterprises they were involved in. Good. Legal income was always welcome. Now that he knew how to get his other money into his legal accounts. But he'd have to pay the taxes on it. He shrugged. Not really a problem. There was a lot of money in those other accounts.

The flight didn't take long and he recognized the pair of guards who met him at the airport. Harthil and Peykan were the ones who usually drove him around while he'd stayed with Erithe and Dantil. Kerit had set out on his way from Beranga with the gear two days ago and would be ready for him on the night after the fundraiser. A quick trip in and out, a short wait and a nice paycheck for their alternate accounts. He wasn't sure he could fit in a trip to a casino to syphon any funds out of his, but just knowing it was an option made him feel better. Maybe once he was back in Beranga and figured out where one was. And the rules of the various games, so the cameras would show him playing, at least a little. Kerit might have to tutor him on those. He could search the net for rules first. In case Kerit wanted to play other games.

He'd messaged some friends once he'd bought his ticket and there were enough people who were willing to go out in a big gang as they'd done at university to let everyone catch up on what everyone else was doing. He'd head out a little early claiming he was tired, then the (hopefully quick) visit to the politician's house and back to Erithe's for a good night's sleep before heading back to Beranga or to meetings with potential clients.

"Aren't you glad you brought the business cards?" Dantil asked as Barrat finished a conversation with an earnest business owner.

"Definitely. This was the second serious one. I might have to delay my flight back home to fit in the meetings."

"How are things going so far?" A raised eyebrow.

"I have one client at the moment. A paintball operation. But the owners' fathers are in business together but the boys don't want to work there. We're meeting late next week. I don't know what they do yet, but I think they, and others from the Commerce Association, are watching me before any real clients come to talk about hiring my expertise."

"Makes sense. Lets them see how you operate and if you can do the job. I've heard of some rich idiots who bought their degrees. Even the Honours designation."

Barrat snorted. "Father could have. But he wouldn't have bothered. Either you have real competency or not. Pretty certificates on the wall don't mean a thing to him."

"So true. That's why Erithe didn't mention me to him until we were sure we wanted to marry. Still had to go through his scut job routine. Thankfully, that only took a couple of years."

"And the stories I heard over the years made me swear to never to work for him." Dantil shrugged this time. Erithe caught his eye and waved them toward the stage area.

"Picture time," he said. The entire family was supposed to have a picture taken on the dais and Barrat joined the second rank with his taller brothers and his sisters' spouses. Mom and Father were seated in front of the group. With at least six inches of space between the chairs. The oldest of his nieces and nephews were sitting on the lower level. There were, Barrat had to admit, quite a lot of family present. And more children deemed too young to attend. He regretted that really didn't know any of them really well. Erithe and Dantil were the ones he knew best.

"Good to see you're better, Barrat," Fraklin, his oldest brother, said. "Any lingering side effects from IC still giving you trouble?"

"Closed spaces are still an issue. I have a big basement in my office building but I don't plan on using it for anything but wine storage." A minute shrug. It would have access to the tunnels. Soon. "The therapists say that might never go away. Otherwise, not too bad." He might as well be chatty. Improving relations with his other siblings might be a good idea. After all, they might know some people who might need an independent analyst.

"You know about the lawsuit mother's championing?"

"She hadn't mentioned anything, but between this and her party I haven't had much chance to just talk with her."

"Seems the IC has a very bad record when it comes to innocents," Fraklin said after they'd been slightly rearranged by the photographer's assistant. "As well as the guilty. Most of the innocents never recover well enough to work and their businesses generally go under since no one in the family was prepared for or able to take on the responsibility. And they don't get much help from any government programs."

"Mother's on the attack?" He grinned for the camera, and inside. The police would be regretting their actions for sure. At least some good was coming out of his ordeal.

"Yes. Her foundation has hired a very prestigious law firm and they have around fifty people signed up so far. From all over the country, I think. All were declared innocent of very heinous crimes after a stay in IC. All their lives and businesses were ruined by the simple act of arresting them. Seems at least half were set up by competitors or people they knew and used to trust. Some of them suicided and their families are looking for justice."

"And Father threw me to them to make sure I didn't arrange my own kidnapping to get drinking money." Several siblings and spouses glanced at him. Father stared straight ahead, ignoring the comments he could certainly hear. The younger members of the family shuffled, but didn't speak. Well trained, he guessed.

"Truth." The pictures taken, they were dismissed to continue to mingle with the other guests. Mother came over and he kissed her cheek.

"Thank you, Mama," he said. "For the lawsuit."

"It actually didn't take as much effort to start as I feared, Barri. All of those families have tried individually over the years to sue IC for the damage done, but made no progress since the judges were taking direction from the police and none of them had the level of funding truly necessary to retain a firm with enough of a reputation to block the police's influence. I made the suggestion to my foundation and they are guaranteeing the lawyers' fees. We've actually raised more than enough to cover them already. We're providing a possibility for justice." She smiled at him. "We'll talk about that and other things in a day or two, shall we?"

"Of course, Mama." He smiled. Shooting all the people in charge of IC wouldn't really stop them. Hit them in the wallet. An acceptable strategy. He'd have to mention it to Kerit. It would depend on the circumstances, but some of their clients might enjoy watching their enemies fail. They'd have to be very careful on the clients they offered that option to.

⁂

Connil looked different, Barrat thought. Thinner, but...

"Did you *have* to call me?" Connil asked as soon as he sat down in the coffee shop. Hunched shoulders. Eyes shifting, looking at everyone with a mix of anger and fear. Thankfully, it was nearly deserted in the pre-lunch lull. Another twenty minutes and it would be standing room only.

"I wanted to see if you were all right," Barrat said calmly. "Everyone thought I was responsible for Vegathic's collapse and I was told we talked in the plaza the day I was kidnapped. I'd just left the building and was cranky, I'm told. Connil, I'm just trying to understand what happened to me. I called hoping that you can fill in some details of that day. If you want to leave right now and never see or hear from me again, that's all right. I've been to the dark hells and don't want to drag anyone through them by my actions."

"I know. It's just..." Connil took a deep breath and relaxed a little. "You had just left the building and I was going in after a quick lunch. You were pissed that Vegathic didn't want you as an analyst, but a puppet. I'd just gotten the assignment to put that report from the dark hells together. We were going to have dinner together that night but I cancelled on you to get a better idea what was in the piles of data on my desk. Got home very late. I left you a message a few days later but you never returned it. I was so busy with the data that I didn't notice. When the crash came, I was taken into Securities custody from the break area on my floor. We were all just standing around watching the market fall. Wondering when they'd stop trading and what was taking them so long."

"That makes sense. Like those "simple" examples they put on the finals in university: There was always something not quite right in the data. Deliberately. Being set up to fail if you weren't paying attention."

"Something like that," Connil said. "There was *nothing* in my damned report that should have triggered the crash. I spent four days after it in custody with Securities Services. Two guys analyzed my report and wondered why I'd said this or that. Someone leaked a different report with a much higher loss ratio, they finally told me." He sipped his coffee. "And you were in Insanity Central for three weeks."

Connil shivered and tucked his hands below the table. Probably so no one could see them shake. Barrat had done the same. "They threatened to take me there, but finally agreed that I hadn't leaked the other report. No one has any idea who did leak it, or where they got the information to build the report in the first place. Most of the numbers were right, but there were some bogus expenses, giant ones, that made the profit margin crater. Ten percent drop instead of one. But even that shouldn't have crashed everything else the way it did!"

"I have absolutely no memory of the kidnapping thanks to the Zeltin the kidnappers dosed me with," Barrat said, keeping his voice neutral. "Might never know who kidnapped me or why. Or if it really was connected with the crash the way a lot of people think. Dark hells."

That seemed to finish calming Connil. He picked up his coffee. "We still live, so we won," he said. Barrat stared at him and Connil shrugged. "Platitude from my father when Securities finally let me go."

"I'll drink to that," Barrat said. They bumped cups and drank. "You're still at Vegathic?"

"Yeah. Since I was cleared of any wrong-doing, they couldn't fire me or I could sue them for wrongful dismissal. Thought about leaving but until my name fell off the news I didn't think I had a chance of anyone hiring me. I'm back to doing analysis again. Spent nearly three months as a fact-checker. Deadly dull but I found a couple of peculators in one of the subsidiaries. And you've set up out in... Where is it?"

"Beranga. Two hours on a plane north-east of here. Nice sized city. I started working with my first clients there last week: a paintball range."

Connil stared at him. "Really? Doesn't sound very profitable."

"It isn't. The fee barely covers a month's rent on the office. But it is a foot in the door. I know some bigger companies and the major local analysis firms are watching how I treat the kids. And it's been fun. I did some paintball at a summer camp when I was a young teen. I'll be going out there once they're open. Right now they have skiers sliding around the trails and buying hot drinks and snacks at the fire pit once they're done. Never learned how to flat ski but I'll likely learn next fall. It's a popular sport there since they get five months or more of snow that doesn't go away inside of a week and there aren't any mountain slopes nearby. A minor downside, but it's a nice city and it's growing."

"Are you looking for an assistant?" A hopeful look.

"Can't afford one, not at the moment. But if you're interested, as soon as I have the work, I can give you a call. There's a second office, small, but okay, on the main floor and another big room upstairs I'm using as a combination exercise area and living room. And there's a second bedroom up there until you get your own place." Having a partner would complicate his other jobs. But it might work out. Laundering the income from a job as an analysis client could be a good way to move his money.

"I'm planning to give them a year to remember what I'm capable of. But let me know once you get swamped and I'll see how pissed off I still am at them."

"Deal. I have two appointments from the fundraiser I went to yesterday. Should be on track to break even this year, even with the start-up costs. At least the office furniture came with, so I didn't have to buy any desks and such, just a coffee maker and a matching set of mugs and small plates. And a viewer for relaxing in the evening. Only downside to living above where I work. I'll have to make sure I keep some downtime, once I get busy, that is."

"All good news, then." They bumped cups again. Connil leaned back in his chair, much more relaxed. Good. His friend was still that.

Chapter 15

Barrat looked over the wall and shook his head. Lothal Pregnor had decent security but it was *not* up to modern standards. Maybe the next person to own this mansion would upgrade it. Kerit sat in a rented van hidden among the trees a short distance away, listening in on his radio and to the local police channels. It hadn't been hard to slip away from the bar. He'd said he was tired from all the events and meetings he'd been to and was going to get some sleep before another day of meetings. Kerit picked him up wearing a suit just like the other guards and had dyed his hair with a wash-out product so he looked much younger. No one paid much attention to them in the busy bar parking lot.

They'd swapped to the van in an old, derelict factory loading area. Barrat changed into his sneaky suit as they drove out to the mansion. A short walk brought him to the wall. He left the suit unzipped until he stopped, then zipped the torso closed and pulled the mask over his head. The suit blocked his heat signature, in case there was anyone with thermal imaging goggles on the grounds. There should be, but Kerit hadn't seen any signs that there were any on his recon of the property last night. So they might or might not be able to detect him. He wasn't stupid, so he wore the suit.

"Going over," he said. A click responded. He double checked that he had everything before starting the climb. Reaching the master bathroom *without* the poison would be embarrassing. He felt the vial containing the blob of adulterated toothpaste in a chest pocket and patted it. Climbed up into the giant bare-branched tree growing far too close to the wall. Idiots. Climbed up the wall and stopped to check on any movement in the grounds. There wasn't anyone out this far and no motion detectors he could spot. *There could still could be tricks he wasn't seeing. Don't assume anything.* Kerit had enjoyed that part of his training far too much, Barrat thought. But it had taught him better than just reading about what devices that were usually found in protecting dwellings would have.

The goggles he wore were also used by the army and the police tactical units for sneaking around in the dark. Everything was faintly greenish and his depth perception wasn't as good as usual. Trees and shrubbery glowed slightly. As far as he could tell, there was no one out this far from the house. The only thing he really had to worry about, it seemed, was someone with a powerful flashlight catching him with his eyes open.

He attached the line and motor onto a thick branch above him, swung down and rolled out his momentum. Coming up behind a tall bush, he moved back to the wall and fixed the lightweight black rope to it for his egress. There were still no guards out here, at least not now. Slipping from bush to bush, he reached the back veranda before any of the six guards on duty came into sight. Two of them, smoking and chatting about what they'd do on their free days as they wandered along the garden path. Well, they'd have a lot of those in the next month or more.

Each had a powerful flashlight that they occasionally waved in the direction of the outer garden. Warned, he turned his head away from them and closed his eyes until they were well past him. They'd swear on anything that no one could get through their security. Another layer of protection for the clients. Then he moved on, staying on the grass to minimize noise despite his soft soled shoes.

The mansion was two stories, with two wings attached to the core building. Built of medium grey stone. Quite pretty, in fact. Despite the scum who lived here, that is. The right wing, with a wrap-around veranda, held the owner's living quarters as well as rooms for guests on the second floor. A study and other public rooms were below and in the central core. The kitchens and other mundane facilities were in the left wing, along with rooms for guards and servants. There was no sign of cameras or wiring on the facade. He moved around the building, keeping shrubbery between himself and the pathway the guards used until he neared his chosen approach point.

The master suite was above this part of the veranda, and its balcony was easy to reach. The ornate stone work of the building had deep mortar lines and his boots and gloves had extensions so he could just climb up the wall. No muss, no fuss. No evidence left behind. An important consideration on this job.

Those paying for the hit didn't want the chance of anyone official to learn what they'd paid for. It was too bad that Pregnor wasn't an honest politician. One who did what his benefactors wanted and didn't change the price of his vote as the whim took him. Death was a fitting punishment. The money the benefactors had to pay to Pregnor's successor would be a lot less. The brothels and liquor suppliers' revenue might go down, but that wasn't really his concern.

Another guard, this one listening to music on a headset and smoking, walked along the veranda and didn't look up. He moved so slowly that Barrat had to freeze and hold his position on the wall long enough to start a cramp in his left calf. Once the man turned the corner, Barrat finished his climb to the upper level and rubbed his cramp for a moment, safely hidden behind the waist high parapet.

A minute later he was inside the master suite and headed for the bathroom. The goggles showed him the surroundings. A huge bed, made up with what looked like satin sheets. A separate dressing room with a walk-in closet. A very thick carpet muffled all sound. Even if the target was sleeping, he wouldn't hear anyone moving around in here.

Pregnor wasn't home, of course. Another late meeting, his official schedule said. An evening at a local brothel was more likely, according to the information they'd been given. His backers knew only too well what Pregnor splurged their cash on. One reason they'd finally had enough of his vices and decided to do something about it. Their operating budgets were being strained by the constant payoffs, Kerit opined. They were still managing to fund their mandates, but the office staffs were being squeezed into shorter hours or lay-offs. That meant it was harder for the organizations to keep their donors happy.

Barrat slipped into the bathroom and picked up the toothpaste tube. Barely used. He looked at the logo and started to swear silently. It was a different brand: Zinger, not Citripow. Different colour and flavor. Their information was a little out of date. But not more than a week and a half, maybe two. A small thing, but given their chosen method to deliver the poison, a disaster.

He took a deep breath. "Change in vector," he said. "Zinger." A click of acknowledgement. Kerit must be cursing now.

Would it be better to abort the mission? Come back tomorrow night? Harder for him to arrange another night out and there wasn't anything on the target's schedule. Could they risk an earlier insertion while he was downstairs and could come up at any time? Would it be dark enough...

"Left pocket lower." Kerit broke the radio silence.

Barrat fished in his two left lower pockets. One each on his torso and thigh. The torso pocket held a tiny penlight. The pants pocket held a small vial of powder and two broad toothpicks. The pure drug. He smiled and clicked twice on his radio. In the instant of recognizing the vial, his heart rate slowed back to normal. It would just take a little longer to set the trap. He had everything he needed.

He took the goggles off, shut the bathroom door and put a towel at the bottom to block any escaping light. Then he turned the penlight on and put it between his teeth, squeezed a blob of toothpaste onto the counter and spread the blob out with a toothpick. He opened the vial and covered the paste with the drug. A few minutes work and it was mixed.

The next time the target brushed his teeth, the poison would start its work. Clots would form in several major arteries. Within one or at most two days, he'd be dead or a vegetable in a long term care facility and someone would be planning a lavish memorial, commemorating his many dedicated years of public service. Someone else would be arranging an election. He hoped there were some reasonable candidates for the public to choose from. Or they might get another contract.

"Inbound. Chase and target," Kerit said. The politician was nearly home. Early by twenty minutes. He mounded up the toothpaste and picked up the tube. Getting an air cavity at the top wasn't that hard but getting all the toothpaste in was time-consuming. He used a piece of toilet paper to clean up the remnants and tucked it, the vial and the toothpicks into his lower pants pocket. He replaced the cap and positioned the tube where he'd found it. Hung the towel back up. A quick look around and all was in order here.

Barrat put his goggles back on, slipped back out into the suite and through the door to the balcony. He reached the side of the balcony in time to hear the chase car coming past him to the garage while the other stopped at the front. He ducked low and closed his eyes as head lights shone from behind him.

Two guards hurried to the front of the house. No one else was around. He dropped from the balcony and moved into the shrubs. Waited a minute, then headed for the wall.

There was another almost encounter with a single guard near an empty flower bed halfway to the wall. Now that the target was home, the pattern changed. A reasonable precaution. But useless when someone was already inside and equipped with low light vision goggles and the guards weren't. He soon found the tree he'd come over and reached for the thin rope he'd set in place at the wall. Clicked the padded black hook to his belt and activated the motor above him. He rose high into the branches, knelt on a branch wide enough to hold his weight and looked around. No guards were in sight or hearing.

"Wall," he said to warn Kerit he was close to departure. He detached the motor from the upper limb and put it and the line in one of the baggy pockets on his vest and jumped to the ground on the other side with an unnecessary roll to finish off his success. Kerit would be ready to leave when he reached the van. He quietly headed down the dirt track with the zipper to his suit halfway down to his waist to start venting the heat contained by the suit.

This wasn't really a public road, and there was no surveillance on it. The target's security head should be ashamed at the holes in his protection. He should be fired for incompetence. At the very least, some entry protection should have been implemented. The lower doors had good locks according to their source, but not the balcony entrance. He shouldn't complain. It made his entry and egress much easier and faster.

Another ten minutes walk and he reached the van. Barrat changed back into his original clothes after a quick wipe down with a damp towel to get rid the sweat. "Didn't really need the heat-concealing suit, Kerit," he said. "That place needs a major upgrade in security for the next owner. I didn't see any cameras on the house at all."

"But it also keeps you from being stupid," Kerit said. "Any other problems in or out?"

"No. Just the change in toothpaste. Why did you put the drug vial in my suit? And when?" Barrat took the other front seat and buckled his safety belt. They'd reached a real road and would be in the city in another twenty minutes. Swap back to the other car and he'd been in bed in an hour. Once the target died, the fee would release from the escrow account and he'd have more money to invest. There were three other companies he'd been looking at in between clients. They'd come through the crash with minimal problems. Decent cash flow, good reserve and a rising dividend with good products that were in constant demand.

"In case. And before you put it on. Check all the pockets next time. There's plan A, then B and you should always have at least a C and D in mind. What could you have done without the pure drug to play with?" A quick glance at him. Part of his education.

"Come back tomorrow or the next night with the right pellet, since there was no alarm raised," Barrat said. "And it would be quicker since I knew the route and the guards' patterns. I know he would be home, but it still gets dark early. Or I could have rigged the car for a brake failure before I left. That would be more obvious than the clots, and the driver would likely die too."

"True. Innocents are not on our list."

"*Maybe* he's an innocent," Barrat countered, staring at the road ahead. "We don't know anything about him other than he's been driving Pregnor for seven years. That's not a sign he cares very much about what his boss does to other people."

"Also true. And the lesson?"

"Always have more tools with you than you think you'll need."

"Good lad."

Kerit dropped him off at the side door to Erithe's house and the guard who opened it at his knock was in shock.

"Mr. Barrat! Are you all right, sir?"

"Yes. Why? Has anything happened?"

"We couldn't reach you at the party you went to, sir. You vanished!"

The back-story. "I left there early, yes," He walked past the guard. "Are Erithe and Dantil still up?"

"Yes, sir. The small parlour on the right, sir."

"I'll go explain what happened. Please stand down any search."

Erithe jumped off the chair she'd been perched on and ran over and hugged him. He felt the baby move. A miracle that he might never know. He felt bad that he'd put her through such worry.

Dantil sighed and picked up the comm.

"I'm sorry, Erithe. I already told the guard at the door to stand down any search."

"Where were you?" He blushed. "A girl?" Nodded.

"You should have let us know," Dantil said.

"No. Someone I knew from before. I hired a driver and he waited outside for me. Did you call the police?"

"No, but if you were still missing by dawn we would have put all our security on alert," Dantil said. He set the comm down. "Well, I think we all should try to get some sleep."

"I'll take a hot shower," Erithe said. "That might let me relax enough to get to sleep. *Don't* do that to us again, Barrat."

"I won't." He blushed again. "I've gotten used to living on my own. No one looking over my shoulder at where I go and when. Lost the habit of checking in. I should have let you know I was going somewhere else."

Erithe hugged him again. "Mom's coming over at ten to visit. She wants to hear all about Beranga, and to tell you more about the lawsuit."

He glanced at the clock. Two in the morning. "Then I'll have to get some sleep fast. Did she think I was missing?"

"No," Dantil said. "We didn't want to worry anyone else."

As he climbed into bed, he smiled a little. But he'd have to be careful during the next few days. Someone like Harthil or Peykan would be assigned to follow him around, he was sure. Not much of a problem. There was nothing left to worry about. Kerit would be headed back to Beranga tomorrow afternoon after visiting a contact, he'd said. Information on another possible contract. Another person could have justice.

Chapter 16

Two days later the news was full of the life and achievements of the target. He died in his office two mornings after Barrat's visit. Within the time frame of the poison's effectiveness. Barrat mentally counted hours back from the reported time of death. He'd obviously waited on brushing his teeth until he woke up. Gross.

Mom was at Erithe's for supper. He was heading back to Beranga tomorrow in the late afternoon and he'd booked an appointment in the morning for a new analysis contract. His second from the fundraiser. He was making good progress on building up his legal business. That he had other clients might help the locals decide that he was competent. He should think about having a few testimonials printed off.

"I'm actually glad Pregnor is dead," Dantil said. "I think a lot of others feel the same. He kept changing his mind on important issues. You never knew until the votes were cast how he felt on any issue. Now they'll have to hold a special election. The fellow who ran against him last time seemed to have some good ideas. He had a decent showing. I hope he'll run again." Mom and Erithe nodded in agreement.

"Was this fellow popular with the voters?" Barrat asked.

"Not really. But he would always be seen to be on their side in some matter just before the election," Mom said. "Nothing illegal was ever proven in any electoral investigation but many people had concerns."

Phonbul came in with the next course. Barrat missed having such a range of dining options. The diner was decent, but his budget didn't allow many visits to the higher class restaurants. Only business meetings were scheduled in those so he could at least write off part of the expense. And he was getting nicely busy now, aside from potential contracts for Justice and Silence's expertise. The boys' fathers sent him a message late yesterday admitting that they jointly owned two hotels in Beranga and were thinking of expanding since the new developments were bringing new opportunities. Did he have any ideas? He'd replied that he might and suggested that they could discuss some ideas after they met about some possibilities for the paintball range.

"Barrat, one of my people sent a query about that new industrial area in Beranga," Erithe said. "She reported that they're cutting the property tax rate for the new commercial developments? It that true?"

"They are. Five years at half the going rate. And there are already plans in motion to start building housing and maybe another set of schools in the next year or two, once the new plants start to hire outside of Beranga and the imported workers need a place to live. The local roads are quite good and there's two railway lines that go through the new industrial area. Last summer and fall they added more tracks going through that area to decrease congestion when big trains come through. That's why they put the development there, I was told."

His wine glass was topped up and he sipped in appreciation. Another thing he didn't indulge in often. With everyone now knowing that he really didn't drink much, he didn't bother keeping up any pretence. The cellar was a good place to store wines but he didn't buy much, or often.

"I joined the Commerce Association when I first arrived and the development gets mentioned at every meeting. They seem to think it's vital for the whole district's financial well being. According to the projections, it's going to double the size of the city in ten, maybe fifteen years. From what I've seen so far, there is a very good possibility that it will."

"Hmmm. I might come visit later in the spring, after I feel comfortable leaving the baby for a few days. Several of our subsidiaries could use a transport node in that area. There was considerable discussion at the last major board meeting. We're shipping a lot of raw materials and products back and forth because we don't have anywhere in between to put them until the factories are ready to use the raw materials and it's actually cheaper to send full trailers for a round trip by rail than to pay storage fees at either end since we can't store that much at most of the plants. Having our own warehouse there might make sense. It wouldn't take long to get something into place, even if it's just a place to park road trailers or railway cars for the immediate future."

Dantil nodded. "Just parking them in a known location would really make it easier to keep track of them. One car was attached to the wrong train and it took three weeks to get it back to where it belonged. Of course the company desperately needed what it carried at the two week mark. No one knew where it was at first."

"Remember I only have two bedrooms, one real bathroom and no separate place to put the guards and such unless they bunk on the couch and floor in my living room," he said with a grin. "There's a great diner down the street, though."

"Cooking is still a mystery, dear?" Mom asked. He grinned at her.

"I can open cans, heat things, cook pasta, steak, bacon and eggs. Not burn the toast. And make coffee, which is the most important skill known. But sometimes I crave dishes that take more effort and skill than I have. Like this." He smiled at Erithe. "Plus it's a good place to hear gossip. I've gotten several clients from meeting them there."

"That's good," Mom said. "And from the fundraiser?"

"A few nibbles and two solid meetings. I'm meeting the second tomorrow morning. His company is based in Jagran, which is about an hour east from Beranga by car. He was dragged to the fundraiser by his cousin, who also suggested it was a great place to do business. I can rent a car easily enough if I need to visit him there. Currently I use taxis or the transit system to get around the city or do grocery shopping. Might buy one next fall, before the snow arrives. I'm not that thrilled with driving on snow and ice but that's a fact of life up there."

"What about buying your building?" Dantil asked. "Is that an option?"

"Still early days for that," Barrat replied. "Maybe once I build up enough for a down payment and can convince a bank I can pay a mortgage reliably without depending on dividend or rental income. So far, things are going well, so I'm not in any hurry. I might move into another area that has more prestige associated with it once I'm making more money. Right now, I'm in what is locally referred to as a "vintage" area, which is actually within my budget. My current lease is only for a year, so I'll start thinking if I want to move in the late fall. The management company has a lot of properties in the city."

He wouldn't move, not with the potential access to the tunnels the building had, but the comment told his family what they wanted to hear.

⋙⋘⋙⋘

Captain Lagrath stared at the potentially career-breaking report on his desk. Now he had to send it up to his superiors and prepare for the fallout from above. No one up the chain would ever want to admit they'd had anything to do with a failure of this magnitude.

Major Peterren nodded when he went into the office and put the report on his desk. He flipped to the end and read the conclusion. "So it's absolutely true. Young Trelner was not involved with the crash. There is still no good idea why it happened, unless Securities Service has a clue after all this time, but he didn't do anything."

"Completely innocent. No idea who kidnapped him or why they let him go, but nothing illegal was done by *him*."

"And IC is now being sued because of us and him. I've heard there are now over a hundred people or their heirs involved in the lawsuit so far. All because you fixed on Trelner as a loose end and I approved the interrogation." Peterren glared at him.

"But his father encouraged us to take him in." He hated the whinging tone in his voice. It wasn't their fault! Young Trelner had looked good for being involved in some way even if he hadn't been aware of it. And Peterren had agreed. Both of them jumping in without thinking: in search of glory with all the uncertainty surrounding the crash and failing completely. Dark hells.

"And there is no real record of that inconvenient fact. What evidence did your mole get? Anything we can actually use?"

"He heard the conversation in the kid's room just before we took the kid away. There's nothing in that statement that shows Trelner asked us to take the kid to see what he'd been up to. No recording of any 'evidence', of course. Trelner the younger is fine, now. Physically and mentally totally recovered. Has his own business in Beranga now. I asked a lieutenant I know there to check in on the kid and he did, not long ago. Then my friend was hauled into his colonel's office and told that if he ever bothered Trelner again, he'd be out the door and in an unemployed line up in a heartbeat." He growled an obscenity.

"The kid must have called the family and their lawyers the moment my friend left. He must have a camera on his door and recorded the whole thing. I don't think we can do anything unless we find him standing over the evidence with fingerprints on every page. Even then it would be very hard to convince anyone it wasn't a set up."

"I'll tell you the same as that colonel did to your friend. Stay away from young Trelner. All of them, in fact. Cut your mole loose. Your new assignment is to find out if there was anything odd in that politician's death. Lothal Pregnor. He had feelers in a lot of companies and lots of people were annoyed at him for various reasons, mostly because he wanted a bigger bribe to vote the way they wanted him to. He's not a great loss, but there's to be an election in a few weeks. Be interesting to see who takes over. But right now the press is suggesting it was a heart attack. We need to be sure no one helped him have one."

"I'll go see the coroner first, sir. See if they spotted anything out of the ordinary on the autopsy."

"Do that. Another debacle like this one," thumping on the report, "and we'll both be looking for new jobs."

Lagrath returned to his office and stopped at Sergeant Cranter's desk just outside it. "Send one of the corporals to bring a car around, Sergeant. We've been assigned to investigate Representative Pregnor's death. He had a few too many friends in the big corporations for upstairs to be comfortable at his sudden death. I'm off to visit the coroner for their first impressions. You and the others, start pulling everything we have on him for a review."

"We're in the doghouse over young Trelner, aren't we, sir?"

"Yes. So I hope this damned heart attack was just that."

The coroner looked over her glasses at her visitors. She was seated at her desk. Thankfully. Lagrath hated going into the working area of this place. "Yes. Heart attack. No real symptoms showing to his staff, but his last medical was well over four years ago. He could have gone downhill that quickly. What seems to be a blood clot blocked one of major arteries in the heart, a few other places in the lungs and a tiny one in the brain. Limbic core, so that stopped his lungs and heart within three minutes. The medics arrived quickly but couldn't do anything to revive him."

"*Seems* to be a blood clot?" Lagrath felt his gut tighten up. Another 'may be this or may not be that' case. Just what he *didn't* need right now. He tried not to growl at the coroner. It wasn't her fault and he'd have more cooperation from her and the techs here by being nice.

He'd vent later. Maybe in the car. After he warned his driver.

"Well, the objects that blocked the arteries *are* blood clots. No doubt about that. I can show the one from the heart to you if you like. How it formed is a bit puzzling. Pregnor didn't have any overt symptoms and his lifestyle didn't include any signs that he might have any activities that could lead to them forming. But, clots like that can sometimes have a rapid onset with no warning signs. Rare but not impossible."

"Are you planning to pursue that avenue?"

"Not really. It was an intellectual exercise, if that. Pregnor had a heart attack and a stroke due to blood clots that broke free from their site of origin. Natural causes. That's what my report will show. I have too many other cases to waste my time on something like this." The doctor suddenly seemed to register what branch Lagrath worked for.

"Is there some reason to believe someone in the corporate world wanted Mr. Pregnor dead, Captain?"

"A lot of people didn't seem to like him for one reason or another, but my team is looking for any sources who might know if there was someone hired to arrange his death."

"Well. There are some chemicals that can cause clots to form without actual physical reasons. I'm waiting on the lab results for anything odd in his blood work. If you don't find anything to change my mind in three days, I'll release the body and officially find for natural causes. After that, it would need to be a very compelling reason for me or anyone else to re-examine those findings." She closed the file and waited. Her expression said it would have to be a rock-solid case and she doubted he could do it. Well, so did he.

Lagrath nodded. "I have meetings scheduled with some of our informants to see if there's any chatter or who might be celebrating his death today with a little too much restraint."

When he returned to the station, the sergeant was staring at a report on his desk.

"Anything I need to know about?" Lagrath asked, taking off his outer coat to hang it up.

"The lads will have the information on the Representative together by mid-day tomorrow. This report is about a body found in the party district two days ago, sir. Older man. Merlg Ratgeth. He's been identified as a snitch the police and our people sometimes heard tips from him. Decent ones, not just smoke to get money out of us. No one has talked to him recently. The last time was a couple of months back, according to Records. That time he gave the city police a tip that a known assassin was in town, looking for a job. Name of Silence. He's very good from what I've found in the databases. But when the patrols arrived in the area, the man was nowhere to be seen. Ratgeth was worried about a possible reprisal and went dark on us. Now he's dead."

"And this happened the same week as Pregnor died. Co-incidence? Or he really died from unnatural causes? The coroner is currently voting for a normal heart attack on this case, by the way. Makes our job easier."

"The snitch's death looks like a simple mugging gone wrong, sir. Wallet and id were missing, one shot in the gut and a fractured skull from hitting the corner of a dumper. Ballistics says there was no rifling on the bullet, so it's likely a homemade weapon designed for close-up work. No brass found near the scene.

"There's a couple of scratches on the bullet but nothing matches any samples in our databases. The police have several file boxes with similar cases, it seems. There were no surveillance cameras at the crime scene and no one but the snitch walked into the alley from what was pieced together from other cameras in the area."

"Check adjacent streets. Maybe someone cut through a storefront."

Private Banthig came up to the desk, holding a report. "I was checking on the dumpers in that alley, sir, and some were emptied the morning after the murder, but before the body was actually found. Someone could have come through a store during the day, hidden in or beside a dumper then gotten into the body of the truck and left at the next stop. No way to tell at this point."

Lagrath felt his blood pressure rising as his private spoke. He did *not* need this shit from the dark hells. Why had he swapped into Corporate Oversight? His days as a patrol officer seemed to be so easy compared to what he had to put up with now.

Chapter 17

One of the footmen handed a message to him when Barrat returned from his morning appointment. Another signed contract in his case. The log-in information was ready so he could see anything in the company's computer network. They wanted to know if expansion was possible and the best ways to do so. And they had a good sized war chest built up so they wouldn't have to borrow much money if they didn't want to.

Garla had been at the party the other night. And she wanted to see him. Today. At a specific coffee shop he thought might be on the other side of town from the address. In... two hours. He sighed. It might be nothing, or an opportunity. He wouldn't know unless he went and talked to her.

"I guess I'm going out again after lunch," he said to Erithe. "Someone from university. It's a bit abrupt, but she was always that way. I'll delay my flight to tomorrow, just in case there's something I need to deal with."

"Is she someone you were interested in?"

"Not in the least." He shuddered at the memory. "She was clingy beyond all measure. Wanted a life of leisure and lots of parties and expensive presents. I'll have one of the guards mention an appointment after an hour so I can get away from whatever she's up to if I need to."

"Good plan." Erithe stretched and grimaced. "I'll be very happy in two weeks. He's doing sit ups right now, I think."

"He might decide to stay inside where it's warm," Barrat said. Then he ducked the sofa pillow she threw at him.

The coffee shop was an independent. Next to a bookstore he'd never heard of. But it was large. And had a dingy air of desperation about it. Two cars in the parking area. When Harthil started to get out to open his door, he shook his head and pulled out his comm.

"Erithe? Can you tell me anything right now about Taltron's Books? It's next door to the coffee shop I'm going to."

"I think the family is part of the IC lawsuit. The name seems familiar. I can have my aide look up more if you need to know right now."

"An update when I get back should work, I think. I see Garla staring at the car from the coffee shop next door to it. She looks pissed. I'll call when I'm heading home."

"He'll have some facts for you when you get here."

He put the comm away and nodded. Harthil let him out and followed him across the street to the coffee shop. Not much traffic at the moment. A good thing.

There weren't many patrons in the shop and he smiled politely at Garla. She'd come to meet him near the door. The table she'd come from had another occupant, a blond girl. Staring at him. Hope, fear and anger flitted across her face. A bad combination.

"Get some coffee and come over. You need to listen to something important." Garla glared at him, jaw set.

"Garla. Drop the attitude and be civil, even if it kills you. Now. Or I walk away right now and don't take any of your calls in the future. Ever. Who's that at your table?"

Garla stared at him, then took a deep breath. "Liselle Taltron. She's a cousin on my mom's side. Her father was accused of... a terrible thing. IC broke him, then threw him out when they couldn't find any real evidence. Like a lot of others."

"So they're part of the lawsuit. That doesn't explain why I'm here." Harthil moved a little away from them, far enough he could pretend he wasn't listening to their conversation.

"Because their business is failing. Someone's targeting them. Still."

"And? How does this affect me?"

"You've helped other businesses turn themselves around. You said so at the party. You're going to save this one."

This was not party-girl Garla he remembered from university. Now she was another predator.

Like Father. Like him.

"I'll listen. I'm not guaranteeing any further involvement. Go sit down. I'll be there in a minute. I need coffee first."

A mulish stare, but she did as he asked. Barrat went over to the counter to get some coffee.

"We're affected too," the male server said as he prepared the coffee. "Some people don't want to get 'contaminated' by being anywhere near the store. And I can't afford to move. I sank everything I had into this shop and I'm barely holding my own."

"You're the owner here?" A nod. *Dark hells.* Barrat paid for his and Harthil's coffees and put a generous tip in the jar. "I don't know if I can help either of you right now."

"Listening is a good place to start."

He took a deep breath and went over to Garla's table.

"Barrat, this is Liselle. My cousin. I told her about you already."

He took a sip of excellent coffee. "What happened and how do you think I can help?"

Liselle looked at Garla, then at him.

"We're still being targeted by whoever sent the accusation to the police. Rumours keep starting and we keep refuting them. Since Dad was released eight months ago, nearly all of our employees, some very long term, all quit without notice and we're down to a skeleton staff. I left university at the end of the fall term and work as a cashier, janitor, stock clerk and I'm trying to keep the account books in order. I was studying accounting, by the way. I didn't know enough to really do a good job when I started, but we couldn't afford to keep our old one on retainer, even if *he* hadn't quit as well. At least I had copies of everything from past years as templates."

"And the rest of your family? Did they pull away?"

"It's just me, Mom and my dad. Some cousins like Garla but most of the others were never close. They've mostly ignored us since..." She stared down at her coffee cup.

"Who do you think wants to drive you out of business and why?"

Liselle looked at him and bit her lip. He sipped his coffee. "There's a competitor, of sorts, that Garla and I think might be involved. We've talked about this a lot over the past few months. We don't have any real proof we can give to the police and we don't have enough free cash to pay someone to figure out if he is involved. His name is Gerath Kaldor. He's the manager of the Big Book Box franchise on the south side of town. He and my dad used to be... sort of friends. There's a bookseller's association and that's where they met. He always said he envied Dad the control and freedom he had here. After the accusation and Dad's release, he offered to buy us out, to give us cash to live on and take care of Dad. We thought about it, but turned him down since the amount he was of-fering wouldn't have lasted very long and didn't even cover all the stock we had on hand. He'd get the store building for free, more or less. My mom is now wondering if we should have taken the money and moved out of Herithan to where no one knows us. She said she'd have to get a job almost immediately to stretch out the money. There's no guarantee how long it would take Dad to get well enough to start another store, even if he wanted to."

"Did Kaldor say he'd keep the name or turn it into another Triple B?"

"I don't know. But I think he's getting near mandatory retirement age for their image. There's a new assistant manager who came about six or seven months ago that might be his replacement. So he might have just wanted the store for himself. So he'll be able to keep earning and not just retire." Garla fiddled with her cup, now half empty.

"And the attack on your father was well before that. But he could have seen it coming if he paid attention to when other managers retired. Does anyone else come to mind? Any other Triple B stores around here? And what about the other independent bookstores in the city?" *Track the competition instead of the money in this case.*

"There are two others, but they are well out in the suburbs at the bigger malls. The other independent stores aren't really a threat to us, then or now. Most of them are way smaller than us, but there's no animosity. And now they're getting some of our customers, but split between them, so there's really no advantage to one in particular. None of them can really expand much since their shops are all about a quarter the size of ours, or they've really specialized in what they sell." Liselle sighed.

"Who owns this store's building?"

"We do. It is paid off. Years ago. We used to own this one, but Vergil bought it when he opened the shop. We hold the mortgage, not a bank. Dad..." she dabbed at her eyes with a sleeve, "thought having the coffee shop next door would be a draw to new customers and give us a caterer next door for book signings and such. And everything was working really well. Until..."

"Who owns the rest of the block?"

"I don't know." Barrat looked at Garla, who shook her head. Confused.

"Find out. Urban renewal is an ongoing issue in parts of the city. Someone could get a lot more money if they controlled the entire block, not just a portion. You need to speak to the other building owners. Ask if anyone's asked about buying them out." He sipped again, giving himself time to think of more questions. "How do the rumours come to you?"

"Most of the time, we don't hear about them until a week or more later," Liselle said. "The damage is done before we can refute it."

"What about the initial accusation? Any idea who called the police?"

"No. They wouldn't say. Why?"

"Separate set of lawsuits," Barrat said. Garla perked up as she understood that idea immediately. Liselle smiled, just a little, then it faded. "IC isn't the only one responsible for hurting people like your father. A personal lawsuit would also give you more cash to work with and show that the recent and old rumours are all false. That should help turn popular opinion around and get people back into the store."

"The officer we asked said the call was to the tip line, not a real report, so there's no way to find out who it was unless they came forward. That's not likely, especially once Dad was declared innocent."

"You'd be surprised what can be done with voice recognition software. And if there's voice distortion on the recordings, which the police do have, it is still real evidence. How are you fixed for employees?"

The question surprised her. "We could use a few more part-time people to cover all the times we're open, but we can't pay them much over the minimum. We also give employees a discount on books they buy, which used to be a great perk that didn't cost us much."

"How is your father?" A gentler voice.

"Some days, not bad. Most of the time, he can't get out of bed. He's given up almost completely in the past few months. I think he feels guilty at how little he can do but he can't face the customers. Not yet."

Maybe he would never recover completely. "And his therapist?"

"The free therapy only lasts two months, which they didn't tell us at the start. Then they quoted an hourly fee that would finish bankrupting us inside of another two months."

"I'll call someone. My therapist works on a different track than the official ones. She's also on retainer to the lawyers for the lawsuit. The money being raised pays her fees, so it won't cost your family anything." He sipped coffee again.

"What's the status of the store? Financially. Are you breaking even?"

"There's some profit most months. Enough so that all the utility and other bills are paid and we can eat. The absolute percentage of profit is getting lower, but with fewer employees and not buying as many books to restock, it's sort of levelled out. Vergil Malern, the owner here, says his numbers are about the same."

"There needs to be a big event," Garla said. "In order to convince the stupid customers that the accusation was false."

"Any ideas who could be a headliner?" Barrat asked.

"Not immediately." The big problem that no one had dealt with.

"Find someone. Set something up as fast as possible. Public relations is critical, for all the businesses who were and are affected. The foundation concentrated on raising money for the lawyers' fees. They forgot about the human angle. I'll go see my mother tonight and I can get her started on that. She can also get the lawyers interested on identifying who accused the innocents. Wave more lawsuits and increased fees under their noses and they'll be eager to jump in."

Movement from his left, towards the counter. The owner. Vergil came up to the table. "That's a good idea, having a big event. I can provide the refreshments if I get some cash up front to bring them in."

"Also possible." Barrat turned to the women. "How about a quick tour of the store?"

"Sure," Liselle said.

Garla looked her watch and sighed. "I need to get to work. I took a late lunch to come here."

They finished their coffees and left, Harthil trailing along behind. Garla and Liselle hugged briefly and exchanged a comment he couldn't make out. Garla headed for a taxi stand just down the street from his car.

The floor and rug just inside the doors needed cleaning. And just about everything needed dusting. The whole place needed a good maid service. Someone should also properly shelve the new books, not just stack them in random order on the shelves, hopefully in the correct section. And they had to get some decent music playing, even if it was just a broadcast station for free. Or a set of recordings. Their footsteps echoed slightly. The quiet was oppressive.

"How many employees do you have?" He tried not to whisper.

"Four part-time, plus me and Mom. She's been trying to do the ordering, which was what Dad was really great at. He had a gift for ordering the oddest books, and they all became hits. We used to have readings here every week, if not more often." They approached the cashier's line. An older woman sat there, looking up with a sad smile.

"Mom, this is Barrat Trelner. His mom..."

"I know. Enough money to give us a chance to stretch out our slide into oblivion."

"I do have a few other ideas, Mrs. Taltron. One is to identify the people who falsely accused people like your husband and add another set of lawsuits for malicious mischief and whatever else the lawyers can come up with. But you have to do your part." He glanced around. No customers were visible. A bad sign but he didn't want to say this with witnesses. "This place needs cleaning as soon as possible. Floors and the front windows at a minimum. Get some cheerful music playing. Stop looking like this is a funeral." He kept his voice low in case he missed someone in the stacks. "Or it will be."

Liselle smiled again. Just that tiny bit. "We tried that."

"And you didn't keep it up. This store looks defeated, so naturally people are going to treat it that way. Same with all the other businesses affected. They have to start believing that they will survive."

"How did you feel when IC let *you* go?" her mom asked. She saw the result of a lot of work, not what he'd been like at first. He resisted a snide remark in favour of the truth.

"I was petrified. A complete mess. Wanted to hide all the time and if anyone raised their voice around me I panicked. I still have problems with small rooms and being anywhere without a window. I sometimes have nightmares that I'm back there. But I didn't let them keep me a victim. That's what everyone has to do. Mr. Taltron may need more therapy to be able to get back to where he was before. Or he might need a good kick in the rear. It's not my place to decide or to take over his therapy."

He took a deep breath as Harthil raised a hand to show his watch. An hour. "I have another appointment. Garla didn't say why she wanted to meet when she left me the message this morning. I will do what I can, and make as much of it applicable to all of those who are part of the lawsuit so I can charge the lawyers for my time, not you or the other business owners. But, Liselle, you need to take charge here. Be perky when you work the cash. Don't let your mother do this. She can do stocking, or concentrate on taking care of your father."

"That's a lot of work," Liselle said.

"And you can do it. Or call and accept the offer while it's on the table."

He looked at her mom. She was crying. "I need some books to take back to Beranga with me. I'll call with the list later today. I loan them to new clients, and sometimes they buy them from me to keep as references." He could afford a few new ones and there were others that he wanted for his personal library.

"Thank you, Barrat," Liselle said. "I'll get the window cleaner out right away. One of the employees knows how to run the floor cleaner. He should be in for his shift soon."

"And have the coffee shop do the same. Looking desperate frightens customers away." He left, the guard close behind.

He took a deep breath as the guard closed the door to the car. "Any thoughts on what you heard, Harthil?" He asked as the car moved into the traffic flow.

"I... I've never been asked for my opinion on anything I chanced to overhear, sir. Never studied any business, just what I needed to keep folks like your family safe."

"But you did overhear quite a bit this afternoon."

"I think you told them the truth about the store. I wouldn't have gone in there to buy anything unless I didn't have another choice. Some folks might still be loyal to them, but not seeing the father in the shop doesn't help the image that everything is okay now. The coffee shop: not so much of a problem, but still, it needs help. Contaminated by the book-store, mostly. Might be someone wanting to buy the block, but the neigh-bourhood doesn't seem like they're in renovation fever."

"And you, Peykan? Any thoughts from street-side?"

"They're both dumps, sir. It's going to take a lot of work to get the places cleaned up so people would walk in, even if they didn't know what happened to the owner. A couple of people went into the coffee shop, no one into the bookstore while I was out here."

"And that's half the problem. Either of you know anyone who needs a part-time job? Minimum wage, but a discount on anything in the store." Peykan thought for a moment, then nodded.

Erithe's aide Larin had a slim folder waiting in the small parlour Barrat used as an office while he was here. "This is all we could assemble in such a short time, sir. We should know much more tomorrow morn-ing."

"Thank you. Have you ever been to that store? I don't think I'd ever heard of it before today."

"Quite often, sir. I've attended a number of readings there. Now of course, there haven't been many events, and the quality of the stock has suffered with Mr. Taltron's illness."

"Just like the rest of the innocents," Erithe said. The aide left.

"Going after the people who made the accusations didn't occur to the lawyers? It seems an obvious inclusion to their to-sue list. Why didn't they pursue it?" Barrat set the folder down on a side table.

"The police claim that it's impossible to trace the calls they received or identify those who called. They do have some who made accusations in person, but most of the false accusations were called to the tip line from public comms. That should have been a big warning sign that there was no proof of wrongdoing."

Barrat snorted. "Of course. But there are other experts out there. I'm sure someone could do it. Maybe not to police standards, but enough to get names so some private investigators can find some concrete proof that the lawyers can use for the lawsuits. Forget about the police for now. They're just trying to cover up their stupidity. Even if they don't have a personal stake in what happened, they're not going to speak up or give any real help to the people whose lives were ruined."

"Do you need to delay your flight again?"

"I hope not. I would like to meet with one of the lawyers and suggest a few options to them early tomorrow morning. Can you arrange something?" She nodded, then smirked.

"And Garla? How does she fit into this?"

"She's not directly involved. She's a relative to the family on the mother's side." A very slight blush sent warmth up his cheeks. Erithe smiled. Dark hells.

"And who else was at this meeting?"

"Liselle Taltron. She left university to help run the store when the accusation against her father first hit. Trying to do everything, and sees nothing but ruin coming. Her mother's not much help nor is her father. Defeated." He tried to keep his voice neutral. Just the facts.

"You've found a real girlfriend?" Both eyebrows went up.

Dark hells. He took a deep breath. "Not now. She's concentrating on her family and their business." He looked at her. "As we should be." No matter what his heart was now telling him. He'd never met someone he was honestly attracted to. But she was under such pressure right now. To look like he was riding to the rescue would put pressure on her to agree to whatever he suggested. He couldn't force this or he'd ruin everything.

His body disagreed. He turned to go upstairs before Erithe saw how interested part of him was in talking to Liselle again.

Chapter 18

He was finally back in Beranga. It felt so much better here. He took a taxi home, since he didn't want to invest in a car just now. He might have called Kerit to pick him up, but wasn't sure if his mentor had returned yet. It was a long drive and Kerit's joints didn't like the cold. Or sitting still for hours in a car.

The stress of being with family was harder than he'd thought it would be. Maybe just seeing Erithe and Cartan's families and Mom the next time would be less hectic. And he'd take just a short holiday with the whole family, assuming Father kept the tradition going this year. With everyone still pissed at him for throwing Barrat to the IC, there might not be much incentive to subject himself to the family's displeasure at such close quarters. Barrat hadn't spoken to his father at any of the 'family' functions. It seemed no one else was talking to him either.

Barrat also had to decide what might happen with Liselle Taltron. Nothing for now, of course, but his meeting with one of the junior lawyers might lead to some fund-raising for someone to analyze the tip recordings and some private investigators to look for actionable evidence. He hoped Kerit had some names for an expert who could access the recordings and provide some answers. The lawyers must know some decent investigators. The taxi stopped in front of the office and he paid the man and took his two suitcases. Waved at the flower shop lady and went in, still thinking of possibilities.

No one had tried to enter the building while he was away, the cameras showed when he checked. Good. He had those new contracts from his trip and he'd have to start working on them early in the morning. A message from Kerit on his office comm said he'd be at the diner in two days. Getting in mid morning tomorrow. Good.

The paintball range was open for skiing and snowshoeing on week-

ends from ten to eight and evenings from five to eight. A warning to
bring your own equipment. Various ski waxes were the only skiing related items listed for sale. Good. The boys didn't need any stock they
couldn't guarantee to sell quickly. Fire pit time was included and hot
beverages and snacks were available for reasonable amounts.

There was also a note attached detailing their efforts. They were
limiting their spending to on-sale snack bars and baked goods they could
eat if no one bought them by the best-by date. They'd dropped the flyer
and note into his mailbox. The boys would do okay now. He might go out
this spring once the range opened up. He had to keep up his long distance practice. His targets, however, would never look like every shot
was in the centre. That would be asking for trouble.

Two weeks later Kerit met him at the diner for one of their regular
meetings. They were fairly open about their relationship. He just needed
to remember not to talk shop unless they were alone.

Really alone.

"Went out to your young friends' paintball range on the weekend,"
Kerit said as he smiled for Bethie, their usual waitress. "Good notion to
use the land for flat skiing during the winter. Yours?"

"At first. They had no idea what they were doing when they had the
basic idea early last spring. Ended up almost broke. They need income
through the year to pay rent to their fathers and cover their taxes. I also
suggested the fire pit and hot drinks. Was it crowded there?"

"Not too bad, given the amount of land they can utilize. About fifteen cars when I got there, a few more when I left. My knees started to
get cranky after a while but my doctor said it was keeping working them
or I'd be in a wheelchair. I did make a suggestion to the boys. Have a
competition: target shooting with the paintball guns and skiing between
targets. They huddled in a corner for ten minutes, then asked if I'd like
to help organise it. For a fee, they were eager to offer."

"And will you?"

"Might do. They're good kids. And I'm a little bored. Fewer jobs in
the winter." Barrat nodded. More chance of leaving footprints in the
snow for any jobs in the north. Sneaking into anywhere was hard.

"We do need to visit a warmer clime," Kerit said softly. "Snathard's
having a warm spell with no rain forecast for the next week. You free for
three days?"

"For this, yes. You have the tunnels picked out?" A smile was the
answer as Bethie came back to refill their coffee cups.

ക്കൈക്കൈ

Welker fumed at the letter, then stuffed it into his pocket. It looked like a card from a friend. He'd been fired by the idiots from Corporate Oversight. No more bonus money to invest or have fun with. Dark hells. He tidied the large parlour without thinking. How could he find another benefactor who'd help him get out of this place? Mastren was a dictator. He'd never advance here, and any reference letter Mastren wrote wouldn't help him get the type of job he really wanted.

Late that night it came to him. Vegathic still had to be riled about the crash. And there were five other big investment companies that might pay well to get some inside information on the Trelners. It was too bad that CO hadn't given him the equipment to see any messages that passed through the system in the basement. He could have done so much better if they'd given him the right tools. Maybe someone else would. Or he'd get enough money to buy a system of his own. The pitiful fees he'd received weren't enough to buy everything he'd need and he didn't have much in the bank. To take a large enough sum out would be suspicious.

He had the day off tomorrow. He'd make copies of some of his better reports, add a few things he hadn't included before because Corporate already knew them, and he'd see if anyone might be interested. He smiled, turned over and slept.

ക്കൈക്കൈ

Nartig Haltarn stared at his boss. "The Trelners are looking for *me*?" He'd been told to get his ass into the boss's office the moment he'd returned from his latest assignment to file all the reports. That trip had been a boring two weeks of guarding someone who didn't try to lose his detail and wasn't really in any danger to start with. That was generally a good thing in their line of work. But being on alert for that long was hard. You didn't get nearly enough restful sleep, even if you were technically off duty.

"Under the alias you used at while following that idiot analyst from Vegathic. From your visit to the gym." Branson said. "Not you as you. Thankfully. Sit." Nartig sat in the more comfortable visitor chair.

"How and why did they connect *me* to the kid?"

"You're an anomaly at the moment. It seems young Trelner was thinking about the kidnapping recently and wondered if he'd been tailed earlier in the day. An obvious loose end but no one thought of it until now, which is very good from our point of view. The sister checked the club records: You came in right behind the kid, said you loved the place but never followed up, so the sister and her guards were curious. None of the police ever questioned anyone at the gym, since they assumed he'd been grabbed at or near home. The Trelners now know the identity was fake, but have no idea who you are." Nartig let out a slow breath.

"The kid's fully recovered from his stay in IC, by the way. And there's no indication that he's having issues from his time with us. His stay at IC is, of course, another issue. We discovered which therapist they used. She's not one of the regular list IC hands out. Since he's doing so well, we might recommend her the next time one of our clients needs help after an adventure." Branson referred to any negative experience their clients endured that way. *Some days my boss is nuts*, Nartig thought. Back to the real problem.

"Dark hells. Are there still any pictures of me from the gym?"

"No, thankfully. All the outside cameras are wiped after a week and so are the ones in the change room. All they have is the name, a scrawled signature and whatever memories the people you talked to have of you. They tried an artist with the people who interacted the most with you. The artist drew three different pictures. None of them really look like you. We don't need to worry much."

Nartig relaxed against the chair back, then sat back up. "How do we know what's going on? Are the police involved again?"

"No. It seems Corporate Oversight turned an employee in the Trelner compound into a mole when they suspected the kid. The mole was cut loose recently, probably since the kid doesn't live in the city any more. Corporate Oversight was stomped on because of the "unwarranted" questioning of the kid and other innocents. Rates of suspects going into Insanity Central are way down in the past months. They need real evidence to send anyone there now, from what I've learned." Nartig relaxed a little. He did not want to end up in IC for any reason.

"Anyway, the mole got used to the extra income and started searching for a new patron. Went to our employer on that op and offered to keep them in the loop on anything Trelner Industries does. Our contact there didn't know why he came to them, by the way. Maybe he sold, or attempted to sell the same information to a number of other companies who lost money in the crash. The mole gave them a couple of tidbits to prove he could deliver. Including the information on the interest in you. They gave him a few hundred for what he brought but declined his further service. After he left that meeting, our contact called me. Normally we'd transfer you to another office, but this isn't much of an issue. Just stay away from that area so none of their employees get a good look at you."

"I can also change my look with a moustache and a slightly different hairstyle," he pointed out. "And with three bad pictures, it makes me look even more different."

"True. You have a week off, then you'll be working with Martan: a celebrity travel gig far away from here. Start growing the moustache now since you may be photgraphed while you're out there. Jula will have the basic assignment details for you when we're done here."

⋇⋇⋇⋇

Captain Lagrath was frustrated. There was no evidence that the politician's death was anything other than natural. Even the coroner was convinced. But something was still bothering him.

Sergeant Cranter came in the office. "The funeral for Pregnor is tomorrow, sir. Did you want the team to attend?"

"We might as well," Lagrath said. "Not in uniform. Maybe we'll get lucky and overhear something useful. Otherwise, the case is closed."

The turnout was respectable, Lagrath thought. Not enough people to overcrowd either the temple or the burial site. The assembled mourners milled around after the ritual ended. His men dispersed to listen.

Two hours later just about all the mourners were gone. They went to their van and Lagrath sighed as he sat down. His back hated just standing around making small talk. "Anything of interest?"

One by one, the men admitted they'd only heard platitudes with a few bad jokes as leavening. Many had come just so their names would be in the reports of the event.

"The lobbyists near me mostly talked about the upcoming election," Cranter said. "Hoping that the new person would support their causes and vote them increased funding."

"Well, we had a day out of the office and it wasn't raining or snowing," Lagrath said. "Let's get back, write this up and head home. If any of you hear something pertinent in the next day or so, let me know. I have the report mostly written for the natural causes option, but I'm still wondering if it was arranged. Somehow."

Nothing came in the next two days. On the third, he handed in the report. Major Peterren looked at the closed folder.

"Natural causes. Some folks seemed happy at the funeral, but their causes hadn't been funded and now they might be, so that's not really a red flag. None of our informants on the street reported hearing anything about someone looking for an assassin."

"Good. We have some little reports to deal with from the crash for Securities. I'll have some of them to you tomorrow. Every team is getting a stack. They think they've found some trading accounts with false identity issues. Track down anything you can on them."

"Yes, sir." Lagrath sighed after he left the office. Anything to do with the blasted crash was suddenly a priority. Again. He was heartily sick and tired of hearing about it.

৵৻৵৻৵৻

Barrat stretched and went to the upstairs window overlooking the street. Early spring here was a mix of melting and freezing that led to many falls, Bethie told him. He'd been lucky so far. However, he had an appointment today and would have to leave the office. He'd use a taxi instead of the bus to get into the Core. Business was decent enough that he wasn't counting every coin any more.

All three representatives of the local analysis firms waited in the Commerce Association boardroom. Three men staring at him. A sense of doom filled the room.

"To what do I owe this honour?" he asked as he took a seat across from them. "Is this a "we want you out of here" speech?" Trying for any response to lighten the atmosphere. First the bookstore, now here. Was there something he wasn't seeing? The country's economy in general wasn't doing that badly from what he'd heard in the news.

"No. There is a major problem with our industrial area." Gandeth said. He still looked grim. All of them did. Serious trouble, then.

"And how do you think I can fix anything, or am I the cause?"

"Neither. But your family might be able to help."

"I moved here to get away from my family, gentlemen. You should know their history. Especially my father's attitude toward investing: Buy Low and do anything necessary to drop the price." Silence while they stared at him. "Why do you and the industrial area need help?"

"Because Norgrant Associates, the company who owns and is developing the industrial area, is about to go bankrupt," Daltons said. "They're overextended by 200%. At least. An idiot vice president has been embezzling from their reserve funds over the past year or two. It's a gambling addiction so there's no chance of retrieving any of that cash quickly. We were told this yesterday morning and received agreement from our principals to contact you. There's no way Norgrant can survive the news reports once it breaks. They'll have to sell whatever assets they can as they have a major payment to make on another development that's five times the size of ours in three weeks. And that means the development here will come to a crashing halt until all the legal wrangling ends."

"Years," muttered Martins.

"Maybe centuries." Gandeth retorted. Daltons glared at both of them.

"They also hold the mortgages on most of the sold lots, just to make it worse," Daltons said. "It seemed like such a good idea at the time, but it's a major reason why the fallout is going to hurt everyone involved. Those mortgages will be called and it will take considerable time to transfer those loans to regular lenders. The interest rates on them will skyrocket because of Norgrant's issues, which will also force some of our clients to put their expansion on hold."

"And that drags Beranga's progress to nothing and all of your clients have invested heavily into the industrial expansion and the new housing plans. They'll all fail in the ripple." *A depression in this city might move further into the surrounding area*, he thought. *Smaller towns were looking to the developments here to provide more jobs for their people and fuel their own growth. Dark hells.*

All three nodded at him. He took a deep breath.

"You need someone to ride to the rescue. You think my father might do it." If they only knew. He managed not to roll his eyes. "I have to warn you that he will not care *anything* about your clients' plight. He might buy out the development and sit on it until your clients caved on whatever changes *he* decided to make to their agreements and mortgages. Those changes would not make your clients happy. He is *not* a good man. He is always after profit and will do just about anything to further his own aims. His philosophy is that he wins, and everyone else can fend for themselves. The weak get stepped on and ground down if they try to oppose *his* plans."

The men sighed, almost in unison. But he'd told them the truth. He wouldn't be responsible for them entering into any discussions with his father without that and stronger warnings.

"Are any of his competitors any better?" Martin asked. "From what we know, they wouldn't care about our clients either. We've heard Industries is holding a lot of cash at the moment from sales of some stocks he bought during the crash. That's what made us think of him. He calls a million a pittance."

"I doubt the other big companies are any different," Barrat said. "How much money would you need to buy out this development from Norgrant? At least enough of a percentage up front so they can make the payment on their other property? More money can come in once the immediate crisis is over."

They looked at each other. "Twenty-seven million in round numbers for the total payment. It's not worth that at the moment, but Norgrant's CEO will insist on getting everything he can to stave off the inevitable. It might let them hold out long enough to sell off something else to get their dammed debt under control. They'll get some cash from the embezzler as his property gets sold off, but their big payment due is ten million. If they don't have at least that, they're finished. And so are we."

"I doubt that my father would go that far. Especially if he can wait and buy the asset for a discount once the news breaks." He sighed now. Erithe planed on coming out early next week for a walk around the site he'd proposed to her for their storage depot. No one here knew she was coming. The way she wanted it. And he had another niece who was now over a month old, which was also a good thing. "I can call someone. *Maybe* they can do something. I can't promise anything. But Beranga and this area needs that development to keep growing. So everyone can win, not just one individual."

The relief showed in the slightest drop of their shoulders. Things were worse than he'd thought here.

When he returned to his office, he stared at the comm for several minutes before picking it up. Dantil answered and put their comm on speaker as soon as he answered.

"Hi, Barri," Erithe said. "Is everything ready for next week?"

"It was, but that's not why I'm calling. Or it is."

"It's way too early in the day for you to be drunk," Dantil said. "Start again, Barrat. Use lots of words this time." Erithe giggled.

"There is a problem with Norgrant, the developer. They may be forced into bankruptcy." Barrat started to explain the very tentative plan which he'd thought of on his way back to the office.

"You think we should buy out the development?" Dantil asked when he finished. "Not Industries? Privately?"

"Yes. It would keep the businesses here on track with their projects, get Industries a very nice place to park railway cars and such, make the rest of the family a decent amount of money and will truly piss off Father."

Erithe giggled. "That's the first thing Mom would approve of."

"I think so too," Dantil said. "We need some solid numbers before we go much further, but we can call everyone and warn them this is coming. We'll have a rough idea of how much is liquid enough to write a cheque."

"The minimum will be ten million, fairly quickly, to pay on their other development. That's due in three weeks. The total might be in the twenty-seven million range, but we may be able to get that lower. I'll have the numbers sorted by tomorrow night at the latest. I'm expecting a courier with all the information within the hour."

❧❧❧❧

He called Liselle later that night, once he'd made more notes on the project. He'd gotten a precis of the entire development project, including all the information he needed to put solid facts into the idea, rather than numbers almost plucked out of the air, by a courier with two escorts.

"How are things going?" he asked, once her father handed over the house comm to her. *Note to self. Get Liselle a portable comm of her own. Maybe.* Even if he had to pay the bills for it.

"A lot better," she replied. He heard a door closing. Good, she was in her room now, away from casual attempts to overhear their conversation. "We're having a reading every other week now. The three teens you sent over are working out really well. How do you know them?"

"I don't actually. I do know their fathers. They're guards and such for the family. They have kids too. And having a job lets them get the things they want that their parents won't buy for them."

A giggle. "Your mom's event started everything moving. The writers were amazing. Quite a few were ones who we'd dealt with in the past. Several announced new books. The reporters were here in droves. We had to send out huge orders once it was over but we had the money in the bank to just pay for them. I...sat and looked at the receipts the next morning. Couldn't believe the total. I didn't think it would do so well. Even Dad smiled. He was able to be there the whole time. It was like. Like before everything went so terribly wrong."

"I saw some coverage in the news sheets." He paused. "But I was wondering how *you* were doing. Not the store, not your parents."

Silence. A sigh. "Better. Some days are still rough. I wake up occasionally with nightmares that it's all starting again. That they're taking all of us to IC, not just Dad." Shuffling sounds as she walked. "It takes me most of the night to calm down. I think Dad's doing better than I am sometimes."

"It will get better. The trial date is coming up soon. I want to come up, at least for a few days during it. Moral support for the rest of the people, if nothing else."

"That's right, you get your own lawsuit. Why *did* you volunteer?"

"I didn't think I had a real choice. My father said the other compan-ies I'd interviewed at were suing the family for huge sums. They alleged I'd done something to Vegathic's computer system and probably theirs. So I went with them and found out after I recovered that my father lied to me. It was the worst decision I ever made. That's when the family stopped talking to my father. They still aren't, by the way."

"But you have recovered."

"I still get the nightmares sometimes," he said gently. "Working out with weights or the punching bag helps tire me on those nights so I can sleep. I tried some medications but those made it worse. I couldn't wake from those dreams. At least when I wake up I can do something else so I don't go right back into the nightmares."

"I think that Dad's had some dreams like that. So have I."

"Maybe you should chat with Doctor Halli."

"I will. Maybe we can have coffee while you're here."

"I'd like that. Or, maybe we could have dinner?" *Was it too soon to mention a real date? Dark hells, he had no idea what he was doing. The profes-sional ladies he'd been with in the past were simpler to deal with. Meet them at a bar, buy them a drink and go to their place. He had transitory physical relief. But they weren't someone who might really care about a future with him.*

More silence. "I would like that, Barrat." Sounds of rapping. "Drat. Curfew," she said. "Let me know when you're going to be in town."

"I will, Liselle." A click as she hung up.

He hung up, then swapped the computer cable to the dark net one. He didn't have voice capability on this machine, but could send and re-ceive messages. One went to the hacker Kerit tasked with finding out who all the accusers were. He'd said he knew someone who could access the dark net. Mama looked like she wanted to ask questions about who that was and how he knew them. The lawyers didn't care how the com-parisons were done, just that they'd find out who the accusers were iden-tified. That he insulated them from any possibly illegal actions was why he also had access to a special bank account to pay the hacker.

A stack of identities were already in the lawyers' hands, who then hired private investigators to look for real evidence and were now build-ing those cases. And they were all happy at the fees pouring into their coffers. Everyone was winning. Except the greedy people who'd tried to ruin lives. He smiled. That's the way he wanted the world to work. Nice when it cooperated.

Any word on Taltron's accuser?

It's the bookstore guy, as you figured already. Easy with just one suspect to match the voice to. *He was stupid to keep floating rumours once Taltron was found innocent. The police should have figured it out without me to hold their hands. What next?*

Send the info to me. I'll get it to the lawyers. There's a good circumstantial case already in process. This should get the threat of IC in play. I don't think he's has enough guts to risk it.

Good enough. I've actually got a dozen more ready to go.

Excellent. Payment will be in your account tomorrow.

The last batch should be done inside the week.

I'll warn the lawyers. Anytime you need a reference, just ask. They might be brave enough to deal with you by themselves next time.

Not likely but thanks. Data's coming your way.

He saw a big file coming in. Excellent.

Chapter 19

The four men around the large boardroom table stared at each other. Damilan Hranthel was at the end of the table, with the ornate chair that meant he was in charge. The logo of the Securities Services filled the entire wall behind him.

"We still have no real idea what or who caused the crash?" he asked.

"Not really, sir," said Vertin Malther, head of their analysis section. He shook his head in dismay. Most of the time, the market was sane. Logical. But not that day. Three of his analysts were currently out on stress leave. He'd managed to keep a handle on his own anxiety though work. His wife didn't agree. But. "But we've been looking into a last straw for the past month. And it's finally paying off."

"And what is that?"

"Our current thesis, as I said last time, is that someone generated the start of the drop by releasing that inflammatory analysis of the Vegathic report to a few on-line forums. We've discovered since then that someone added fuel to the fire by shorting a number of stocks, including Vegathic's. The shorting orders started coming in near close of trading, two days before the actual crash. Just a few at a time, and scattered among twenty different companies that were already on most analysts' watch lists. Everyone, it seems, expected those stocks to go lower within the month. The total number of shorts didn't signal any problems because we've only looked at the overall totals in the past. We should be looking much closer and Somners' programmers are developing and testing code to do so. We plan to track the numbers to see what the variation is over the next few months." The other men nodded in agreement.

"I've got a team going through last year's data to get an idea of the numbers from different times and situations." Kartlin Somners said. "The day before the crash, the top predators noticed those shorts and started adding their own late in the day. Early in the crash, about an hour in, a number of buy orders hit the system computers. About sixty of them within a half hour. All the buys were for prices considerably under the asking prices of those stocks. The system tried to find those stocks at the requested price and that's when the market started to go out of control. Investors, especially those with smaller portfolios, saw the bid prices dropping and started to panic. They decided to sell before the prices went down further. Which, of course, caused the prices to drop even faster. A cascade, like a major dam breaking apart and releasing all the water in one big wave."

"Who made the original shorts? And those buy offers?"

"We discovered that most of them were from fake accounts," Julin Bethnil said. "All of them were built up over the past year and a half, we've found. Modest trading, mostly good results, but no brokers, and no trail back to whomever actually set up the accounts. All of them tended to buy the same stocks on the same day, which confused Malther's analysts, who were compiling the data. At first. The rest of the market had what we think is about the normal number of shorts the day before the crash. Once we deleted those accounts from the totals."

"What about young Trelner? Any sign he was involved in any of this?" Hranthel leaned back in his chair.

"None at all, sir," Bethnil said. "Judging from the financial records that we saw thanks to Corporate Oversight, he didn't have the resources to fund even one of the fake accounts. So, he's still in the clear. The only way he could have been involved was to have set up the scheme in the first place, and his time at IC disproved that possibility. His involvement was truly peripheral. Someone might have rigged the kidnapping to hide that he'd done some illegal work for them, but there's no sign of any payments in his financials. It could be a different fake account but there's no evidence of anything illegal. There's no sign that he's accessed any trading account but his own, very small one since he recovered. It originally held nothing but Trelner Industries stock. That's been changing in the past few months but we can account for all the new money. He's also accepting partial payment in shares from public companies to diversify his portfolio for work he's doing for them. Nothing illegal. He's working with the lawyers in the suit against IC and can access one of their accounts, but none of that money is going into his pockets. Bribes to informants, I think. They're trying to establish who might have called in the bogus tips to the police."

Hranthel shook his head. "That's now all water in the sea. But how can we stop such a crash from happening again?"

"The automated trading halt is the easiest of the methods we've thought of to implement, sir," Somners said. "That will replace having three analysts watching monitors and sitting next to a kill switch. All three have to agree to shut the market down. They've come close a few times, but never actually hit the button. My team has been gaming scenarios over the past two months, using the actual data from the crash. Current plan is that drop of a hundred points in an hour triggers a half hour halt with no new orders being accepted until the market is back up. Two hundred points in three hours will also trigger a halt that takes a vote of the directors to start up trading. That will give you and the other directors a chance to review the situation and decide if trading will be allowed to start back up and when. With the new code to track short orders, that data would be available for the directors in real time to aid in their decision. A sudden uptick in short orders for multiple companies would be a definite signal that someone was planning something."

"Agreed. When can you have the trading halt code up and running?"

"Three days, sir. We're double checking the short compilation at the moment. There's also a "cancel order" section we want to implement in case of sellers' remorse when we do halt trading. That will save a lot of the little investors from the results of their panic. That code will be finished in two weeks, possibly three. More testing is needed to be sure it does what we want."

"And what else can we do to slow down any conspiracy?"

Bethnil spoke into the silence. "Faked accounts have been a problem for years, sir. Criminals often use them to hide money and anyone can start up an account with minimal identification and a handful of cash. Many new accounts go through a bank or a broker, but it's the completely on-line initialization that's the hardest point to monitor for fraud. We asked Corporate Oversight to look into all the accounts that shut down that day or placed short orders. They're the ones that found the majority of the fake accounts. About fifty of them so far and there's still three boxes or so of files to be processed. Whoever opened those accounts used names of people who either never existed or had been dead for several years. They were opened early in the new year to give the longest time frame possible for trading. Since they weren't people who would get notices and such for filing tax returns, there was no warning that their tax identities were faked. So there was no chance the fraud would be discovered before they caused the crash. Even the Tax Office hadn't realised yet that there *were* fakes. Their people assumed that those returns were late in being filed. They were from all parts of the country, so no one tax office saw all of them. And, many people don't bother to file on time. This was a very well thought out plan, sir."

Malther nodded when Hranthel looked over at him. He and Bethnil had already discussed the issue. They hadn't seen any other sources of trouble accounts.

"In person start-up means their face is known, and those who set one up where they bank aren't likely to be fake." Hranthel nodded. "Any ideas how to slow these other ones down?"

"Going to a registry office with identification and getting finger-prints of the owners seems to be the best of the ideas we've tossed around," Bethnil said. "The account doesn't truly activate until that is done. They can transfer funds or stocks in, but no buys or sells would be possible. However, it's a nightmare according to our legal team. The gov-ernment and military spooks will have trouble, but they can label those prints as "report clean" in the system and not mention that they're doubled up. There's a few other classes of people who are living under assumed names that we also have to account for. Legal is discussing pos-sibilities with the police, several major law firms and Corporate Over-sight. It will take several months, possibly as much as a year to get that system in place. If we even can, that is."

"Well. Somners, implement the trading halt system. That we can do without bothering any judges. Then the remove order and short order tracking modules. The fingerprints, that's going to be a harder sell to the public, even if Legal thinks we can do it."

"Maybe not, sir," Malther said. "It could be widely accepted if we re-veal what we think happened, and then put out ads to tell individual in-vestors that the various measures will keep them safer. We should also run the information through all the brokerage and bank account man-agers. The little investors are the ones most likely to panic and start selling so they'll welcome the news on the remove order module. I don't think the backlash would be too bad. You or one of the other directors need to make a statement on the stop order system. You could start lay-ing the groundwork for our other theory then, just to get people worried about the fake accounts and how much damage they did."

"Any other questions or concerns?" Hranthel asked.

"How much did the big investors make in profit so far?" Somners asked. "Round numbers."

"So far, about ten million or more in current profits have been paid out in special dividends, sir. That's split between the big six and the next ten." Bethnil said. "We also have breakdowns on the activity during the crash of the top twenty investment companies and none of them had more than their usual number of short orders just before the crash. Our best guess is that the people behind it, if anyone, might be shareholders in those companies. No direct connection to the management, just shareholders along for the ride. Invisible. The bogus accounts we found so far totalled under a half million in assets at their peak. About two hundred thousand in start up funding. Most of them sold and closed out early in the crash, going to cash, then withdrawing most or all of it. It looked like the investors shut down in a panic after they sold and stuffed the cash into their sock drawer. The rest sold off everything and cashed out the moment the markets re-opened. It wasn't until we found that they were the source of the shorts that we realized what happened."

"Could this group crash the market again?"

"No, sir. Not with the same tricks, at least," Malther said. "Once we get the automated halt in place my teams are going to start trying to think of other ways to protect the market from attack. Right now we're depending on two teams of three analysts watching trading indexes and the composite level." The four men nodded in agreement.

"We need to worry about the next attack, not obsess about the last one. I'm sure they're planning something else. I just hope we can see this one coming." Malther looked around.

Silence filled the room.

✎✎✎✎

Erithe and her entourage appeared in the airport lounge slightly after lunchtime. Three security guards, one of them female, his sister and her maid. Plus Larin the aide to carry her briefcase and run errands. A small group, his sister told him when they made the arrangements. His definition of small was very different now.

After a brief hug, Barrat surveyed the group. "I have a proper car waiting outside. With a driver. You can keep the car and send him away once you're at the hotel if you want."

Svent nodded. "We'll keep him as a spare for information on local conditions and routes."

The aide and one guard headed off to collect luggage.

"Your assessment of the situation is interesting," Erithe said. "There is considerable interest among the family, but what happens will depend on what I see. What is currently known to the locals?"

"That there's an "interested person" arriving to confer on the idea. That's all that I told them." Barrat said. "I did notice that I was followed once I left my office to come here, so there should be someone reporting back to the Commerce Association people about now. They should have you identified later today if not immediately. I thought it rude to try to lose the poor men given the situation. The major companies are all trying not to panic about what's going to happen if we can't come to an arrangement. Norgrant's embezzler is poised to ruin a lot of people's dreams here."

The luggage appeared on a large cart with an airport minion pushing it. "We'll go to the hotel first for some lunch, then we'll tour the industrial area," Erithe said. "Tomorrow morning they can talk to me and try to convince me there is hope for the development."

In the car she smiled. It was a large one with seating for ten. The driver headed for the hotel. A window kept him from listening in. "As I said, there's considerable interest. None of us want to give Father more money to play with, so everyone's been doing side investments of our own and taking Industries dividends in cash for other purchases. Dantil and I can bring two million easily. Add in the rest of the family and we can put twenty-one million on the table in three days. In cash. More will take about a week. We've had several discussions via conference vid once you sent the numbers."

"And in return?"

"The lawyers also suggested we form a holding company, as you suggested. Trelner Holdings is the current favourite for the name. "

"Tweaking Father's pride. Maybe not such a good idea." But the whole plan was his idea. What *had* he been thinking to propose such a wild plan? It wasn't the result of alcohol poisoning since he hadn't had anything but coffee in days.

"He never wants to be *seen* as petty," Erithe said. "Especially by outsiders. Many people will think it's a front for him, which could work in our favour in the long run. No one will want to annoy us."

"Is Mom investing too?"

"She is. With considerable glee in her eyes at the name. We, well, the holding company, can become the owner of the development, hold what mortgages are already in place and the development can go forward as before. As the mortgages swap to regular lenders, that will pay back our investment. And we will acquire a lot for our rail storage yard and set it up essentially for free. We'll still charge Trelner Industries the full rates for storing cargo and such, of course. Good business, as Father would say, if it were anyone else doing it." She shrugged.

"And me?"

"Some shares in Holdings as our consultant. And any fee for the work you do can be in shares or some cash and shares. We guessed you didn't have much spare cash to invest at the moment."

"True. Things are picking up though. I can put in twenty thousand and not short myself. The two leads I have from the fundraiser paid well, and I have more clients here who are happy with my work."

"You are doing well." She smiled at him, then looked out the vehicle window. "It's a pretty city."

Barrat warned her about what the Core meant to the locals as they pulled up to the third best hotel in the city. She looked at the facade with a slight frown. "I know it's down from what you're used to, but they're poised to build another, down near the industrial area, as a convention and meeting venue. And a smaller one, with one and two bedroom suites that can be easily converted into apartments is in the design stage. And on hold for the moment waiting for the panic to die down."

"And?" She arched a brow.

"They're my clients. The parents of the two young men who run a paintball range. My first clients here. I suggested they consider the other venues. Which is partly why I have some money to invest." She smiled again as her door was opened by one of the guards.

The manager was at the main desk. So were two bellhops, who headed for the main door with trolleys.

"Mrs. Hathner, I am Centhral, the day manager. We have three suites for you, all adjacent. The centre one is for you, the ones either side for your staff." He raised a hand and the minion behind the counter handed him a key-card, which he passed to Erithe. "This is for your suite. The bellhops have the cards for the other two, and an extra card that works on all three for one of your guards. If there is anything you need, our staff is only a comm call away. The dining room is currently open for luncheon, or room service is always available."

"Thank you. I'm sure I will enjoy my stay."

Centhral smiled and bowed slightly. "There is a small workout area in the lower level, with a steam room and a hot pool."

Erithe smiled. "The dining room will suffice for now. My brother and I will be going out this afternoon if anyone leaves a message."

Another smile and bow. The bellhops returned with loaded carts and led the way to the elevators. Once the suites were opened and the luggage deposited, Larin the aide passed discrete thanks to the bellhops and they vanished. Erithe's room had connecting doors to each of the other rooms. Svent remained on duty near the corridor entrance and everyone else vanished to unpack.

"Very nice view," Erithe said. She crossed to the window and looked out. A small balcony held a tiny table and two chairs. "Does this place have secure rooms if needed for our discussions?"

"They do. These suites also have built in soundproofing and can be rendered inaccessible to radio or comm traffic." She nodded and kept watching the scenery while the unpacking noises continued.

Barrat joined her at the window and pointed. "That cluster of tall buildings is the main part of the Core. This hotel just on the outskirts, but inside the boundary. The Commerce Association building is the short sandstone one two blocks over. They're right on the boundary. There's actually a bulge so they were included. The discussion on where the official boundary should be was quite spirited at the time, I've been told."

"And your office is where?"

"Over in the plebeian section of town. Vintage, that is, older and not yet renovated. Back behind us. Very middle class. I can give you a tour of the office once all this is settled if you have time. Being there actually helped how the important people in town saw me. Fiscally responsible, modest and so on. Not someone who starts out with a sack of diamonds and ends up in the compost pile."

Larin the aide reappeared from the left hand room. "All is ready up here, Mrs. Erithe. Would you like to go down for lunch?"

"We shall."

An hour later they were back in the car, minus the maid and one of the guards. The driver went through the Core at Erithe's request with the dividing window down and pointed out landmarks.

The industrial area was mostly deserted. "Ground's still frozen," Barrat said in response to Erithe's Look. "Which is a *very* good thing in relation to this visit and our purchase. The big building boom is about two weeks or so away. Everyone's booked equipment, paid deposits and is bringing in supplies. You'll probably see stacks of building components in most of the lots."

"That's why the timing is so critical," Erithe said, nodding. "We'll need to do this quickly and fairly quietly to prevent Norgrant's creditors from jumping on the sale." He nodded in agreement. "I'm amazed none of them have noticed the slowdown in progress."

"I think everyone involved with the project has been lying through their teeth to their suppliers and anyone else who might talk to the wrong people. We're good for another two weeks, until Norgrant has to make their instalment payment. If they can make that one, they have a chance to get ahead of their debts without defaulting."

"So, take me to the parcel that is our "reason" for being here. Larin, make sure we have pictures of the site and the surrounding area to show everyone." The aide nodded and held up a camera.

Ten minutes later, with only one minor halt due to a doubled freight truck full of crushed rock pulling into another bare lot, they stopped at the edge of a grassy field with a few thin trees. Tall stakes every five metres marked the edges of the lots.

"This is the one," Barrat said. They left the car and Larin took the lens cap off his camera and moved to one side.

"It is certainly large enough for a quite a few rail cars," Erithe said. "Where are the main tracks?"

"At the other end of the parcel," Barrat said. "There's even a spur started from them. One for each parcel, I was told. And there will be a control tower built in the middle to ensure everything gets where it's supposed to be and not run into anything else. You'd want your own engine or some sort of hauler unit, just to move things around in here if you're parking a fleet of rail cars. And a good sized crane to move loaded containers from the rail car to a trailer truck and back. Computer inventory to keep track of where everything is. I've estimated about two million for the rails, engine and crane. And pavement. There's some nasty clay under the shrubbery, I'm told. Spring and fall rains make it prone to become slippery mud. There's a company dredging the nearby river to decrease the possibility of flooding and turning those rocks into gravel. Everyone's buying it. Since it isn't travelling far it's reasonably priced."

"And we can put in a small building for switching or sorting cargoes, keeping personnel warm and dry and a paved parking lot for the road trailers," Erithe said, shading her eyes. "Maybe three or four people. Flexible hours since the trains could come through at any time."

"We'll need a security fence of course, but that cost will be shared with the neighbours." He pointed at a pile of at least ten meter long steel girders in the adjacent lot. "On the left will be a packaging plant. Stationary and such, I heard. Boxes of loose things like pens come in and store ready packages go out. I'd never really thought about how such things are done." Erithe glanced at him. He shrugged. He'd never cared. Maybe she hadn't either. It wouldn't surprise him.

"On the other side of us is a construction company, with a bigger lot since they need a lot of material and component storage. They assemble panels for a house, actually fit it all together inside their plant building, then the sections go out on a trailer truck to a site with a foundation and such in place, and in three or four days the house is ready for a family to move in. It'll be the noisier neighbour, but the rail cars won't care."

"Do they have a source for lighting fixtures?" One of the subsidiaries she and Dantil supervised.

"Probably. I'm not sure who they use. Haven't met them yet. I was told their current facility is on the east side of town but housing development are spreading that way. They're starting to get noise and transport vehicle complaints, even though they build a decent number of the houses in the new areas. People knew the plant was there when they moved in, but rationality seems to be lacking in the grumblers. The company wants to build their new plant somewhere where that won't happen any more. Then they can sell off or lease their other property for a small shopping area, which will be needed in that area very soon, since none of those developers thought the people who live there might want to shop near their house, not a half hour away. It's what I plan to suggest to them, if I can get a foot in the door. I'd thought to go see them as their new neighbour once we finish buying out the development and everyone's calmed down."

"It is human nature to complain about everything," Erithe said. She headed for the far side of the parcel, with Larin now at her side. To see the rail lines for herself, no doubt. His sister left nothing to chance.

The next day started with a lavish breakfast. Barrat arrived by bus to find the sitting area of Erithe's suite filled with heated tables full of food and ten desperate business owners and the three advisors sitting on the edges of their seats. He took a cup of coffee and a plate full of pastries and took a seat somewhat behind his sister, next to Larin, who had filled at least three pages of notes. So far.

Waiters eventually came with more coffee, tea, pastries and sweet breads. They took away the breakfast dishes and brought lunch a few hours later. Barrat looked up from his own copious notes, started during his first cup of coffee.

"I think we have a rough agreement," Daltons said. "Norgrant's CEO, Trang Senthen, knows we're meeting. He and his people would like to see you, and us, tomorrow morning if possible."

"A good idea. I will contact my associates this evening. And our lawyers will get a summary of our discussion. If all is in order, we will have a cheque for ten million here within the day of signing as a down payment." Everyone's tension level dropped. Their trip into the dark hells was on hold. They might be able to sleep tonight and not writhe in agony with stomach cramps.

The owners left in ones and twos, so there would be no sudden exodus to alert anyone. If any passersby cared that the future of their city and the surrounding area was being decided in a hotel room.

Gandeth was one of the last to leave. "And what do you get out of this?" he asked Barrat with a wave of his hand.

"A modest investment of mine gets me a few shares in the holding company, once the price is set, plus some extra shares as the "facilitator" and the one who came up with the general plan that was presented at this meeting. I expect I'll get some more mundane business out of it as well once word gets out. Do you have any objections?"

"No. It's a good plan. Solves our problems and it will net you, your sister and her investors a tidy profit. I'd guess they'll reach payback in less than a year as the mortgages transfer, and cash out entirely in two. Or they might keep a small stake just to scare off the other predators."

"That's what I suggested as well. Good, stable dividend income is always a good thing."

"What will they, you, invest in then?"

Barrat smiled. "No idea. But it will be fun finding out. As the cash comes in from the final sale of the lots and the transfer of the mortgages to more standard lenders, it will be invested in something fairly liquid. No sense in just letting that kind of money laze around. It should always be working."

"So that eventually, we don't have to." Gandeth smiled and left.

Erithe smiled after the door closed. "An amazing opportunity," she said. "And it just fell into our laps."

"Well, mostly. At first, they wanted me to contact Father and have him bail them out. I told them it would not be in their best interests to let him know anything about the opportunity. But we aren't him." He paused. That didn't come out the way he thought it should. But it was the truth.

"So, where are the pictures of my new niece? That's your real reason for showing up here, wasn't it?"

Erithe smiled and reached for her briefcase.

Chapter 20

The comm on his desk chimed and Barrat picked it up absently, not quite taking his eyes off the report he was proofreading. It was early summer and he wanted to get this completed so he could have the week-end free to get some practice with his new rifle in preparation for a job. They couldn't get very close to the target and the possible distance was on the edge of what even his new toy could reach with any accuracy. The target didn't come out often or on a regular schedule and his people swept the local area to check for people like him before he did so.

Two others had turned down the job when they couldn't guarantee just the target would be dead. Personally, he thought a bomb under a manhole cover would solve the problem much easier. His guards must be complicit in their boss's unsavoury habits, given how little evidence was left for any honest investigation to find. But the job was for just the boss. No one else. A complication, but if he could ...

"Trelner Consulting," he said. "How can..."

"Barrat? You need to come home. Now." The voice was hard to recognize at first. Breathy and a choked sob.

"Mama? What's going on? Are you all right?"

Silence. Then some background noises he couldn't identify.

"Barrat, it's Erithe. We just received a report from one of the doctors working with us on the anti-IC lawsuit. We asked him to analyze your medical file as well, just to make sure nothing was wrong."

Muffled sounds in the background. Was someone crying?

"And? Why is Mama upset?"

"Dantil's with her right now." The sound of a deep breath. "Someone at That Place was trying to kill you, Barrat. That's why you lost so much weight and your mind was so fuzzy. We don't know the person's name yet or why he hated you enough to do this but we know the times and dates when he was on duty."

He nearly dropped the handset in shock. Dark hells. How many others had been damaged by that one rogue?

Kerit dropped him off at the airfield the next morning. "I'll drop by the office to take the mail in and such every couple of days. Don't worry. And the job can wait a week or so. Revenge jobs are never time sensitive. If things go longer, I can subcontract it or do it myself. I'm also tracking down a few more victims of the steak knife mugger."

"I'm not surprised. Whoever is responsible, they're a real idiot for using the same sort of weapon all the time. I wonder why none of the police departments have caught on."

"Because they're so scattered," Kerit said. "Once things calm down I want to visit some people who bought those businesses with the drug kit. Find out what they know. And if they paid for the deaths."

"They are the most likely to be involved," Barrat agreed. "Still, I shouldn't be home long this time. I think mostly Mom wants to hug and cry all over me. I think she and Erithe need to talk to my therapist. I hope they called her in, so first thing I'll suggest they do so if it hasn't already been done."

"And a quick visit with your young lady? And dinner?" Kerit smiled at his blush. "Fly safe."

There were three guards instead of the usual two waiting for him at the airport. Harthil and Peykan nodded. The third was a newer man he hadn't met before. Ragnal. Erithe's paranoia was working overtime. Mom was at her house, alerted by the guards on his arrival, no doubt so she could meet him.

There was a lot of crying by both women. Dantil arrived from the office and Barrat nearly had broken ribs out of that greeting. Eventually everyone calmed down.

"What actually happened to me there, Mom?" Barrat asked. "What Erithe said didn't make sense over the comm."

Dantil sighed. "It seems that at least one of the techs in the IC doesn't like rich people. Your identity was well known there, we found out. Because of the crash, we think. Or as a Trelner son. The tech was the one in charge of monitoring your cell, swapping fluids and such and giving you the interrogation drugs as ordered."

Barrat nodded. "So he gave me fewer nutrients and more plain water? No wonder I lost weight."

"And he changed the dosages on various drugs," Erithe said. "There's also a record of the times he shocked you without orders, mostly while you were in a drugged sleep so the cameras wouldn't show anything odd. I think no one really double checked those logs before. Our doctors started looking at every one of them once we found out what happened to you. They've found a number of other cases, some as bad or worse than yours, with similar weight loss and fuzzy minds. All were business owners. Mr. Taltron was one of them. Most were innocent of the charges against them."

Barrat took a deep breath to calm himself. "The shocks made my mind fuzzy for some time after the actual jolt," he said after another long moment. "I think that's the root cause of a lot of the problems people have after being held there. I didn't try to fight the interrogators, but if the innocent people tried to fight or refused to obey orders, they'd get shocked more, and suffer more damage. Same if they were guilty, but no one really cares about them."

"That's what the doctors found," Mama said. "The doctor who examined your files left here and I had to call. I'm sorry I was so..."

"Caring," Barrat sat next to her and put an arm around her. "It's okay, Mama. Last time I was here I asked Svent to show me some footage from when I was first released. I wasn't me when they finally let me out of there. I'm just glad you found Doctor Halli to help me."

"I called her after we hung up," Erithe said. "She came over at once. I think that's why we're calmer today."

"The lawyers contacted IC last night about that tech," Dantil said. "They called me just before you arrived with an update. The tech has now been identified and is in custody. I think they're going to try to pin some of the worst damage to the innocents onto him, but all the plaintiffs have copies of their medical records so they can't change anything in their copies and be believed. He can't have been assigned to *all* the innocents. The statistics are very much against it, given how many suspects are in there at any time. At least, how many there used to be."

"The main trial is due to start next week." Mama sat up straighter and blotted her eyes. "Even if those people assign some blame to that wretched tech, the system can't be allowed to continue."

"They've already changed some procedures, the lawyers reported," Dantil said. "They need some actual, verifiable facts, not just verbal accusations before anyone is taken there for questioning. Especially for those accusations called in on their tip lines. The person might be taken into custody, but any questioning is just words, no drugs or shocks. Not until they do a proper investigation and have some sense of what happened and if there's any truth in the allegations."

"That's a relief. It also shows they already know what the result of the trial is going to be. What happens with my report?"

"The tech's being charged with multiple assaults," Dantil said with satisfaction. "One count for each shock, and about one count per day on changing the fluids to starve you. Any of the other people in the suit that he harmed will be added to that one."

"And we and the others are filing a malicious civil suit against IC, since the tech was able to do this and the supervisors didn't realize what he was doing," Mama said. "The doctors traced his work back four years so far, I think. That trial will be in the next month or three. You should come home for that. We'll need to show some footage and you might have to testify about how you were treated."

"Then that's what I'll do, Mama," Barrat said. "In the meantime, there's paperwork to deal with for the Beranga development. That final parcel in the industrial area has an interested party and I brought their bid along." Mama smiled at him.

"How's Father dealing with everyone else being involved with Holdings?" Barrat asked Dantil and Erithe the next morning at breakfast.

"Pissed," Erithe said. "He's hinted several times that with his money and clout added, there are many more possibilities for some "real" deals. Not the piddling twenty five million we paid to Norgrant, but serious challenges that need his expert hand to truly make a killing."

Barrat smiled, but his heart was sad. He was his father's son. The thrill of the hunt would always be with him. *Had* always been with him. That's why they fought all the time. Each wanted to be dominant. Needed to win. The only difference was that Barrat's other wins resulted in funerals and happy survivors. His father's pile of money was bigger. For now.

❦❦❦❦❦

Liselle looked nervous. The dress was slightly out of date, but the colour suited her so well. A rich blue, which made her eyes look bluer. He smiled at her. They were at the back entrance to the store, which was the easiest way to access their living quarters above.

"What did you have in mind for this time?" she asked as the driver, Ragnal, closed the door.

"A nice supper, then I understand you like music. There's a concert that I have tickets for. Not right up front, but very nice ones."

"Garla told you about the group?" The car purred off.

"Yes. When I asked you what you'd like to do, I didn't get a real answer. So I had to improvise. And we aren't going to talk business either. My sister Erithe suggested that caveat."

"Neither of us has really dated much, have we?"

"No. I was afraid of predatory females for years. You were just starting to be independent. Then we both got blindsided."

"And now we're here," she said. A smile. This would be a good evening, he thought.

The restaurant he'd picked was about halfway up the snob scale and had reasonable prices. They were seated immediately and Liselle looked around at the decor. Medieval inspired, the reviewers said. But with all modern amenities and decent sized portions.

The concert was well attended, since the guest conductor rarely left his own group. Barrat knew there were reporters for the society pages there. They might rate a line at most, he guessed.

His notoriety rated three lines. And a small picture of them. Fortunately, Liselle didn't mind. He hoped her father didn't either. He'd been accepting so far.

≪⌒≫⌒≪⌒≫⌒

Two months later Barrat looked at the cheques. Four thousand from the tech, after all of his assets were sold and another eighty thousand from IC. For his pain and suffering. The main lawsuit changed the lives of hundreds of families. Thousands of people. The judges ruled that anyone who could demonstrate incapacity as a result of IC's interrogation could apply for a share of the settlement. He had more money to invest in Trelner Holdings and in his own trading portfolio. There were two new applications from businesses in difficulties. He would do the analysis to determine if the companies could be saved. Some were starting to refer to them as champions of the little companies. Others swore at them for taking away victims. Father was likely among those.

Barrat celebrated the end of his first year in business with an excellent cash flow analysis. His official accounts held more money than he'd imagined he ever would in such a short time. The renovations on his apartment building were progressing well. The elderly lady who owned his office building was considering selling it to him. For a slightly inflated price, but having access to the tunnel system as long as he wanted to stay here was worth it. He looked out on the snowy street and raised a rare glass of whiskey.

And he had, possibly, a woman who might be interested in building a life together. He sipped the whiskey and smiled. It was odd that he'd been so eager to leave Herithan and now he was there at least once a month. When could he manufacture another excuse to go visit her?

Chapter 21

Barrat stood behind the fully leafed bush and stretched now that he was out of the line of sight of anyone at the remote mining camp. The recon went as planned, always a good thing. The scum were there. No sign of the boy they'd kidnapped, but there was no way Barrat could get close enough to see him without eliminating at least two of the guards, possibly more. That many dead would mean the next step was to bring the boy out with him.

The most secure place to keep the boy was in the mine itself and this was the only person sized entrance he saw near where the men stayed. He'd left five cameras in place. The batteries should last about a week with motion sensors to cut down on filming while no one was outside or at night. He'd be back here a few days after that to retrieve them. Easier the second time. He hoped. There was a slightly overgrown road that led up to the camp, but the thugs might have their own gear in place to detect intruders.

Ten men here. One of him. And Kerit, of course. His partner was down the hill on another old road. As close as they dared bring a vehicle without chancing that anyone up top might hear it and panic. Barrat thought they *could* take out the guards late at night and rescue twelve year old Carlon, but Magin Garthil, the boy's father, wanted more. The people who'd organized this were those who needed a severe lesson in proper behaviour. Silence and Justice would give them that education. No matter what was happening to the boy in the meantime.

In a way, he was glad he didn't have conclusive evidence of what they'd done or were doing. He could leave the animals alive when he left the area. He hoped Kerit would explain why they couldn't just raid this place and leave the bodies for their resupply men to find. That's how this location had been found. Very poor planning on their part. Somewhere in the nearest large city would have been much less obvious. Someone must have been watching a stack of idiot spy movies, where every villain had a remote lair for holding prisoners and plotting world domination. The real reason wilderness lairs were so popular in movies was that it was very expensive for a film crew to shut down a large enough area in a city for the sequence to be believable. Plus out here they had wonderful scenery. If they cared to pay attention to it.

He clicked his radio twice. The signal he was heading back. He tucked the camera he'd used to get layout pictures into the pouch around his waist and pulled out a slightly used but still bright orange cap and vest from a light pack. A hunter, checking out places to put a deer hide come fall. If anyone noticed him, that is. This wilderness area was popular on the weekends but during the week, even in the summer, few tourists or hikers came out here. Another reason for their timing for this trip.

A half hour later he reached the road and started jogging west. At least climbing and sliding down was faster than going up that miserable hill had been. He hadn't wanted to chance the road in case the scum had cameras or motion sensors. He would have set up some elaborate systems to ensure a warning, not just on the road. Kerit spotted him a few minutes later and handed him a chilled sport drink when he reached the truck. Barrat doffed the cap and wiped sweat from his forehead. Stretched and sipped.

"The boy must be up there, Kerit," Barrat said. "The mine entrance has two guards, both armed with pistols. We could rescue him during the night. Use dart guns if we want to keep them alive for a trial. Hold all of *their* men as insurance against the union behaving itself or they're handed over to the police with all the evidence needed to get them into Insanity Central to talk. We could take down the entire union that way. Without all of this skulking around. Far simpler to deliver the message."

"Let's get under way and I'll explain. You've never encountered this kind of assignment before. Part of why I suggested we take it." Barrat stretched again before getting into their rented truck.

They were most of the way to the main road before Kerit spoke again. Neither was paying much attention to the beautiful scenery around them. "Kidnappers come in two basic kinds, Barrat. For most, it's a business move. They don't ever harm the kidnapee and let them go in decent shape. Ensure that the person never sees anyone well enough to identify them. They confine the person, but they're given food and drink, maybe some novels to read. No one beats them up unless it's provoked. Even then, not much damage is done and nothing permanent. Often the person is given sleeping pills in their meals but just at night so they don't fret too much. Most families in this type of situation don't bother calling the police because the chances of getting the person back actually falls dramatically if they do. Most kidnappers walk away if the police start nosing around. Most of their victims die if they can't get out of the place they're kept. Sometimes the kidnappers leave the door unlocked when they pull out but some victims don't even try to open it. They just die if no one finds them in time."

Barrat turned to look out the window, absently noting a deer just inside the tree line. "I didn't go anywhere near the door while in IC. Not after the first shock. Possibly because it didn't have any way to open from the inside."

"And while the other guys had you?"

"No idea what I did or didn't do after I activated the memory block. When I woke up, I was tied in a chair and blindfolded. Webbing for the restraints I think. Couldn't do anything but knock the chair over. It was metal so it wasn't likely that it would break. I don't think they beat me because I didn't have any obvious bruising or pain when they let me go. Just muscles like over cooked noodles when I woke up in the alley. I had to protect us from this part of my life, so I used the failsafe after talking to one of them. The Zeltin means I won't ever remember what happened after that. I'll never know unless we can find those people. The odds are slim that will ever happen. I've mostly accepted that."

"That's also the basic reason your father didn't contact anyone official when you were taken. A family without their own security teams might call a firm like Branson's and those with security might do the same, to facilitate the money transfer and pick up the person when they're released. It's hard to tell at the outset which type of kidnappers you're dealing with so most families are cautious."

"And the other kind? Not very nice, I imagine?"

"They're the meanest people you'll ever see, lad. They have a cause they devoutly believe in and kidnap people to force the family to do things they wouldn't do without the threat. The person they take is beaten, maybe raped, and is constant fear for their life. The scum often amputate a minor body part just to show the family they're serious about their demands. They never let the person go without a big ransom."

"And we have type two here. That dammed union wants extravagant concessions and they'll get them because Garthil loves his son." Barrat paused. "Are they planning on returning the boy or do you think they'll keep him to make sure his father doesn't do anything they don't like for the next few months?"

"I would guess they'll keep him for a short time after the deal is signed, then they'll give him back. A month tops, but likely quicker. There's too many chances for Garthil to do something that would queer the deal if all he got back was a body. They'd also have to provide proof of life on a regular basis if they keep him. I can't imagine the guards they have out here want to bother with a long term hold. Certainly not into the local winter, which is worse than Beranga's up here, from what I've heard. But they grabbed the boy out of his dorm room. That shows they have people who can get into a boarding school with decent outer security. And they could go after other targets from his senior staff if we just took Carlon away. No way to protect everyone with the union intact. So, he contacted us. A referral, of all things. One of the spouses of the steak knife killer's victims."

"Mr. Garthil wants them all put down," Barrat said. "But not with anything obvious. Keep this union and others wondering and looking over their shoulders. Wasn't there was another union you helped deal with last year? You didn't say much about it when my memories returned."

"Yes, while you were in IC. Pretended to be you. Simple bullet job for a smaller union, but those people took the warning. All the larger unions are getting out of hand from what I've heard on the news. Too much clout and too many greedy leaders who are grossly overpaid for what they actually do. Our efforts are being funded by several business owners who see their future and don't like what's coming. They have the same union in their factories and their contracts renew later this year. Any thoughts so far on how we can complete that part of the deal?"

"A glimmer. Have they drawn up the new agreement yet?"

"Mostly, from what my contact at their headquarters said." Kerit's eyes asked why he needed to know but didn't speak. "Garthil wants his son back so he's not interested in dragging out the negotiations much longer. He does not want to get another toe. Or a finger."

"I need to get to my computer to check some legal wording," Barrat said after a few minutes of thought. "I have the glimmering of an idea, but it might not be possible to implement. Or if it might work for all the clients." He turned his attention to the road but wasn't really watching it as he developed scenarios in his head.

The motel parking lot was mostly empty, as it had been for the past three days. Kerit pulled in next to their room. The small motel Kerit picked for the base for this part of the operation catered to hunters in the fall and skiers in winter and the owner had smiled when told they were here to find some good places to set up come fall. Be something or someone no one thinks is up to anything else, Kerit taught him. The owners thought they were father and son. Barrat wished that was really the truth.

Kerit lounged on one of the single beds, reading a novel about spies, making occasional snorts of amusement. Probably at the idiotic trade-craft of the hero. Barrat noted the title as he sat down at the desk and opened a cheap computer that had nothing of value stored on it. It connected to the general web without any problems and he started to search for the wording he had in mind.

Four hours after their arrival that he shut the computer down and picked up a sheet of paper from their tiny printer. Barrat coughed to attract his partner's attention. The older man looked over from his book with a raised eyebrow.

"Their legal department should bury these clauses or something very like them into the fine print of all the new contracts. They give Garthil Appliances a perfect way to negate the agreement with the union whenever we choose. And it will all be perfectly legal." Kerit's eyebrow rose. "Read it. Then I'll explain, so you can explain it to Branson. I'll have to be involved in my public persona in order to get Holdings involved and I don't want to chance any of my wording choices to give them a clue who I am. You can say that we know that I'm someone who can help them with an overall plan."

"And intimate that we've used your skills before. Risky if they talk about our involvement."

"But it will allow me to interact with the owners. But not to pass messages through. We'll keep using Branson's people for that." Barrat grinned. "I know just the employee to be our contact." One of those agents didn't like that he and Kerit were involved. It was petty revenge but Barrat also didn't like the man for some reason he couldn't rationalize or explain.

Kerit rolled his eyes and sighed. Then he moved his bookmark and shut the volume. Then took the sheet and started reading. Twice. He put the page down and sighed.

"Start explaining, lad. After we get Garthil and his friends' approval, you'll need to contact your family and see how much they can raise to fund all of this. Six companies will need a lot of cash to buy out."

"We might not have to do it all at once, since the other union contracts don't renew for a few months, but we should have enough time to fill the war chest. Again."

❧❧❧❧❧

"Are we sure we want to get more involved with these two?" Nartig asked Jula as he stared at the recently arrived document. "They're assassins. Killers. This is a kidnapping. Do as they want and they release the boy. Simple."

"All I know is that the boss said we're getting a call from that number at nine tomorrow morning. Silence will explain the general plan to you. Then you get to go explain it to Mr. Garthil." Jula fiddled with her earset.

"Did they at least get eyes on the boy? Carlon?"

"No. He's deep in the building they found, but they've set up cameras to monitor and get facial recognition on all the guards. Those men are also on the hit list. Dead or disgraced was how Martan described what Mr. Garthil wants. There are several other business owners involved now, to spread out the fees. All deaths will be covert, so they and we don't have to worry about Corporate Oversight or the police. All of our new clients have the same union at their plants and they're very worried about their children's safety."

Nartig groaned. Jula's tone said she approved of this operation. It was paying very well, which might be why the boss took the job. At least by the time the assassins were done with the union's leadership, no one would be capable of seeking revenge on anyone. Corporate Oversight might look the other way, or they could all be arrested on murder conspiracy charges. Why had Branson taken this job? Moving up into a different sort of clientele? Dark hells. He'd rather just do bodyguard work for the moderately rich and clueless on their vacations. After this assignment was over, he would think about what he wanted his future to look like. There were several other companies he respected who did much the same thing as this one. But he wouldn't leave just yet. He wanted to see Carlon at home first.

The next morning he waited until the comm chimed and activated his recorder as soon as he picked the handset up.

"This is Silence," said the voice, distorted and an impossibly high tenor. "Thank you for being prompt. Do you have the document we sent? It is a way for our clients to negate all the contracts once they are ready to shut down the union for good."

"I do. Thank you for providing the clauses. However, no one here speaks that level of legal. How or when do they get activated?"

There was a chuckle and the voice explained. Nartig was happy he was recording this. Maybe he'd just play this to the client. It seemed overly complex, and he didn't want to miss anything. The firms' lawyers would have to be able to understand the plan to properly implement it.

"So any other company that's dealing with the same union will cave immediately for the same terms and put these same clauses into the fiddly bits at the back of their agreement. The union will assume correctly that Mr. Garthil told them what happened to his son and what might happen to them and their families if they tried to fight it. At the end of this mess, the owners will have formed a holding company that owns 52% of all of their companies. And Trelner Holdings, which does not include Vanthin Trelner or Trelner Industries, might be brought on board to front the buyout money in return for a chunk of the holding company's stock. Securities will likely sign off on the agreement, but shelve any announcement and their four highest ranking officials will have to be in on it. According to your expert, they don't like what's happening with the big unions either."

Another chuckle. "Truth. Any questions?"

"Not at the moment. Wait, who does own Trelner Holdings? I don't think I've heard of it. I know about Industries, of course. Everyone does." And he knew much more from what young Barrat had told him thanks to the truth drugs they'd given him.

"It is privately held by the *other* members of the family at present. No public stock offering is contemplated at this time. None of the holding companies like the one they help form are public and plan to stay that way so they can keep control and not have to worry about the market's ups and downs."

"Damn. I'd buy *that* stock in a minute."

"Most would. We'll be following events and let you know if we need anything else. By the way, contact Barrat Trelner at Trelner Consulting in Beranga. He has the ability to pull all the analyses the family will need to make this work. And he's your only way into Trelner Holdings."

"Have you worked with him before?" A click. Nartig sighed and hung up. Now to pass on the explanation. How was the kid involved with these assassins? Had they worked together before? Probably not. He'd been released from Insanity Central, not gone directly to jail. But now? What had he been up to the past two years?

⋰⋱⋰⋱

Barrat nodded. "I'm starting to be pretty sure he was one of the people who kidnapped me, Kerit. Any chance of getting a picture? I did see him briefly at the gym. Wasn't paying much attention to anyone there because I was really pissed about the stupid Vegathic offer. I think he also questioned me at wherever they held me. They were using distortion on their end but his voice cadence and word choice sounds about right."

"What about on the street? When did you spot him?"

"I saw a shadow coming toward me from across the street. His head was down so I didn't get a good look at his face. He moved in where a streetlight was out. Must have very good shoes as I didn't hear him at all. I *was* paying attention. There was a second man waiting in the alley behind me that I missed entirely. He could be either one of them. No way to know unless they tell us."

"I'll have someone get a camera on him in the next few days. Try for another voice sample. What do you want to do with him if he was involved?" Kerit sipped at his coffee.

Barrat sighed. "Nothing for now. There's too many complex details to finishing the current job to worry about who paid them for my kidnapping and understanding why they did it and what they hoped to learn."

"Good lad." The warmth in Kerit's voice helped him relax. But once this was over, he'd be having a late night chat with Haltarn, with vials of the IC truth drugs and some Zeltin in *his* pocket and a gun in his hand.

Five hours later Barrat's office comm rang. He smiled and answered. It was the CFO of Garthil Appliances. Now he had to pretend he'd never heard any of this before. Mr. Farnal started to explain why he was calling and Barrat made some pithy comments as the grieving and furious man laid out what had happened and why.

"You mean an assassin told you to call me and get my family involved with an insane union who's already kidnapped and mutilated a boy? Your CEO's son? And he's still alive?"

"Yes, he's alive. For the moment, anyway. Or he was yesterday, from the latest picture. Have you worked with these men before?"

"You expect me to admit to conspiracy to commit murder on an unsecured comm?" A pause.

"Why did you start Trelner Holdings? I should warn you I've already talked to the president of the Beranga Commerce Association. We have colleagues in common. We needed to know if we could trust you with Carlon's life."

He huffed. "It was about the only chance I had to stop a local depression from starting when Norgrant, the developer, was close to bankruptcy. We kept a huge industrial project from failing. And it was the right thing to do."

"So is this. Six companies are involved now. The same union has their tendrils into all of us. Carlon Garthil, a twelve year old boy, was kidnapped and unless his father gives these slimes what they want, he'll die. Mr. Garthil contacted the assassins before the others joined with us. They're pretty sure where the boy is, but his father wants to break the union. Their leadership has gone past any semblance of reality with their proposals. We can't afford to sign the contract, but we have to in order to free Carlon. The scum from the dark hells cut off one of his toes as an incentive to settle quickly." Barrat heard the pain in the CFO's voice. He must know the family well. Probably called uncle by the missing boy. He took a deep breath and focused. He was an outsider, a financial analyst, not an assassin who already knew everything about the job.

"That's conspiracy on a massive level."

"It is. I have also contacted Damilan Hranthel, head of the Securities Services. He doesn't like how the bigger unions are behaving either. He's seen what we want to put into the contract to start breaking them. We hope that the rank and file will vote in sensible people during the next elections. Without the current scum still around."

"Does *Hranthel* know about the assassins?" That could be a problem. He and Kerit needed to stay in the dark to be safe. He would have to watch what he said when he went to their headquarters.

"Of course not. He'd be legally constrained to warn the union. He only knows that Branson Security is involved in trying to find evidence of wrong-doing by the union. No one's mentioned Carlon to any law enforcement agency."

"He's much safer that way," Barrat agreed. "I'll consult the members of Holdings. I won't mention the assassins until I get an idea of how much they're interested in funding your plan. Send me the rough figures, especially how much we'll have to front to get this in place and when everyone has to renegotiate. We may need to liquidate some of our other holdings in order to have enough cash available to put this in place without borrowing money."

"I'll send it to you immediately." Relief saturated his voice. "Thank you for listening. I'll tell Mr. Garthil and the other owners once I hear back from you."

The line reverted to the "awaiting a code" signal. Barrat leaned back in his chair and looked at the big calendar he used for generally planning out his assignments. This one would take a lot of time. At least thirty men were on the list Kerit was compiling. Some would be easy to destroy. Others needed a longer timeline, especially since if only one police officer looked at any of the deaths and started a list of the dead union people that person knew or was associated with, the clients would all be in IC, telling them everything. A risk, but the suffering they'd stop was worth it. He hoped.

Time to call Kerit to come in and help with the filing. A good cover, since he sometimes used terms that his clients didn't understand. And he couldn't justify a permanent receptionist at this point. Maybe by the time this was over, he'd have to think about hiring someone. And find someone he could trust absolutely. Or he and Kerit would take a well deserved holiday.

Chapter 22

Barrat looked at the list of union officials and thugs who were on the disposal list, then up at Kerit. "This might be impossible to keep covert, you know. Forty-three people to destroy. So far."

"Yes. Some will actually be easy and be very unconnected to the union and their activities. Turn the page." He did. The same list, but it was ordered very differently. "The first section is about half of the thugs. Branson's people followed six of them to an illegal brothel. All that's needed to take them out is to drop send a message to the right police office when we know that they're inside. As a bonus, some kids get a chance to reclaim their lives and I'm guessing twenty or more men go to jail. For a while, at least."

They might not last very long, Barrrat mused. A lot of inmates celebrated those who committed murder and robbery. Using children in brothels was not on their happy list. Most lasted a week in the general population, if that. Their killers always had a long list of witnesses that they were somewhere else at the time. No one really cared.

Barrat nodded at Kerit. "And the union won't admit they know the thugs with those charges. Good enough." He looked at the rest of the list. "And a heart attack for the president. But down a few months. Why should we wait on him?"

"We do need to stretch things out," Kerit pointed out. "I'd thought about a gas explosion in their headquarters, but we can't be sure all the people who work there are involved."

"No innocents. Right."

"We'll go over each name and set up a timeline in a few days. Some hits may be opportunistic. The union has a couple of resort properties on their books. A wonky furnace could be a useful cover. Or a car accident on bad roads during the winter. Lots of accidents are possible then."

"While drunk. Their bar tabs are truly impressive, according to Branson's report. And the blood alcohol levels would make the deaths invisible. That also keeps the police interest down."

Kerit smiled. "The rest of the thugs are harder, but concentrating on the leadership makes the election much easier to trigger."

Everyone stared at him. Mom sat down abruptly. Dantil opened his mouth, then closed it. No one on the video conference call said anything.

"Yes. We've been asked to help break a union," he said. "I think it's possible. But the timing is tricky."

"And Securities is on board with this?" Dantil found his voice.

"It seems so. Mr. Farnal, the CFO, said they have it in writing, and in a recorded comm call."

"How does the plan work?" Sathira's voice was not her usual brusque tone when speaking to him. He wasn't sure why she'd been so aloof toward him all these years. Her oldest daughter was actually the same age as he was but they'd never been close. Not even at the boarding school they'd both attended.

"The contract currently on the table will kill the company in about two years, since they'll have to raise prices to cover their inflated costs," he started. "No one else will, so their market share goes poof except for very loyal repeat buyers. The plan is fairly simple. When the revenues start to fall, Mr. Garthil will cut back all workers to the normal work week. No overtime at all. About a month after that, all the union people will be laid off since they can't afford to keep production going."

"That's far too simple," Fraklin said into the silence. "The plant closure shouldn't be seen to be the company's fault to keep the union from becoming suspicious of a conspiracy." He paused. "Does this union send in bogus safety violation reports? They're always a nuisance since they're about trivial problems, but we've run into them with some plants. Waste of everyone's time to show that there was never a problem in the first place."

"I'm not sure," Barrat replied. "How could those reports help?" Since he'd never had to deal with union reps he hadn't thought about that possibility. He didn't smile visibly.

"If Workers' Health and Safety can be brought on board, one of their people can pull all those citations out of the files and claim the plants are unsafe. *They* shut everything down and put everyone out of work. Then Mr. Garthil can claim there's not a lot of money available to fix anything, since they'll have a huge amount of inventory stashed away by that time if their sales go way down because of the increase in prices."

"The union has to top up the unemployed benefits," Carthan said with a smile. "And their top management has probably used a big chunk of their reserves to line their pockets. Have the investigators find out exactly what the union owns. Art, property, airplanes. Anything. If it all went on the block at once, it would be harder to sell. Plus, anyone trying to sell a house and move once everyone is laid off will have trouble if there's a lot of them at once. That will really get the regular workers pissed at their leaders."

"I can pass that on. So, at some point when everyone is out of work, Mr. Garthil announces that he's selling part of the company to a consortium to get money to get the plants back in operation. That triggers the time bomb in the fine print. The contract is null and void if Mr. Garthil's family ownership drops below fifty percent of the shares. They'll own forty-eight percent. But eventually a big chunk of the holding company. Since they are two separate entities, that ownership doesn't count."

"Poof," Carthan said with a snort of laughter. "The union doesn't have a valid contract and has no way to force Mr. Garthil or the other owners to come back to the bargaining table. They may do something desperate at that point."

"This is all supposed to just trigger a union election?" Erithe asked. He nodded. "And with a new union board, the companies will no doubt bring back their old agreements, which gave everyone a decent living."

"That is the plan." More silence. "Actually, they could dissolve the holding company once they have a new contract in place, but I think they'll keep it running. And we'll own a bunch of shares so they'd have to buy us out. Any comments about the plan in general?"

"I'd like to see the numbers first," Fraklin said. "But I think it's doable in general. Could be very lucrative in the long run. And it will help build up our reputation, once word gets out."

"How did they contact you?" Sathira asked.

"Mr. Farlan knows someone in Beranga, who mentioned Trelner Holdings as a possible source of money. I'll soon have the information to do a formal analysis and show the effects of the new contract. That will be shared among the other companies who have the same union. But we have to agree to help them first."

Erithe kept staring at him. "There's something else you haven't mentioned, Barrat. You weren't as focused on the Beranga deal. What's different about this one?"

He took a deep breath. "The union kidnapped Mr. Garthil's son. Carlon. He's twelve. And the bastards cut off one of his toes and sent it to his father. That's why he'll do anything the union wants. He's signing the contract in two days. Carlon should be released by the end of the week, maybe a few days later. There's a security firm involved to pick him up."

And do other things, but he wouldn't say anything about the deaths that would soon follow.

More stares. "You should have said that at the beginning," Mom said, then turned to the camera. "We *will* do this. Industries will be paying out another special dividend within the week. See what else we can turn into cash in the next month. Keep everything in very short term investments. Do not mention this to anyone outside of the family. The union cannot get a hint of what is planned. Agreed?"

A chorus of yeses. Then the icons began to vanish. Mom came over to him. He stood. "Are you all right, Barri?"

"I will be, Mama. I'll ask Doctor Hallie if she knows anyone in the area to help Carlon." She smiled and hugged him.

He pulled his comm out and entered the code.

"Mr. Farnal? It's Barrat Trelner calling."

"Yes?" The tension in that simple word was almost unbearable.

"We're in. I'm in Herithan at the moment. Can you courier the information to me here?" He gave Erithe's address.

"Of course. I'll pass the word onward." Relief.

"Now comes the hard part," Dantil said.

•ઈ•ઈ•ઈ•ઈ•

"We just heard from the thugs," Mr. Farnal said. "They're going to give us Carlon's location later today."

Nartig gave a silent sigh of relief. "They want some time to get all of their gear and such clear of the area." His voice sounded professional.

"Ten days since we signed. Mr. Garthil was starting to worry again."

"That's why they waited," Nartig said. "Keep you all guessing. I have four men with me. Can we borrow six or so from your people in case they're trying something?"

"Of course. We'll come over to your headquarters so we can leave as soon as we have the location."

Nartig paused. Might as well find out. "Have the assassins been informed of this development?"

"They have. They'll go in later and remove all of their surveillance equipment once Carlon is back home."

"Good plan. But everyone else needs to keep their kids close. They shouldn't let their guard down. Not until this is all over."

"I agree. Mr. Trelner mentioned a therapist," Farnal said. "She's not available but gave us another name. That person is on her way here. First thing she insisted was that Carlon isn't going to a hospital. We're getting his doctor to come make a house call to check on his general health."

"A good idea. Hospitals just magnify the trauma. We have some female guards on our roster. I can have a team here in a day. That might help."

"A very good idea. I hope to see you soon." More relief in his voice. The call ended.

Nartig rolled his shoulders to drop his own tension levels. He'd call Branson and pass on the hopeful news and arrange for the extra guards.

❦❦❦❦

Barrat's car door was opened by his escort. He smiled at the man. Nartig Haltarn. He did seem more and more familiar. But Haltarn remained aloof. Monosyllabic responses to any questions he asked.

Mr. Farnal waited just inside the main doors. Haltarn faded away. "Mr. Trelner. Good of you to come so quickly. We'll talk more in my office." A quick look around. No one was nearby.

In the elevator, Farnal relaxed. "The other companies have copies of your analysis. We're having a video conference with them tomorrow."

"How is Carlon doing?" Five days after his release.

"Sleeping a lot. But only in the closet. The therapist said to let him stay there as long as he wants. He's starting to eat more, thankfully. Either they didn't feed him much or he just couldn't force whatever they fed him down."

"He feels safer in the closet. I can relate. Panicked when I heard loud noises. And even guards I'd known before still terrified me."

"Branson's sent over two female guards. Carlon does better with them than the men. Those are on outer security."

"A good choice." The elevator door opened. He might have responded better with female guards as well. He put those thoughts away. He had to be the outside professional now.

❦❦❦❦

"So, how was the trip?" Kerit asked him once they were in the car and away from the Beranga airport.

"Good. I'm glad you're on all the communications and not me. That last video conference meant I was talking a lot more than I'd thought I would have to. No one mentioned us, by the way. I think they talked about our plans before I came in. Sensible of them, since that way they're all safer if I told anyone what was going on."

"Truth."

"I did get three job offers, though. Full time, nice salary and stock options." He shook his head at the thought. "They really liked the analysis I did on Garthil's. I think they saw their own ruin if the union isn't stopped."

Kerit laughed this time as he rounded a corner. "What did you tell the eager owners? And did they get suspicious?"

"Said that I had several ongoing clients and that Holdings was keeping me busy enough. That I enjoyed the challenge of different projects instead of a single employer. Slightly peeved but one of the others started asking some questions about the analysis. How are Branson's people doing on the lists?"

"Not bad. The thugs are easy so they've been concentrating on them. Their focus has been on security, not in following people, so they're building their skill set on the thugs. By the time they get to the upper management, they should do okay." Kerit looked at him via the mirror.

"I think they're talking to other business owners about unions in general. A lot of them could be facing the same sort of problem."

"Could be a major issue, but we'll see how others react. We'll need to get started on the thugs in a week or two. I found a good cop in the city. Worked in Vice, but now he's mostly working a desk because of someone else's mistake. This should get him back on track."

"Good. We'll have someone from Branson's be sure some thugs are at the brothel and then we'll spoof a call to that officer. I had Haltarn as a driver," Barrat said with a grin. "He doesn't seem to like the idea of taking out the union thugs and their board. He's pretty stiff around me, so I'm really thinking he was one of my kidnappers. I know it's petty to insist he stay so involved, but I'm getting some satisfaction."

"Any chance he's cluing in on your other involvement?"

"No. One of the other guards might also be involved, but he might be a better actor, or he's more relaxed since he's not around the office much. Saw them talking very seriously when there wasn't anything crucial going on."

Chapter 23

The Garthil Appliances workers crammed into a section of the stadium's parking lot, not the stadium itself, which Davon thought was a bad sign. A stage was set up near the main entrance. Davon turned to his buddy Merlid after they left the school bus that brought them here. Both started to work for Garthil Appliances right out of school and worked their way up to supervising production lines over the past twenty years. They'd been proud of the union in their early days but the latest agreement made them both worried. It was too good to be true. Some workers went on a spending spree when the first checks came through. He and the others who had seen bonuses come and go paid down on their debts, to the wails and pouting expressions from their offspring, who wanted the latest clothing and music crazes.

"Any idea what's going on?" Davon asked. Merlid had an uncanny ability to be around the union stewards and be ignored, allowing him to hear all sorts of gossip that the union board probably didn't want anyone to know. He spotted several other friends in the crowd. They'd get together in a day or two to discuss whatever they learned today. "This isn't the usual rah-rah show. We'd be sitting in the stadium, not standing out here. At least it's not raining." He pulled up his coat collar anyway.

"You're right," Merlid replied. "I've got absolutely nothing on this. My sources are as confused as the rest of us. Upper management went somewhere last week. Not a big resort, I heard. All three plants, not just ours. Maybe some other bodies but that's unsure. There might have been an outside analyst. Someone new was spotted at corporate headquarters just before they left, but no one I know heard a name. Been there a couple of times. Youngish man, dark hair and a good suit is it for identification. Carried a case, but only one security of his own. The rest was all company guards, and they were told not to talk about him. And they haven't. That's a very bad sign."

"Well, I've got a very bad feeling about this gathering." They both looked around at the milling crowd. The younger workers were smiling and happy about getting out of the plant and still being on the clock. The older ones looked as worried as he felt.

"Me too." Merlid shook his head slowly. "We're screwed, I think."

"We figured that contract was too good. Now we find out just how bad the fallout is going to be."

The press of the crowd behind them forced them fairly close to the stage. Enough to see the set up. No one official was up there yet, just some security guys. Armed, but fairly heavily. They usually just had pistols. Not automatic weapons. *Dark hells.* What was going on?

A camera system came on line so everyone could see the speakers on the big screen if they were near the back of the crowd. A guy in coveralls came out and tested the microphone. Great. He could count to ten. Before they had a chance to get bored, Mr. Garthil and all their plant managers and sub-managers came out and sat on the right hand side of the stage. The union president, Trather Wakin, came out with a couple of his top advisors and sat on the left side. Twice as many management people as union. Also not a good omen, Davon thought.

"He's got no idea what this is about," Merlid whispered, staring at Wakin, glowering at the management people. The crowd, seeing that the show was about to start, shuffled a little closer and mostly shut up to listen. Someone stepped on his foot, then apologized.

Mr. Garthil stood and went to the lectern. No one to introduce him. Guess they figured everyone could recognise who they worked for.

"I thank you all for coming here today. You are all on the clock for the travel time and for this meeting." There were some happy cheers at that. Time off the line *and* pay. Garthil's face didn't change from a serious one. The cheers subsided.

"I think we're beyond screwed," Davon said quietly. "I thought that contract was too good to be true."

"We've finished some long term forecasts," Garthil said. "That's where the senior management was last week. And... the news is not good, I'm afraid." Complete silence. Not even the wind dared make a noise.

"Due to the drop off in sales resulting from our recent price hikes, we have set a new work schedule. Everyone *will* be getting the standard thirty-five hour work week. But there can and will be no overtime, replacements for those who quit or new hires. We simply don't have the orders to justify our current level of production. We are only selling half of what we did in the summer and expect that to drop further. We have to reduce production and cut costs to keep from raising our prices again. That would only drop our sales even further."

Davon looked at Wakin's face. Shock, then anger. Same as the other union officials. A sullen murmur from the crowd. They wanted more big, bloated paychecks. That was *so* not going to happen. Maybe never again. Dark hells. He was glad he'd resisted the kids' whinging.

"Management, and especially sales, are going to be working harder to try to get some new orders, but, since they are on salary, they'll also be working longer hours. We're going to be stockpiling product so that we can keep everyone employed, despite the slowdown."

"For a while," Merlid muttered. Davon sighed. Too good to be true, as they'd feared. Dark hells.

"If anyone wishes to leave to seek work elsewhere, we're prepared to lay you off so you'll be entitled to work replacement funds until you can find a new job. See your union stewards in the next week if you want to take advantage of this offer. We'll try to process those forms as quickly as we can. I truly thought that we could make this contract work. I am sorry that market conditions won't let us do that. I wanted to tell you all in person, not hide behind my managers. The buses will take you back to the plants when we're done here. Clock out at your regular time. Those on the evening schedule will only work a half shift tonight."

"Crap," Davon said. "Glad we didn't go wild on spending." There was now a solid murmur as the workers started to vent at each other.

"I doubt that any kids will get hired next summer," Merlid said. "Assuming that *we're* still working. Cheaper than paying us, but there's a lot they can't or don't know how to do."

"Truth. I was hoping to get Halin into shipping next year. I think there's going to be a lot of people moving out of the city if things don't pick up quick."

"I think so too. But I can't, unless I want to lose all the equity we've got in the new house. Too many places go on the market at once and the prices will crater. We'd get nothing. Better to stay here and tough it out, I think. The wife was talking about quitting her job at the daycare. That's not going to happen now. Can't afford to let our income drop very far."

Davon looked back at the stage. President Wakin was talking to Mr. Garthil. The old man looked shrunken and apologetic at first, but rallied and said something, then left, followed by his managers. Wakin glared after them, then the camera system shut down.

There had to be a lot more going on than any of the men and women now moving toward the buses knew about. Dark hells. Davon hated politics with a passion. Who ran the city and province was the most he wanted to care about. The union was supposed to be looking out for their members. Doing the right thing. That hadn't worked out this time, had it? He turned and shuffled toward the buses with the rest of the workers.

❖❖❖❖

Magin Garthil hated playing submissive to the animals who'd kidnapped and tortured his son. At least that analyst, Trelner, had given them some good suggestions to help the boy recover. He still didn't remember his own kidnapping, but his stay in IC had put scars on his soul. Like Carlon had. The therapist Trelner recommended to them was hopeful that Carlon would recover fully. But his missing little toe would always be a reminder of the horror of that time.

"We'd still be running at full capacity if you hadn't insisted on such a big pay increase," he growled, staring at Wakin as the workers slowly headed toward the buses, many of them arguing. "People simply aren't buying our appliances. They're buying ones that are cheaper. Simple economics. I don't know which one of your people came up with this idiot idea. We've all made a decent income for the last forty years. If nothing changes, we won't last another five months. Think on that, in your fancy resort chalet." He stormed off.

When he arrived back at his office, one of the Branson men, Haltarn, held out an envelope for him.

'Stage one is complete. You'll see an item in the news sheets tomorrow. Five of the animals who guarded your son were arrested in the early hours at a local brothel in regard to a call to their tip line. Eight children so far were rescued and nearly ten thousand in cash was seized. Other bank and investment accounts of those arrested are being isolated and seized by the police. The building will be purchased by a concerned citizen and demolished. All of those funds will be divided among the children concerned via a trust fund.

The IC will doubtless obtain many more names from these five. The others may choose to run, but we can arrange to reveal them in whatever local jurisdiction they flee to.

More items will be activating in the next month. It will seem a run of bad luck, not a concerted effort to eliminate the top men of the union. Please burn this and flush the ash once you've read it.

Justice'

"Do you want us to try for a fingerprint on the letter or the envelope?" Haltarn asked. Garthil shook his head.

"No. I doubt there is any evidence on either. These men are doing my work. My revenge. All is in preparation, he says." Magin went into his personal washroom and lit the paper in the sink. It burned brightly and soon only a thin film remained. He ran the water and watched it flow down the drain. He could pretend that his tears were from the smoke, but in truth, there wasn't any.

Magin smiled at the news story the next day. The five men were named in the news reports but there was no indication that they belonged to the union or what they might do for a living. All were taken to the Interrogation Clinic for questioning on other patrons or brothels in other cities. He put that section to one side. Carlon might want to see it, but he would ask the therapist first. It could be too soon for his son to think of revenge and justice rather than shame at what had been done to him.

❧❧❧❧❧

Barrat rolled out from under the vehicle. The idiots parked and left it, completely untended, in a commercial car park while they ate and drank away the evening. It was, in fact, past two in the morning when they finally returned to it. He'd placed a small camera to watch for their departure and waited in a rented work truck with a covered storage area two rows away. He stifled a yawn. The lightproof cover meant he'd been able to keep working on another project in relative comfort, thanks to the inflatable mattress he lay on.

The four men were relatively ambulatory when they reappeared. No one fell down but two were leaning heavily on each other. The least drunk one poured himself into the driver's seat. He didn't hit anything on the way out of the mostly empty lot, which Barrat regarded as a minor miracle given his first three attempts at backing out of the stall. He could have just driven forward and saved himself the difficulty.

The cameras in the lounge and their bar bill would be convincing evidence for the accidental deaths that were sure to follow. Any hint of brake failure would be hidden in the mess that would be left when they crashed. And this late at night in the middle of the week, there were few other people who would take the isolated road to the local resort chalet the union owned.

According to Branson's information, these men were supposed to be coming up with proposals to increase sales and get the workers back to overtime status. The average worker's pay dropped by thirty percent with the "normal" workweek restored. Many of them had ordered new cars and charged other expensive items when the first of the bloated paychecks had come out. Some were trying to sell or return the vehicles, he'd heard. The next time he was up here officially, he might buy a car. Buy Low and Buy Smart worked very well in this situation. And having a vehicle at the office could make his life easier. He could also afford to buy and maintain one without dipping into Justice's accounts. He'd have to ask Kerit about models and reliability.

Rental cars could be noticed if they had corporate stickers on them. Wrecked Rentals was their usual source, since their vehicles had no identification and standard personal ID plates. Most of them were in pristine condition, despite the name of the company. He was in one now, in fact.

He shut down and packed his computers, opened the storage area lid and retrieved the camera, then headed off at the speed limit in the general direction of the chalet. Halfway along the side road, he let the truck roll to a stop. A broken railing showed in the headlights. The cliff here was forty feet or so, he recalled from the topographic maps. Good enough. He drove on the far side of the gravel road, so he wouldn't drive over any of the wreck's tire tracks. It would look like he'd been a very cautious driver who didn't want to be anywhere near the edge with an uncertain roadway beneath him. There was another way out of the resort area, mainly used by the forestry service, and the tires on this vehicle were the same brand as those used for the resort. No one would remark on their presence, even if the investigators noticed them.

Time to work his way back to the city and one of their rented rooms. He yawned. It would take an hour to reach the city and another hour or more to store the work truck at one motel, change his clothing, then access the somewhat battered four-seater, also from Wrecked Rentals, and get to where they actually were staying. He debated getting coffee on the way to help him stay awake, but decided not to. Limit any and all exposure to people and cameras while on mission. A good rule. And coffee now meant it would be harder to get to sleep and there were several items on their agenda for tomorrow, or really, later today.

Once he woke up and showered, Kerit turned on the noon news program as they ate some lunch courtesy of a run to a big grocery store, not their motel's problematic dining area. The ratty motel room's beds were lumpy and the sheets were none too clean. Both of them looked little better than vagrants. Barrat hadn't shaved in three days and the resulting beard itched as usual. But fake facial hair had a tendency to look fake, so Kerit insisted he forgo shaving until they were ready to leave here in a few days.

'Police were on scene at the wreck early this morning, after the morning supply run was heading to the resort area and spotted where the vehicle went *through the guard rails. All four men were found dead at the scene and likely died in the crash or slightly thereafter from a combination of injuries and hypothermia. The coroner will have to wait until they thaw out to complete the autopsies. Cause of the accident is unknown at this time, but alcohol is being considered as a major factor. There is no evidence that the driver attempted to brake or make the turn. He might have been asleep. At least one person in the vehicle was not wearing a safety belt.'*

The older female reporter sensibly stood well back from the edge, but her camera person edged forward to show the wreck. It had flown out a fair distance and knocked several smallish trees over before coming to rest. Either the brake line had failed much earlier on or the driver hadn't even tried to slow. The sleeping theory was reasonable, given their condition when they left the garage. Either way, the result was the same. Four more names checked off on their 'to do' list. Two other thugs had been arrested as a result of IC's questioning and several others were now officially wanted by the police.

'Rescue teams said they will have to cut down one tree as several major branches are embedded in the engine compartment so it can't be brought out of the ravine until they are removed. Back to our news team in the station and the weather outlook for the next week.'

"Well?" Kerit asked after muting the sound.

"Went well," Barrat said. "I cracked one of the brake fluid hoses above the reservoir. A tiny one, but it sufficed. They tended to speed and were very drunk. Went off the road about where I thought they would. I'm not sure that anyone actually needed to help them along."

"How are you feeling about the deaths?"

"Fine. Why are you asking?" Kerit hadn't asked him that question for four years. "And why now?"

"This is a complex operation, Barrat. More so than any other we've done together. And, given what happened to young Carlon, you could be resonating. That's not a good thing in our line of work."

Barrat turned from his meal. Saw the concern in Kerit's eyes. "I admit that I feel bad for Carlon. At least Branson's people, or whoever it was, were decent guys. Their job was to find out what I knew about whatever it was they were paid to. That's all they did. I still want to know why, Kerit. It must be part of the Vegathic collapse but we have no proof of anything we've posited. But *these* men are scum. I know some of them have families. I'm sorry for them if it's a good relationship. But not sorry enough to stop the operation. If they are as good at being spouses and parents as they are at all the heinous things we've found so far, the families will be far better off without them."

Kerit's smile returned. "Good enough. Who's next on the list?"

"The president of the union. Trather Wakin. It's time for him to start having chest pains. I'd thought to put the drug in his mouthwash. It absorbs easily through mucus membranes. His wife has a different brand. I'll need to check out their bathroom to be sure. Thought to do that on this trip if we have time. This way there will be a decent time line of symptoms before his actual death. Less interest from the autopsy."

"Should work," Kerit said. "Conflex raises blood pressure and doesn't show on all but the most rigorous drug screening."

Barrat smiled. "And it messes with adrenal function, which is another plus. With all the stress of his job of gouging business owners and terrorizing kids, elevated blood pressure and angry outbursts are to be expected. And he might make some other mistakes that will help the plan."

"Let's go have a look at his home security this evening," Kerit said. "Then we'll plan the approach."

"If it's anything like what they have at their headquarters, it shouldn't be a problem," Barrat said. "And I'm thinking of buying a car when the workers start seriously downsizing after everyone shuts down. Maybe you can tell me what sort I should look for."

Kerit smiled. "You don't want flashy, not with your public persona. Mid size. We'll go through a middle class neighbourhood once we've swapped to the other car. I'll point out some that would suit you. Don't buy red or bright yellow. People tend to remember them. Black, dark green or blue are very common and there are thousands of those colours on the roadways. Count them in traffic or a parking lot when you get a chance. You'll be surprised."

Barrat nodded. It would take them an hour to get to one of their other vehicles and change so no one would notice two scruffy men in nice car. Being invisible took work but was very necessary in their line of work.

Chapter 24

All the news sheets showed huge headlines. Magin shook his head and tried not to laugh. The rest of his family didn't know everything that the analyst had proposed, so they were all aghast. The lad was fiendishly clever, but that's what he needed to destroy this union board. Even if his advisor was a Trelner.

'Garthil Appliances' plants shut down due to safety violations!'

'Workers survived unsafe conditions for years! Workers Safety and Health finally acknowledges hundreds of complaints from the union!'

"Their past tactics begin to backfire," Haltarn said once they were alone in Garthil's office. He'd become the regular contact between Branson and the two assassins he'd hired. Haltarn wasn't happy but the killers insisted that he be their liaison. No one but them knew why and his boss insisted he take the role to keep them happy. Magin didn't care who carried the messages, so he hadn't commented.

"They do," Magin replied with a smile. "Three months now since we went to the shorter work week. The last of our allies signed the same contract a month ago."

Late fall now. The current total of union dead or in prison was seventeen. One or two a month were having accidents. The most recent was due to a faulty furnace in a fancy cottage one of the union executives bought last year. Only one casualty there: two others survived but were off work and in hospital with what might be permanent brain damage. The cottage was now for sale by the widow, but was actually owned by the union. Silence had commented that it would come out before the sale finalised. Most of the deaths never made the news sheets beyond the obituary pages. The only ones that had were the thugs found in a brothel one night.

"How many of your workers have resigned so far?"

"In all our plants, about a hundred, maybe a few more. Youngsters or single people with few ties here and they've all moved away, from what I've heard. In our allies, more, I believe. It seems most of them waited until they could get work replacement assistance before they left. With this shut down, all of our line workers will be laid off. Same with our allies. Maintenance and perhaps a few line workers to deal with the most serious of the safety issues will be the only ones left. All the managers will remain at work, trying to sell off our stockpiles of goods. We could sell them for less than our normal asking price, but it seems young Trelner has dropped our reserves with his suggestions on buying up raw materials while they're cheap. We cannot afford to give any more discounts. And the *cost* of dealing with the safety issues may further erode our bank accounts if the union comes up with anything else."

"He's a sneaky one," Haltarn muttered.

"Did you know him before this?" Magin asked.

"Not really, sir. Most of what I know came out in the news when Vegathic failed and the stock market nearly did. What will it cost to get even one plant back into operation? And how much time?"

"Not that much to have them all running, actually. Mostly making copies of the existing paperwork, documenting that the "safety issues" were repaired right after the complaints were lodged. Of course, there are a few things that were so idiotic that we never bothered even acknowledging them. The type of toilet paper in the men's washrooms was one." He chuckled. "They said the brand was too soft, if you can believe it. Not manly enough."

Haltarn stared in amazement, then chuckled as he shook his head in disbelief. Magin smiled briefly.

"Those will need a bit more work to ensure that when we do want to restart the lines, there will be no sudden issues. I was told that most of the Workers' Safety and Health inspectors are trying not to stagger around their offices laughing their heads off. In public, they're all serious and grim. Not commenting on anything relating to our factories, which they shouldn't anyway."

"Once the union caves, you'll begin operating within a week or so?"

"About that." Magin sighed. "Perhaps a bit longer. It will take a little time, since the machinery of the production lines need to be checked first, then the various components moved from storage to the line. Then the people for that line come back. And supply people to bring more components and others to take the finished products to the warehouse." He sighed and looked down at his hands.

"There are some very good men and women who belong to the union, Haltarn. I'm hoping that they will band together and take back the union from the animals who sabotaged their lives. That's really why I asked Silence and Justice to target their leadership and their thugs. The other owners and I decided that there *must* be an election in the near future. It will be the workers' choice what happens to our futures."

⋙⋘⋙⋘

Davon and Merlid stared at the plant manager. Everyone was crowded into the cafeteria this time.

"All the safety issues the union has brought forward over the past years were recently reviewed by Workers Safety and Health. They've shut us down," the manager said. He looked rumpled and untidy. Davon had never seen him look other than calm and controlled, his suit pressed and clean. "Mr. Garthil didn't want to use up any of the reserves doing a big announcement like last time. We'll need every penny we can lay our hands on to fix the problems so we can bring everyone back to work."

"All *three* of our plants?" someone from the side called incredulously. Davon couldn't see who'd spoken. The workers shuffled and some men near him started swearing under their breath.

"Yes. And while WS&H were at it, they looked at all the safety citations for any company with workers that are from our union. They've shut down ten plants already. I just finished a conference call with Mr. Garthil and the owners of four or five other companies. Another four plants are on thin ice. They may shut down in the next few weeks. We think that at least three thousand people will be laid off because of this." Murmurs of shock echoed through the room. He mopped his forehead with a paper towel, staring down until the noise subsided.

"We have until the end of the late shift to shut down all the lines. When we're done here, go to your stations and process what's left on the conveyors. Nothing new gets started. Once you're finished, clean up and pack any parts remaining to be returned to the warehouse. Tidy your work areas and ensure all the tools are racked. The late shift will run further clean up and shut down the rest of the systems. Personnel is gearing up to start filling out the lay off notices. You'll have them as soon as we can get them printed off. Mr. Garthil contacted the work replacement department and alerted them before this meeting started. They're bringing in extra people to expedite the processing."

"I thought all of those citations were listed as work completed?" Mrenth, the head steward here, asked. "That's what I was told."

"That's what we thought too, Mr. Mrenth. I don't know what started WS&H off on this idiocy. Maybe some new hire who piled all the past citations together?" He shook his head and rubbed his eyes. "I may know more in the next few weeks. When I know, I'll inform you so you can pass the information on. I believe Mr. Garthil will notify your leadership directly, but redundancy is never wasted in this type of situation."

"So all the union people go on the unemployed line. What about management? All of you get to keep your cushy jobs?" Mrenth growled.

"Sales will keep going, mostly to find buyers for what we have in the warehouses. The company needs cash to deal with the repairs and such that WS&H have mandated. We're not sure the extent of the layoffs but we'll let people from just about every other department go. Your people will get a top up from the union emergency funds. Unlike the rest of us."

Davon looked at Merlid as the workers began to leave the lunch area. "We are so in trouble. Meeting tonight at your place?" Merlid nodded. He had no idea what they could do at this point but at least they could all vent about their idiotic union officials. What had Wakin and the board thought would be the result of their stupid wage and benefit increases?

❧ ❧ ❧ ❧

Barrat looked at the news sheet. The next step was complete. Three thousand or more people were suddenly out of work. Late fall. The worst time to lose a job. The union couldn't afford the top-up for long. Not unless they sold off some of their fancy cars and the resort chalets kept for the top management. That was where huge amounts of the union reserve funds had gone over the years. He glanced at the big yearly calendar on his wall. Nothing but his "official" business items showed but he knew what was planned for the union. It was about time to refill Wakin's mouthwash. He'd been to his doctor twice now with mild angina. Time to up the dose. And he could be there in both personas, cutting down on travel costs and time when no one knew where he was. He'd caught sight of a watcher last week hovering across the street. He was one of the union's dirty tricks men, who was also on their list. Too bad he'd choked on a chunk of beef in his hotel room after ordering room service. Two days before anyone noticed as the "Don't bother me" sign was on the knob. He did feel sorry for the security guard who opened the door for the maid.

And he would look for a car. A five or six hour drive home, but worth it. He'd have to take out some cash to pay for it. That would get him a discount, he was sure. And he'd have to arrange for insurance and the registration as soon as he bought it. More details to keep track of.

Wakin snarled when he heard the news. Their headquarters security was *very* substandard. A trusted contact maintained the feed, once Barrat had put the microphones in place. This had been relayed earlier than the usual summary. Nothing was said about the possibility that the dead man had help in choking to death. The sedative decayed in five hours. It was much easier to force the lump down someone's throat when the target slept.

⋘⋙⋘⋙

Barrat and Kerit sat together in the diner a week later, watching the special news report on the wall mounted vid unit. Everyone else there was also staring raptly at the screen.

"This is the scene outside Garthil Appliances main offices," the reporter said. "It doesn't look like anything is wrong, but this business and several others are partly responsible for the sudden collapse of our local economy. Many locals, including many of the older workers, say that it is the fault of the union, not the company, for requesting such large increases to the pay and benefits package in the latest round of collective bargaining. The first sign of the collapse was that the company stopped all overtime, only allowing a standard work week."

The camera panned the front of the building.

"All six companies that employ this union are shut down now. The effect of so many people laid off in such a short time is causing other problems. Not many homes are listed for sale right now, but at least seven or eight hundred laid off workers have already left the area. The rental market is beginning to reel with the sudden influx of empty units. Some people are threatening their landlords to lower their rent, or they say that they'll move. Even those with stable jobs are getting nervous about the continued health of the local economy."

The view changed to the station's news room. Their lead, an older woman trusted by anyone who saw her, sat behind the desk.

"Parint, we've heard that in the latest poll many local residents fear that there will be a general recession in the area. Do you have any information on that?"

"I do, Cari. What they fear is possible, our economic experts say. But it is also possible that it won't be as bad as some fear-mongers are saying. There are currently three thousand or so people out of work. Many of these workers will have to cut personal spending because of debt ob-ligations and the need to keep feeding their families. They won't be pur-chasing expensive items and may try to sell or return items they bought when the bigger paychecks began. If enough people move out of the area, there won't be the same need for just about every sort of service. Bars and restaurants may go down first. And if *those* families move, schools and other businesses may lay off workers. But there are still thousands more people who are still happily employed and will stay that way. We just can't be sure what panic will do to their spending habits. If they keep their spending the same, it will mitigate the loss from Garthil's employees. The union people are all getting work replacement funds based on their last few checks, so won't be badly affected. They'll have about three quarters of those paychecks, if not more. If the rest of our local workers don't keep their heads, well, it could be devastating."

Bethie filled their coffees. "What a mess that is up there. And what are the companies doing to help them out?"

"The union is topping up the cheques to the people laid off," Kerit said. "Heard Garthil's people are trying to sell their stock of appliances to get enough money together to fix at least one of the plants so they can get some folks back to work."

"But the companies can't survive with the union insisting on the in-flated pay and benefits," Barrat said. The view changed again to a cemetery.

"We're just outside the Shady Rest Cemetery, Cari," A different re-porter said. A younger woman dressed in black to fit in. "The funeral for Trather Wakin has just ended. You can see the mourners, mostly from the union board and a few of the stewards leaving the site." The camera obligingly shifted to show the black clad men and women. The widow had a veil pulled down to hide her face. "His death from heart failure was not completely unexpected, I've learned from speaking to those in at-tendance. He has been suffering from angina for some months now from the stress of what's been happening. He and other union leaders were at a retreat in the mountains to discuss ways to resolve the slow progress of Garthil's and the other companies in addressing their safety concerns and opening the plants. My source said the union board were consider-ing loaning the companies the money needed to do that from the union reserve funds."

"That is totally unprecedented, Vitani," Cari said. "Did they give any reason for the offer?" The vid swapped to her as she spoke, then back to the reporter.

"I've heard several theories. In fact, my source said the loans would be secured against stock in the affected companies," she said. "Still, it is in the union's best interests to have all the affected plants up and running as quickly as possible. They can't keep the top-ups forever."

"As we all hope," Cari said. "We'll update you as soon as we know more."A commercial started.

Bethie was now filling other coffee cups. Barrat looked at Kerit. "I think this is their new plan to have the union take over the companies legally. Ingenious. They have one person with a brain in their midst. I wonder if we can figure out who it is and arrange a special accident. They must have talked about it in the board room."

"It seems to be a decent plan. Using the company's own money to buy their stock. At least it won't happen now."

"Not this time, but every company dealing with a union should make sure they read the very fine print in any new contracts. I'll mention it to Erithe when I call her tomorrow. She can spread the word through Legal and to her friends."

❧❧❧❧❧

Pawthel Beldran, the new president of the union sat fuming at the news conference two weeks later. That coward Garthil had caved again. But not in the way any member of the union board ever expected. They hadn't gone for the union funding proposal. It had been a last ditch attempt to wrest control from Garthil and the other owners so he hadn't had much hope they'd go for it. Dark hells.

"I am announcing that I have sold a portion of the company to a consortium with significant assets so that we can fix all the safety issues. My family will be left with a minority stake in the company and we will sign the final papers at the end of the month. It is hoped that we'll be able to finally fix the safety issues and get the plants back on line, at least on a part-time basis, so that some of our workers can be back at work soon."

There were questions, mostly about this consortium. Who were they and what kind of money were they bringing to the table. None were answered. Garthil tottered off, leaving the audience and local reporters arguing about who could be coming to the rescue.

Back at the union offices, now unfortunately minus some excellent pieces of art, Beldran rubbed his hands together as he glanced at their contract, flipping through the end sections he'd never seen as a junior member of the team. Back to the good times. Great times. Then he noticed a sentence in the interminable clauses that filled every union document. Filler no one ever expected to use and usually meant nothing. His mouth dropped open and he blinked rapidly. He guessed that no one, including their lawyers, had ever read this far into the document. The ingrates. It couldn't be... This agreement was null and void if the original owners' stake dropped below fifty percent. The moment the sale was finalized there was *no* contract with the union. He shouted and his aide rushed in, then rushed out to call all the other officials to get to their headquarters as soon as possible.

The next weeks were full of bad news.

Several other major officers in the union died and their funerals were tiny. General workers were not encouraged to attend. One committed suicide, but that was because someone leaked to a local reporter that the paedophiles arrested earlier gave his name to the police and they were on their way to arrest him.

Pawthel Beldran looked at the empty seats around the executive table and sighed. There was no hope for it. He'd have to call for elections. He couldn't just appoint new members to the board any more. They'd managed to promote some assistants but they'd run out of them in the past months. The lawyers he consulted shook their heads in sorrow. And they said the same clause from the dark hells was in *all* the recent contracts. Likely those companies were also going to be part of the consortium. The families would own stock in the holding company but their personal ownership of their companies would be forty-eight percent. Enough to negate all the contracts.

Dark hells, he thought. *Why hadn't this been noticed months ago? They would have had a chance to work around it!*

꧁ ꧂ ꧁ ꧂

After the elections, the new board nodded at each other at their first meeting. Davon still wondered why the heck he'd volunteered to run. Merlid was to blame, he decided. None of the previous board was re-elected. Those people had ten percent of the vote, if that. All the new board members came from line or supervisory positions in the various plants the union controlled. All the office staff were replaced the next day. So was the law firm. No doubt there were some people working here that might have been honest, but no one who had worked at the union headquarters was trusted by the rank-and-file anymore.

Trevar Galarn, their new president, was from one of the other companies the union used to have contracts with. Davon liked him. Merlid said he'd heard good things about him, which did a lot to reassure their people. That the old stewards *didn't* like him was a bonus.

He guessed that first meeting would take at least three days to go through everything on Galarn's list.

"On the top of my list is retiring all the factory stewards who have or had serious ties to the old administration. All of you must know people in your plants who can do the job. If a plant wants to keep a steward, they'll have to vote. A clear majority, not a fifty-one percent squeaker. Eighty or they're out."

"There might be one or two good ones," Davon said. "But I agree. I've got someone in mind who'd be way better than our last guy." Since Merlid suggested he run for the board, setting him up as a steward was a good way to thank him. He grinned.

"Everyone contact your buddies and get us some names." Garlan looked down the table and everyone nodded. "The union jet is for sale. I understand it should go quickly. That will give us some cash to keep the top-up fund solvent. I don't want to have to borrow money to keep our people comfortable."

"What about the other stuff?" a woman down the table asked. Marithe, Davon thought her name was. They needed name tags for a couple of weeks to keep track of who was who.

"Other stuff?" Garlan asked.

"The art in my office is real. No idea how much it's worth. Plus there's at least one or three chalets that we, the union, own. Kept hearing how they'd go for working meetings." A soft growl from everyone. "I can have a look through the asset lists and see what's there."

"A very good idea," Garlan said. He looked at the large painting on the wall behind him. "Anyone know an art expert?"

"My cousin's an artist," said someone. "I'll give her a call this afternoon when we break and get some names."

"We'll also need someone who knows real estate," Davon said. "There's a big firm that has lots of buildings I've heard of. I'll call around to find someone."

More changes: Board salaries were slashed in half. No one minded. It was still more than what each of them had earned at the plants. Union dues would be cut in half. The reserve fund was still in danger of defaulting, so the list of properties for sale was increased, even though few buyers were interested in the still depressed region. However, since no one was working at the moment, it didn't really matter to the income level.

Two weeks later Davon accompanied a real estate rep for the walk-through of the chalets and other properties before they were listed for sale. He hoped they'd be able to continue the top up until everyone was back at work.

"Dark hells." The car stopped in front of a three story building that sat in a huge lot nestled in mature trees, with a terrific view of the mountains. "*This* belongs to the union?"

"It is." Taritha Helker, the female rep, looked over at him. "There are three others in this area, sir. This is the largest. You didn't know?"

"Dark hells." Davon turned to Merlid. "You know about them other than they existed?" Merlid shook his head, eyes wide. "Get pictures. Lots of them. Nobody's going to believe us without them."

"Right." Merlid shook his head and pulled out his camera. "Glad you suggested I bring it. Should have brought more storage disks."

"Do you have the keys?" Taritha asked.

Davon pulled a large ring out of his outer pocket. Four sets of keys were on it.

The door opened into... He didn't have the words. "Dark hells," said Merlid. "Should have brought a video unit."

"I take it that no one from the union was aware of the... extent of the former board's... um. Indulgence?" Her eyes were wide. He was sure his were wider in shock.

"Not a whisper," Davon said. He shut his eyes for a moment. "We'll have to come back with a video unit. Or two."

"Since it is fully furnished, that would raise the price of the property," Taritha said. "Or your board might consider selling the contents separately. Rental is also a short term option, at least for the winter and until the plants are fully operational again. Many people seek week-long or even longer term rentals on properties like this. That would provide some cash flow for your members."

"Yeah," Merlid said. He moved from the entryway into the room on the right side. "We need an inventory, I think. Bring another couple of guys with us." This room had what looked like a well stocked bar at the far end. Slightly dusty since no one had been here for at least a month.

"Look at this, Davon. How much do you think these cost?" Davon and Taritha came over. She picked up a bottle of whiskey. Unopened.

"This is, I believe, two hundred. Perhaps more."

"Per case?" Merlid asked hesitantly. Afraid to know the answer. Well, so was he.

"No. Per bottle. When one of our vice presidents retired last year, we chipped in to get him a bottle."

"Dark hells," the men said in unison. Stared around at the room.

"This is just one of the chalets. One room." Davon couldn't think properly. He had to call Garlan and warn him what they were finding.

"Our firm has a local estate evaluator. Perhaps they could help. He has considerable contacts with auction houses and buyers. For many sorts of items."

"Like art?" Merlid asked. She nodded.

The two men stared at one another, then around at the room again. "I'm thinking that's a really good idea."

Garlan answered his phone. "Hi, Davon. You get to the chalets yet?"

"We're in one of them." A sigh. "Sit down if you aren't. We started with the biggest one. It's huge. Three story and fully furnished. A big lot. There's a bar in the living room with bottles that cost two hundred each. And more paintings. Not prints on the walls." He set the comm on speaker so they could all hear.

"Dark hells," Garlan said softly. "I'm... I'm..."

"Wait til you see it in person," Merlid said. "I didn't realise how much all this was. We're getting a video unit sent up. Should be able to send you a copy tonight. Warn the other board guys."

"We have estate evaluators available," said Taritha. "I think by selling some contents from the various chalets, that will alleviate any immediate cash flow issues with your top-up funds."

"You think it's worth that much?" Garlan managed to say.

"Yeah," Davon said. He walked to the bar and counted what was in view. "Got maybe twenty bottles of whisky with names I know are expensive. No idea what might be in the storage area or in the cupboards. We basically came in the front door and our brains stalled out. Then I called you. Figured we all need a warning."

"You may also be able to sue the old board members to recover some funds," Taritha said. "I doubt any vacation properties they owned directly were paid for out of their pockets."

✦✦✦✦

"Mr Farnal, good to hear from you. Is everything going well?" Barrat asked. He sipped his coffee.

"Very well, in fact. I wanted to update you and your family on the latest news. Mr. Galarn, and two of his people from the new board, met with the presidents of the six companies two days ago. He was very upfront about the changes they're making in how the union is run. They've received warning calls from three other unions in the past week."

"Why? What are they doing?"

Apparently the others are upset at the cuts in dues and salaries for our union's officials. Their members are reading the news reports and are starting to ask their officials very embarrassing questions. The story on the vacation chalets and other properties spread all over the country. And beyond, I believe."

"Holdings was happy our bid for them went through so quickly. A discount on what their current value is, but Mr. Galarn didn't want to mess around with selling them piecemeal. How are the safety issues?"

"We finished all of ours and everyone else is within a week of settling everything. That's why Mr. Galarn wanted to meet. He brought a new proposal for everyone to consider." A chuckle came through.

"Can I guess what it looked like?"

"I'm sure you can."

"The old contract, more or less? Minus the padding at the back?"

"Yes. It went from thirty pages to ten. Quite a relief. Our lawyers are making sure there aren't any odd bits, but we should sign within a week, maybe two. Another week to get the lines checked out by the mechanics and we should be up and running soon."

"Excellent. That should give everyone in the area cause to relax. What about the people who left?"

"Most have jobs now, I would guess. There are still a number of unemployed people in the area, so hiring will fill in the gaps. All in all, it seems to be ending."

"And the good guys won," Barrat said. "The other unions may have their own troubles soon if their members are paying attention. I'd guess they won't be making any outlandish proposals at their next rounds of renewals."

Another chuckle. "I would agree with that assessment. Thank you again, Mr. Trelner. I'm not sure we would have survived without your family's aid."

"That the sort of thing we do, Mr. Farnal. Take care."

The connection ended. Barrat turned off the recorder. He wanted to play it for Kerit when he came over next.

Chapter 25

Barrat smiled at the news report as he finished a late supper. His fee was a modest number of shares of the holding company, as he had little money to invest openly. More than at the end of his first year of business, but still a pittance compared to where he wanted to be.

Trelner Holdings was still the major shareholder of that holding company, but that would change as profits allowed the business owners to redeemed those shares. Then Holdings would be ready for the next big deal. Smaller ones were possible, given the size of Holding's bank accounts and their temporary investments. Some of them were all the resort chalets the union used to own. He'd suggested those purchases. Once the local economy rebounded, they'd sell easily, their management company assured them. They had been all rented through the winter skiing season. All the bills were being paid with a little extra and that was the most important fact right now. The sale prices were where they'd make their profit.

It was now mid spring. And the weekend beckoned. Maybe he'd go out and play at the paintball range tomorrow. Hide and seek was a great game and kept his skills sharp. That everyone there thought he was a very bad shot who kept trying (and failing) to hit anyone but was very sneaky was a bonus. However, he always hit what *he* aimed at. He'd bought an expensive paintball rifle through the range two weeks ago.

One more thing to do before he went to bed. Time to check in to their dark net account and see if anyone needed Justice. It had been a few days and it was his turn. He and Kerit limited their time on the dark net, in case someone was watching for them. So far, their involvement in the union's troubles hadn't been officially noticed.

He padded down into the office and swapped the net connection to the one that ran through the splitter box in the basement. He logged in and saw two messages. The first was from a contact, the other directly to him. Well, Justice.

The initial paragraph of the earlier one started with whinging. And it continued for the entire screen. Barrat sighed after skimming it, trying to figure out just who the person wanted dead, or why. Even how much they were willing to pay. On first read, he was willing to remove the sender from annoying him further. The next section was written after the first by at least a day, he guessed. And it *was* revenge. The husband had taken the considerable family savings and vanished. With someone, identity unknown. No idea where they were or who the new lover was. And the enraged wife offered to split the insurance money and said savings once the errant spouse and the tart were dead in an accident so no one would question her inheritance.

He started to delete the message, then saved it. Kerit might find it amusing. Maybe they should find out who the woman was and have the police in her town pay her a visit. In the event that she found someone else to take the hit. Finding the lovers would be difficult as neither of them likely had any trade-craft or it was just from vids.

Most people weren't aware of how much work setting up new identities was. Just running away to a resort in another country was the most common 'escape' such people decided on. He shook his head, drank some coffee and opened the next file.

The second was also a simple hit but the sender wanted a rifle shot. Out in the open. The more witnesses the better. With video for proof of death before they released the payment. Barrat froze as he read the name of the target. Vanthin Trelner.

The hit was on his father. He stared at the screen. The screen blanked since he hadn't done anything for fifteen minutes. Barrat picked up his coffee and stared at it. The thought of drinking it made him nauseous. He put the cup down, took a deep breath and stared at the message again.

His mind stalled again on his father's name as the victim. When he was able to think, seemingly hours later, he looked for the sender's information. There was a link to an article about the collapse of a company. Engineered by his father, it seemed. He'd then bought the remnants for pocket change and the value had tripled in the two years since the takeover and was likely to go higher. The message said it had taken him this long to raise the money. Several other business owners were chipping in to raise the fee. They'd all been targeted recently. Barrat knew his father had become much more ruthless in the past few years. Especially after his kidnapping and the family's anger about Barrat's stay in Insanity Central.

Was he to blame for his father's ruthlessness? No, he decided. Father was showing the family that he didn't care what they thought of him. That they didn't want him involved in Trelner Holdings. He'd concentrated on making himself richer than they were. That everyone else in the family also owned Trelner Industries stock and kept getting higher dividends and increased net worth from his efforts seemed to have escaped him. Barrat forced himself to only think of this message as any other they'd received in the past years. People were seeking Justice. Could he, and should he, give them closure?

Looking at Father's will might be instructive in any case. Would the family be better off if Father was dead? Would small business owners like the ones in the message be safer in the future? He blinked. He had to think of the target as just a nasty guy named Trelner. Not his *father*.

Again no. The clients and every other idiot business owner would still be at risk. Vanthin wasn't the only predator in the markets, just one of the most successful. They'd still be vulnerable to take overs and all the tricks that predators used to isolate and identify a company that had value or was in their way.

Trelner Holdings couldn't help every company in the world avoid the consequences of the stupid business decisions their management kept making. Most of the tentative requests they received were turned down after a cursory examination of their finances. They'd dug their own graves. His advice was generally to sell, if they could. Otherwise, head for the bankruptcy courts and try to salvage what was left.

If he didn't take the hit on his father, there were many others who did the same sort of work as Silence and Justice. The sender would just find one of them. Who would do the job and not worry about anything other than what location gave him the best access to take the shot.

He shut down the computer automatically. Went upstairs and lay on his bed. Stared at the ceiling until dawn came.

Kerit stared at the message. "Not what I expected when you called for me to come in today," he said.

"Or what I expected to see as a request. And if I don't take the job, someone else will. They want a shot, which means it doesn't matter how many guards Father has standing around him. Line of sight..."

"Is the sniper's friend," Kerit finished, then sighed. "And most oth- ers would fire through the extra bodies without a thought. Dark hells, Barrat. Okay. Let's look at it as a normal contract. Be Justice, not Barrat. Think about what he's done and who he's hurt. Is his death justified un- der our normal criteria?"

"I tried that," Barrat said. "While staring at the ceiling most of the night. And the answer is yes. He's destroyed countless lives, all to make his company and the investment side bigger and more powerful. Have more money and crush anyone who stands in his way. Manipulate everything and everyone he needed to get the results he wants. But he's not unique in that. Idiots are always at risk from their own stupidity." He looked down at his hands. "We did the same thing with the union. We broke them and killed their members for the benefit of the six company owners."

"Yes, some suffered, some died. But the only ones who died were those that were guilty and would never face an honest jury. Now, every- one's back at work and the holding company will ensure that they're safe from any other takeover scheme. Some workers left, but most stayed. And in the last two months, two other unions were forced by their mem- bers to hold new elections and dumped their old leaders. Dropped their union dues and cleaned up their ranks. So far. That operation made and will continue to make a big difference to a lot of people. A very positive one. We made that difference possible with what we did."

"I know," Barrat muttered. "And I know there are five, maybe six others just like Father. Eliminating him won't stop the others from chan- ging how they do business. And removing all of them just gives the slightly smaller sharks room to operate and become bigger sharks to re- place them. As well, it might make the clients happy to watch his fu- neral, but they still won't have their companies back. These people are looking for revenge, not seeking real justice."

"What does your father's will say? Who gets control of Industries if he's no longer around?"

"I think Mother has a copy from the lawyers, but it's from around ten years ago. He rewrote it after my grandfather died, I think. He might have changed it in the past year or so since we stopped talking to him. The old one says that his personal shares in Trelner Industries will be di- vided equally between all us kids. Mother gets her settlement and my aunt gets a couple of odd properties left over from my grandfather's will. There are specific bequests for anything he held personally. I think Frak- lin gets the CEO slot since he's the oldest. He's not as ruthless as my father so the company might slip down a notch if he's running it. It's hard to tell what changes he might have made."

"The whole mess around your kidnapping isolated him, didn't it?"

"Yes. The rest of the family was pissed at him for giving me up to IC. They stopped going over to the house for the weekend, that sort of thing. There hasn't been a family vacation since then. Whenever I go back there, I stay with Erithe and Dantil. Mom comes over and so do Carthan and Hethane. When I have business in a city where one of my siblings live, I've tried to stay there, about half the time now. Getting to know them as adults is helping deal with how isolated I felt growing up. Doctor Halli suggested it. It was very hard suggesting I visit the first time, but it's become easier. We almost have conversations now. That's a big change from what we had before this."

"And that's when your father became more vicious."

"Yes."

"How about this scenario? He's lonely now. The family shuns him, so he's focused all his energy on work. To him success is defined as building the company up further. I think he does have an alternate will, with a firm he doesn't usually deal with. That gives everything he controls to someone else, or a charity. Even worse, one of his competitors."

"That could be contested, Kerit. And we all own shares in TI, from grandfather. I'm not sure on the total, but there might be enough to keep control of the company, no matter what his will says. None of us has ever voted against his proposals, even now. I can ask Erithe or Carthan to check on who the major shareholders are. I can also use some of Justice's cash to start buying up shares to increase the number we control. And I don't need the dividend income from Industries to live on anymore since I have lots of legitimate consulting money. I can reset the automatic buy order for any dividends and suggest everyone else do the same. That won't get us a lot of shares, but any extra will help if all of his shares suddenly vanish from our control. Everyone was taking the dividends in cash to have money for other investments, and to fund Holdings."

"That's a couple of things to do. Will you warn him?"

"I... think so. But I'll tell the clients I'm checking out the possibilities for a shot. Just to give me some time to decide if I can do it."

"Or I can," Kerit said gently.

◈◈◈◈

Nartig Haltarn swore at the letter he'd just opened. "Why do they keep doing this to me?"

Jula turned from her desk. "What?"

"That assassin, Justice? He's just sent this letter to me. Wants me to take a copy of a message he just received to Vanthin Trelner. That someone's taking out a hit on him."

"What?" Jula blinked, then stared at him. "Why you?"

"I have no idea why they keep harassing me. I wish they'd stop. And there's a draft enclosed to pay for two hours of my time. At bonus rates, at that. Dark hells."

"Talk to the boss," Jula advised, then turned back to her radio link. Martan was on the stakeout he'd take over in a few hours. Maybe not once the boss saw this.

"I have something you need to see." Nartig held up the envelope. "It's from Justice."

"A new contract for us?" Branson grinned. "That last one was very lucrative, you know."

"I know. And the fat bonuses for our work, which were very nice. But this contract isn't for us. It's a hit on Vanthin Trelner and Justice is the one who'll do it. He wants to warn Trelner for some reason I can't guess."

Branson sat back in his padded chair. "Is this a joke? If so, you have..."

"I wish it was." He handed the letter to his boss. Branson read it, at least twice by his eye movements, then put it down on his desk.

"We'll deliver it. There's no risk to us. We're busier than ever, since some other business owners know that we helped find evidence against the union leaders. They don't know the truth about the deaths, but our reputation is significantly higher than this time last year."

"You think the assassins will call on us again for leg work?" Dark hells, he wanted nothing more to do with them or the Trelners. Now both of them were in his face. Again. Would it ever stop? Maybe he should start looking for another job.

"Possibly. I don't really want to follow people just for them to kill again, but delivering this message isn't an issue." He picked up the bank draft and a slight smile resulted. "Especially at the bonus rate."

"How can I get in to see him? I doubt he takes many appointments from people he doesn't know. I doubt he would see us as having enough clout. Or he'd fob us off on some underling. Should we try for his security head? That might be easier. He'd be happy to hear the news."

"I know some people. Former clients, who do know him. One is on the board at Trelner Industries, I think. I'll give her a call first. I can't reveal the nature of the message, so I hope she won't just hang up on me."

Two days later, after several rounds of comm calls and consultations with previous clients who knew Trelner and the draft deposited in the company's bank account, Nartig waited outside Trelner's main office. The aide on the desk guarding the door offered coffee but he'd refused.

A low tone from a comm and the aide stood. "He'll see you now, sir." Nartig rose and headed for the door but the aide reached it first and opened it for him.

Trelner didn't look much like his youngest son, Nartig thought. Barrat was more like his mother in appearance, but the kid was full of the same fire as his father. Even though the kid hated him. Every question they'd asked him about his relationship with his father made Nartig grateful his own parents had always supported him and his choices.

"Well?" Trelner said. Sitting behind the desk, two large screens full of market data. Barely paying attention to him. "You're from Branson Security. Why did your boss pull in favours from one of my board members and several others I know to get you through my door?"

Nartig took a breath. "My company was asked to bring you word of an assassination contract, sir. On you."

Trelner blinked. The only reaction. "So some whingers think I'm a target?" A snort of derision. "Finally grew some courage, did they? Which snivelling coward is it?"

"I don't know that, sir. And it seems to be a consortium, not just a single individual. The message we received didn't list any names." He pulled the slim envelope out of his jacket pocket. "This is what we were asked to give to you."

"By whom?"

"The assassin, sir. Who is considering the contract, he says. He may be trying to make you death more "sporting" by warning you. I don't pretend to understand why he sent it to my firm. The contract specifies a bullet, not poison or other covert method, by the way. And they want video as proof of your death."

An eyebrow rose slightly. "It's harder to get close to me, and the whingers don't want to get their own hands dirty."

"Since the method is so overt, they obviously don't care if there is an investigation, sir. Whatever reasons they have for seeking your death, they believe that going to jail is an acceptable risk. They are probably some suspects that the police and Corporate Oversight would look at very closely. Perhaps take some of them into IC to determine the truth."

"Which assassin is it?"

"We don't know," Nartig lied. "We received the message and a bank draft two days ago. While normally we wouldn't pass on something like this, it was determined that it was, indeed, a credible threat. We have not informed anyone else, including those we asked to arrange this meeting, about the nature of the message. The assassin stated that reparations to those wronged might be enough for them to cancel the contract. He seems to be giving you some time to decide if you want to die. He must be very good at his job. He's very confident he can do the job, even with an explicit warning."

"Give that thing to me," Trelner said. Nartig handed over the envelope. "I would guess there are no fingerprints or anything giving any clue as to his identity? And are you sure he's male?"

"No, sir. Most assassins *are* male, so we tend to default to that."

"Give my your card. I'll contact you if there's something else I want to tell you."

Nartig handed over his card. "Our main office always knows where I am, sir." A wave of Trelner's hand and Nartig left, shutting the door behind him.

"Hold all my calls," came from the comm. The aide watched him leave. He'd relax once he was out of the building. Maybe.

⋐⋗⋐⋗

Barrat tried to keep his mind on the analysis he needed to finish by the end of the week: three days away. It wasn't working. Haltarn should be giving his father the letter soon. Then he would send word of what happened to the dark net account. But did he want to know what Father said? He shut down the computer, locked the front door and went up to his weight room.

Sweaty and tired two hours later, he padded into the bathroom, stripping off the exercise gear as he went and dumped it in the hamper. The hot water from the shower brought some relaxation to his muscles but he stared at the ceiling most of the night. He'd check the dark net in the morning. Could he actually pull the trigger and kill his father? He finally slept, but not well.

⋐⋗⋐⋗

Vanthin stared at the message after the security man left. The assassin had fortitude, he'd give him that. Warning the target? He'd never heard any of his ilk doing that. Should he inform his security? A news announcement on the market monitor caught his eye. Trelner Holdings was bailing out another loser with production problems. They'd bought twenty percent of the company stock and would have a seat with veto power on the board. And the financial analysis that showed them the way to prosperity was done by Trelner Consulting. Barrat was becoming known for taking his payments in shares, not cash. Or not entirely in shares. He still had expenses after all.

His youngest son was finally fulfilling his destiny. But not for him. Never for him. He'd been so angry at the boy about that damned kidnapping. Sending him to IC to get the truth shattered the already precarious family cohesion completely. That hadn't been the reaction he expected. His *wife* was the only one of them he saw these past months unless there was a major board meeting and his other children needed to report on the subsidiaries they managed for him. And Carithe only slept and ate at his house to keep her own settlement in force. He growled. He wouldn't tell *them*. They didn't care. He'd fix them.

He picked up the comm and called for Berhan, his head of security. He could manage the company from the house for a week or two while his security ran down the cowards who wanted him dead. Then the assassin would go bother someone else. Or maybe he could outbid the whingers and have the assassin eliminate them. But with poison or some other covert method. He had no intention of being seen as a suspect by the police or Corporate Oversight. He knew far too many secrets to risk a trip to Insanity Central.

Chapter 26

The head of the Securities Service, Damilan Hranthel, looked at six stacks of files on his boardroom table. Then at the eight analysts, clustered at the other end. Their leader, Vertin Malther, sat to his right.

"And what was so important you had to summon me without notice? Those do not look like they have much impact," was all he said. No reason had been given for this meeting, just that it was crucial.

"We swept for recording devices ten minutes ago," Malther said. "And found two devices. That's why we didn't book anything formal. We finally found evidence of the *why* behind the crash, sir."

"Excellent." *At last.* How had been just over two years ago now.

"The scheme is quite ambitious, sir. It is a two step plan. The crash was part one and it worked flawlessly. They never intended a second try with that system, so the holes we plugged were a waste of time in that respect. The next step, however, is even more catastrophic. But now that we're aware of what's planned, we can stop it."

"What is your best guess when they seek to implement phase two?"

"Originally, we felt it would still be several months from now," Malther said. "However some new information recently came to light that indicates it may be much sooner than that. We can still halt trading in time to save them."

"Them?" Hranthel glared at his subordinate. Plain speaking was the norm in the office, not vague hints or generalizations.

"The six major firms who hold direct or considerable indirect control of fifty five percent of the securities market," Malther replied. "We discovered that there are a dozen or more people in a consortium who seek to take that power for themselves."

"Is Trelner involved? He's been very ruthless of late but hasn't crossed any legal lines that I've heard of. And Corporate Oversight keeps a close watch on him now."

"He's one of the targets, sir. Not part of the problem. And his death might be the triggering event for stage two. Without his hand on the market, we believe that the other five would have a much harder time mitigating what happens when the next event hits."

"His *death*? Are you sure?"

"Yes, sir. There is an assassination contract on his life. That's the new information we just received. We have several officers who troll the dark net for information. The parties behind it are supposed to be families who lost control of their companies because of Vanthin Trelner's direct intervention in their affairs. And the contract was accepted by Justice a few days ago. You've heard of him." Malther pushed a document over.

Hranthel sighed after he scanned it. "The union collapse. Eighteen dead or in prison. We didn't even try to stop them or inform the police. We didn't officially know what they were up to but it was pretty obvious once the deaths began..."

"Thirty four, sir," came a small voice from the end of the table. "Possibly more. We feel all the union's troubles, including accidents, deaths by what looked like natural causes and suicide, were due to Justice and Silence. They acted together in that case, and several others we've managed to trace back to them. Other times they run separate operations. This matter seems to involve Justice alone, unless he's already consulted with Silence. The contract was offered directly to Justice, not both. The fee offered reflects that. Silence may still be involved in an auxiliary capacity or to help arrange travel or a safe house. We can't be sure."

"Even the *suicides* and the union president's heart attack were their doing?" Hranthel asked. Unwilling to let the past be dismissed so quickly. "Why wasn't I told of this before?"

"Deniability, mostly," Malther said. "But we believe the death toll was all due to their efforts to break the hold the previous leadership had on the union. We haven't asked directly, being officials who are constrained to report crimes to the police or Corporate, but one of our people spoke with Branson. He intimated that his people provided reports on their surveillance of all the dead to the assassins. Mind you, ten or so of them were the thugs who beat and raped the kidnapped boy that started the whole thing. Several were arrested in a child brothel and died in prison. IC was able to get enough information from them for the police to arrest three dozen other paedophiles and find another two dozen children and young teens who served in nearby cities. Those children now have a substantial trust fund and many were reunited with their families."

"In any case, how can *we* contact Justice to let him know what's going on?" Hranthel tapped a finger against the table. "If we can convince him, or them, that they've been lied to, we may be able to find these people before they can wreck the economy."

"It is possible, sir. Branson had a contact method back then. A comm account that isn't registered anywhere. They left messages via the dark net and set a time for the assassins to call back. That's usually within two days. What I *don't* know is if they'll believe what we've found out."

"Then why don't you convince me, and then you'll try to convince Branson. Hopefully he and his people can convince Justice we're not trying to apprehend them, just whoever hired them."

One of the analysts from the end of the table, a middle aged woman, stood and went to the side lectern, activating the projection system.

"I'll describe the first stage in light of our new information to begin with, sir, then go through the second stage and the specific evidence we've found so far."

"Go ahead." Several of the group shifted their chairs to see better.

"We started to refer to their group as the cabal, to have a quick reference term for them. These men are mid-tier rich. Mostly inherited money, although some have gained their wealth through real estate or the market. None or very few have truly worked for a living, we believe. They resent people like Vanthin Trelner, who took his father's mid-tier industrial company and turned it into one of the top tier investment companies, despite the name. The cabal set up and funded fifty-seven fake accounts for phase one. For the next phase, we believe they are using names of their low level employees, since it's become harder to establish truly fake accounts thanks to the more stringent identification requirements we implemented after the crash."

"Employees? How did you isolate those from all the legitimate accounts in the system?"

"With considerable difficulty, sir. We found those accounts because there is no mention of those accounts in the tax filings of the employees and the address the statements were sent to were not their home addresses, but busy post office boxes in large cities. It's these accounts that are critical for phase two. Just about all the earlier fake accounts were cashed out just before or during the initial hour or two of the crash. We believe that money was funnelled from them into the employee accounts from the amounts and the timing of the purchases. They all bought Trelner Industries and the other five big investment companies stocks as the market went down. Nothing else. Even if Trelner Industries, for example, went down in price over the day, it rebounded and went higher in the days after the crash. The cabal's accounts had over five hundred thousand since they all sold everything early in the crash. All the new accounts are set to reinvest all regular dividends so the number of shares they control continues to grow. The special dividends after the companies sold off some of their buys also meant those accounts grew."

"Many small investors bought into the big six," Hranthel said, frowning. "They figured that those companies would not fail, no matter what the market did. Or that we'd bail them out. That wouldn't happen but all six were able to get loans or used their reserves to continue their buying spree. And they all released more shares from their pool to attract new investors when we allowed trading to resume."

"And that is what the cabal counted on, sir. By now, all of their employee accounts, as well as their personal accounts, will hold a sizable percentage of the big six's common shares. We aren't sure if we've found all of their accounts, but you see the number of files we do have." Each of the files was thin but there were fifty or sixty in each stack. Dark hells.

"Do they represent enough of a voting block to take control of each or all of the companies?"

"Not with the accounts we've found so far. All the cabal members must also own a considerable number of shares in their own right. But if they can sway others, unrelated to them, to their way of thinking, they could call for a no confidence vote of the boards," the analyst said. "Yet, there is another way they could cripple those companies. One that is far worse for our economy."

"How can they hope to do this?" Hranthel asked.

"By forcing the company to cash in their shares for redemption. There is legislation in our code that allows an individual investor to request the company to buy their shares at the current price, which is then fixed in respect to others seeking that same option in a one week window. No matter what the share price drops to, the company is obliged to use *that* price, not the one at the time of the stock sale. And with such a high percentage of small investors seeking to cash out, the share price would fall very quickly as other small investors panic."

Hranthel nodded. "Have someone look into who put that clause in and when. Someone from the cabal might have done so, but don't limit your thinking to them." Malther nodded.

"The result of that code is that the affected company has to start selling off *everything* they own to get the cash," the analyst continued. "If it was only one company, the others would chuckle and buy all of their assets on the cheap. We'd be down one big player and nothing would really change. Some smaller players might have enough in their reserves to move up into the higher levels. If *all* of them are trying to sell, the market crashes completely, since no one else, not even all the governments, has the cash available to mitigate the drop. We'd shut down the market when it started down, but the companies would have to try selling personally once the buy-out clause was activated and wait for the market to reopen to post the sales."

"And the cabal sits on the sidelines with the payouts and other cash and pick up the pieces," Malther said. "Or then calls for new board elections and take over the big six that way. When it is over they end up as some of the richest men in the country and since, according to their plan, we'd know nothing about their connection to the fake and employee accounts, we'd have to sign off on it."

"And you think we can stop it? How?" Hranthel asked.

"By letting the big six know what's being set up. But it is critical that we stop the hit on Trelner, sir, or convince the assassin and Trelner to co-operate with us and fake the death. Legal suggests that we need to allow the operation to start, then we can stop the cabal's operation, to prove they are actually breaking laws and various securities regulations. Conspiracy, which is about all we could charge them with at this time, is a slap on the wrist and we might not be able to ban them from having any trading accounts or work in the securities' sector unless we have that evidence. Legal is unsure if what we currently have is enough to get the suspects into the Interrogation Clinic. If we do get them in, we'll have all the information we'd need for conviction."

"How likely is it that the assassin will cooperate with us?"

"I have no idea, sir," Malther said. "I don't know how much you've heard about these two and how they operate. By their nature, they're never in the news sheets and I doubt they'll ever be caught."

"I've only seen the odd report or two from Corporate Oversight."

"Justice generally works with another assassin named Silence, as you know. From police and Corporate Oversight records, Silence is an older man, likely military trained. Justice is his protege, likely in his mid to late twenties, given when he was first noticed. They may be related but no one is sure and there are no good descriptions of them. They seem to work though the dark net for much of their contact with clients and the occasional collaboration with others for specific tasks."

"Justice has been active for five or six years. Small hits at first but he now has a decent reputation. Some sniper work but he's also very good at getting in and out of guarded locations. He might do all of that type of work now since Silence is older, likely in his mid to late fifties or possibly older. I think we can get Justice to agree because all of his known hits involve finding real resolutions for people who've been screwed over by competitors or the legal system. He won't take the job unless the target has broken the law or caused grievous harm to someone. They do their research before accepting a contract, I've been told by one of our contacts with dark net access. Won't take revenge jobs at all, so we were surprised when he took this one. It looks like revenge from our group discussions. Anyway, the officers that I've talked to also think they've even sent warnings to police and to some of proposed targets in the past. They've helped specific officers or detectives to solve mysterious deaths. Their information has *always* been correct and no one is sure how they learned of it." Malther looked around the room. The others were focused on him. He took a breath and continued.

"I did wonder when the innocents sued IC if he might have been behind it, but that idea didn't hold up. It was Mrs. Carithe Trelner, on behalf of her son Barrat. Since he did voluntarily submit to the questioning, they started a separate suit for the damage IC's idiot tech caused. He was given a decent payout, but Mrs. Trelner is a major power in the charitable community. She held a number of fundraisers scattered around the country to provide for the lawyers' fees so the plaintiffs would get all of their settlement instead of losing half or more to the lawyers. The foundation also paid for extra counselling for those affected and their families and funded the search for who had made the unfounded accusations on the tip line. The entire program was *very* well funded, sir." Everyone nodded. "I think they even have money left over so they are still funding therapists to help the last of the innocents."

"Even before the trial started, IC drastically changed their intake requirements: real evidence was needed, not just a call to the tip line," one of the analysts said. "CO and the police didn't like it and their rate of case closing dropped by at least half for a while, but it's back up to near normal now. I think they had to relearn how to do proper investigating, not just grab people and let IC sort out who was the guilty party."

"I don't know how Justice feels about Vanthin Trelner," Malther said, "but he did work with Trelner Holdings, which is the rest of the family, in the union operation. Possibly other deals they've been involved with, but we don't have any firm evidence on that connection. I don't think Branson would volunteer that information, but they've been growing recently, so I suspect they may still be involved with doing background work for the pair. We can't be sure and we don't want to spook the assassins by going for a warrant to force Branson to tell us more."

"How do we tell the big six we need to have a meeting with them?" Hranthel asked. "None of them seem to like the others, from what I've seen over the years. Some respect, but that's predator to predator, never friends who work together."

"We've already discussed that, sirs," the analyst said. "The easiest way is to call them individually and not tell them anyone else is coming. Stagger arrival times and which door to come to and that should do it."

"Good enough. Now give me the details on those stacks of files."

⋅⋅⋅⋅⋅

Haltarn groaned. *Not again,* he thought. Another note in his mail slot. He should have gone to the workout room first this morning.

"It's not from Justice this time, at least," Jula said from her desk. "It's from Mr. Trelner, to go to Justice."

"That's supposed to make me feel be better?" He sighed and picked up the message. Then he turned to the nearest computer. He wasn't sure he wanted to know what Trelner said. Or what the assassins' reaction might be when he told them.

⋅⋅⋅⋅⋅

Barrat listened to the message relayed from their unlisted messenger account for any contact with Branson's. It was Haltarn, with a reply from his father. Haltarn would be at his comm at nine tomorrow and the next three mornings to take their call. Finally. It had taken longer than he'd thought. Maybe Branson's had trouble getting through Father's office door.

Kerit grimaced when he came in to "help" with the filing. "Do you want me to get him to read it?" he asked. "Faster than having him send it to a post office and one of us travelling to pick it up."

"You're right. Slipping our message and the draft into the post bags was discreet and easy. Having him send it to a drop would take a couple of days and I want to know what he says sooner than that."

"Okay. I'll run the call from my place. You want to come over? Then we can discuss it and maybe send word back at the same time."

"And we'll need to send another payment to Haltarn for his time."

"You really enjoy using him as our go-between, don't you?" Kerit smiled as he said it.

"I do. Petty revenge, I know. I want to sit him down with some truth drugs and some Zeltin so he forgets the visit. I really want to find out why they kidnapped me. At the very top of my list, as soon as this is settled."

"Good enough."

⋙⋘⋙⋘

Nartig sat at his desk, staring at the comm. *Would they manage to call today? Or when?* He hated sitting around waiting. The message was in the centre of his desk, still unopened. Branson hovered nearby.

The comm buzzed, startling both of them. Nartig picked the handset up, then activated the speaker function. "Good morning. This is Haltarn." Trying to sound pleasant. The boss smiled. Customer relations belonged in the dark hells. Especially with this customer.

"This is Justice." The same weird modulation as before. "Who else is there, Mr. Haltarn?"

"It's Branson," said the boss. "There are some odd things happening at the Securities Services building. We thought you might be interested."

"Our message first. Open and read it, if you haven't already."

"I hadn't," Nartig said. He ripped open the envelope and took out the sheet. Unfolded it. Two sentences. No signature.

"I don't fear cowards. You will fear me."

What sounded like a chuckle came from the speaker. "About what we expected," Justice said. "But now he is warned. That won't help him survive my attention."

After several moments, Nartig shifted on his chair. Both of them must be there, discussing their response. If only they could determine their location, the police could arrest both of them. Make the world a safer...

"Please relay to Mr. Trelner that we received his message. He'll get our next one directly."

"I'll see him as soon as possible," Nartig said.

"And now, Mr. Branson, you had a comment?"

"There have been several very high level, very quiet meetings at Securities in the past week. Rumour says they finally know the why of the market crash. I don't know if you followed that news story, but they did determine how some time ago."

"We know about the trading halt software. A decent partial solution. What else have they discovered?"

"My contact isn't sure. They are not highly placed so they weren't included in any of those meetings or the research behind them. But at least eight very senior analysts were very involved. We can let know you know more if you like. There might be information you need."

Silence. Another discussion, no doubt. "Unless you have some in-formation regarding a contract for our services, we have no further in-terest in the Securities Services. Our own investments are well protected. Goodby." A click as the call disconnected.

Nartig and Branson stared at one another. "Well, maybe they won't be bothering us any more," Nartig said hopefully. He didn't really believe it.

⚓⚓⚓⚓

Vanthin grunted as the security man put a typed sheet on his desk. He picked it up and read. "About what they expected," he said and snorted. "My people have put new procedures in place. I'll be safe enough. And if it was my family that arranged it, they'll get a surprise if I die."

"Then my work here is done," the security man said. He sounded re-lieved. Idiot. "Good luck, Mr. Trelner."

"You don't need any luck if you've done proper planning," Vanthin replied. The man left and Vanthin returned his attention back to the markets. Time to take a little more profit from his crash purchases. But he'd have to declare another special dividend if the market kept going up. He had a lot of cash in the investment pool. One of the board made a tentative "suggestion" of another special dividend at the last conference call and several others agreed. He tapped and another set of figures came onto the screen.

"Don't want to give those ingrates any more of my money," he growled. "Hmmm. There was a few companies the analysts thought might be ready for harvesting." He turned to his comm. "Have Mr. Rithards come up in two hours with his top picks for immediate pur-chase," he instructed his aide.

⚓⚓⚓⚓

Barrat bit at his lip. "I wonder what those analysts found," he said after Kerit disconnected and shut down that comm line. It was spliced directly into the system so it was untraceable.

Kerit sighed. "Does it matter to the current job?"

"Not really, but I am curious since it was the crash that forced me into IC's clutches."

"Chase that down on your own time," Kerit said. "We should drop in to check on his security updates. You have any reason to visit the family? Or another client nearby?"

"I do need to go visit a couple of newer clients to see how the plan I put together for them is working out. Happy clients mean referrals. And I think Mom has another fundraiser happening in two weeks. I'll double check with her from my office comm. It wouldn't surprise her for me to come since I've been finding clients that way."

"And Liselle might want to see you again. It's been over a month." Kerit chuckled. "We should go out to the mountains this weekend. Practice. With the new silencer I just bought, no one more than six feet away from you will hear anything. That will make it harder for the police to determine where you were, which gives you a bigger escape window."

"True. I haven't done any shots over a mile in two months. The video feed messes with the scope so I'll need to use it as well. We'll just need to be sure the mountain side doesn't have any climbers on it. Hate to scare anyone like that, although they might think it's just a rock flaking off."

"That could be our next message," Kerit said. "A close miss, just to make him feel confident, dismiss your expertise and lower his security."

"I'd really like to make sure he really doesn't have a new will first," Barrat said. "That would make my life a lot easier if he does have to die."

Chapter 27

V anthin stared around the conference table as he entered the large conference room. His five main competitors were already seated, all of them glaring at each other. Damilan Hranthel, the head of the Securities Services sat at the head of the table and some flunkies, some seated, the rest milling about like sheep waiting to be told where to go filled out that end of the room.

Hranthel stood. "Thank you all for coming in this morning. I know that none of you expected anyone else to be here, but there is some information we want and need to share with you and this was the easiest way to do so. It regards the crash: the why and how. We have information on the next attack on the markets and *all* of your companies."

Silence. More glances at his competitors. They were silent. None of them blustered without a very good reason.

"The real Vegathic report was just that," Hranthel continued. "A minor drop that really didn't make any difference to the company as a whole. But the response to it was planned and calculated. Short orders went in for a number of companies in the two days leading up to that announcement. Several pundits were leaked a very different version of the report and that's what started the hysteria. We eventually tracked down every report made, who made it and where they sourced their information. We finally tracked down all of their informants. Corporate Oversight's officers were very helpful in collecting the data we needed. There were a number of fake accounts we discovered, as I'm sure you know. Those accounts started to underbid a group of twenty companies, including Vegathic. From that start, the crash was almost inevitable."

"And why *did* they crash the market?" Vanthin said. "Not that we're complaining about the chance to buy good stocks at bargain prices."

"Their aim was to raise money to buy shares in your companies, gentlemen. Each of you released more common shares to encourage new money to invest during the aftermath of the crash. This group, which we're referring to as the cabal, plan to take advantage of the shareholder buy out clause in our governing legislation. It is our guess that they control, more or less directly, at least ten to fifteen percent of each of your companies." Some shifting around the table. Vanthin stayed still. That would be a huge payout, if they had to make it. And it was likely the other sheep would panic, and *that* would be an unmitigated disaster.

"They have a number of accounts they control completely as well as their own personal ones, and if the news goes public that some people are asking for your companies to cash out their holdings it will cascade. That will cause the same sort of panic as the crash did, and we wouldn't be able to stop it. Any investor has the right to do sell back their shares to the issuing company. Shutting down the markets wouldn't help since there is no one with the economic clout to buy enough of your stocks to actually pay out everyone who asks. All six companies will fail. The cabal have divided you all up and we think they will call for new board elections, which they would be on as concerned major investors. They might have direct or indirect control of enough shares to vote you out of your positions, no matter what percentage of your firms that you and your families control personally."

"So?" Montrason asked. They'd crossed paths occasionally. Tough and determined. All six of them were, he had to admit. None of the people around the table lacked the determination and will to win. That's why they were the biggest of their kind.

"Our current plan is to let their scheme start, then we'd close the markets and arrest the cabal members and their hangers on. Inform the public of the scam and finally, rescind *all* the cash out requests as part of a criminal conspiracy, thus illegal actions. Let everyone calm down for a day or two and reopen the market."

"Do you know *who* these schemers are?" Vanthin asked.

"We know some of them at the moment, Mr. Trelner. Not all. Corporate Oversight is following the ones we know of, very covertly, so we can find the rest. All of their known communication channels are being monitored as well. We have received information that has led our analysts to believe that your death, Mr. Trelner, is the starting gun for this scheme. As the Vegathic report was for the crash."

"Should have known the whingers didn't have the balls to attack me.

What about the shooter? Do you know who it is? The idiots who gave me his message said they didn't."

Several eyes bugged out around the table and among the flunkies behind Hranthel. He snorted in derision. No real balls among them. That's why they worked for Securities instead of out in the real world.

"Pardon me?" Hranthel said after several eye blinks. "You know about the plot, Mr. Trelner? How?"

"The shooter sent a message saying he wanted to warn me. Make it more interesting for him, no doubt. The message came through one of the security firms. Told him to take his shot. Nothing's happened since. Been four days now."

"Dark hells," Malther said, then looked at his flunkies. "Our information was just that a contract was placed, and that an operative named Justice has taken it. He, and we aren't completely sure that's correct, has a record of not taking contracts that aren't justified. We don't know all of his kills, but there are a considerable number of them. He is not an amateur, Mr. Trelner. We planned to ask him not to kill you, but to make it look like he tried in order to start the cabal's agenda. We'd allow the police to report your death. Our legal department wants more than the slaps on the wrists the cabal would get for the illegal accounts they've set up to hide their total investment. Conspiracy to commit murder and defrauding your companies would allow greater sentences. It is likely they would all visit the Interrogation Clinic to determine their guilt in other matters. We have considerable evidence of their guilt already so a judge will grant that request with no hesitation." A few smiles from his competitors.

"Hranthel, have you contacted the assassin yet?" Montrason asked.

"Not yet. We planned to send a message tomorrow that we wanted to talk. It takes several days for any contact to be returned, we were told. I just hope he's not in the city already. You should be more cautious, Mr. Trelner. In case."

"My security is good and already prepared for a shooter. I have a vest for times I'm out in the open. Your little meeting disrupted my guards' plans to keep me safe. I planned to run the business out of my home for the next week or so while they run him down. I'll have a sprained ankle from a slip on a freshly waxed floor if anyone from the office asks."

"What about your family?" One of the flunkies asked. "If you aren't available, sir, they might be targeted, thinking that their deaths would distract you from dealing with the sudden cash out requests."

Montrason snorted. "Not likely. You have ice in your veins, Trelner. I'd bet against anyone's death putting you off your game." The others nodded in agreement.

"Still, warning your family is a reasonable precaution, sir." Hranthel glanced around the table. "In fact, you and your families should all be taking more care, gentlemen. In case more than one of you has been targeted. The hit on Mr. Trelner is the only one that *we* know about. If one of you dead can start their program, having several or all of you out of action would insure complete success from the confusion."

Calculating looks from all.

"You're sure about all this?" Warens asked. Hranthel and the flunkies all nodded. "I, and I am sure I'm speaking for all of us, would like to see the numbers and the basis for your suppositions. To see if there is anything else we can do to protect ourselves and our companies."

"Of course." Six briefcases appeared on the table next to each of them and the flunkies stepped back. "Each case contains the same type of information. Names of the suspect trading accounts in your companies but not the names of the cabal members we know about. Just so you don't try to take other matters into your own hands."

Warens smiled, echoed by the rest. Of course, they'd be very good. Especially since lots of official people were now watching their every move.

On their way out, Hranthel walked next to him. "Will you warn your family about the contract?"

"Maybe. I want to look at your information first."

⋐⋐⋐⋐

The fundraiser was profitable to the charity and as a source of business opportunities for him. Barrat arranged two appointments in the first half hour of mingling. Mom smiled as they danced together. "I'll be at Erithe's tomorrow afternoon at three. She and Carthan found some oddities in the investor list for Industries that they want to discuss."

"I'll check with her on timing when I get back there, so I don't book anything on top of that meeting. I've heard a rumour about Securities: They're still rummaging around in the crash data for some reason. It should be considered old news by now. If it is true, Holdings will be all right since we have no exposure to the market. Industries may have some trouble but I'm sure Father has plans to cope with anything."

"I heard about it as well," she said. "No details, of course. And I think I've found the firm that holds Vanthin's new will. But it might be a smokescreen. He's been more secretive the last few days. And the guards have been totally rearranged and a dozen more of them appeared two days ago. Any idea why that could be?"

"No," he lied. It was a good thing that Father was taking the threat seriously, but guards couldn't stop a bullet from the distances he would use. Even if he wore a vest, it wouldn't matter. Head shots were more effective anyway. Even though the funeral would be closed casket.

A commotion at the entrance drew Mom's attention and the musicians faltered and stopped. Four men, three in uniform. He stared, almost recognizing them. It was... Captain Lagrath. And Sergeant...Cranter. With friends. He wondered who they were after this time. His heart sank as they headed toward him.

"And the cause of this disturbance, Lieutenant?" Mom's voice could freeze lava in an instant.

"It's Captain, Mrs. Trelner."

"For now." There was still ice in her voice. The dancers rearranged themselves to get good vantage points. Several grinned in anticipation.

"We have reason to believe that someone has put a death contract on a member of your family."

"And you had to disrupt this event to inform me and my son of this fact?" Lagrath's jaw worked. He was not happy to be here.

"Are the two of you the only members of your family here tonight?"

"Yes," Barrat answered, Mom still on his arm. "Are we under arrest for attempted murder, Captain Lagrath? And how are you, Sergeant Cranter? It's been a few years since we last met." A few murmurs from the crowd, more jaw working for the captain. Barrat tried not to smirk.

"Where is your father?" Lagrath turned to him.

"At home, I believe," Carithe said. "He generally doesn't care to attend events like these. Barrat had some business in the city and I prevailed on him to accompany me here tonight since we don't often see each other. Is the contract on my husband, or on me?"

"Or me," Barrat said, just to complete the set. "You could have contacted our security people and apprised them of any threat. They are quite competent at what they do."

"When you have them around," Lagrath growled. Barrat nodded, acknowledging the point. "But our information is that only Mr. Vanthin Trelner is the target. A very notorious assassin has been hired."

"And again, why did you come here to inform us?" Mom said. "Did you contact the main house? I am sure they would have relayed a message to my detail if there was any danger."

"We are here to take both of you into protective custody." Lagrath said after staring at the audience and taking a deep breath.

"Why?" Barrat asked. "We have our own security people here, at the main house and at other family residences. What do you expect will happen tonight?" More murmurs from the crowd. This would top the society pages tomorrow. Mom would double the donations to the charity with one interview for the morning papers. He noticed several reporters busy taking notes in the background. Others had their cameras aimed for footage for the late evening news programs.

Lagrath growled again. "I have my orders. There are cars outside to take you to a safe place."

"We could end up safe at our family compound, or would we be drugged and taken to your headquarters or the Interrogation Clinic instead?" Barrat asked. One of the reporters pulled out a comm.

"It would be a safe house, sir," Cranter said, with a sideways look at his boss. "Nothing would happen to either of you."

Barrat looked at his mother. "Shall we decline, Mother?"

"Yes, we shall, dear."

"Then we do. I'm sure all of these witnesses will be sufficient if we're killed on our way home. Everyone will know that you tried to do your duty. It's all our own fault, not yours." He turned toward the reporters. "Please make sure your reports and articles reflect that we refused to go with them." The reporters all nodded. "Thank you." A few on-lookers giggled and smiled.

"My superiors were very insistent that you come with me," Lagrath said. His jaw was grinding. Very bad for his teeth.

"And we refuse, Lieutenant," Mom said. A man came out of the crowd. Barrat didn't know him offhand but Mom smiled at him. "Unless we are under arrest and in that event, we will contact our lawyers and wait for them to accompany us."

"As your personal attorney is not present, perhaps I may offer my assistance in this matter, Carithe?" He smiled at them and at the officers.

"Indeed, Harthal. Perhaps you can explain to the lieutenant what the words "we refuse to accompany him" means." Another round of giggles made Lagrath flush, which led to more murmurs from the crowd.

"Is there some further explanation that you do not wish to make in this very public venue due to sensitive information, Captain?" Harthal asked. "If that is the case, I would suggest that there are smaller rooms here, and with Carithe's security to accompany her and her son, that information could be shared and this impasse concluded."

"I hope you really know what you're doing," Lagrath said. A jerk of his head and the sergeant and the rest of the officers turned and headed for the door. Too bad it wouldn't slam. One of the waiters standing near there hurried over and held it open for them. They all ignored him as they left. A brief titter came from somewhere as the door closed.

"Well," Mom said into the silence. "I think we need more champagne. And music, if you please." Waiters headed for the side tables to refill their trays and the crowd started to chat about the visitation and its implications. Harthal bowed his head slightly.

"I would be cautious, Carithe," he said softly. "I've also heard some rumours. Vanthin is the target and the assassins might not care who else is nearby. You and Barrat might also be targets."

"I'll speak to him tonight or tomorrow morning," Carithe promised. The foundation's president came toward them trailed by a pair of reporters, with three others close behind. They headed off to the side of the room to fill tomorrow's society pages.

"Is there any word on who the assassins are?" Barrat asked Harthal. And who had spread the word? The people from Branson's? Or were there moles in Father's security? Not impossible if he'd just hired more people as Mom said he had.

"No, that isn't known. I heard of the rumour from a client, but I don't believe rumours unless there are independent sources. Two points now, but the police seldom act like this without real facts to back up their belief. At least when taking people off to Insanity Central."

"I'll contact our security and get more men here for when we leave. Check our car and that sort of thing. It's been in the parkade with all the others. If someone wanted to plant a bomb it might be possible, but there are guards out there to prevent any tampering."

"A good plan. And... I may have a client or two who could use the services of a discreet analyst. How long will you be in town this trip?"

"At this point, I'm not sure, sir. I don't have any security where I live but now might be a good time to arrange coverage, at least until this is all sorted out." He pulled out another business card.

Harthal nodded as he took it.

Chapter 28

Barrat went to the main house the next morning with Erithe and Dantil. They'd warned everyone else to increase their security last night as soon as they'd returned from the fundraiser. Carthan and Hethane were also on their way in. As their car stopped in the basement garage, the other one pulled in.

Mastren was confused at their arrival. They ran into him on the main level, warned by the guards on the front gate, no doubt. It satisfied Barrat on several levels to see him flustered and inarticulate.

"Where's our mother?" Erithe asked.

"Her suite, I believe, Mrs. Erithe."

"Good. We're going up to see her. Have someone fetch us coffee."

They walked past him, still stunned.

Mom was talking to someone on the comm when they arrived. She smiled and indicated the large computer screen. She hung up after a warm farewell. "The conference call is almost ready, dears."

"Did Father say anything this morning?"

"I haven't seen him yet," Mom said. "Though Mastren has probably reached him by now to let him know you've all arrived. He went somewhere yesterday morning, but not, I believe, to the office. I didn't see him even at dinner but he was home for the rest of the day."

The rest of the family logged in and Mom provided a precis of the captain's statements last night. Most had already seen the coverage in the papers. The few who hadn't planned on having words with their aides about their future job prospects.

Father stormed in just after Mom finished.

"What are you all doing here?" His jaw was set and he stared at all of those he could see. His children and their spouses stood but Mom remained seated.

"Getting ready to arrange your funeral, Father, unless you've paid off the people who want you dead," Fraklin said from the screen. "Were you planning on telling us you received a death threat, Father?"

"I get them by the truckload. No one ever said anything before."

"No *assassin* ever sent you one," Barrat commented. "At least, not that any of us were ever told. The officers from Corporate Oversight showing up at the gala last night meant that the threat is much more serious than something scrawled in crayon, which covers most of the ones you get." He'd seen some come through the mail room when he was an intern. He'd read all of them, fascinated by the bluster and needing a dictionary to understand some words. Other suggestions, he'd decided, were not anatomically possible even if one were a contortionist.

"So, the whole family is in on this?" Dark hells, nothing but bluster.

"Yes. Where were you yesterday?" Carithe asked.

"At a meeting."

"I'm guessing you were at Securities or Corporate Oversight," Barrat said to get him talking. "The ranking officer last night was with Corporate Oversight, and he wouldn't do something like that on his own. Not with his history with this family. So, Father, why don't you have some coffee and tell us why someone wants you dead this time." Barrat tried to keep his voice calm and rational. At least for now. Ranting and yelling back at his father for being stupid and obtuse would be counterproductive. But enjoyable, he had to admit.

To everyone's surprise Father went to a chair near Mom and sat next to her. "I didn't say anything when I returned here because Securities has some idiot idea I wanted to think about. That the big crash was part one of some huge plot by a bunch of whingers who think they can take me and five others down with the push of a button."

"Or a single shot?" Dantil asked.

Father waved away the suggestion. "I haven't finished examining their evidence. The guards are on higher alert. I didn't think any of you cared what happened to me. Or if you did, it was because of your inheritances. Which are not the same as you think."

"We knew you changed your will, Vanthin," Mom said. "And I have observed the guards closely in the past few days. A definite change in procedure and the fact that ten guards showed up at the gala and insisted we take a different car to ensure Barrat and I returned home safely was a very good indication that something was and is terribly wrong. Do you *know* who is trying to kill you?"

Father seemed put out at Mom's comment. His surprise ruined? Or that they didn't seem to care about inheriting? They did have enough shares with some loyal friends to keep control, no matter what the will said. But there were some odd things in the general shareholder lists. He wondered if those names would match up with what Securities had found.

"The killer didn't say. Just that it would be a bullet. He intimated if I paid off the whingers they might cancel the contract. I told him to take his best shot. I have a story ready to go out that I've sprained an ankle to keep the idiot investors from worrying that I'm at home, not in the main office as usual."

"A good plan," Barrat said. "But maybe that was just a fake out, to polarize your thinking, while he does something else."

"Like what?" A high powered scowl in his direction.

"No idea," he said cheerfully. "Mess with a car? Infiltrate the new guards you've hired? Could be anything."

"What did Securities tell you, Father?" Fraklin asked.

Silence. Father stared at them. They stared back. Father broke eye contact first. Barrat almost didn't believe it.

"They seem to think the real group behind all this own, control or influence up a significant percent of Industries, *as well as* our five biggest competitors. On my death by the idiot assassin and some upsets in the market, they demand to cash out. Five companies our size could absorb the collapse of one, which would be fine, but Securities think all six of us are targets. They don't know why I was picked to start it all, or if the CEO's of the other five are also being set up to be killed."

"Maybe this group doesn't like you the most?" came from the screen.

"Aside from providing information on their theory, what is Securities planning to do?" Mom asked.

"Ask the assassin not to kill me," Father said. "It's supposed to be someone called Justice. The idiots from Branson's didn't tell me that, and *they're* the ones in contact with him."

Barrat stared. Securities knew about the hit, and wanted to call it off? He had to contact Kerit very soon. For all he knew, Kerit planned to do the hit by himself to spare him making the decision to kill his father. It would be like the man. And it would be the wrong thing to do. Maybe. They didn't have enough information to make the decision at the moment. What in the dark hells was going on that they didn't know about? Who had sent the message to them if it wasn't cranky business owners? The names had all been from people Father had bought out. They needed to do some more research. Quickly.

"Any word from the assassin yet?" Fraklin asked.

"Not that they've said. And they'd send someone to bring the message the moment it arrived, I was told. Branson said it would take at least a day for them to hear back from him or his partner. At least they're smart about security."

"What about the plot itself?" Erithe asked. "How did the crash benefit whoever is behind this?"

Father stood so everyone here and the camera could see him. He stared at them for so long Barrat wondered if he was just going to leave. Then he explained. It was a good summary. And it explained a lot. He and Haltarn were going to have a long chat very soon.

Mastren came in, supervising a footman pushing a trolley full of coffee and various nibbles. Father immediately went over for coffee. The rest looked at each other. The footman, Welker, was dismissed after he parked the trolley. He nodded and left. Mastren left after fiddling with the coffee urn. No one spoke except for banalities about coffee for several minutes.

"It sounds so..." Carthan said after Dantil checked the hallway to ensure they were alone.

"Insane," Father agreed. "But all the investors that Securities says are fake are in the company database. I checked. Bought most of their shares the day of the crash or were in the queue when the markets re-opened. One thing Securities suggested is that we block all of those accounts from performing any real actions. They think we should let them input their orders and think the fakers have done their job. Their coders say they can shut down the market within a minute, but they seem to think letting the scheme run for a little while is best. To establish the whingers' guilt. I know what I'd consider if all these officials weren't involved."

"What?" Barrat asked.

"Contact that killer and have him take out his employers. He must know who they are. Not sure how to do it, but I'm sure someone in the company knows how to send a message."

"But Securities is contacting him directly. They would go through Branson's to establish credibility. " Mom said. "So the inciting incident for all this..."

"Is my death, apparently." Father seemed proud that the cabal thought him too dangerous to let live. That he might spoil their plot. His ego was... "Securities wants to have the killer fake a shot and they'll put out a report that I'm dead. Then the whingers activate their plan and once it's underway, Securities shuts down the market, each of the big companies shut out their investor lists and Corporate Oversight arrests all the whingers. Market reopens a day or two later. Once the sheep change their underwear. Fairly simple, but the timing is tricky."

"Do they want to start this early or late in the day?" Barrat asked despite himself. This was beyond strange.

"There seemed to be two schools of thought," Father admitted. "One is around lunch, the other late afternoon. Just to limit the time until the market usually closes, I think. They'd likely leave the market closed for a day or so once the plan is active, so they can finish tracking down the whingers and take them over to IC to be sure they've found all of them."

"Is the family at risk?" Fraklin asked. "If so, we need to get the older kids back from university or where they work and the younger children from their schools."

"Securities doesn't think so," Vanthin said. "But I wouldn't trust that. I doubt this assassin would target the children. Maybe they have others who aren't as picky. Shareholders with trustees can be worked around in the grand scheme of things. All adults..." he glanced at Mom, "should take precautions."

"That's why the lieutenant showed up at the fundraiser?" Carithe asked. The hand holding the cup and saucer trembled once as she set it down on a side table.

"Yes. You two were the only ones out that night with minimal security. Saw in the papers what you told him." A snort of approval.

"We also called in for reinforcements before we left to return home," Barrat pointed out. "And would have gone there with more security if we'd known about this earlier." Father ignored the comment. He wasn't very surprised.

The conference didn't last much longer. Barrat was silent on the drive back to Erithe's. He had to warn Kerit not to take the shot.

He had his chance after they arrived. Phonbul had several messages for him. One from Kerit. Thankfully.

"I'm going to deal with these before lunch," he said, waving the papers as Erithe headed for the nursery and Dantil for their office.

He entered the code for Kerit's home number, which could forward his call anywhere. After two rings, a familiar voice answered.

"Things are complex here," Barrat said. "I may need to stay a few more days. Don't get any more flowers until I return." The mention of flowers referred to the hit and the rest meant stand down. "There may be some documents on the way." Information on the hit incoming.

"Okay by me. Don't want to have those pretty blooms wasted," Kerit said. "I'll check the mail in two days, just in case something comes in." He'd wait two days, and if he didn't hear anything in that time frame, he'd go to ground and swap out all the passwords and locations of various items. And would be cranky if he had to pack up all the toys. Again.

"Good idea. I'll contact you as soon as I know when my flight is."

"See you soon, lad," Kerit replied. Barrat set the comm down. One major hurdle down. Now to find out what Securities wanted them to do.

✦✦✦✦

Nartig groaned again at the sight of an envelope in Jula's hand. And the smirk on her face. As he reached for it, Branson came into the operations room.

"That's very important, Haltarn. Possibly the most important document we've ever had to handle." Branson was paler than usual.

"For our allies?"

"Yes. We need to stop Justice from a fulfilling a contract."

"Whose?" Nartig had a very bad feeling.

"The one on Vanthin Trelner. You know, the one Justice just accepted."

"Dark hells."

"Very much so. Set up the call."

✦✦✦✦

Kerit listened to the relayed message from Barrat again. Strange things were happening, it seemed. He hadn't left for the capital yet and decided to stay in Beranga. For now. He went into his basement to check on chatter from the dark net. Someone had to know something. Or there might be a message from Barrat, assuming he could access the dark net without anyone from his family being aware.

Nothing. Securities was playing this very close, he decided. He almost went back upstairs after stashing the other cable away. If things were tense, Barrat might leave a separate message on their private comm. He could listen to it here, but he was restless. Retrieving it from the same cubbyhole as the cable, he tucked it into a pocket and left the house.

The Beranga Shopping Centre was the biggest in the city. Lots of people with comms to hide his signal. He stopped in the food court, and bought some coffee. Made his way into the middle of the seating area and slipped the comm out.

One of the older models without any fancy location software, the unit drew a few glances from younger diners.

"Old comm for an old fart," was one comment he overheard from a nearby table. Kerit didn't let his amusement show. Be what people expect and they never remember much else about you.

There was only one message. He faked dialling a number but played the message instead.

"This is Haltarn from Branson's. Securities has given us some crucial information about your hit on Vanthin Trelner, Justice. It's a set up to completely wreck the economy. My boss has seen some of their data. This is real. Very real. You were lied to by the people paying you. Please stand down until we can talk. I'm in the office from nine tomorrow. Someone from Securities will be here to explain. Your fee will be covered, whatever happens."

He shut down the comm and sipped his coffee. No wonder Barrat called. This was getting much stranger. Kerit wondered if this had anything to do with Barrat's kidnapping by Branson. Who *had* been their employer on that job? Questioning Haltarn was quickly moving up their "to do" list. They had his apartment address, so that part would be easy. A few minutes with a truth drug and a little Zeltin and all the details would be revealed. Then they would decide how to proceed.

The next morning at nine he had the call ready to go. Distortion software up, the comm linked directly into the computer system. The recorder started up. He clicked on the code number.

"This is Silence. Explain. Five minutes." he said when someone picked up on their end. If Securities was trying to trace the call, this limited the risk they could do so.

"My name is Vertin Malther. I'm with the Securities Services. We've been trying to figure out the source of the crash since it happened. We found evidence that a small group of disgruntled investors that we're calling the cabal used a series of fake accounts to short the market that day. They manipulated buy orders during the day that brought the market further into the abyss. The Vegathic report showed the true state of that subsidiary, but a different one, much more damaging, was leaked into several investor forums from accounts controlled by the cabal. The difference made many people think there was a cover-up and they were more prone to panic. Then the hysteria spread into the smaller investors. And, well, the market collapsed."

"And now?"

"The cabal used their profits from the crash to buy into the top six investment firms. Trelner Industries is one of them. Their plan seems to be to start another crash, but they have more legitimate looking fake accounts this time plus their private holdings. Together, those accounts hold over a solid percentage of all six major investment companies. The plan is to start the crash, and when Securities shuts the market down, to have those accounts request a cash out to redeem their shares. Once that news becomes public, many more small investors will join in, not realizing what the effect will be. The six companies' share prices will fall quickly and the payout will potentially bankrupt each of them. I don't know if you're familiar with the regulations governing such an option?"

"Not as such, Mr. Mather. Keep talking."

"The cash-out clause freezes the share price. And, within one week, any *other* investor can also ask for a cash-out with the same price. If only one firm was targeted, the market would survive. All six go down and it is absolute chaos. We think their plan is intended for the cabal to take control of these firms through proxies and votes of non-confidence of the current boards. There's currently fifteen people that we've found so far in this group but we think there might be a few more. Enough board positions that they can take the top spots in all of them. We want and need to stop them to protect thousands, maybe millions of people and require your help to do so."

"Renege on our contract? We do have a reputation for completing our assignments. Our word is well regarded in our profession."

"You've been lied to by your employer, so that should mitigate any backlash. The death of Vanthin Trelner seems to be their go signal. We aren't sure why he was chosen or if he's the only one. Legal says the plot has to start, allowing the first stage of their plan to activate, so that we can get them on more than just conspiracy charges. We want you or Justice to take a shot, but make it look potentially deadly, not truly fatal. After Trelner's death is announced to the reporters, you get paid by the cabal, and later that day or the next we shut down the conspirators. Trelner appears alive and well once the plotters are in custody and the clean up work begins. Members of the cabal are already under discrete observation by Corporate Oversight. We will take all of them down."

Kerit didn't respond immediately. What was really going on? He had to talk to Barrat before he gave a final answer. See what he thought about this whole thing. What had he already learned that he couldn't trust to an unencrypted system?

"We will confer. Expect a call in two days at this time."

"Where is Justice? Is he here in Herithan already? Can you..."

He disconnected the call and stared at the wall. What could they do? He had to

⚜⚜

The four men stared at the comm in Branson's office as the call ready tone came on. Nartig glanced at his boss after he disconnected. Who had their contact at Vegathic really been working for? Could he be one of the conspirators? And how did the kid's kidnapping fit into this?

Mather leaned back in the chair. "At least they're not dismissing the idea out of hand," he said. "I'll take some coffee now, if you don't mind."

"Always in order," Nartig said, forcing some cheer into his voice. "I'll get some for everyone."

He left the door open and shut it on his return. The boss looked pale. Nartig handed out cups from the tray and let their guests have first crack at the sugar and cream.

"We may have some other information Securities need to know," Branson said slowly. "Before the crash, we were asked by a high level employee at Vegathic to keep an eye on the analyst who wrote that report to ensure that he didn't slack off. Then he encountered Barrat Trelner leaving the building from his interview. We were asked by our contact to discover what Trelner knew, if anything, of the analysis."

Malther looked at his colleague. "The kidnapping? Was you?"

Branson sighed. "Yes. Dark hells, we were responsible. On orders from our employer. We were told to find out what young Trelner knew and find it out quickly. We used several drugs on him and found that he knew nothing except that his friend, the analyst who wrote it, was working on a big project with a specific deadline. They had a tentative plan to meet for dinner, but the analyst cancelled as he'd just been given the data that morning. He said they'd get together later in the week once he had a good start on the report. He didn't quite understand why there was a deadline by what we learned in monitoring him. It was due the day before the crash. Plenty of time for any final changes to the rigged one. They probably had access to whatever he had on the company servers."

"Agreed. It was impossible for them to meet since Trelner was in your custody. Why did you use the Zeltin?"

"We didn't want anyone to know what we'd asked him about," Nartig said. "And he wasn't harmed at all, not while we had him. IC, on the other hand..."

A wave of Malther's hand dismissed that line of distraction. "Vegathic was worried about the report? Who in specific was your contact there?"

"Petran Caldith. A vice-president in their analysis department. All of our contracts and such have Vegathic logos. The comm number is listed to them and the cheques were from Vegathic accounts. We were told our company was used to ensure there was no internal leakage of their data. I was... concerned once the market crashed, but I was assured by Caldith there was no correlation between our actions and the crash. We were instructed to let young Trelner go and ensure his safe return to his apartment the day before the crash. So we did. He reached home safely, about one in the morning. Went to bed quickly and we stopped observing him."

The other man looked at a paper from a folder that hadn't been opened before. "Caldith's one of the cabal. Fairly high up, we think."

"Dark hells," Nartig said. "We were set up. I guess they decided on the fly to involve the Trelner boy in their scheme since they met just outside the Vegathic building. Try to pin something on him to distract any investigation into who else might have leaked the report. And it very nearly worked."

❧❧❧❧❧

Barrat took Peykan and two other guards with him to go to the bookstore. He knew he was safe from Justice, but couldn't be sure anyone else hadn't been hired. They'd seen nothing on the dark net, but since they'd sent a direct message, the cabal might know of others with their skill set. The vest under his coat was moderately uncomfortable. Liselle understood there was a problem since the news had made the front sheets so they'd have coffee in the shop next door instead of a walk in the park before an early dinner as they'd originally planned.

They'd put an additional entrance from the bookstore directly into the coffee shop, he noticed. And everything sparkled and a sprightly tune played, not loud enough to be distracting. Excellent. There were even a decent number of heads who were *not* employees visible in the stacks. Even better.

Liselle wasn't working cash today. A bouncy young woman was. She beamed at him when he entered.

"Welcome to Taltron's Books, sir. Do you need help in finding anything today?"

"I've got him, Anthie," Liselle said, coming around a bookcase, neatly full. "Hi, Barrat. I'm glad you could come over with all the excitement."

"The store looks great," he said, taking her hand briefly and an even briefer kiss to her cheek. "How's your dad feeling?" They headed for the office first. The two guards split up and shadowed them. A woman with a stack of books headed for the register.

"Much better. Doctor Halli is helping him so much. He's started looking through the publisher's catalogues last month. Found some books he insisted we bring in. And they're selling well. Very well." They went in the small office and closed the door.

"And total sales?"

"Rising every week," she said. "The readings have also been going very well. I met your mother at another one two weeks ago. She left late just so we could chat with her. Mind you, we were exhausted but I do want to meet her again. So did my mom and dad."

"Should I worry?"

"No. She and my parents seemed to be chatting a lot. I'm sorry you couldn't come, but I did get the flowers you sent last week. We put them up by the register for some extra colour."

"Deadlines," he said. "I need to keep my clients happy so they give me good referrals so I get enough work to take little vacations to come see you." A brief hug stretched out and the kiss was even better.

A tap at the door gave them enough time to move apart. Mrs. Taltron came in, smiling. "I'm glad you came for a visit, Barrat. Dad's been saying he wants to ask you some questions on that analysis you did for us."

"Coffee comes first, Mom," Liselle said. "Then interrogation. We're civilized." The look on her face warmed his heart. He still had to be wary, but Liselle was the one woman he wanted to keep in his life.

"Oh, all right," Mrs Taltron said. "Shoo and let me get some work done. I have a poetry group wanting to set up a multiple author reading in three weeks. Barely enough time to get the books in and arrange the advertising." She indicated the door. "Out. Now."

They reached the packed coffee shop and the server, who was *not* the owner this time, got their usual orders ready. Plus plain coffee for the guards. Barrat paid and they found a small table near the back. Plenty of cover from the street and the guards split up to keep an eye on them and the rest of the customers.

"I should be able to go back to university this fall," Liselle said. "Now that all the payouts came through. I'm glad we were able to prove that scum was the one who called the police on Dad. To think that we considered him a friend." Tears threatened. Barrat took her hand.

"The past is that," he said gently. "Look toward the future."

"You say that. So does Doctor Halli."

"One guess where *I* learned it from," Barrat replied. "I try not to think about what happened to me in IC. Most of the time I can. Sometimes it comes back. About all I can do about those times is to remember that it *is* past. For your family, it's almost past. Every day you all survive is a win. I'm glad you're going to be able to go back to school. Same one?"

"I was looking at other schools," she said with a blush. "The accounting course at Beranga College is well respected and my credits would transfer with no problems." He blinked. She looked down and away from him. "But I..."

"*I* think that could be an excellent idea," Barrat said with a smile. "I hadn't thought of that possibility. I wasn't sure if or when you'd be able to resume. Or if you could get away from the store."

"It was a faint hope for so long," Liselle said. "But now I have practical experience that should make the corporate classes easier. Reconciliations were a nightmare before this. Now I don't really need to be that awake to do them."

"The campus is on the other side of town from your office." Barrat sensed she was working up to something. "I want to live on campus to make getting to classes easier, but... I do want to keep seeing you. Weekends at the least."

"Do your parents like the idea of us?"

"Mom is on side. Dad... he's in the "my little girl is growing up" phase. But by the time the semester starts, he should be okay. I talked to Doctor Halli about it. She didn't laugh out loud but I knew she was inside."

"He may start the grilling today, then," Barrat said. "I've been with other women, Liselle. Paid ones for the most part. I've never been in a relationship like we have. The women I went to university with were looking for a fancy house, jewelry, and an allowance. Not love. Not a family."

"And you haven't been with anyone else since we met. At least that's what you *said*." Brows arched up.

"I've been saving money so I can keep coming back here. I chose Beranga mostly because it was far away from all of my family, but I keep finding good excuses to keep seeing them. And you."

"Business trips are wonderful things."

"This one has been up and down," he admitted. "Very up, at the moment." She smiled at him.

"We read about the death threat on your father in the news sheets," she said. "He didn't tell the family anything about it?"

"He came clean this morning," Barrat said. "That's why the extra guard. The whingers, as he calls them, might be after the rest of us. I don't think so, but we aren't taking chances. I'll likely have a guard or two when I head back home. I have no idea where I'm going to put them, other than in my spare bedroom. They'll insist on staying at my office, since my apartment is right upstairs. That would seriously impact any visits." She looked frightened.

"However, the whole thing should be resolved in a week or so, Father says." He couldn't say anything about what Securities' plan was, not out here in the open. "With the news of a possible hit going public, Father's plan is to have the police track down the whingers and get them under arrest so no one can pay the assassin, so he won't bother taking the shot since he won't be paid." He wished he could tell her the entire plan.

∽⌒∽⌒∽

"What the dark hells is happening with Trelner?" The top six members of the cabal seldom met in person, but the stories in the recent news sheets had them all worried. They'd come too far to let anything stop them now. Too much work had gone into this plan.

Caldith shook his head. "Someone must have heard rumours on the hit and sold the information to the police for a lighter sentence or cash. Everyone needs to double check their security. I know a company that's good at not asking questions if we want an outside audit."

"We should keep things in-house for now," Melkin said. "We can't risk any leaks. What we need to do right now is to determine if we should put stage two on hold or not. If Securities knew what the plan is we would have heard about it. We have people in there for that very reason. Everyone takes a deep breath and relax. It's..."

"If we keep on target, that gives Securities and Corporate a shorter time frame to figure out what else we're doing," Jonarth interrupted. "If we wait, there's more of a chance they'll get wise to our employee accounts. Or to do something else with the market code. The automated trading halt is going to give us some trouble. We can't control what the individual investors' panic will do to the rate of the market fall."

"True," said Caldith. "We should contact Justice and tell him something that will reassure him, no matter what we decide about the timing. If we decide to postpone the plan, maybe we should tell him that things are too hot for us right now with all the publicity. We'd contact him when the hit is back on."

"We do not want to mess with them," Terbei said. "I've heard some other things, now that his name's out there. We need to find who leaked the hit information and make sure no one can trace the offer back to us."

"But first we need to decide on timing," Renten said. "All in favour of staying with the original timetable, raise your hands." Four hands went up, including his. Two stayed down.

"Why not stay on schedule?"

"I think a short delay is best," said Jonarth. "We're already planning everything happening in a week or so. I say wait. Two weeks max, so we're still mostly on target. Everyone and their guards are running around on high alert right now. Two weeks makes it into sleep deprivation time. The guards and everyone else will assume the hit was called off and relax. And none of my people have seen Trelner in his office lately. That'll make the shot impossible, and that's what we've insisted on, so Justice won't try for anything else. He'll *have* to wait until Trelner comes outside. And he won't chance killing any innocents. That's well established in his history."

"Same thoughts I had," Terbei said. "We shouldn't delay long, just long enough to lull everyone, especially Trelner, into thinking they're safe. If he stays in the house, there's no good way for a shooter to get to him. Justice might pull out of the contract if he couldn't deliver. All we have is the contract, but we haven't paid him anything yet. Not even into the escrow account."

"I agree with the short delay," said Melkin. "And with the extra security, it would be very hard, if not impossible to change to a covert method. The only way Justice could get close enough to Trelner to poison him or something like that would be to join the new guards he's hired. And he might refuse or need a long delay to make the arrangements. Plus their security might be looking very closely at any new hires."

"It sounds like we are agreed," Renten said. "Caldith, can you send the message?"

"First thing tomorrow."

◈◈◈◈

Kerit checked his dark net account late that night in case Barrat found access to an unmonitored computer. There wasn't a message from him, but there was one from their employer. The cabal. A trite name but he supposed it made sense to have a short label for them.

"A two week delay since he's hiding in the house," he mused after reading the overly long message. All they'd needed to do was to send one line, maybe two. "Need to tweak their noses. Who's the leak and where's our money? That should do."

He typed for a few minutes, going back and changing a few things before he sent it. He sent an update of the documents through the messenger system as well as a copy of this message to Barrat's dark account, then downloaded the original message and a variation on his reply and printed them, using gloves to pull fresh paper out of their special package. He'd drop the envelope in the mail tomorrow for Branson's. That should stir the idiots up.

◈◈◈◈

Barrat spent the next two days working in Erithe's second floor sunroom. He'd brought his main computer along this time and it was easier to get started on the analyses that he needed to do than sit around waiting for someone to take a shot at his father.

Dantil knocked on the door in the late afternoon. "The assassin's sent another message. We're all meeting at the main house tomorrow morning. The others will conference in."

"Good." The cabal must have contacted Kerit.

"The Securities people are sending someone in the grocery truck," Dantil said. "I guess they *really* want to know if the assassin's going to play nice with us."

The man from Securities introduced himself as Vertin Malther. Barrat ended up sitting next to him around the conference table. A large screen at the end of the table with a camera currently showed Fraklin, with smaller icons for the rest of his siblings and their spouses. Haltarn was also present, sitting next to Father. Barrat wasn't sure he wanted him around, not any more. There was something in the way both newcomers looked at him that he didn't like.

Father sat at the head of the table, naturally. Malther turned to him. "There are two main items we need to discuss, Mr. Trelner. The first is to discuss what you were sent from the assassins. I was present and spoke to Silence on a conference call at Branson's offices. Justice was not present and we are sure that he is in Merithan by now. We asked if he was here but Silence ended the call before answering. I explained our rationale and plan and Silence said they would confer. This letter reached Branson's yesterday. It has not been opened. We hope it includes their agreement."

At Malther's nod, Haltarn took an envelope from the inner pocket of his suit coat and handed it to Father. He ripped it open and there were two pieces of paper.

"This one is from the whingers to the assassin," Father said. His eyes flickered as he skimmed the content. "Telling him to stand down for two weeks, it seems." That sheet went to Malther. The second received the same quick scan. "This is the reply, which is simple: we agree to the delay but put the half the fee in an escrow account in the event of a default. He didn't include the number."

"Not unexpected," Malther said. "And quite reasonable from their point of view. I don't know how many people decide not to go through with a contract once they realize it's really going to happen. Two weeks delay isn't a bad option. The cabal would assume no one knows we're in communication with the assassin or that we know the cabal's entire plan." He turned to Father. "What measures are you and the others taking to protect your companies?"

"We aren't sure exactly what the others are doing, Mr. Malther. Likely the same as we are. All the target accounts you provided the names for can be frozen very quickly," Fraklin responded from the screen. "That includes log-ins, trading instructions and most important, the cash-out activation. Our experts have set up a fake website for when one of those accounts is logged in. It looks perfect but just records everything, including the location of the person who logged in. The cabal might have automated the log in procedure to activate all the accounts in a short time frame. This method prevents anything from hitting the system in the event they go live late at night, for instance."

"Technically, the separate sites are illegal," Malther said. "But Securities will sign off on it for now. I'll check with the other companies to see what they're doing tomorrow."

"Good, but now we have you on record as agreeing, just in case," Father said with that "I've got you now" smirk that Barrat had seen far too often. Justice was totally ready to eliminate this...

Malther pulled a document out of his jacket. "This is from Securities. A blanket pardon for acts done to protect the market and our economy. It expires in three weeks. But our people will be watching everything that all six companies do very carefully. Behave yourself, Mr. Trelner." A snort answered that comment.

"So," Barrat said. "*Are* the assassins going to cooperate with your plan? What contingency plan do you have if they decide not to play?"

"We should get their decision soon," Haltarn said. "It might be in the next envelope. Or if Justice is here in town already, which is likely, it may take them some time to confer and pass information back and forth. Have your guards noticed anything odd in the past few days? Someone walking or driving past the grounds often?"

"Nothing like that, and they're also scanning the local rooftops for lines of sight since a shot was ordered," Dantil said. "For this house and on all the company offices and our homes. Nothing so far. We've increased security on all family members, including our younger members. Those in university are studying at home for now, and the boarding schools have increased their security. All of our kids have a screamer at all times. We're as prepared as we can be."

"That must be why they wanted to wait two weeks," Father said. "Let us get complacent and drop our guard. That won't happen now."

"But we should make it *look* like it's happening," Barrat said. "Once they think we're complacent, that would be the time to strike."

"I agree," said Haltarn. "Show the cabal what they expect to see."

"I believe you said there was another matter," Mom said. "If we are in agreement on what we'll do for the next two weeks."

"True." Malther looked past him at Haltarn, then focused on him. Barrat's danger sense went off. "We also know who kidnapped you, Barrat. It was part of the cabal's plan. Improvised, to be sure, but it was one of them who ordered it."

Barrat went cold inside. That person would die. He didn't care what it might do to Securities' investigation.

Erithe was sitting next to him and took his hand. "Who took me?"

Haltarn took a deep breath. "Branson's. And I was..." Barrat was on him in a second, his hand around Haltarn's throat.

Dantil managed to pull him off and held him in an iron grip. Malther helped Haltarn stand, wheezing.

"What's the name?" Barrat growled.

"We're not going to mention that information just now," Malther said. "He's one of the cabal, that's all you need to know at the moment." He looked over at Haltarn. "Could you explain what happened?"

"Sure," Haltarn said, rubbing his throat. "We had no idea of the bigger picture at that point. We only figured it out when all this came up. Please sit down, Mr. Trelner. We had no idea that Corporate Oversight would be involved or that the crash would be blamed on you."

Father stood and went over to Haltarn, who immediately folded over, Father's fist in his gut. Malther sighed and knelt beside him, helping him to sit up while he whooped in air.

Father came over to him next. Dantil released him and moved to one side. Barrat was surprised at the fierce hug. "Those bastards are going to pay," Father said. "Starting with Branson's." Father let go of him and turned to the men. "So *why* was Barrat taken?"

Malther helped Haltarn into a chair, still winded enough that he couldn't talk yet, then turned to speak. "It seems that Branson's was hired to ensure that no one interfered with the analyst or his report, since its release was their signal for part one of their plan. It had to be released on that particular day because of the short orders to be in place first. Your son met with the analyst outside Vegathic's headquarters after his interview and they spoke. Once Barrat was identified, their employer wanted to know if the analyst told him anything about the report or made any arrangements to give you any of the data. Mr. Haltarn was ordered to follow you, and see what you did. You went to the gym and he followed you in, saw you speak to your sister and make arrangements to meet up later in the week. That interaction made their employer even more suspicious."

"Then you were Kintol. Who said he loved the gym and never followed up." Erithe headed for Haltarn but Dantil stopped her.

"Yes," croaked Haltarn. "We were given orders to take Barrat that night. When he came out of the building and headed toward the bars, it seemed ideal. We discovered very quickly he had no knowledge of the report. The kidnapping scenario was implemented to distract attention from his disappearance. I was not in favour of the plan, but I did as I was told. We let him go on orders from our employer, and our people made sure he reached home safely once he woke up. We were as surprised as anyone at the market crash the next day. Looking back, it was all part of their plan to ensure panic and distract everyone from looking in their direction. Some of them must have leaked information on the kidnapping into the hysteria after the crash." His voice steadied as he spoke. "That's what brought Corporate Oversight into thinking you were involved. Why they suggested taking you to IC."

Silence. Barrat was surprised that he still wanted to pound Haltarn into the carpet. Revenge. It was a very good thing he didn't have a pistol or a knife with him. He shut his eyes and turned away.

"Get out of here," Father said. "I don't want to see anyone from your organization here again. Give whatever comes from the killers to Securities. If I see one of your people in my house or offices, no one will ever see them again. Understand?"

"Here's my contact information," Malther said. "I have a car on standby to pick us up." Sounds of people moving. No one came near him and he heard some comments from the screen that he ignored.

"Barri?" Mama asked gently. "Do you need some quiet time?"

"No, I need to hit something, Mama. A lot."

"All right, dear. Go kill a punching bag." A quick hug and she left. He opened his eyes and saw Carthan near him.

"I'll help you," he said. Barrat nodded.

"And soon we'll get the bastards," Father said, still within arm's reach of him. "Destroy all of them."

⋞⋟⋞⋟

Barrat left the room, escorted by his brother. Vanthin scowled. The bastards would pay, all right.

"Does anyone know how to access these killers?" he asked, looking around the room and at the screen. "I don't want to be on the far end of the information chain any more. If we can talk to them directly, I'd be more confident of our success in interfering with the cabal's plan."

"I know about the dark net," came from the speakers. The picture flipped to Sathira. His oldest daughter. The one who was always proper and followed the rules.

"How did that happen, dear?" Carithe asked.

"That's not important now, Mother. What matters is that I *can*. What's the names of the assassins?"

"Justice and Silence. Have you ever heard of them?" Vanthin asked.

"Yes. They were involved in a situation that Holdings was involved in. One of the business owners contacted them long before we were involved. For some reason, *they* suggested that Holdings could help them. None of us had any direct contact with them. They don't take contracts unless they're very sure the hit is justified, Father. Do we know what they were told about this situation?"

"That some whingers whose businesses failed and I bought up a few years ago finally raised enough money to see me shot," Vanthin said with a shrug. "For the record, I have never enticed anyone into making the stupid decisions that sent their company into near bankruptcy. That they did entirely on their own. I only reaped what they sowed." His glare dared anyone to comment. "Like the gambler from Norgrant that you started with."

"Can you contact these men, dear?" Carithe said. "If we have our own channel of communication, we won't need Branson. We can send copies of what we discuss to Securities as necessary."

"I know someone who can. I've used this person to find facts and such against my local competitors. He's very good with the diplomacy needed for the dark net's denizens."

"Good," Vanthin said. "Tell them we want to put contracts on all the cabal members. Last one to die should be the one who ordered Barrat's kidnapping. Or maybe just maim that bastard. So he lives but can't ever walk again."

"I'll start the process, Father. I'll send word to everyone when I hear back. Tell Barri we'll see him soon."

The others soon logged off. He took a deep breath and faced his wife. "I was so pissed at Barrat the summer he graduated. Thought he spent all his time drinking and lying around, supported by that apartment building and any dividends I paid out. Not doing anything for what he was trained for."

"He couldn't *get* a real job, Father," Erithe said. "And he'd heard and experienced what it's like for your children to work at headquarters. He wanted no part of that particular dark hell and I don't blame him. I plan to have my children's first jobs in places that won't be what I and the rest went through. Vegathic and the other big companies he interviewed at wanted a puppet with the Trelner name who mouthed scripted platitudes at shareholder meetings. Not doing analysis. The slightly smaller companies where he sent resumes thought he was working for you as a front man, to give you inside information on those companies so you could take them over. None of them would hire him. That's what his five months of job searching did for him. When he recovered from the brain damage at IC, I found him a small job doing an analysis for some friends with private corporations. They were and still are, too small for Industries to bother with. That's the type of client he decided that he wanted to work with."

"And then he moved to Beranga."

"You know who his first clients there were?" Carithe asked. He shook his head. "Two young men who opened a paintball range on their fathers' land. He was paid four hundred to help them develop a business plan. But that was the start of his success."

"I know he's doing much bigger companies now. Word is it was his plan that bought out the industrial area in Beranga. Got you all to start Trelner Holdings. Hmph."

"Companies come to us now," Carithe said. "They wouldn't if you were involved, Vanthin. They don't trust you or your methods. But as a result of our helping all those companies we also have a network that the cabal won't expect to be used against them. And there is enough internal capitol in our war chest to fund some large share purchases since we are looking for another deal but haven't settled on one. With fairly minimal effort, we can bolster support to prevent the type of crash Securities is afraid of. With Securities' approval, nothing will show in the market data. But if each of the six targets release more shares for our friends and their own to purchase, it will dilute what the cabal controls and limit what the damage another crash can do."

"A good plan," he admitted. He glanced over at the clock. "Lunch in an hour. Barrat should be tired by then. I'm going to send word of these developments to the other five myself. See if they want to contribute to the contracts on the cabal. Let your allies know about the share plan." He smiled at her and she returned a small one back. That hadn't happened in a long time.

❖❖❖❖❖

Barrat was covered in sweat and his shoulders were screaming in pain, but he didn't want to stop.

Carthan grabbed his gloved hands. "That's it for now, Barri," he said. "Shower off. Lunch is soon."

"I don't know if I can eat anything," Barrat admitted, his torso glistening with sweat. He brushed his hair from his eyes with a forearm. It fell back into his eyes as soon as he moved.

"You won't know until you sit down. Shower. Now." One of the guards came over and helped Carthan remove the gloves.

"Your clothing is waiting in the change room, sir."

Barrat nodded and headed for hot water.

Carthan was waiting when he came out into the hallway. "Just enough time to get upstairs. I got an update on what happened after we left." He proceeded to do just that as they walked.

"*Sathira* knows how to access the dark net?" She always seemed so proper, never a hair out of place or a smile for him. Her oldest children were fairly near him in age, but were never encouraged to associate with him during the family vacations. He'd stayed at their home once and felt stifled with the formality and the staff's attitude. And hers. So he'd never asked again. Maybe once this was over he'd ask again when he was working near there.

"She says that she knows someone who can," Carthan said. "Father wants the assassins to hit the cabal instead of him. The only problem is that Securities won't tell him who's *in* the cabal."

Barrat snorted. This was getting way crazier than he'd ever imagined. "But if we know the names on their bogus accounts, maybe we can trace them ourselves. Or let the assassins do it."

"Good idea," Carthan said as they arrived in the dining room.

"Are you feeling better, dear?" Mom asked, coming over to him.

"I think so. I also think dropping Branson from any further work with Holdings is in order. I can't believe they'd do something so stupid."

"Or criminal. And we'll sue them for everything they have once this is over," Father said. "Get some food into you. It will help."

Barrat sat in his usual place next to his mother. Father's attitude confused him. After years of "*You're weak, the baby, never going to be good enough,*" approval was not what he ever expected to hear from his father.

Mastren began to serve once Father sat down. Nice to know some things would never change. Erithe and Dantil, conversing quietly in a corner, sat down just in time to be fed.

Father raised an eyebrow.

"We were discussing what to tell our allies in Holdings," Erithe said.

"We've had excellent success with our efforts there, but part of that was due to Industries *not* being involved. How can we explain that we need them to buy that stock right now?"

"Don't," Barrat said after everyone was silent and thinking. "It's too complex and we need to worry about people who can't keep secrets. I'm sure there are cabal informants in a lot of different firms across the country. Some might not know just what they're involved in. Have our friends buy shares in the other targets. Family buys Industries, none of the others. And we tell as many as possible of them face to face, if we can arrange it. Keep as many people in their offices unaware of what's going on. I can see a lot of them in the next week or so, since we should be checking in around now to see how the realities of current growth match the projected growth from the analyses I did." It would also get him out of this house, so he could act.

"A good plan. You'd take security with you of course," Father said. "Before today, I would have suggested Branson but that's not possible now. We have some new hires who might suit. Berhan will arrange it."

"After we do some extra digging in their backgrounds," Mom said. "In case they're plants for the cabal."

"Or Securities," Hethane said. Everyone looked over at her. "They'll want to keep tabs on Father, at least. I can understand them watching all of us to be sure we don't do something to cause their plan to fail."

"True enough." Father nodded and went back to eating.

✦✦✦✦✦

The cabal met to share the message from Justice. Melkin took a deep breath. "Do we have enough cash for the partial payment?"

"That's not a problem," said Caldith. "We have more than that in one of our alternate accounts. Did he give the account information?" He was handed the sheet. "I can arrange the transfer tomorrow morning. Is there any fall out from that idiot from Corporate Oversight showing up at the fundraiser?"

"Not really," Renten said. "Everyone I've talked to seems to think the hit is because Trelner bankrupted several firms and bought them up for next to nothing. No one knows which companies, and he's bought up ruins enough times over the years to make the potential list a long one. It's a good cover and it's holding up well. That's why we chose it, after all."

Caldith nodded. "I was approached some time ago by one of the servants in Trelner's mansion. I declined his services at the time, but it might be an advantage to have a source to confirm what's going on inside the house. Our outside watchers have discovered there were several meetings in the past few days, with the adult children resident in the city going to the main house, and the others probably attending via conference calls. We need to know what Trelner is telling the family and what they intend to do about the threat."

"Can you assure us the mole won't reveal who we are?" Terbei asked.

"Not a problem." Caldith smiled. "He's not really as bright as he thinks he is. By the time he starts actually thinking, he'll believe that he's working for Justice and will get a big payday and references for a better job. He did provide a communications channel when we last met, so I'll have someone contact him tonight, tomorrow at the latest."

All of them nodded. It would be a reasonable ploy by Justice, to get information on any new security protocols so he could take the shot. If the mole didn't like his employer, he wouldn't look closely at what he was asked to do.

Chapter 29

Barrat and his shadows were at his third city so far. There were three companies in this town who had dealt with him or Trelner Holdings in one way or another. So far, no one had balked at his request for their allies to buy hidden stock in one of the other five companies. He hoped the cabal wasn't too involved with these companies. But they were too small, he figured. If the cabal had an in with Securities or Corporate Oversight, they couldn't report there were any stock buys since nothing would show up in the market data.

Sathira reported that morning she'd sent a message to and more importantly, received one from Justice. Well, Kerit pretending to be him.

The next city on his list was Beranga. At least he'd finally get to talk to Kerit and they could really compare notes and decide what they'd do.

Barrat sighed as he dumped his case onto his bed in the late afternoon. Noise from the other bedroom was the two guards sorting out the rented cots and sleeping bags he'd asked Kerit to source.

Harthil stood in his door. "You trust this Kellman fellow?"

"Yes. I met him when I was fourteen at a summer camp and we reconnected when I moved here. He's retired. He ferries me to and from the airport, picks up the mail when I'm away and helps around here when I need reports proofread and such. He was bored and I need occasional help. Can't afford someone full time yet. Works out well for both of us."

"He'll be here tomorrow?"

"Yes. In the morning. I have an appointment at the Commerce Association in the late morning tomorrow and three in the afternoon. There's a list in my briefcase."

"He drives you?"

"Sometimes, mostly before I bought my own car. One of you can drive tomorrow, if you're so worried. He's perfectly capable, despite his age. Just don't ask him to climb stairs too many times in a day. Can I finish unpacking now?"

Harthil vanished and he heard them talking quietly.

Peykan was in the reception area when Kerit arrived the next morning. Barrat came out of the small kitchen with a mug of coffee when he heard the door chime.

"You weren't kidding about the threats, lad," Kerit said. "Getting enough sleep?"

"Trying, but it's a complex issue. Coffee's ready."

"Good. Think I'll need it today." Kerit moved slower than normal, with a slight limp. "Been damp the past few days."

"Grab your coffee and come into the office, Kerit. We'll use my car to get to the appointments. There's two guards with me."

"Serious goings on, I see. Be right there, lad."

Barrat went into the office but didn't shut the door.

"You were in the army in your youth, Mr. Kellman?" Peykan was at least being polite.

"Twenty years in and I feel every day of it now. And it's Kerit, please. Hate titles after that long in the services. You good with that toy?" Each guard had a pistol. In case, they said. In reality, they'd go down quickly in a blitz attack. But he had to keep the family happy and that meant towing them around, at least for the next few days.

"I keep my clients safe," Peykan said. Condescension dripped from his voice now. Barrat smiled. Kerit would be too. An old man, almost doddering. A good cover. They were so exposed on this operation.

"Good. Wouldn't want to lose the lad. There's always something of interest lately. Helps keep you young, to learn new things." Barrat heard coffee pouring. Soon Kerit was at the door with a twinkle in his eye, now that neither guard could see him.

"Have a seat. I need some reports checked over," Barrat said as the door closed. "I've been too busy to worry much about grammar. Or if they have too much jargon for the average person to understand."

"Got something for you," Kerit said quietly. He handed over an older comm. No tracking capability. "So we can chat without people worrying. You should be in a crowd, just in case."

"Far easier than trying to access the dark net away from here," Barrat said. "So. The plan is for Justice to fake the shot. Securities is right. This cabal is dangerous. And I was told Branson's people kidnapped me for one of their leaders. The fact that I ran into Connil was a fluke but that person seized on it to help distract everyone from what they were doing. And Nartig was the one in at the gym and one of the ones who tranked me on the street on my way to meet with you."

"Makes sense," Kerit replied. "On my end, the deposit went into the escrow account the day after I requested it. I can take it at any point. They don't have much experience with that type of payment system and didn't check the fine print. Do you know *who* ordered the snatch?"

"Not yet. Corporate Oversight and Securities want to arrest all of them. Him, I want to suffer. If I can arrange to take a second shot that day, I will. Father suggested that the family hire us to take out the cabal. But let that one live in agony."

"That wasn't mentioned but it has merit. To the real plan: How can we be sure your father survives the shot?"

"A short load on the bullet and he wears a vest with extra plates over his heart. The distance I've calculated should give a flat trajectory. And he'll need two bags of real blood in case they have someone on the clean up squad. His by preference, but at least the right blood type. Corporate Oversight and Securities should arrange for the ambulance staff and some police to show up. I think a hit as he's leaving the office for lunch would be best. There's a good rooftop a half block away. I can rig a line easily to get down and away. I'd be homeless with an older shopping cart, which lets me take everything away with me. I don't want to chance leaving *any* evidence, Kerit. The police will be all over this, as will Corporate Oversight and Securities. We have to be very careful. Not let them know when the hit is, for one thing."

"I agree. Any idea on how we get you away from the boys out there to make the shot? We could drug them but that might backfire."

"I have an idea in the files," Barrat said. He pulled several folders out of a drawer and laid them open. "I also have the names of the accounts being used to arrange the collapse. Could you trace their connections? We're guessing that they're employees of the cabal. The ones we've checked are real people this time. Securities has the cabal's names but won't tell anyone else. Especially not Father."

Kerit snorted. "Already have the dupe account names from your sister." A slight squeak meant someone was right outside the door. Able to hear them if he leaned close to the door.

"I can look at the files today, if you want," he said, sipping his coffee. "You want me to keep coming in every couple of days?"

"Yes and yes. If your joints are too cranky some days, Alicial from the flower shop can take any mail. Just give her a call."

"Good plan," Kerit said as Barrat pushed his secondary computer over. "I'll get on these files. You going out soon?"

"In a few minutes. Be about an hour, maybe a little more. The ones I need you to review are on the desktop. I have another couple of meetings this afternoon. You should come along to those so we don't get lost. The guards don't trust my driving and I don't trust they're ready for the street system here. The Core is fairly easy to find from here. Only two turns to get to the Commerce Association so we'll be okay."

Kerit stood and picked up the computer. "I'll be here when you get back. Want some lunch then?"

"Order in some sandwiches and such from the diner for all of us," Barrat said. "The guards don't like me being out in the open."

"Sure thing."

Kerit opened the door and Harthil was over in the waiting area, sipping his own coffee. He smiled, went to the reception desk and opened up the computer, then set the folders to one side.

A few minutes later Barrat left out the back door, trailing the guards.

◈❧◈❧

The lad was clever, Kerit thought. The files on the computer didn't really need editing, but it was a good cover. There was one called Future plans. He opened it and started to read.

'My idea to get away: Justice wants a hostage against a double cross or the police trying to catch him. Gives the family incentive to help. We'll use a series of instructions to get me near a tunnel access to break contact with anyone they have following me. Then you can pick me up and we get to work. Ideally, I'd like to hit the one who ordered me kidnapped before Corporate Oversight shows up to arrest him. We need to identify that one. I think he must work at Vegathic.'

Kerit snickered as he took a portable drive out of his pocket and set it on the desk so he could move the files. He'd have a locator detector and a spare set of clothing in whatever vehicle he rented for the pickup. A lead lined box would prevent any signal from getting out. And he'd bring along a med kit and an emetic in case the guards forced Barrat swallow one or implanted a device. He turned to the next file. The list of the account holders, plus the names of people who'd bought substantial blocks of Industries stocks in the past two years. He saved that one to the portable drive in case it was different from the list the sister sent him. He'd look at it at home and start tracing where all the people with fake accounts worked.

◈❧◈❧

Welker stared at the oceanfront postcard on his nightstand. From his aunt? He didn't have an aunt named Jolena. The message was also confusing. Then he noticed a pattern of capitalized letters. Not just the first letters of the sentence or names.

He checked the door. No one was around. He got out a pad and pencil, then stared at the pad. *Gotta make sure I don't leave any evidence.* He pulled a sheet of and started writing down the capitalized words.

'I Know You Want To Escape. Need Information On Trelner. Death Frees You. Reply This. Justice.'

Reply this? Then he noticed there was a postbox number below the signature. Here in the city. The staff dining room had buzzed with the news in the morning paper. How had Justice known he wanted to leave here? Maybe he'd ask. First he had to think about this. Selling information to Corporate Oversight hadn't made him much money. But to sell it to an assassin? He'd have to think a lot about what was best for him.

An assassin would have a lot more cash available than the police or CO might have. Late that night he wrote a short note. Going to the coffee shop would still work. He went there a few times a week, so he could drop off reports as soon as something important happened.

Welker finished clearing the dirty dishes and leftovers after another of the conferences in the small drawing room. The tech was disconnecting the screen and computer used to allow everyone in the family to attend. He hadn't managed to hear anything. *Again.* Justice was going to be pissed. He needed to know more about what the family was doing so he could eliminate Mr. Trelner. Lots of small business owners would sleep sounder once he wasn't around to trick them into losing everything.

He headed for the drop point at the local coffee shop. He tucked the brief message into the corner crack in their patio wall. He read two sections of the paper until he finished the decent coffee and left.

'I don't have much yet. A dozen more guards were added recently. Mr. Trelner hasn't left the house recently and it seems he doesn't plan to until the whingers, as he calls them, get arrested. He's told the office he sprained an ankle but that's a lie. He's hiding from your justice. He thinks nothing will happen if the whingers aren't around to arrange to pay your fee. He is so arrogant. There have been two meetings in the past few days with the rest of the family attending by conferencing. No one is allowed near the door but the guards once those begin. I could place a monitoring device in the room if you send me one. I haven't seen any of the guards with any sort of detection equipment in there but I don't know where to get one and stay discrete.

The family must have spoken with the police or Corporate Oversight, but again, I can't monitor many conversations. No one is talking about any plans at the meals, although as time goes on, I may be able to learn more when they relax their guard.

The list is the names of the new guards and the regulars. Mr. Barrat left the city a few days ago. Holdings is having him review the progress of the newer companies, at least that's what they're saying. He's grumbling that he has to take security with him. Another idiot.'

≪⑤⑥≪⑤⑥

Caldith smiled as he read the note. A listening device might prove useful, since the idiot couldn't deliver anything valuable by himself. He made a mental note to have one sent to him at his next pickup. A modest payment for the lack of information would encourage him to do better.

≪⑤⑥≪⑤⑥

Kerit sat down at his basement desk to log into his dark net account. This was the strangest operation they'd ever done. It would be best for them to go dark for at least a year once this was over. Possibly two. Corporate Oversight had too much information on them. They might have to change out all their aliases and possibly their accounts. That was more difficult now that Securities was close to requiring positive identification when a new account was set up. Maybe start some small accounts before that happened. He'd heard rumours about fake fingerprints from his time in the army. Surely someone in the wider world had the technology working now. He'd look into that possibility once this mess was over. He finished settling in front of his computer and hooked in the other cable.

To work: sending the message to the Trelners to get Barrat away from all their security so he could take the shots. He wished he could see their faces when they read it.

≪⑤⑥≪⑤⑥

Sathira's image on the screen mostly filled it. Another conference call, but everyone was at their homes so any outside watchers wouldn't see all the cars arrive and suspect that there *was* a meeting. Erithe and Dantil sat next to him on a large sofa in their home office. Barrat returned here two days ago, tired from trailing his guards around. Soon, though, he'd be out of here.

"I received a response last night," Sathira said. "Not exactly what I expected, but the assassins *are* now convinced they were lied to and are willing to go along with the ruse." The tension in the room went down. "Justice is now prepared to fake Father's death. The shot will occur when he leaves for lunch on whatever day is chosen. A bit later than usual so there are fewer people to get in the way. Father will need a bullet proof vest with three extra plates over his heart and two blood bags with real blood in it and something to blow the one on his back open when he falls down. But not the front, which confused me, then I realized the bullets they use would normally go right through someone." She looked shaken, then took a deep breath. "Securities and CO should know the general method but not the exact date so they can arrange transport for Father after it's done." She looked unsettled. That was very rare.

"Makes sense," Father said. "It has to look good for passers-by. Won't be fun to just stand there."

"They also said to reassure the cabal, a group of people from some companies you took over a few years ago should be arrested as the whingers who set up the hit. That should happen at least four or five days before the hit. Without a possible paycheck, the public will believe that Justice would stand down. In reality, the cabal knows they've already paid half the fee and will pay the rest on completion. Security would lessen and you'd be back at headquarters so Justice could make the shot, which he can't do until you are out in the open."

"Also sensible," Dantil said. "What do we tell Corporate Oversight?"

"We have them arrange for the arrests of the whingers. They can tell them it's a mistake after Father gets shot. We also tell them the wrong day for the hit." She paused. "Justice said that if he sees too many police around the area on the day, he'll abort the agreement. He'll shoot to kill. A head shot. There's no way we could protect Father from that."

Silence.

"Then we must be sure of our security," Mother said. "Sathira. No one outside of you and Vanthin will know the exact date."

"I agree," Sathira said. "A few guards will know the time frame, and Corporate Oversight will have to arrange for an ambulance and so on who will be prepared ahead of time. We can't risk some uninformed idiot proclaiming the truth at the wrong time. "

Barrat nodded. Just as he and Kerit had planned.

"There's another... concern. They still... don't quite trust us." A snort from Father. "So they also want a hostage. They want Barrat."

More silence. Barrat let his eyes widen. Erithe grabbed his arm. He took a deep breath.

"They said he'll be fine," Sathira said quickly. "They'll have a very secure room with food, water, light and some books to keep him occupied. They'll let him go a day or so after the hit."

"But a locked door," Barrat said. Another deep breath. "They want *me*? Did they say why?"

"No. Maybe because the rest of us have kids?" She shrugged. "They'll send instructions on where you should go in a later message. We should put a tracker on you before you leave."

"Not a chance," Fraklin said as his image replace Sathira's. "This *is* about trust, everyone. They're way out in the open here. Trusting us not to mess up their work. I looked into these two, back when they were involved with the union problem. They are, well, honourable. The only people they kill are evil. They also don't renege on a deal. If the hit is supposed to be covert, it stays that way. There were no investigations into any of the union deaths. Not one. I have a contact in the police and he checked the files. No one is sure of their total body count but it must be high. They are very useful in their profession, and as links to other experts we may need to consult at some point."

Sounds of agreement.

"Let them know we agree," Barrat said. "I'll take my own sleeping pills, though."

"You don't have to do this, Barri," Mom said.

"I do. Small spaces haven't been as much of a problem lately. And we shouldn't tell Corporate Oversight about this either. Everyone can think that I'm here at Erithe's, working on some really detailed analysis for Holdings." And he wouldn't be in any dark holes for long, if at all. Not unless you counted the tunnel system.

❧❦❧❦

Welker swore the next morning, when he received the listening device in a package allegedly from his mother. There was another meeting last night. And he'd missed it. Well, at least he had the device now, and could read up on how best to use it. From what he'd seen, there was a meeting every few days now. And there were more guards stationed around the outer walls. Every vehicle was searched completely before they were allowed in. The cooks were cranky because they had to feed so many people and there were cots in the gym since they'd run out of bedrooms. He was glad he hadn't been tossed out of his room or given a roommate, but his single bed and dresser barely fit.

❦❦❦❦

Nartig swore under his breath as he woke. He'd been dreaming of the kidnapping and its aftermath. Again. This time, he knew what they'd forgotten to mention. The mole that Corporate Oversight had in the house. Someone in the domestic staff, he guessed. Not one of the guards. Invisible to most of the people who lived there.

He rolled out of bed and dressed, then headed for the office. Branson might remember more of what the mole had relayed to Caldith.

Branson also swore, which was unusual for him. "We can't call the Trelner's directly. I don't think the name of the mole was ever mentioned to us." He turned to the comm and looked up Malther's contact information. A few moments later, the call was completed.

"Mr. Malther, we know there was a mole was in the Trelner main house. He was relaying information to Corporate Oversight after the market crash. Captain Lagrath must know who he is. Caldith, and thus the cabal, also know who he is and if they activated him, they could learn that we know exactly what's going on."

Nartig heard Malther swearing. Branson held the comm away from his ear. "He's upset. No one at Securities knew Corporate Oversight had someone inside the Trelner compound back then, it seems."

"Well, this might help us get back onto Trelner's good side," Nartig said. "Might not, but at least it's a step in the right direction."

The swearing stopped and Branson put the handset back to his ear and listened without another comment, then hung up.

"He'll get the name from Lagrath and call the Trelners to warn them. About all we can do for now."

"Any new assignments today?" Nartig hadn't realized how much of their recent business was due to Holdings and their network of business dealings. Five operatives were in the gym right now, working out while they waited for something real to do.

"A few. We'd turned down other clients in the recent past because we were so busy with Holdings. But it's picking back up. You're on a surveillance with Martan tomorrow night. Divorce evidence."

❦❦❦❦

Berhan set down the comm. It was a very *Good Thing* that Mr. Malther hadn't called Mr. Vanthin directly. That would have set off an explosion the mole couldn't help but overhear. A footman. Welker. He didn't know all the house servants other than to recognize them as the people moving around cleaning and serving. He headed over to Mastren's office. He'd have the employee files. A search of Welker's room would be next.

Welker was on duty, so Berhan found his room and slipped in. A cursory search found the listening device and the instruction manual wrapped in a dingy undershirt. He sighed. Now he'd have to tell Mr. Vanthin. He returned to his own office to think about a way to use the mole, just once, to reassure the cabal that all was going according to their plan. They'd be less likely to start improvising that way. Then they'd get the name of the man who worked at Vegathic. Then Mrs. Sathira could send it to Justice. Another problem solved.

Berhan slipped into Mr. Vanthin's office just after lunch.

"Any problems?" His employer asked as he stopped in front of the desk. Hard eyes glanced at him, then back at the screens.

"Yes, sir. A potentially large one. But I believe we can use it to our advantage." Berhan waited until the coffee cup was set down. In case. "It seems Corporate Oversight had a mole in the house during the time Mr. Barrat was under suspicion in the market crash. They forgot to tell us that." Trelner's scowl deepened. "However, we just heard from Branson's by way of Securities. It seems the mole, once he was cut loose when Mr. Barrat moved to Beranga, tried to find another patron. Somehow, and we're not entirely sure how, he contacted someone in Vegathic. The same someone who hired Branson's to keep an eye on the analyst and kidnap Mr. Barrat."

A thin smile. "And he can tell us the name, since Securities won't."

"Yes, sir. I'd like to stage something he can record and send to the cabal. Just to reassure them we have no idea what's going on. In two or three days, once he has time to set the device. Then I'll have a little talk with him." Mr. Vanthin smiled with him.

≺৯৵৵৵৵৵

"We have six cabal members' names that we're fairly sure of, but none of them work at Vegathic." Fraklin grumbled at his computer screen and the camera. "Sathira, any word from Silence on the list?"

"A few other names. Again, no one at Vegathic. We're having that fake meeting tonight?"

"That's what I've been told. You know, Father's really enjoying this. He wants to help interrogate the footman to get the Vegathic contact."

Sathira rolled her eyes. "And he always thought Barrat was immature. They are so much alike it's no wonder they don't get along. That was one reason I tried to keep him away from my children. I didn't want them to pick up his bad habits."

"Barrat doesn't actually have many of them," Fraklin said. "He's a very good analyst."

"I know that *now*. Back then, I didn't want to risk contaminating them. I hate how ruthless Father is."

"If he wasn't, Industries wouldn't be where it is today. I just hope we can keep it going without him."

"And that event will be years from now."

Chapter 30

The news sheets led their editions with headlines about the group who ordered Vanthin Trelner's death. Five of them, who had lost control of their businesses at least three, or in one case, six years back. Each family made statements saying they had no idea who wanted Trelner dead. It wasn't them, despite the arrests.

Vanthin smiled at the headlines. His wife came into his study. "It's in play now," he said. "The whingers are in police custody."

"I know. Sathira just called. She has the instructions for Barrat. He's to go out this evening."

"He'll be fine," Vanthin said.

"You said that about the IC, as I recall." She closed her eyes and took a deep breath. "But I trust these killers more than I do the police. That is a very sad tribute to the police."

"The assassins do seem worthy of that trust. How many died in that union job you helped deal with?"

"Over thirty of their top people and their worst thugs, and without those deaths the union members wouldn't have had any way or incentive to replace the corrupt officials who'd been stealing from them for years."

"We've had less trouble with the unions lately in the manufacturing subsidiaries. They sent a set of reasonable offers a few weeks back. Mind you, we cut them back some, but that just put them on par with that union. No one complained much, at least not where anyone gets the wrong impression."

"Then the whole sordid thing served its purpose," Carithe said. "What did Berhan say about the plan?"

"He doesn't want to trust Justice, but I've overruled him. He's co-ordinating everything with Securities and that Corporate Oversight lieutenant who bothered you at the fundraiser. Lagrath, I think."

"He *is* a captain, you know. I just said that for effect at the time."

"Turned a pretty shade of red, I heard."

She smiled at him, the way she had long ago. He'd missed that smile but hadn't realised it until he'd seen it appear again. Then it faded.

"You're worried about Barri," he said.

"Yes. He's grown up so much in the past two years. And I feel so... frustrated? I'm not sure what word to use. That we missed his childhood because we were so busy with work."

"That's why none of the kids work as hard as we did back then," he said. "They saw the effect first and second hand."

"Maybe we should have a vacation together next summer." They smiled at one another. "By the sea side. That was my favourite place."

"I'd... like that too." Vanthin said. He didn't know what else to say but Carithe's smile held him in place.

❧❧❧❧

Barrat dressed in dark colours by choice. It would be harder to follow him at night. Svent appeared in his room at Erithe's with a variety of tracking devices and a hopeful expression.

"We went over this already," Barrat said. "The assassins need to trust that no one will mess up their plan and timing. That means no effort to follow me. Are we clear on this?"

"Yes, sir," Svent muttered.

"But I will take a screamer. Openly. So when they let me go, I can call for a ride without trying to find a comm."

"A good plan," he said. A screamer was set on the desk. "Where are you supposed to start from?"

"The Batith Mall. I'll pick up another set of instructions from there they said. Do the police or Securities have any idea what's going on to-night? I don't want to waste the whole night trying to lose a follower or three."

"Not to my knowledge, sir."

"Good."

"I suppose you're going to refuse to tell me what the instructions are," Svent said.

"That's very true. I don't want to risk the assassin killing my father." Of course, the instructions that Sathira was given mentioned the mall, and specifically a high end men's store. But that wasn't where he would start his journey.

Svent insisted on driving him to the mall. Barrat didn't object since he had no other way to get there without being on a bus or driving himself. But he would have Kerit do a sweep of his clothing once they met up, just in case. He left the car near the food court entrance and Svent drove away: cursing under his breath, Barrat was sure. He didn't put it past the man to have some men already in the mall to see which way he went. That would just make it a longer time until he was able to slip into the tunnels for the actual rendezvous.

About half the tables were occupied and Barrat spotted one with the tray still on it. He went over to it and pulled the napkin out from under the tray. He quickly balled it up and took the tray and its contents over to the waste bin. Then he slipped into the washroom, to study the instructions that he'd write on it once he was out of everyone's sight.

The napkin was blank to start with, albeit with some grease stains. Barrat pulled out a cheap pen and wrote a set of cross streets on it in case one of the guards caught up with him and demanded to see the note. It was a few blocks away. He tucked the napkin in his pocket, pissed for good measure and headed out. He didn't notice anyone behind him, not at first. They were good. He sighed. This was going to be a long night. He should have had a nap this afternoon instead of finishing off an analysis for Holdings.

It took two more sets of bogus instructions before he managed to shake the tails. Three of them. He'd have words with Svent, Berhan and some others when he returned. Or maybe they were Corporate Oversight or Securities, following anyone who left the compound. He didn't want to waste time finding one of them to ask. The entrance to the tunnels in this alley wasn't obvious and he slid the door closed with relief. He pulled a tiny pen light out of a pocket and started to jog. Twenty minutes later he was in another alley and saw the back end of a nondescript dark van. *Finally,* he thought.

He climbed in the back and the van sedately merged into traffic a minute later.

"That took longer than I expected," Kerit said. "Trouble?"

"Three tails. Maybe from our security, maybe from Securities or Corporate," Barrat replied. "I'm not sure who they were so it took time to make sure I'd lost all of them before I came into the tunnels. You brought a detector?"

"In the bag, along with a complete change of clothes. The box is lined with lead, so if there is something, it won't reveal our location."

"I also have a screamer," Barrat said. "For when I need a pickup."

"Good idea. Put it in the box, too."

Barrat ran the detector over his clothing but the device remained quiet. "Looks like I'm clean. I'll change anyway. They might have something on a timer." He swayed a little as they went around a corner.

"Good. There's a wig for you to get into the motel. Everything's set on my end. Anything new?"

"No. It's a relief to be out of there, though. Everyone was so... I'm not sure what they were feeling. Clingy?"

"Loving, caring what happens to you. It's quite common in families, despite what they've been like to you in the past."

Barrat climbed into the passenger seat as they went up a ramp to the speedway to their first stop. "That's still a strange feeling coming from the family. And Father's been so... approving in the past week. That's seriously confusing me."

"Well, it looks like you'll have him around for some more years so you can build a better relationship than what you've had." Kerit said.

"I suppose." Barrat exhaled. "It was easier to think of shooting him when I was sure he deserved it."

"How he's acting now doesn't mean he didn't do all manner of things to deserve a bullet, or that he made your life miserable for years," Kerit pointed out. "And he's still is one of the most ruthless predators around today when it comes to business acquisition."

"True. But he's not an anomaly. He's a successful predator. Like us."

The motel they stopped at was clean but elderly. The slightly battered van fit in with the other vehicles in the lot. Barrat picked up the box with his clothing and followed Kerit to an end unit on the main floor.

"I limped a lot when I registered," Kerit said softly. "The lady who owns the place put me in this room without me asking."

"How long will we stay here?" Barrat asked as Kerit unlocked the door with a key hanging from a large fob.

"Til mid-morning," Kerit said. Barrat set the box down in the unpacking area. Several mid sized suitcases were there, plus two slightly worn backpacks. The two beds were small but the room itself was clean and smelled of laundry soap, not spray cover-ups. "Then we'll take a bus into downtown. Our changes of clothing for the hotel are in the backpacks. Everything else is in the other hotel room. Fairly central to both hits. You sure you can get in place for the second?"

"I think so. I want to do a dry run tomorrow night so I'll be sure of the line of sight. The first is easier since I can be there in good time. I want to find the best route from there to the secondary. If I miss him there, I can try when he leaves for the day."

"If Corporate Oversight hasn't picked him up by then," Kerit pointed out. They went to the tiny table near the window. "Don't shave tomorrow morning. I have a new beard for you to wear tomorrow night, and as a hostage, you don't get a razor."

"True. I'm just glad I don't have to spend the next few days in a tiny room with a locked door. I should pick up a thick novel from a used book store to pass the time." Kerit grinned and pulled one out of a pack. Barrat looked at the cover. The rippling pectorals and the scantily clad girl attached to the hero's leg meant he was not going to enjoy this.

"You have a sick sense of humour, my friend. Truly sick."

"Think of it as window dressing. And it reads pretty quick so you can skim it and still be able to describe most of the action if anyone asks. You can start on it tonight."

❧❧❧❧

Barrat knelt on the rooftop, hidden behind one the crenellations. His clothing was all second or third hand and he smelled horrible. His incipient beard itched under the fake one. He had looked and acted like a street person to make the approach to this building. A derelict shopping cart was tucked between two dumpers in the alley below so no other homeless person would find it. He hoped. If it vanished he'd have to find another way to hide his rope and rifle. The rifle could break down but the rope would have to end up in a dumper or down a sewer. He might need it at the second site so didn't want to abandon it early.

It was twenty minutes before Father would come out of their corporate headquarters. No one else knew the hit was today but them and the cabal. And the cabal would be surprised at the results. Kerit would relay the footage of the hit to their contact as soon as Father went down for the rest of their payment. With any luck, the money would be theirs before his second shot.

His rifle was assembled and a small bag of sand lay in the low section of the wall as a rest. Barrat snugged the rifle to his shoulder and looked through the scope. It was bulkier with the video attachment but that was why he was here early to accustom his eye to the change.

"Ready," he said.

A click from Kerit. He activated the video camera to ensure the feed was recording. A double click. Good. One less thing to worry about.

The main doors of the building were sharp and clear with a quick adjustment. A few employees, taking an early lunch, trickled out of the building. The plan was for Father to leave a little late, just to ensure most of the employees were gone and Justice could have a clear shot. Injuring a bystander was not acceptable to either of them. He was a little surprised that Father didn't want anyone else hit. He pushed those thoughts aside. Nothing mattered right now except the shot. His breathing slowed and so did his pulse.

The lunch rush started. He recognised several people from his time in the mail room. Most were unknown to him. The numbers faded to a trickle. Father appeared, talking to one of his top analysts. The guards were down to the usual three instead of five. One was right in front of Father as the doors opened. He looked around and nodded that there were no obvious threats. Father looked up toward his building and moved to the side slightly. How cooperative of him.

Barrat took a breath, held it and aimed. Let the breath out slowly and the rifle fired.

When he saw Father fall backward and the screaming started, he ducked behind the wall in case someone looked this way and started breaking down the rifle. The video unit had transmitted the hit to one of their servers in real time, so he didn't have to waste time on that task. He was sure the police and Corporate Oversight would be swarming the area quickly.

Kerit was in their hotel room about three blocks away, watching the hit. Now he'd send a copy to the cabal. On Barrat's part, he'd head for the second location for the other shot and then on to the motel, assuming the van would be where Kerit left it.

Once the rifle parts were stowed in a ratty sack, he took the small sandbag he'd used as a rest and headed for his rope. As he moved across the roof, he activated his headset and clicked once to let Kerit know he was on his way. A double click came seconds later. The shot had hit exactly where he'd meant it to. The triple layer of plates plus the vest would protect Father. Kerit had tried a similar shot with the same equipment a week ago and there would only be a bruise.

Barrat rappelled down the rope and detached it. There was no sense in leaving any clues for the police. He coiled it quickly and stowed everything into used garbage bags and put them at the bottom of his shopping cart. On the top were two bags half full of recycling, an ancient sleeping bag and some scavenged food he did not intend to eat. He wasn't risking any chance of food poisoning at this point. He headed away from the building. Time to go dark again. He shut off the radio and tucked it into an inner pocket of the coat.

♛♛♛♛

Vanthin thought about courage as he waited for the elevator near his office. The vest and extra plates made him look stouter than he liked. He'd worn the vest to work this morning and taken the rig off in his private bathroom until it was time to leave for lunch. The bags of blood attached at the front and back of the vest bothered him. It was going to be messy but that was necessary to convince the cabal, and any bystanders so they'd start their plan. He'd worn an older suit today, since it would be ruined no matter what happened. His valet had looked oddly at him when he pointed out which one he wanted, but had the sense to keep his mouth shut.

He had to stand out in the open and wait for someone to shoot him. *Was* this a good idea? He could go out another door and bypass the assassin. But. Barrat had gone into their hands, not knowing what might happen to him. His youngest son, his *baby* had shown true courage. Twice now. His own father couldn't show less.

His top analyst waited for him on the main floor. Vanthin had told him they were going to lunch today to discuss some new opportunities now that the whingers were out of the picture. He just wanted another shaken witness to be interviewed on a live broadcast. His guards tended to be silent and stoic. Pathos and shock would not be on their faces. Grim would not be suitable. He needed a different face on the news feeds.

The guards ensured no one was close as they left the building. Vanthin had a hard time not snorting in disgust. He glanced up at the building he'd been told would be where the assassin waited. Hmm. Berhan was blocking his view. Anyone else would shoot through the guard, but not this man. Someone else with honour. It didn't seem possible given his profession.

Vanthin moved to the side, forcing analyst over. Then there was a heavy push against his chest and he fell backwards.

⊰⊱⊰⊱

Berhan swore as Mr. Trelner fell backwards. Idiots! Why hadn't he been informed that the hit was today? Had the assassin changed his mind and taken the shot for real? Mr. Trelner wore an older suit, he suddenly realized. And was fatter than usual. He must be wearing the reinforced protective vest.

He'd heard nothing of the shot. The analyst was kneeling beside Trelner, trying to staunch the bleeding from his chest. That couldn't be allowed if the plan was in progress. Ragnal moved the analyst away and put a finger on Trelner's throat, then shook his head. He moved the body a little to reveal more of the spreading pool from his back. A quick nod meant his boss was still alive. Dark hells.

Passers-by started to watch the drama. Berhan took a deep breath and activated his comm to bring the police. He noticed several people calling as well. Some would call the media instead of the authorities. Good. They needed all the public documentation they could muster to pull this off. He just hoped the body didn't start to twitch. Or sneeze.

⁕⁓⁕⁓⁕

At the ping from his work computer, Caldith turned to see that he'd received a new message on his alternate account, open for just this message. He opened it quickly. There was the video. Trelner fell down, a pool of blood spreading beneath him. A short message was attached.

'*Our work is done. Send the rest of the payment.*

Good luck.

Justice'

He smiled and sent an acknowledgement. He shut down the alternate account. It would leave no trace for anyone to find. Then he picked up his comm and called Jonarth to send the rest of the fee. He'd go out to lunch now and by the time he returned, the market should be reacting to the news and their automated buys and sells would be hitting the market in an increasing wave. The crash would stop quickly, since the trading halt software would do that, but by the evening, their cash-out orders would become public knowledge and the true wave of destruction would begin. In the next week, there would be a lot of board elections called.

The news was full of Trelner's death. No one had seen the shot itself, but plenty of people sent in footage starting just after. Justice had shut down his feed moments after the body fell so he (or she) could escape before the police showed up. Sensible. Too bad they were so fixated on killing only the guilty. The cabal had an extended list of those who had annoyed them in the past. They had thought to use another assassin, but he only did muggings. Harder to explain a rash of them among a group. But they were so common that no one had ever detected his work.

The restaurant brought in a large screen so those who cared, mostly the people in the bar, could watch the unfolding events live. He was content to listen to the commentary. Pundits were starting to predict any number of terrible outcomes to the incident, including the collapse of Industries without Trelner's ruthlessness. A camera truck was now in place outside Trelner Industries headquarters and there were a lot of police keeping everyone away from the tarp covered body. There was a trickle of blood escaping from underneath. Excellent. It was all going as planned. His comm buzzed.

"The orders are starting to go in," Melkin said. "Because a lot of people are at lunch, it hasn't made much difference yet. I expect the real drop to start in about an hour."

"As we anticipated," Caldith said. "I'm heading back to the office in a few minutes. Jonarth should have sent the payment by now."

"Good. We'll need to stay on top of things. They're just removing Trelner's body now, I see."

Caldith caught a glimpse of the screen as someone left the bar area. The black body bag was on a gurney, heading for the coroner's transport. That would be a quick autopsy. Shot through the heart was the fairly obvious cause of death. But procedures had to be followed, he thought.

The waiter brought his bill and he paid. Eager now to return to his office and track the chaos.

❦❧❦❧

Captain Lagrath saw the start of the news coverage of Trelner's 'death' and swore. His comm rang and he picked it up.

"This is Malther from Securities. Did you have any men in the area?"

"No. We thought the hit was going to be two days from now. At least that's what we were told."

"Same time frame as we were told." Malther sighed. "Best to get over there and at least make a show of searching for Justice. I would guess he's long gone by now."

"Truth. I'll take a couple of squads over there. There aren't that many roofs he could use. Most buildings have sealed windows these days. He wouldn't leave any holes for us to find."

"We're monitoring the market. There's a little activity from the suspect accounts, but the cabal hasn't really started their next step yet. They may be waiting for the official announcement. My boss will be calling the Trelner house in a few minutes to find out what else they've hidden from us."

"I'll give you a call if we find anything. But I doubt we will."

His men arrived at the site and Trelner's body was just being removed. The regular police had a cordon well outside of the area so no passerby could see the dead man still breathed. And the tarp would disguise any small movements.

"Lieutenant Orthil," he said as he stopped just next to the coroner's van. He pulled out his identification. "All in order?"

"Yes," Orthil said. "He's grumbling that we took too long to get him out of here. Has to piss. I told him he should just do so. Very common for it to happen. He said he'd never be that crude."

Lagrath choked back a laugh. Not in keeping with the gravity of the situation. "We had no idea it was planned for today. Any luck with witnesses?" Orthil grimaced.

"None near here. Not even his guards heard anything, so he used a very good silencer. Trelner came out of the building, were partway to the car and he suddenly went down. From line of sight, I think that five story has the best angle. Not too high, so the short load on the bullet wouldn't matter. I sent two men that way looking for someone moving quickly away from there. No one they talked to saw anything. They just looked around the building but didn't go into it."

"He was likely well away before anyone knew to pay attention. Any cameras near there?"

"Some, but also a bunch of alleys that aren't monitored. We can't get the funding. I'll have someone at the station start to check on all cameras in a four block radius of there. Do you want your men to canvass the building's tenants?"

"We'll do that. I'll check the roofs and their access first. I doubt he left any sign beyond a scuff mark, but we need to go through the usual procedures in case the cabal is tracking our response."

"When will he head back to his house?"

"A few hours. Mrs. Trelner will be escorted to the coroner's shortly and they'll take him home in the trunk of her car. At least, that's the plan I was told. I have no idea what else they've done behind our back. They must have figured out how to contact Justice on their own."

Orthil's radio buzzed.

"There's been another shooting, Lieutenant," the dispatcher said. "The Vegathic Building. Only one down. He's still alive and we have medical on route. Your people are closest to the site."

Lagrath swore. "One of the top people we're very interested in talking to works at Vegathic," he said. "I heard he was the one who authorized the boy's kidnapping."

"Shit." They looked at each other. "Tell half your men to come with us," Orthil said. "Not that I think we'll find any trace of him there either." They both sighed. Such a great chance to rid the world of at least one assassin. Wasn't likely now, but they had to keep trying.

"As soon as I tell the other half what to look for around here."

⚜❧⚜❧

Barrat quickly scaled the fire escape on the building they'd chosen for his second shot. The angle wasn't ideal but he really wanted to take Caldith down before he could help set the cabal's plan in motion. It also meant he had to be in place before Caldith returned from lunch.

He saw no one, as he expected. He glanced at his watch. Nearly time. He didn't have much leeway this time, since every traffic signal on his route was red as he approached it and he couldn't run, not pushing the dratted cart *and* stay in character. And he couldn't abandon the cart just yet. He took a deep breath to start lowering his heart rate from the exertion and stress. All would go perfectly here.

At least he knew where to set up already. That had been an energetic evening, the one after he'd vanished to become a hostage. The concern of the family for his safety had been heartening. But they could never learn of his true involvement or he'd be on the outside of the family forever.

He set up the rifle and put one of the fully charged bullets into the chamber and another two in the clip. In case. The video unit stayed in the bag. He wouldn't need pictures of this hit to remember it. He placed the sandbag on the top of the just under chest-high wall. He had to stand for this shot. Less stable, but it was the shortest building in the area with the necessary line of sight.

He took another deep breath and started to scan for his quarry. The people streaming into Vegathic's headquarters made him worry. Where was Caldith? They had timed his lunches for the past two days. Always returned at quarter past. After the usual rush for the elevators died down. He might be late watching any coverage at Industries' site on a restaurant screen. It wouldn't matter soon.

Barrat caught sight of Connil, heading inside. They had to get together soon. The amount of work he had was becoming a bit too much for one person if he also wanted to have a social life once Liselle moved to Beranga. Maybe Connil was tired of working for a giant by now. He and Kerit would be dark, so that would help keep that aspect of his life quiet. He'd still need to keep in practice, and paintball alone wouldn't be enough. There were subtle differences in the aiming and trajectory that could mean a miss or worse with a real shot. Combining work trips with a stop to meet up with Kerit could work. They'd have to talk about it once they were back in Beranga. Without the security men tagging along behind him.

The flood of employees thinned to a trickle. Good. He swept across the plaza. Caldith came from the left each of the two days they'd observed him. Hopefully he was a creature of habit in where he had lunch.

There? He zoomed in with the scope. Yes. Finally. Dark hells. A man on his off side, who would take damage from the bullet if it went through the pelvis as Barrat planned. He'd need two shots then. One for a lower leg to drop the target, then through the hips and spine, destroying his ability to walk forever. It wouldn't really matter. He'd be in prison. It was harder to arrange something this debilitating in there, so any retribution had to be now.

The two men approached the door. A breath, then he fired. Caldith went down and Barrat loaded the other bullet. Another breath and it was over. He watched for a moment, not hearing the screams that would be echoing. Justice prevailed. The other man wasn't injured, still standing, looking down in shock. Good.

The rifle was in the bag in a few minutes and he picked up the spent casings. Then back to the fire escape. There were more people around than he'd planned on and they might notice him rappelling down. He shrugged and started down the stairs. He made it to the cart and hid the rifle and rope. As he prepared to leave, two security men from the building came around the corner and started toward him.

"You. Stop right there," one called. They stopped about three arms' lengths away from him as his aroma registered.

He hitched at his pants as if he'd just pissed into the trash.

"Not doin' nuthing," he muttered. "Gotta piss someplace."

The two guards looked at each other. Then one grimaced, probably at the stench coming off his clothing. "Get out of here," he said. "If we find you here again, you'll wish you'd stayed away."

Barrat hunched over, still not looking directly at them. He started pushing his cart down the alley toward the plaza. A bold move, but the police would soon be here and would be far more interested in people quickly heading away from rather than toward the site of the not-quite-dead man's pain.

The sounds of a siren sent him down another alleyway a block later. In character, since the homeless were often singled out for abuse by police. He was faintly surprised the two guards hadn't beaten him up on general principles. The smell from his clothing, noxious as it was, might have saved him. Bruises might be difficult to explain once he got back to his family. There was sure to be pressure for another medical exam no matter how well he said he'd been treated.

A crowd was starting to gather on the plaza, so he started muttering and those near him moved away. The faint sound of more sirens started over the chatter and questions. The signal changed and he headed away from the crowd now. Three or four blocks to go. Then he'd go into the tunnels.

He reached a tunnel entrance and paused. No. Not yet. He had to get further away from here first to establish that he had left in case the police tried to track everyone who showed on their cameras. There was a bottle depot two streets over, he recalled. That would be a good place to leave the rickety cart, with dozens of others so it wouldn't stand out. He fed the rope down into a sewer grate. That left the rifle and video scope. Easily hidden on his person under the layers of clothing he wore.

A little more work and he didn't clank when he walked. There were only three other homeless people at the bottle depot and he waited patiently in line and didn't comment when the sorter underpaid him. He just tucked the money into his pocket and left, abandoning the cart with the others. Someone would take the sleeping bag before the police thought to check here, if the two security guards even mentioned seeing him. Now he could head down into the safety of the tunnels.

Another quick change: his coat was reversible and he took advantage of an alley with no cameras and a space between two dumpers to do so. A dark winter cap helped hide his face. He couldn't do anything about the smell just now. A long shower with lots of soap would take care of that problem. He headed into the tunnels three blocks later. Now to head for the van. His stomach growled and he pulled an energy bar and his flashlight out of a pocket.

Chapter 30

Carithe stared at the coverage on the screen, not hearing the door to her suite open. "Madam, the police are here to escort you to the... facility." Mastren's voice was surprisingly gentle.

"Have my team meet me at the front door in five minutes," she said, turning slightly. She was surprised there were tears streaming down her cheeks. She reached up to touch one. After years of sniping at one another, she hadn't thought she could be moved to tears. But...

She sat in the back of the car and didn't see any of the streets, buildings or other cars. She remembered so many things.

The police escort made it possible to approach the building through the crowds of gawkers and reporters. She did not look at the sign that said 'Herithan Coroner and Forensic Department'.

The reporters tried to get close enough to shout questions but she ignored them, possibly for the first time in years. She didn't blot the tears away. His reaction to them would tell her a great deal about his attitude.

Her team, packed closely around her, escorted her into the building. Few of them truly understood what had happened today. Patyrn would explain as soon as possible to the others.

"Mrs. Trelner," a man in a suit said gently, "Please come this way. We have a place set aside for you to wait. Are any of your children coming to be with you?"

"No, sir," Patyrn said after she didn't reply. "We thought it best they stay indoors. There was word of a second shooting but no details were available when we left the compound. Our car is reinforced."

"Not a fatal one, it seems. Otherwise, the victim would be here." The man looked around to see if any staff were nearby. "We'll speak more in a few minutes." He led them into a maze of corridors to a door labelled as a staff lounge. She took a deep breath and went in. Her men stayed outside, ready to keep her safe.

"About..." Vanthin had some exercise clothes on that did not suit him at all. "You're crying, Carithe." He came over and stood in front of her. "All this sadness is for me?" He looked uncertain. "I... It was hard."

Her view of him was obscured by a sudden rush of tears. She didn't want to admit to her feelings in words, so she just hugged him.

"I thought about leaving some other way. But Barri..." His arms came around her and their tears damped them both.

It was twenty minutes later by the clock that someone knocked on the door. "Enter," Vanthin said. It was the Corporate Oversight captain. Lagrath. He was upset.

"We weren't ready for this today," he said, scowling. "Why?"

"Because Justice didn't trust you," Vanthin said. "You would have tried something clever to catch him or his partner once he'd shot me. He told us directly if he saw police around, he'd kill me for real. A head shot, not into the vest. We believed him. So. Who was the other person shot?"

"A member of the cabal. He works, well, worked at Vegathic. He's the one who ordered your son kidnapped. Did you share the employee files we gave you with the assassins?"

"Of course," Carithe said. "The man is alive?"

"Yes. He'll never walk again, I was told. One shot through the knee to drop him and a second through the pelvis. Shattered it. We think it might have been Silence who took that shot, or maybe the one on you, Mr. Trelner. It's our understanding that Justice is younger and the second hit was technically more difficult."

"But you're rounding up the cabal tonight?" Vanthin asked.

"Tomorrow morning, I was just told. The crash hasn't progressed the way Securities or likely the cabal planned. You should look at the trading history once you're back home. Just don't log in *as you* in case a mole in your corporate headquarters is monitoring your computers."

"You can borrow my system," Carithe said. "When can we leave this place?" A slight shudder.

"In a few minutes. Your car is in the underground parking area right now. We think putting that Mr. Trelner into the trunk, then having the car pick you up out front would be best. Do you, or can you say a few words to the reporters before you leave? Securities thinks it would be a good idea, Mr. Malther said a few minutes ago. There are still a dozen or so waiting out there. I don't think they'll leave until you do."

"It would help the plan," Vanthin said. He looked at Lagrath. "Put some padding in the dratted trunk. At least I won't have to wait for an hour for the police to finish taking pictures that only show I was shot."

"Head for the car, dear," she said, patting his arm. "I need a few minutes in the washroom to get ready for the photographers."

❧❦❧❦

Barrat stretched. The van was where they'd left it and he climbed in the back first, changing clothes and storing all the noisome gear in doubled heavy duty garbage bags. He combed his hair and cleaned the dirt off his face and neck with a damp towel stored in a plastic bag. Now he was the youngish man who belonged in the cheap motel. He noticed a small cooler on the passenger side floor when he sank into the driver's seat. His feet were tired from all the walking he'd done in the crappy, second-hand shoes. The exercise shoes felt heavenly.

He opened the cooler to find several sandwiches and bottles of water and juice and smiled. Kerit was amazing. He ate half a sandwich before starting the van. Rush hour traffic made the trip a bit longer than he liked, but he ate another sandwich and drank some water since the speedway was stop and stop traffic.

When he reached the motel, he parked and made it into the room without getting too close for anyone to smell the residue of his previous clothing, then took out his unregistered comm to call Kerit to confirm all was in motion to get him back to Beranga.

"The money's ours," Kerit said. "Saw some coverage on the second shot on the viewer. You did well. We do need to go dark for a while."

"I know. At least a year, I thought. It's not like we really need the money at this point, is it?"

"True. We should keep the skills up, though." That meant his skills, not Kerit's.

"Of course. Had some ideas on how, but we can discuss that later. You plan to head home tomorrow?"

"Purchased my bus ticket yesterday. Easier than driving. The rifle and such will fit into the bigger suitcase there. Bring everything in the van tomorrow at two. Rendezvous at the Magrethi Mall, west side, north corner of the parking lot. We'll leave the van there. Your fingerprints could be in the back, but not the front, if you haven't cleaned it out yet."

"I thought a delayed fire would take care of any evidence," Barrat said. "Or I can leave it in the Slideway once you're on your way. The choppers will dispose of it for us." They'd actually bought this van, not rented one. In case it was noticed officially.

"Better. The motel might recognize the plate number if it's on the news. I don't think anyone will notice, but it'll be good for parts. Or they'll sell it to someone for other nefarious activities."

"True. I'll see you soon. Take care, Kerit."

"You too. When do you plan to reappear?"

"In two days. I might keep the van at the motel til then. Drive it through one of those nice, camera-less alleys, then leave it in the Slide-way, come back and take a half a sleeping pill. When I wake up, activate the screamer and wait for a ride home to the family. It'll be hard keeping track of what I do and don't know, so I won't follow any of the news in the interim. Maybe get another of those thick books to keep me occupied."

A snort of laughter. "Good. We'll talk soon."

"And I won't have those guards following me everywhere when I get back. At least, I hope not."

Kerit chuckled. "That'll make seeing your young lady much easier."

❧❧❧❧

Jonarth didn't realize Caldith wasn't on line for nearly an hour. He was tracking the market. The sudden drop hadn't materialized. Their buys and sells were logged in, but the public wasn't panicking. Few investors were selling at the lower prices they offered. It was more or less business as usual. Which it shouldn't be. His comm buzzed quietly.

"We have a serious problem," Renten said. "Caldith was shot this afternoon as he was heading into Vegathic from lunch."

"What? Who shot him?"

"The consensus on the news is that the same person who shot Trelner did it. So Justice or his partner. No one from Securities has commented, other than platitudes. And the market isn't going down."

"I know that part, idiot," Jonarth snarled. "All of our sells were listed, though. I'm tracking my share of them. The idiot investors should have sent the market into a tailspin with the level of sells and the low offers we've got in place."

"I don't understand either. But why would Justice shoot Caldith? Did he mess up the payments?"

"No. Caldith called me from his office before lunch and said to put the second payment in. He'd seen the video on Trelner's death. I did, and it was transferred out about ten minutes later. That was when Caldith was away for lunch."

"About the only thing I can think of is that someone from Branson's put two and two together and told the Trelners that he was involved in the kidnapping. And he was shot in payback for that? And who did it? Maybe we should send a query to Justice. Maybe he heard some chatter."

"The timing's weird for that," cabal3 said. "But. Since Justice has no idea *we're* the ones behind the plan, he wouldn't know Caldith was involved. Just saw the chance for a double payday. Confuse Corporate Oversight and the police that the hits were related." He paused. "Maybe. We should confer tonight. There's no use putting any of the cash-out orders in place at the moment, since there's no real crash to encourage the sheep to panic. The plan is busted, as far as I can tell. All these months of work, and it's all been for *nothing!*"

Jonarth nodded. "I agree. No sense in showing Securities the whole plan. It looks like the market will shut down as usual. We'll talk later. We have to come up with a new strategy to take control of the big six. Maybe we should target them one at a time. Start with Industries, maybe." He disconnected and stared at the market data. It didn't make any sense. The market should have crashed or been shut down within two hours of Trelner's death.

He snarled at the screen.

Chapter 31

Corporate Oversight seemed to be shutting down for the night. Streams of men headed for home or other entertainments. But their strike teams were waiting for the cabal to finish their meeting. More evidence of what they intended to do.

Captain Lagrath smiled to himself as he listened in to the hidden device, along with Malther of Securities. These trials would be very satisfying. And the Trelners might have enough evidence to launch a suit against the cabal's assets for the kid's abduction by Branson. It wouldn't hurt for them to try, at any rate.

"Should one of us go see Caldith?" Melkin asked. "I haven't seen any indication that he's in any kind of custody. Just one regular police officer hanging around for a statement once he wakes up, from what one of our people reported."

"The news is full of pundits wondering if the Justice shot him too." Renten said. "So, no. Very bad idea. No one knows we're linked in any way. Let's keep it that way."

"I agree," Terbei said. "We should ask Justice if he went for the double payday though. It would be expected, I think."

"But four or five people were arrested as the ones who authorised the hit," Jonarth said. "How do we explain how they have access to the dark net in jail?"

"Easy," Jonarth said. "The ones who hired Justice aren't in jail. The ones who were are just guys who made too much noise so Corporate picked them up with no evidence. They can hold people for a week without charges now, remember. They wouldn't send them to IC, but a small cell and interrogators yelling at them for hours isn't going to cause any severe mental problems that would come back on them."

"Makes sense," Renten said slowly. "But we need to aim for a cranky tone. I can write something tomorrow. I'm guessing Justice is dark for now, until he can get well away from here."

"Agreed. At least he did the job we paid him for. Besides, if Caldith is tagged for anything, we don't have to split anything with him. Melkin, have you finished wiping his computers? We'll split those accounts among us unless he's just seen as a victim."

"Good idea. That's why we have each other's codes, after all. It'll take me a minute or three to finish up." Sounds of walking, then a chair screeched a little. "Why don't you all get some coffee while I get this done? Made a big pot so there's enough for everyone."

More noises of movement.

Lagrath snorted as the cabal members started trying to explain to each other why the market hadn't crashed. They became quite loud and were reduced to being insistent that the plan *should* have worked after a while. Malther smiled.

"I'm truly amazed that *our* plans all worked so well," Malther said. "The market is fine, we have excellent information for the arrests and trials. All the cabal will end up in IC so we'll get maximum sentences once they finish explaining all the details. The innocents will all get the accounts that were set up in their names and the big six owe Securities a big favour. About the only minus I see right now is that Justice and Silence remain at large. There's no sign of them, I've been told."

"I wouldn't count on the six being eager to repay you," Lagrath said. "As for the assassins, I don't think we'll hear anything from them in the next year or more. They took an incredible risk. I would imagine Trelner arranged an extra payment for them for Caldith."

The cabal members returned to their homes in the early morning to find the police waiting for them. None of the neighbours realised what happened until they watched the morning news.

⋙⋙⋘⋘

Erithe sighed. The news was full of announcements. She held her daughter on her lap and bounced her occasionally. Dantil sat beside her.

"The big news of the day is that Vanthin Trelner is alive. Bruised from the shot to his chest, but hale and ready to take on the market. Corporate Oversight reported today. It was part of a joint operation...." The pundit kept talking but Dantil muted the sound. A picture of Father from his home office filled the screen. He was smiling broadly.

"It's over. Hard to realise it's only been a few weeks since we heard about this," Dantil said. "There's a big news conference scheduled for early tomorrow, then the market will open after lunch."

"That should reassure the investors," she said. "But I'd bet on some selling out anyway. I heard from some of our allies a little while ago."

"How are they feeling about the cash they invested?"

"Some may keep the shares, or at least a percentage of them. They were promised a one percent bonus if they return the shares, so a few will take advantage of that offer."

"We also have to decide if Holdings wants to return the shares we bought," she said. "Industries does have enough cash on hand to redeem them all. We might need the money for another deal, after all."

The comm rang. Dalton rose and picked it up, then swapped it to speaker.

"You're the last I've called, except for Barrat. He's still with them," Sathira said. "I just got a message from Justice. The hit on Caldith was a gift for Barrat as he was the mastermind and the one who ordered his kidnapping. They're letting him go sometime tomorrow."

"We'll have to send them a nice thank you," Father said. "An amazing shot, Berhan told me. Mine was simpler, he said. I'm still surprised Justice didn't shoot the man beside Caldith."

"They never cause harm to an innocent," said Mom. A hmmph. Was she sitting *next* to Father? She turned to Dantil. He looked confused as well. "I am glad that no one else was harmed in this. But I'll worry until Barri returns. But I am not as worried as when he was in That Place."

"Anything else?" Dantil asked.

"What about that mole, Welken?" Fraklin asked.

"Welker," Father said. "One of the footmen. Been here for five years, Mastren said. He's been arrested and is heading for prison. A small fish, but he could have ruined everything if he'd been a better spy. Berhan growled at him once and he wet himself. Then he told us everything."

"Good thing he *was* incompetent." Sathira said. "I'm off. Let us know the minute Barrat appears."

"Of course," Father said. Clicks on the line until everyone disconnected.

Chapter 32

Barrat woke up and blinked. Faint light from either side of him. Night time. The alley. A minor headache. He really hated sleeping pills. He checked his pockets and found the screamer. Pushed the button and twisted it. He sat up and leaned against the building. From his location, it would take about fifteen minutes for a car to arrive. The van was long gone. He'd left the keys in it and walked away mid-afternoon near the Slideway. Then he'd gone to a nice park. A walk there with Liselle would be nice. They could have a picnic in a day or so, once everything and everyone was calmer. He still might have to tow a guard or two around until he left here, but at least they could have some quiet time together.

The sound of sirens broke into his reverie. Coming closer. Did Corporate Oversight or the police know about his hostage status? That hadn't been part of the plan. He glanced down at the screamer. The only way to shut it off what to break it, and that was deliberately hard to do.

The sirens moved away from him. Good. His heart rate went back down. He started to review his story. And maybe he could get something to eat once he was back somewhere safe. The odd meals he and Kerit had over the past few days had been mostly edible. The ones from the hotel room service were the best, but eating from street vendors for the past two days hadn't really been filling. He didn't want to risk showing up on any surveillance systems so that limited what he could purchase.

The screech of tyres at either end of the alley heralded his ride home. Measured footsteps echoed a little. "Mr. Barrat?" a voice he knew. Harthil. One of the men who'd been with him.

"Over here," he said. He started to stand and Harthil was quickly by his side to help him rise and steady him after. "I'm okay. Sleeping pills make me a little off balance for a while."

"Good. We've sent for the doctor anyway." Harthil kept a hand on his arm and they headed for the middle car. Barrat wasn't surprised.

"What time is it? I didn't bother to take my watch with me. And is my father all right?"

"It's about eleven. All is well with the family and Mr. Vanthin, baring a bruise on his chest. The markets didn't crash and the cabal were all arrested. It's been two days since the fake attack on your father. Six days since you left the house."

"That's all good news." They reached the end of the alley and Barrat settled in the comfortable back seat with relief. "Could someone call in that I'm hungry? The meals were not that good."

"What were they, sir?" Peykan asked.

"Army field rations. Dark hells. They should go on strike for better food if that's what they're expected to fight on. I think we have a subsidiary who does prepackaged meals. Maybe they should put in a bid." The driver snorted as they pulled away.

They went to the main house, which he mostly expected. He didn't expect everyone local to be there, and awake, waiting for him.

Mom's hug was first, then Father. His ribs creaked. He took a deep breath and held it as Dantil approached.

"We've sent word to everyone else that you're all right, dear," Mom said. There were tears in her eyes.

After more hugs from the family, they moved into the small parlour. Food smells drew his immediate attention.

"Everything went as planned?" Barrat asked as he took a pair of sandwiches and sat down next to the tray. Toasted ham and cheese and mustard on rye. One of his favourites.

"It did. Mostly," Vanthin said. "I had to walk out from behind Berhan so I was in the clear. I have a bruise the size of my hand on my chest and a bump on the head out of it. Berhan is mad that we didn't tell him it was the day but he's getting over it."

"And Vanthin complained it took the police far too long to get him out of there," Mom said. She was sitting *next* to Father. Close to him. What had been going on between them while he was away?

"The crash didn't happen, thanks to the spoof sites the companies all used," Dantil said. "The cabal was arrested the next day. The whingers were released with profuse apologies by CO."

"And twenty thousand each from me," Father said. "They'll probably waste it, but that's what they agreed to when we signed the contracts."

"Securities wanted to wait until the last one of them was out of surgery before arresting them all," Erithe said. "Barrat, Justice gave you a present, it seems. Caldith was the one at Vegathic who ordered your kidnapping. We discovered who he was from our mole and sent word to Justice. The mole was one of the footmen who Corporate Oversight turned when you were first suspected."

Barrat swallowed a half-chewed mouthful. "Which one?"

"Welker," Dantil said. "He didn't gather much information to send to CO so they fired him when you left for Beranga. He tried selling the same reports to Caldith at Vegathic and he relayed that to Branson. We don't know how he found out about Caldith. Dumb luck maybe. Someone at Branson's finally remembered that little fact and they sent word to us. We let Welker set a listening device and played out an "everything is going according to the cabal's plans" family meeting and let him send it on before our guards had a little talk with him. Then we sent the name to Justice. In case he wanted to send the cabal a message for lying to him about their motives. It seems he did. Sathira has arranged for a thank you payment for that shot. It did make the cabal confused on the day, thinking that Justice had doubled up on his assignments."

Barrat nodded. Seeming to take all the revelations in to make sense of what happened while he was away. He had to admit that it was confusing to remember what he should know, not what he did.

"Why was he, Caldith, in surgery?" Barrat asked around a mouthful of almond pastry.

"After shooting your father, Justice went to the Vegathic plaza and shot Caldith," Erithe said. "Two shots. One in the leg and the second through his pelvis. He'll never walk again, the doctors told us."

"Good." He stopped eating. Had that shot really been justified? The rest of the cabal were as guilty as Caldith was and he hadn't tried to shoot any of them. It had been revenge. Pure and simple. His rage. And Kerit hadn't tried to stop him. They'd have to have some long talks when he got home. About a lot of things. To bad that he couldn't mention anything of what had happened to Doctor Halli.

"The list of charges against the cabal members is considerable," Father said into the silence. "And they're all in IC at the moment. That fellow from Securities said that the fake employee accounts will be given to the people whose names are on them. Taxable benefits, so no one, not even the tax people, are complaining."

"Can you tell us what happened from your side, Barri?" Mom asked.

"Boredom," he said, relieved at a question he knew a simple answer to. "Total boredom once I woke up, Mom. Backing up. Svent dropped me off at the mall but there were at least three people following me. I don't know who they were, but I thought they might be police or from Securities. The second note I found included a little earpiece. One of the assassins told me where to go to lose them. They assumed I had some sort of tracker on me. Woke up in different clothes. They were a bit large."

"Berhan was to blame on that angle," Father said. "I've had words with him on the danger he put you into."

"They weren't too mad, I guess." A small sip of coffee.

"Was the voice altered when they talked to you?" Dantil asked.

"Yes. A tenor voice that high isn't possible. Not in any male over puberty, anyway. I reached their van eventually and got in the back. It was a cargo type, with no way to see who was up front. There was a sleeping pill bottle with one in it. I was told to take it. We drove for a while, then I went to sleep. When I woke up, I was in a little room. Two lights, one with a dimmer switch, food and water, a camping toilet and two books. Boredom ensued."

"What books did they give you?" Hethane asked

Barrat sighed. "*Romances.* Very thick ones. I don't understand why they picked those. But reading them gave me something to do. And that's about it." He'd found a second in a used book store and read parts of both, especially the endings, with love triumphing over disaster, while he waited for other things to happen. He'd left them in a dumper after he abandoned the van in the Slideway.

"And when did you leave there?"

"Earlier today, I guess. I woke and found another sleeping pill on the table. With a note, saying that when they knocked on the door, I should take it. They must have had a camera system in there to keep an eye on me so I didn't wander away."

"Could you have escaped?" Mom asked. "If you had to?"

"The walls looked like standard interior ones, and the door was the same. I could have. The meal kits had plastic utensils I could use to start a hole, so it was possible. If the food and water ran out, I would have started remodelling the wall."

"But that was not necessary," Erithe said. Relief in her voice. "Then you woke up in the alley?"

"Yes. Not nearly as smelly as the one Branson's people left me in. Thankfully. I woke wearing all my original clothes. I found the screamer in my pocket and, well, here I am. I heard some sirens while I waited for my ride. I wasn't sure if you'd told the police or CO about that part of the plan, so I didn't try to attract any attention from them."

"No. They all think you were working at Erithe's," Father said. He sighed. "Well, that's that. Now we can all get back to work tomorrow."

"We can talk about our other plans later," Mom said. "We have all the papers, so you can read up on events. I'm sure you want a shower, Barri."

"Yes. And to shave. I hate beards. I'm not sure I can sleep right now, since I just woke up. It may take a couple of days to get my sleep schedule back to normal."

"True. Dr. Rethennel is waiting in the medical office. Just in case."

He finished the pastry. "Don't let Mastren take that tray away."

"He'll take it to your old room. You'll stay here tonight. Erithe brought you some fresh clothing for later," Mom said. "We'll schedule a general conference call for tomorrow evening. That will give you a chance to catch up on everything that happened."

"Good," he said. There was another round of hugs and everyone but Mom left. She sat down next to him.

"What's changed with Father?" he asked quietly. "I know he was acting different before I left, but he seems even less like himself."

"He's been lonely," she said, "for some time now, not just when you were kidnapped. We've been talking since the shot. The way we used to. And he'd like us to have dinner with Liselle and her parents. Soon. Before you go back to Beranga."

"He *approves* of us?" Was the world ending?

"He's thinking about it. All of this made him start to question himself, Barri. He told me when I went to the... coroner's office to fetch him that walking out the door so Justice could shoot him was the hardest thing he'd ever done. He considered going out some other door."

"But he didn't."

"He won't tell you," she frowned. "At least I don't think he will. Not now. I think he admitted it to me because... The enormity of what had happened was still uppermost in his mind. Now, he's had time to process those events. Lock his feelings away, to some extent. He was very worried about what the assassins might do to you, Barri. Leave you locked in that little room, with no way to truly escape. Kill you."

"I could have left, Mama," he said, taking her hands.

"He also realized how brave you were, to let CO take you after the crash. You didn't know if you would survive That Place. And then to let the assassins take you." Tears started to fill her eyes.

Barrat felt terrible. He'd just thought the plan as the easiest way for him to get away from the family, not what effect it would have on them. He hugged Mama until she pulled away a little.

"I don't think Father will mention it either," he said. "Everything turned out for the best, Mama. Doctor Halli taught me that the past is that. The future is what we make of it."

"I'm glad we found her," Mama said. "I've had several chats with her over the past months. She does help me gain perspective on events."

"Maybe another one in a day or so?"

"Perhaps. I'll see how I'm feeling after some sleep."

"A hot bath will help relax you."

"Having you home is the best way to relax me." She rose and headed for the door. "See Dr. Rethennel and then get that shower. You smell."

"No, I probably stink." He stood up. "At least I can't smell it anymore. See you in a few hours, Mama."

❧❧❧❧

The next few days were somewhat chaotic. Father insisted on the dinner with Liselle and her parents before he returned to Beranga. There were reporters hanging around outside the compound asking everyone they could about the truth of the assassination attempt.

Just before he left, there was a family dinner scheduled with a conference call afterwards. The older children were home from boarding school and university so the table was at almost the full extension. The younger ones were in the nursery as usual. The stiff formality of the past years was gone when they finished lunch and it still confused him. Barrat was about to enter the dining room for dinner when he had another shock and stopped out of sight.

"It's time to redo my will again," Father said to Mom. "I was beyond pissed when I did that new one last year."

"I know, dear. Your father's influence and training was not good for our marriage. Or our children."

"Especially for Barri," Father said. "The old man kept telling me that the youngest was the most likely to be soft. Taken advantage of. The rumours of his drinking in university didn't help change my mind."

"He didn't mention anything like that with Carthan?"

"Some. But then the rest of the kids were fairly close together in age. Sibling rivalry gave them skills they needed to survive. Barri was so out of sync with the rest. Don't know why the older grandkids didn't bond with him. The older ones are near enough in age. Past is, I suppose."

"And can't be forgotten. He was surprised at the change in us when he returned, and your attitude toward him even before the assassins let him go. He doesn't quite trust that change, dear. He's almost waiting for you to yell at him. Another dominance battle to show that you're in charge and he'd better behave and do as you say. Or else."

Two dears in a few minutes? Were they... reconciled? The world was ending.

It had to be.

"I know. It's hard, knowing he's the best chance of Industries growing and succeeding once I'm gone. And he's spending his time doing business plans for paintball ranges?" The confusion in Father's voice stirred something deep inside himself.

Barrat headed back towards his room to think. Father thought *he'd* be in charge of Industries eventually? Not Fraklin? He almost ran into Erithe around a corner, obviously heading toward the dining room.

"Anything wrong, Barri?" She took him by the shoulders to stare at him. He waved a hand toward the dining room.

"Um. Father. Mom. Dining room. They're talking. Still. It's…"

"Been going on for some time now. Maybe it's the new normal. We'll have to see." She took his arm and started to tow him back to the dining room. Hopefully they were making enough noise to warn them this time.

❧❧❧❧

Barrat packed his suitcase. Again. He was getting better at not having everything wrinkled and unwearable when he unpacked. Erithe knocked at the open door.

"All set?"

"Just about. I'm looking forward to a few days without drama and revelations."

She laughed. "It has been intense lately. I'll be happy to get back into my usual routines. When is Liselle moving to Beranga?"

He blushed a little. "Term starts in three weeks. She's coming out a bit early so I can show her around the city. She'll stay at my place until the dorms open up." A pause. "But her parents don't know that part. Yet. Maybe never. Okay?"

She smiled.

Beranga's trees were in full fall colours when Liselle arrived. It looked pretty. So did she. She was nervous as she came out of the arrival area. He was there thanks to Kerit's driving skills. He'd been too nervous.

Barrat smiled as she recognised him and smiled back at him. Their kiss drew some glances and chuckles.

"How much luggage do you have today?" he asked.

"Three suitcases," she said. "And they're full. Way too full. I had to pay over weight charges."

"But you're here, and that's the most important thing." They hugged. "Let's get the bags and we'll head to the office. I wasn't sure how tired you might be, so I haven't planned much for today." He turned and they started walking toward the luggage area, the other passengers bustling past them.

"Getting to the airport wasn't much of a problem. Stopping Dad from putting just one more thing into my bags: that took some effort. I thought they were going to explode as it was. He didn't act this way when I went away before, so I'm not sure what's different this time."

"Maybe because he knows it might be permanent now," Barrat said. "He seemed okay the last time I was over." Just after he'd returned from his "captivity". He had to explain why he hadn't returned several calls. She forgave him, thankfully. The dinner with all their parents had been stressful, but at least they'd been able to sit next to each other.

"Doctor Halli said he might regress once I started packing," Liselle said. "It became real, not *sometime* that his little girl was growing up."

"Well, we'll go back for a visit during winter break if not before. That'll make both of your parents happy and get us away from the snow for a week or so."

"And yours?" He shrugged.

"I'm still getting used to my father approving of me," Barrat said. "He called the other evening. Just to chat. Ask about how I was, if there were any side effects from the assassins' little room. It made me wonder if he actually cares about me." He shuddered theatrically.

"Highly abnormal for a parent." Her eyes filled with laughter.

Kerit waved from the edge of the car park. "Come on, kids, time's a wasting!"

The End?

Made in the USA
Columbia, SC
12 April 2018